ETERNAL LIGHT

DESCENDANT

Also by Kastie Pavlik

Children of the Morning Star Series

The Arrival Reawakened (1)

Confessions of the Second Born (2)

Last Born Daughter (3)

Eternal Light Descendant (Final)

Additionally

How to Make Lemonade

Praise for *The Arrival*

...providing a degree of psychological and philosophical dimension...there is still some fresh blood to be drawn...

~The BookLife Prize

...an author with a genuine flair for originality and character driven narrative storytelling. A deftly crafted and unfailingly compelling read from beginning to end...

~Midwest Book Review

...gorgeously written, with a great page-turning plot and complex characters...

~Serene Conneeley, Into the Mists & Into the Storm Trilogies

...the premise is clear, and so well thought, not good nor bad, vampires [s]imply are...a great start to a new series...

~Ruth Miranda, The Blood Trilogy

Pavlik's descriptions are scrumptious, a delight to the senses...a new world of vampire mythology where love and faith in the Almighty are pivotal pieces of this delightful page turning puzzle.

~M.K. Deppner, Photographs of October

Praise for *Confessions Of The Second Born*

...the world Kastie Pavlik creates is nothing short of fascinating...it left me craving more...

~Ruth Miranda, Heir of Avalon Trilogy

...infused with powerful darkness, aching light, and scenes which threaten to rip the reader's heart out...[y]ou'll want more when you finish...

~M.K. Deppner, Photographs of October

...kick-ass new characters, lots of action, a little romance, a plot twist or two, and lots of magic and intrigue...a new spin on vampires and their history, lore and world... Jonathan's...back story is fascinating...

~Serene Conneeley, Into the Mists & Into the Storm Trilogies

Praise for *Last Born Daughter*

Prepare to have your heart ripped, because that's how Ms Pavlik rolls and I love her books for that.

~Ruth Miranda, Heir of Avalon & The Blood Trilogies

... a compelling world that will draw you in and make you cheer for your favourite characters – then break your heart when you realise not all will survive. It's a masterfully crafted tale of love, loss and sacrifice, perfect for fans of vampires, myth, legend, and paranormal romance and suspense.

~Serene Conneeley, Into the Mists & Into the Storm Trilogies

Thrilling…devastating, but satisfying. A riveting read you'll have trouble putting down.

~M.K. Deppner, Photographs of October

…I dread and thrill in equal measure for where Pavlik will take us. So much hangs in the balance, and with an ending to Last Born Daughter that left me in stunned silence, this series still has so much more to come.

~Julie Embleton, Turning Moon and Voyager Chronicles series

Praise for *How To Make Lemonade*

Beautiful prose and an unexpected story…Ms. Pavlik delivers unique twists and leads the reader through the darkness toward the light…or does she?

~M.K. Deppner, Photographs of October

I simply could not put it down…I was left replenished, satisfied, my thirst slackened by this fresh glass of lemonade!

~Ruth Miranda, The Preternaturals Series

ETERNAL LIGHT DESCENDANT

ETERNAL LIGHT DESCENDANT: Children of the Morning Star
Book 4

Copyright ©2021 Kastie Pavlik

ISBN-13: 978-1-7376818-3-0
Library of Congress Control Number: 2021917639

Printed in Fairfield, Ohio
The United States of America

Editing Services: Magpie Press
Original Photographs and Illustrations by: Kastie Pavlik
Email: *kastiepavlik@gmail.com*
Instagram & Facebook: *@kastiepavlikauthor*
www.kastiepavlik.wixsite.com/author

TIM

SLIDE

∞

And neither the angels
In heaven above,
Nor the demons
Down under the sea,
Can ever
Dissever
My soul

~Edgar Allan Poe, *Annabel Lee*

TABLE OF CONTENTS

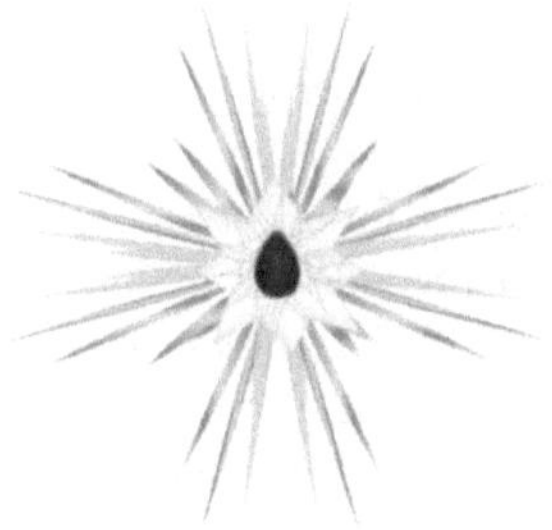

Chapter One: Black Shuck Redux

I

ALEXANDER

Animus Hollow, Summer 2006

Someone Powerful had locked Hawkiel's Celestial Landing Point. The Hollow's white swirls disintegrated upon hitting material that resembled the arc casements. Alex shifted focus to the angel's Unofficial Secondary CLP, but the Hollow wasn't normal there, either. The mist clung to him with gelatinous fingers as he fought to reach an anomalous milky portal.

Screams from the Realm of Man punched through the surface and kicked his heart into his throat. White became crimson. His fangs descended. The whole of his body ignited. The screams were shrill and feral, and filled with a despair that grated his very essence and propelled him across the barrier and onto the Isle of Wight.

Alex landed on his knees at Salea's feet. The crooked grin on her lips faltered. Bright red blood dripped off Corben's outstretched claw onto his cheek. Movement in his peripheral jerked him to his feet—Donovan leaping into the Hollow with a body slung over his shoulder.

It's Paresh! No! No! He spun on his heel, but a sickly sweet voice stopped him cold.

"She's gone Papa Alexander. The. Great," Salea cooed. She licked her bloody fingers one by one. "Donovan didn't want to share his *prize* with us."

Feigning a dramatic pout, she flipped her hands out. "She wasn't much fun to play with anyway. And definitely not as durable as Lior."

Gone. Wasn't.

Panic twisted his gut.

Gone! Wasn't!

Rage scorched a path up his throat.

Bring her joy.

His roar was a gutturally foreign thing as trees, buildings, and the gilded river swirled into a blood-tinged blur. Salea and Gabriel's words collided and slid apart, coated in the oil of an unacceptable reality. He visualized Paresh, haloed in golden light, smiling and laughing, happy and curious, alive with wonder. He was numbed to the familiar weights of his revolver and the Cataclysm. And deafened to the gunshot that fired over chiming silver blades.

Centuries of battle-earned muscle memory and instinct moved him autonomously. He saw only Paresh's body thrown over Donovan's shoulder. Her blood slicking his back. Her lifeless, too-thin frame——

A wind gust carried his fury over the report of another explosive silver bullet and subsequent chorus of the Cataclysm's song. Aegis cloaks might protect against his seething aura, but nothing could stop his weapons.

Salea dodged the first shot but doubled-over when the second pierced clean through her abdomen. Corben's predictive abilities failed against a dually armed opponent faraway in memory and too fast to sidestep. The Cataclysm bisected him at the waist on its second return. The sight of him ripping apart into two gory chunks returned a shred of sanity.

Salea blanched when Corben collapsed. Blood trickled from her mouth as she glared pure hatred at Alex.

"You're only alive because of me!" Alex screamed, cocking the hammer.

"It's all on you then." An unsettling smirk tugged at Alex's gut as she directed his sightline to the blood trailing from the shore into the Medina River.

All that blood… Alex mentally fell to his knees. "The baby——"

"Shoulda thought 'bout it a bit, ya think? Mama Raven takes kill orders for a reason." Salea scoffed bitterly. "Even mine."

The white veil split open and she stepped backward into it, sing-songing, *"But not anymore!"*

Without lifting his gaze, Alex aimed and fired. Salea grunted as the Hollow swallowed her up. Cold damp seeped into his pants as he knelt on the shore and his weapons clattered against the rocks. An immovable lump lodged in his throat. His fingers scrabbled over the blood trail. *"The baby…!"*

Tears and snot splashed into Paresh's blood and released the scent of her innocence. He buried his face in his hands and leaned back on his heels, the whole of his body heaving under guilt's weight.

Orders are orders, Raven said in his mind.

Bring her joy, Gabriel added.

You're only alive because of me!

It's all on you then, Salea finished.

And it was. Endymion and Paresh, his hunters, the Arc of Celestial Night, Ambrosia—the blood of those killed by the COMS—all of it stained his hands as much as it did Salea's. He should have shot her twice in the head instead of deluding himself into thinking that healing and sleep might rehabilitate her.

A distant police siren wailed and was getting closer. Modern society came with too many eyes and cameras, and the COMS cared little about exposure. He wiped his eyes and collected his weapons.

He stabbed a dagger into Corben's heart for good measure and wrapped his remains in his cloak. A quick chemical burn destroyed the DNA evidence. He heaved Corben's remains over his shoulder and fled into Animus Hollow.

He'd rather face *Someone Powerful* than return to Eric and Jonathan without Paresh—or with the grim new truth. He went back to Hawkiel's CLP on Marblehead Island in Massachusetts. The barrier was gone. Formidable waves crashed onto giant boulders as the Atlantic Ocean reflected the sun's illusorily peace.

Raven's blood scent weighted the air despite strong gusts of salty spray. He dropped the cloak holding Corben's corpse to inspect a large dark circle in the grass. Raven might not be dead—yet—but she'd lost a lot blood. It was still wet, too. He'd been *right there*, at the gate—

And he'd lost both of them.

Mama Raven takes kill orders for a reason...but not anymore!

Alex grabbed his head and screamed, kicking at nothing and everything, desperate to escape Salea and his guilt. "Stop it! Stop it! *Stop it!*"

He snatched the communicator from his pocket and opened the frequency Raven used as High Commander to monitor all Vampire Shadow Hound channels. Donovan's frantic voice rattled his jawbone.

"*...parley, of sorts!*"

The bones in the hinge of his jaw cracked as Alex growled through clenched teeth, "*Where is Paresh?*"

A static charge zapped the communicator. "A-Alex? Where's Raven?"

"Don't act surprised. I am going to tear you apart—"

"N-no! You have to help me! They want—they want her back!" Panting and garbled, Donovan tripped over his words. "I can't stop…get them off me…they'll take her! Pare—"

Hope alighted in Alex's heart. "Is she alive?"

"…safe passage! They're after me," Donovan cried. "*Get them off me…we'll parley!*"

Alex charged into the Hollow after Donovan's energy signature and arrived at the fixed point in Sunset Grove. An uncomfortable sensation of déjà vu prickled his skin—the forest was silent.

The Hollow opened and Donovan slammed into him, fumbling with Paresh's bloodstained body. "Keep them off me and I'll come back to talk to you—*only to you.*"

He dove into a new portal, his red cloak fluttering in a wake scented of the purest blood. Alex lurched to grab him, but the fixed point reopened and a trio of hunters crashed into him. He shot each one in the head, not in the mood to ask first. All three had gone AWOL during the mansion invasion.

Blood from their skulls pooled onto his pants. He groaned and leaned back on his palms, his finger on the trigger. This day couldn't get any worse. But it would. He knew it with certainty.

Cheery yellow beams darted through the swaying branches high above, offering a moment to delay reality—just one. The nightmare didn't need to be real yet. Everything was fine. Paresh was with Eric and Jonathan, slurping up homemade soup in Vermont, and Raven was sneaking up behind him to wrestle him into a headlock and mess up his hair—her most nefarious goal in life.

Ruffling his blond spikes, he whispered, "You'd better come back to me, Raven. I can't do this alone."

The brutal memory of Raven's anger surged forth. Of her boots cracking his ribs. Of her beating the shit out of him in a forest a thousand miles away. He wiped his face and kicked the bodies off his legs, disgusted to see the Crimson Guard's crest and uniforms. He tried Donovan on the communicator and failed. Seneca came to mind next, but Kestrel was Raven's First Officer. He needed her security clearance and discretion.

"Kestrel, as VaSH High Commander, I hereby issue a confidential order to destroy the corpse and DNA on Marblehead Island. Go fully armed but withdraw immediately if you encounter an enemy. That is all."

"As you command." Succinct, no questions, no bravado, no curiosity. Kestrel's loyalty and skillset suited her to command the Wraith Reapers and support him as High Commander.

New tears stung his eyes. Raven had planned for the inevitable conclusion to her role in Hawkiel's prophecy. Alex hadn't known what to expect when they reunited, but it hadn't involved her disappearing with massive blood loss.

What happened to you? A future without Raven was supposed to be far away. Not here and now.

He sniffled. That damn angel held the fates of the people dearest to him in the world. He stacked the dead rogues behind the fixed opening and walked down the trail to the southern clearing.

The mammoth silver maple stood proud, majestically bathed in golden light. Sour thoughts churned as he fixed a hard glare upon the tree. Gabriel had known. About the baby. About Paresh's death. Yet instead of warning them, he'd said to bring her joy. What good had that done?

"If I had an axe, I'd chop you down!" he yelled. He sat at the edge of the path and crossed his legs so that no part of him entered the circle. He dropped six empty casings from his revolver and chambered one exploding silver point. He fired at Grandfather Wisdom.

Click.

"You got lucky there, Ol' Gabe," he muttered. He fired again. Another dry shot. This wasn't as cathartic as he'd hoped. He should've loaded all six.

He cocked the hammer. The barrel rotated. The weight felt right. He coaxed the trigger and laughed aloud when the report echoed and scattered birds like bats from the canopy. Irrational relief trickled down his spine as their silhouettes faded. He swapped out the spent casing with six new rounds and aimed again. Between chunks of old, gray bark, the tree's trunk glowed like a halo, and a concentrated beam as bright as a star shot out from the bullet hole.

Curiosity drew him over. He'd shot into a hole stained with Paresh's blood—the one from the dagger that had pinned her right wrist. The bullet's heat must have reactivated her—

"Crimson Commander."

Gabriel's thundering voice pushed Alex back. His arm swung through the concentrated beam and brought forth memories of biting swords, shields of searing light, and gore-slimed mud. Beastly growls rose sharply above the metallic clang—

"*No!*" Forcing the Great Holy War from his mind, he instinctively grabbed his arm and discovered a blistered burn. Scowling high into the branches, he screamed, "*Why didn't you tell us?*"

"I have no compulsion to speak with you in your violence," Gabriel replied harshly, "but *she* insisted."

"She...?" The air in his lungs disappeared. A new silence crushed down. The light—

It's Paresh.

He flattened his palm against the bark. "You have her?" His voice cracked with emotion. "She's there? She can hear me?"

"I am the protector of souls. I hold them both in slumber. Her desire for you to know this was made clear to me."

"You have them both..." Falling to his knees, Alex sucked in a ragged breath and blew out a relieved cry. He braced himself against the trunk and wept.

"She feels your love." Gabriel's tone softened. "That is all I can offer to her in this type of stasis."

Alex wiped his cheeks. The light was fading. "Wait—no! W-what do you mean?"

"As long as she has *Strength* or a *Bridge*," Gabriel said, "and until the final cell in the Sacred Vessel has degraded, I may hold them here without sending them...*up*."

No, no, no, no. Squeezing his eyes shut, he tried to think. A shaky breath crossed his trembling lips. "Wh-what does that mean?"

In the lingering silence, he hung his head, too scared to peek and find the holy light gone. Swallowing over a painful lump, he willed his fingers to dig in and search for Paresh's soothing essence. Even if he only imagined it, he needed to feel her. *Just once more. Please.*

"I may only say that you must protect the Sacred Vessel's future at difficult and great cost," Gabriel replied at last.

Tingling heat seeped into his fingertips. He choked on a heaving sob and gripped the bark. No, once wasn't enough. She couldn't go.

"She yearns to take your pain. I feel it strongly—her love," Gabriel said. "I've done all I can. It is up to *you*."

Alex whispered, "I love you, Paresh."

Her warmth faded and the light behind his eyelids darkened. Both her essence and Gabriel's presence vanished.

But he couldn't let go.

"Thank you," he cried, repeating it again...and again. Grief and hope scraped his throat raw, but even then, he couldn't stop.

☽ ❋ ☾

Alex was nearly delirious when the unwelcome pattering of dust kickers sounded on the southern trail. A vice screwed onto his heart. The slinking mongrel stopped at the clearing's threshold. He was drenched in Paresh's blood scent.

"Are you alone?" Donovan asked.

The urge to tear Donovan apart warred against Alex's willingness to break his connection. As long as his fingers were wedged into the trunk, he could imagine the tingle of Paresh's warmth. But that was a dream. It was time to wake up. It seemed so wrong for the sun to rule such a somber day.

"I killed three of my own," Alex croaked. "All of them abandoned their posts when you invaded the mansion. Traitors. Rogues. COMS."

Thick tears splashed audibly at his feet. He silently pulled his gun from its holster, spun around, and aimed at Donovan's head. Throwing his hands up, Donovan ducked. His Aegis Cloak was gone. He wore his usual black garb, half of it clinging to his body and caked with blood.

"Pow. Pow. Pow." Alex popped the gun up with each repetition. "Three headshots. Three dead."

Donovan hesitantly got up. Alex's pupils dilated and focused on the muscle movements under Donovan's jeans. The instant he flexed to firm his footing, Alex fired an exploding round into his thigh and lunged. He forced Donovan flat onto his back and pressed the hot barrel against the bastard's forehead.

"*Where is she?*"

Donovan gritted his teeth and struggled to fight back. Hatred spilled into his aura, but it wasn't directed at Alex. "*Corben wasn't supposed to kill her!*"

Alex cocked the hammer. "Good thing he's not around anymore."

Donovan yelped in pain. "Honorable Judge Alex didn't offer rehab to the rogue Elder?" He lifted his head against the gun to get into Alex's face. "Or is that only reserved for insane immortal fourteen-year-old girls in love with Lucifer?"

Bones cracked under Alex's knee. Donovan howled. "Those explosive silver fragments burn like hell when they enter the bloodstream, don't they?"

"You and Raven are fucking perfect for each other!"

"Maybe," Alex said, pressing his full weight into Donovan's chest. "But she honorably parleyed with you and I lack her motivation to keep you alive."

Sinking into agony, Donovan groaned through shallow, labored breaths. "Then you'll...never find...Paresh."

Each word ran a cold shiver down Alex's spine as a pit opened in his stomach. He wanted so badly to pull the trigger. "You'll talk for the Chthonic Knights. Then Master Jonathan and Eric can take turns killing you. I'm good with watching."

"Liquid silver's not going to cut it, pretty boy. The *only* way she comes back is through me."

Alex's finger twitched. An unnerving light glinted in Donovan's eyes.

"I heard what that angel said, and I know you'll never help me revive her. Just as you know, I'll never give her up. So it's a draw until one of us determines the next move."

"My next move?" Alex shifted his weight. Another rib cracked. Donovan whimpered. "Letting Eric shred you to pieces. He'll take his chances knowing we'll find her."

Donovan struggled to throw a deliberate look at the giant silver maple. "Knowing her soul…is right *there?* And that *they* won't tell you where she is?" He licked his lips. "I don't think so."

Alex tapped his communicator. "Let's find out."

"You're…supposed to…protect her!" Donovan screamed, slapping wildly at Alex's face.

"Yeah, *her*, not you."

"You dense asshole!" Donovan spat a mouthful of blood. "Do you think killing me counts as a *great cost?* If you don't *protect* me…her body will be worm food…*Strength* and *Bridge* be damned! Do you really think I'd put her anywhere you'd think to look?"

Alex went rigid. "N-no——"

"What do you think that fucker meant? You need her to save the damn world as much as *Lucifer* needs her to end it! Corben's stalled everything! *No one* can make a move now."

That disturbing gleam resurfaced in Donovan's eyes. Alex knew he wanted to smile, but wouldn't dare without a clear victory. He was addicted to Paresh——if he couldn't have her, no one would. This was the ultimate power play.

The lump returned as bile scorched Alex's throat. Donovan was going to win——there weren't any cards left. Liquid silver wasn't an option without Endymion alive to bring him back if it killed him. He shoved off Donovan and swung away, screaming and fisting clumps of his hair.

As long as she has strength or a bridge…I may hold them here without sending them…up.

"Up…" As though entranced, Alex trudged over to the tree. "No!"

You must protect the Sacred Vessel at difficult and great cost.

"*No!*" He sank to his knees and holstered his revolver.

It is up to you.

He stroked the splintered crater his bullet had left behind.

Until the final cell in the Sacred Vessel has degraded—

His vision churned into a watery mess. Donovan's limping shadow loomed and the smile in the bastard's voice broke like ice against the back of his neck. "I believe we have security details to go over, Commander."

II

LUCIEN

Location Unknown, ca. 2000 B.C.

Dark becomes light.

Voice in head. *Morning Star—Lucien, eradicate humans.*

Different voice. *Alone. Hurts.*

See. *Mountains. Snow. White.*

Feel. *Blistering. Cold. Biting.*

Hear. *Howling. Whistling. Screeching.*

Smell. *Sharp. Woody. Invigorating.*

Taste. *Cool. Energizing. Crisp.*

Dark shapes in rows. *Trees. Conifers. Piney. Needled.*

Investigate. *Trees block wind.*

Wood. *Soft. Breaks. Scented.*

Snow. *Melts. Powdery. Thick.*

Lift branch. *Snaps. Snow falls. Action. Reaction.*

Arm. *Scales. Armored. Teal.*

Fingers. *Pointed. Sharp. Claws.*

Crawl under branch. *Dark. Shadow. Shelter.*

Nature. *Camouflage. Protect. Defend.*

Trees. *Safe.*

Nature. *Home.*

Lucien. *Sleep.*

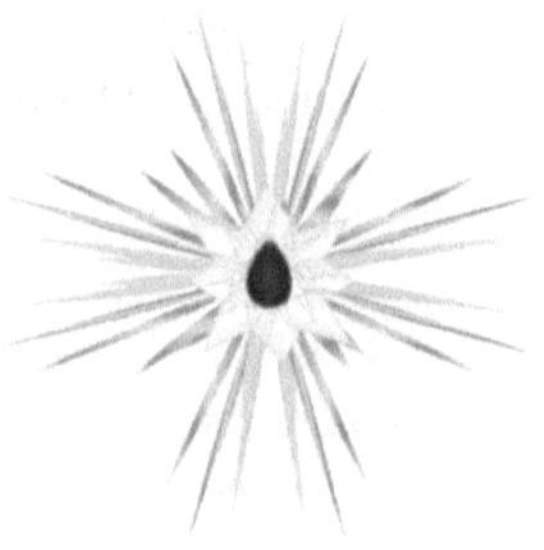

CHAPTER TWO: HOMO SACER

I

KESTREL

European Continent, ca. 150 A.D.

Kestrel and Lior inched beyond the sightlines of the Heavenly Host and human soldiers onto the burial ground and found the stone marker they'd left a decade earlier. They'd underestimated the reach of the Host's protection behind the War's front line. They dug quickly.

Their first attempt at desensitizing their bodies to the pain of the silver wielded by the Host and Rainne Blood Pathos had failed. But, they'd adapted—she was focusing on physical sensation, while Lior trained on the light spectrum. Subsequent attempts were promising. The soil burned worse as they burrowed closer to their hoard. Sacred ground increased the potency of scavenged silver.

Kestrel scooped muddied coins out. She secured them in a crude leather pouch as Lior crawled into the hole.

They locked eyes. Kestrel began to backfill. The purified dirt singed Lior's skin. She didn't stop until only his nose and mouth were visible. Curling over his makeshift grave, she covered up with their crimson cloaks and guarded Lior. He slept for one day.

A dull rain started an hour before Lior was due to awaken. It was hammering when his breathing changed. She carved soil away from his face while under the cloaks before uncurling to dig by the armful to get him out quickly.

Mud and stones were embedded into blistery raw skin that oozed blood and sweat. He faced the torrent and panted as it cleansed his tortured body. The aftermath was always worse for him. Sleeping in hallowed ground required a mastery of mind over body to condition his sight.

Again, they locked eyes, his swollen and amber, hers sleek and golden, and nodded to each other. They visually searched in opposite directions. The Host's patrols were gone, but they were on a grassy mound devoid of trees and large stones and needed cover for fire. Kestrel nudged her chin at the telltale smoke of a settlement blooming in the distance. Gingerly draping Lior's cloak about his shoulders, she pulled the hood over his dripping curls. They'd travel slowly until he fed, but she'd be at his side.

A swollen and weeping sky hid the moon when they arrived at a roundhouse beyond a village's protection. She eased Lior down to the grass and entered.

Unlike most human dwellings, which consisted of small spaces divided by walls, beams supported a thatched roof over a single room with a central fire pit. Goats were in a pen that spanned the length of one side. All had stiffened and fainted. She'd never seen humans living with livestock, but they were asleep on the far side. She sliced the throats of all eleven occupants and returned to Lior to bring him inside. She pulled a few bodies close for him to feed on and took a fired clay pot outside to collect rainwater.

Lior's skin was finally regenerating when she returned, but his fingers were stripped to muscle from laying out her silver coins. She darted in low and grabbed his hands, concern drawing her lips tight. She pointed for him to feed, and took over, tossing the coins into the water to clean them. Once his fingers were healed, she gave him his bag and he arranged his smelting tools. As he set the ladle into the fire, she gathered another batch of bodies for him. She ached to drink with him, but that would be counterproductive.

He gave her a grateful nod and let his cloak slip off his shoulders. Large swathes of inflamed blisters marred his naked frame, but, as his strength returned, and he drank harder and faster, a fresh layer of skin formed. He settled at her side and quietly watched her wipe and dry each coin.

The silver stack didn't look like much, but it was more than they'd used in one sitting. She unclasped her cloak and laid flat on the dirt floor. Lior's newborn fingers traced the last set of skeletal vines he'd tattooed. The skin was angry red and oozing bloody pus. His gentle touch filled her with longing, but he was ready to carve.

Sucking air in, she tensed and gritted her teeth. The first slice was always the worst. She breathed deeply in through her nose and out from her mouth, closing her eyes to link her mind with the sensation.

Lior carved channels into her skin that he cauterized with boiling liquid silver. The stench of her burning skin roiled her stomach, but she forced herself to embrace the process. She needed to *feel*. They both did or this was never going to work.

II

KESTREL

Marblehead Island, Massachusetts, Summer 2006

The sun had yet to set on the small, wave-battered island, but it was sinking closer to the horizon. Kestrel was shocked to find a bisected corpse and a large pool of Raven's blood untended in daylight. It wasn't like cleaning up an arc explosion in the Arctic—people lived here. Tourists visited the lighthouse.

Alex's recklessness rang her internal alarms, but that wasn't what seared her silver vines with Hellfire. Raven might have come here to meet Hawkiel, but she'd met Lucifer instead. Kestrel anxiously gathered the loose evidence and burned the DNA trace.

After depositing Corben's traitorous remains at the Arc of Mourning Eidolons for cremation, she called Raven on the communicator. It didn't go through. She tried Alex and failed.

Something was desperately wrong. The Commanders were supposed to be in Vermont with their trinity. Why was Raven's blood at Hawkiel's CLP with a dead Elder that smelled of an English river and *Paresh's* blood? And why had Alex's energy signature come from Sunset Grove?

She took Animus Hollow to the forest. It'd only been a few days, but she'd acclimated to the pitter-patter of wildlife that came with Lady Paresh's essence. The silence was harrowing.

Her silver vines tugged south, but the immediate air smelled of coagulating vampire blood. She found a trio of Crimson Guard hunters, each with a silver bullet in the head.

Alex never shot to kill like that.

She unsheathed her sword and studied every shadow, highlight, and twitching leaf as she padded soundlessly to the trail. Pressing her palm to a tree, she flooded her aura high into the leaves of the canopy and deep into the roots. It fed back an organic map and vibrations of holy light and bloody violence at the spiritual nexus known as

Grandfather Wisdom.

The tree's roots intertwined with others for miles, tying every tree in Sunset Grove to its giant ruler. Somehow, it *spoke* to her and what it said jolted her in place. She caught herself on her sword and gasped for breath. It couldn't be true. She raced south.

She'd sensed two humanoids in the southern clearing. As she emerged into the sunny meadow and saw Donovan standing over the Crimson Commander at the base of the mammoth trunk, her heart sank.

It was true.

Firming her grip on the hilt, she charged and leveled the blade to stab Donovan directly beneath his heart. Gripping his shoulder, she seethed into his ear, "Move and I twist the blade."

Shock and pain plastered Donovan's nauseating smile into place as his eyes swiveled and Alex whipped around, terrifyingly pale, screaming, "*No!*"

"She's d-dead!" Anger chattered Kestrel's teeth. "And her blood is all over *him!*"

"Don't kill him!" Alex yelled, fearfully staring at the blood dripping off the tip of her sword. "That's an order!"

Fiery talons of rage climbed her spine as garnet color draped her view. "Why? Make it better than why you saved Salea after she murdered Lior, because my vines and the holy light of that tree are screaming for his blood."

Confusion contorted Alex's face as he glanced at the beastly tree. His eyes swollen with sorrow, he shook his head and shot hateful daggers at Donovan. His lips trembled when he spoke. "Donovan hid her body."

"You like to dig, don't you, Kestrel?" Donovan sneered. "Or...was that only an excuse for your extracurricular activities with Lior?"

Kestrel went numb. It was a foreign feeling that she didn't like. Each breath was gruff and heavy as she searched for words and only managed to scoff from sickened disbelief. She called for Master Jonathan.

"*What are you doing!*" Alex lurched for her communicator,

She snapped her fingers against the hilt. Alex froze. "One twist and he's dead."

Master Jonathan's voice was strangely empty when he agreed to meet at her location. To Alex, she reported, "He and Lord Eric will be here directly."

"Yay," Donovan said, glaring over his shoulder. "And to think, I was going to draw you a treasure map."

"You *shut up!* And you! Shouldn't have called them!" Alex huffed at

Kestrel. He jerked out his revolver and unhinged the Cataclysm. "Keep your hand steady. I'll go for non-lethal strikes. I cannot permit either one to attack him."

A new anger flared in Kestrel's belly. "You would attack your masters? For this rogue? Are you as daft as Raven says? You can't kill *them* either!"

"Raven is gone." Alex ground his teeth. "Until I find her, you are acting Commander of the Wraith Reapers."

Resting his arm on Donovan's shoulder, he aimed the gun at the southern trail and displayed the Cataclysm in his left hand. "When I fire, it's going off in your ear, you bastard scum."

Donovan's lips parted, but he shut them at the deadly gleam in Alex's eyes. "You say another word and she finishes what she started. I have no more patience for you, even with what Gabriel said."

Kestrel gave him a visual query.

"You said the tree wants blood? Well, her spirit's in there, in stasis, and I think that's her telling you she wants him dead," he said, "but Gabriel wants us to save her. At this point, if Donovan cooperates, Gabriel gets his way—which is my preference, for once, but if not, then Paresh gets her revenge and goes—"

He choked out, "*Up.*"

Another horrified expression lit Donovan's face. Blood trickled from his mouth. He was as rigid as a plank.

"Lungs burning yet, traitor?" Kestrel tightened her grip on his shoulder. He gasped and coughed, and once he started, he couldn't stop. Blood bubbled up his throat and spurted off his lips.

"Good thing my hands are steady," she whispered.

"What the hell?" Master Jonathan hesitated briefly in the shadows of the trail, but his temper quickly consumed his aura and shot out to encapsulate their death triangle.

A bullet cratered the grass by Master Jonathan's foot. "Stay back! Especially Eric," Alex warned. "Trust me or I will fire again."

"*Then fire,*" Eric growled, storming into the clearing bearing a monstrously demonic façade.

Alex shot again but couldn't aim fast enough. With a frustrated shake of his head, he clenched his jaw and threw out the Cataclysm. He pleaded silently with Master Jonathan.

"My sword is a twist from his heart!" Kestrel yelled. "I will kill him if he twitches, my lords. I am Acting Commander of the Wraith Reapers. Listen to the High Commander—we have both received celestial messages!"

Kestrel heard Master Jonathan tackle Eric just before the Cataclysm sang over them. "Stay down until he gets it back or it'll hit you on the return," Master Jonathan hissed.

Kestrel yelped as Eric's fury blasted her vines with startling power. "Speak fast, Alex. He dislodged the silver in my back. My hand won't stay steady forever."

"I...uh..." Alex panicked.

"Raven's missing," Kestrel started. She mouthed: *tell them.*

Alex holstered his weapons. He skirted Donovan with another glare and his voice squeaked over the lump in his throat. "Look, coming from Gabriel, okay? You *cannot* attack him. No matter what. And believe me, I know that restraint is impossible, but, ah—"

His voice shook as he deteriorated into a blubbering mess. "I...P-Pare...she's...*dead.* Gabriel's holding her—*both of them*—in stasis, there, in the tree, until we find her body."

Eric's wrath flickered into numb shock and then...nothing. Kestrel glanced back. Both of her lords were gawking at the giant tree as though she and Donovan no longer stood there. She followed their gazes and gasped.

Beneath the furrowed gray bark, the tree shone like gold. The energy coming from it was pure and light, and full of affection—warm like a lover's embrace—flowing directly to Eric.

Whispering, "No," repeatedly, Eric collapsed.

"You guys can resurrect her, again," Alex said.

"You make that sound easy." Master Jonathan's voice was hard and gravelly. "We need to know where to look."

"I know," Alex replied quietly. "Your hand steady, Kestrel?"

"For now."

Alex shot Donovan in the other leg, knocking him off his foot. Kestrel lowered with him, taunting, "Easy, easy. Sink too fast and the blade kinks up just so—" She sucked her teeth and whispered, "and *I* get to kill you first. But...you might prefer that, so how about we hold it steady and give them that fun?"

"You're a fucking sadist," Donovan snarled.

She grinned. "Sticks and stones you predatory creep."

Addressing the group behind her, she said, "Lucifer was on Marblehead Island to meet Raven, not Hawkiel."

"*What?*" Master Jonathan and Alex demanded in unison.

"It was vile and sulfuric, like Old London when he was there with

Salea, but concentrated."

"Salea was on the Isle of Wight…with *him*." Alex pointed at Donovan. "Raven lost a lot of blood, but I don't think she's dead…or, at least, she wasn't."

"She's not dead," Donovan said through clenched teeth. "Lucifer needs her, too, and no matter how big she talks, Salea would rampage if he killed Raven. *So*, if ya'll'd stop maiming me for a few minutes, maybe we could work out those details? Eh, Lexy?"

"What *details*?" Eric growled.

"He needs protection," Master Jonathan surmised grimly.

"Ah!" Donovan declared, his expression turning Kestrel's stomach. "Ding-ding! John-boy gets it."

He spat a mouthful of blood onto Grandfather Wisdom. "Remove your sword. Now."

Kestrel twisted the blade a smidge. As Donovan howled, Master Jonathan quietly said, "Release him."

A knot coiled up her insides. Every part of her screamed that it was wrong. All of it was wrong. "If the COMS want her back that badly, perhaps we should hand him over. They'll be far more persuasive than us. Less honor. More brutality."

She leaned in and whispered, "You're more scared of them than us aren't you, coward?"

"They're insane, hooked by Salea—even Lucifer. She's in his ear constantly. He lets her do whatever the hell she wants." Donovan spit another mouthful. "You thought she was a monster before? She flicked the fetus into the river without a second thought and probably would've killed Paresh if Corben hadn't struck first—Lucifer *needed* her alive."

Eric's murderous rage slashed into her vines. He was up and charging and no one could stop him. Yanking the blade free, Kestrel turned into a bracing stance against Donovan's back and instantly took a full force hit. Eric easily crushed them both into the tree.

On impact, blinding light flashed and an ethereal voice wholly imbalanced with nature bellowed, "Protect the Sacred Vessel's future or doom every soul on Earth."

Alex and Master Jonathan stared at each other as though afraid to breathe. She could feel Donovan's bones cracking and hear hers creaking.

"Eric, stop!" Master Jonathan raced over to pull him off. "That's not Gabriel!"

"Then who the hell is it?" Eric yelled.

A blue glow reflected off Alex's blond spikes. "Mi...Michael."

Kestrel dragged Donovan by the arm as Eric and Jonathan drifted away from the tree and followed Alex's gaze. High above the silver maple, a bright blue star hovered, crackling with energy and emitting a fierce holy essence that could easily liquefy her vines. It morphed into a humanoid form with flowing robes and six colossal wings and stared at them with flaming eyes that flickered orange, blue, and white.

Jerking Donovan down with her, Kestrel dropped to a bended knee and bowed her head. The appearance of the princely warrior seraph, the Archangel Michael—the Angel of the Apocalypse—meant the balance had shifted into a terrifying new direction.

Lucifer was, indeed, active on Earth.

III

LUCIEN

Location Unknown, ca. 1901 B.C.

Sounds. Footsteps. Close.
Crunch. Crunch. Crunch.
Human walking on snow. Wearing animal skin.
Wearing human skin messy.
Fur clean and warm. Take and wear. Lucien crouch.
Pain. Hunger.
Human not see. Lucien ambush.
Feed. Take fur.
Human. Prey.
Eradicate.
Lucien predator.

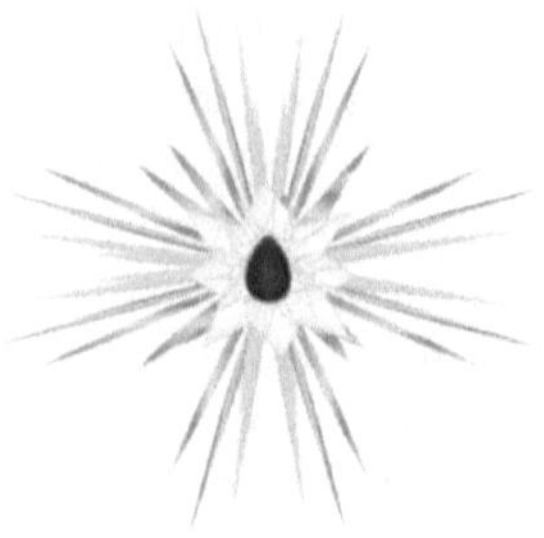

CHAPTER THREE: CUSP OF DARKNESS

I

RAVEN

Location Unknown, Summer 2006

The agony of her new reality throbbed at the surface of consciousness as she drifted from the twilight of sleep and waking. Masculine voices tugged at her heart with certain familiarity—one soothing and one coldly apathetic. Her eyelids struggled to part into blurry vision that dipped into shadow and light. Movements as simple as a finger twitch invited agony's embrace. The voices quieted. Her muscles instinctively seized.

He'd heard the changes in her pulse and breathing.

Tears dripped onto the down-filled futon beneath her. A door at her back creaked open. She squinted through the misty haze and her vision began to clear. Beyond a glass wall sat a sunlit shrub—a squat evergreen, no more than a half-foot tall, with pointed oval leaves darker than Alex's eyes and clusters of small urn-shaped flowers paler than the pink of her hair. It sat atop a bed of veiny and mottled serpentine rocks, and redwood planks lined the walls—

She squeezed her eyes shut and held her breath as he knelt behind her and enveloped her in his lavender scent. She couldn't face him— not even his reflection. But in her private darkness, another betrayal looped as Not-Hawkiel's wings spread wide over the crashing roar of the Atlantic. Instead of a sky smeared with color, she harkened back to the inky, salty night of Salem 1692 and a moon that dusted everything in monotone. As sickening as it was, she preferred that to the cheery sun that had framed Lucifer's devastating revelation. She shuddered at the feel of his hand running down a blood-slicked primary feather.

Shattering her world hadn't been enough—Lucifer added another surprise. Tears stung her eyes anew. She refused to appease her burning lungs. Why was she trying so hard? She was out of moves. No plan. No backup. No one knew she was gone. Not even Alex.

Finally choking in Endymion's scent, she gave into desolate sobs that jarred an aching frame literally ripped open by the Devil. She pulled her knees up to become as small as possible so the Earth could swallow her up and erase her from existence.

Endymion patted her hip. It was a simple gesture—*I'm here*—but it backfired and turned the projection of her memories to the bloodstained white silk in Lady Rainne's smoke-filled chamber.

She cried harder, folded smaller, and wailed louder, her voice an utterly unrecognizable thing—much like everything she'd ever known. The Prince of Lies had plotted her entire life and primed her for this—with Gabriel's misguided blessing.

And what about *him*? How long had Endymion been part of it? From the beginning? Had he killed her a thousand years ago to resurrect the future soldier that Lucifer wanted? Is that why Salea's village was eradicated? *Because of her?*

Her head was not a safe space. She peeked at the shrub instead and traced the branches, slightly red in color—

The peridot orbs in his reflection captured her gaze.

Neither spoke.

Neither moved.

They were connected, but disconnected, physically separated by her wings and emotionally distanced by a thousand years of deceit. He restrained his aura and she cocooned herself in hers. It was the only thing left that was hers—solely hers—and had been from the moment of her creation.

Dropping his stare, he granted a merciful release. "'Tis the rarest plant in the world." He spoke softly, coaxingly. "Raven's Manzanita. A symbolic way to keep you close while we were apart. Humans know of only one naturally surviving in the wild, but this one is far older and blooms eternally."

He paused. "Like you."

The guy was a frightfully skilled psychopath.

Alex was right, but it didn't change Endymion's love for her or hers for him. She hated that she was relieved that he was alive, despite his treachery, and that meant she needed to stop wallowing or she'd drown. Their mutual emotions could work to her advantage, but only if she focused. The real Hawkiel was out there and so was his brother. The Nation and the world were worth fighting for regardless of the personal cost. She'd never expected to survive anyway.

An IV line led from her arm to an empty blood bag. That explained why she wasn't healing. "Thirsty. Throat sore," she croaked.

He patted her hip again. "Of course, my dear. I'll be a moment."

The color of the manzanita's flowers was the same as her hair, but the saturation was near white. She huffed in frustration and smacked tears off her cheeks. *You're the VaSH High Commander. Act like it.*

He returned with a tray and steaming tea set. He wordlessly set up a folding tea table and arranged the pot and bone China cup.

"May I?" In an uncharacteristically vulnerable gesture, he offered his hands, palms up.

She grimaced as she tried to rise up on her elbow. He braced her shoulders and alleviated the burden on her inflamed musculature. Her wings opened autonomously and propped her up.

Moaning through the pain, she managed to get somewhat comfortable, but his fair hair and silk robe haunted her peripheral. Her gaze dropped into her lap. The fire in her shoulders zipped down her arm and into her fingers as she reached for the cup. She pulled back with a groan.

He knelt beside her and streamed blood from the kettle into the cup. The charge between them spoke of words he wished to say, yet he remained silent as he gently positioned the cup into her hands and supported her as she lifted it to her lips. The warmth of the liquid greasing her parched throat made her moan in relief. Something finally felt *good*.

His palm was like fire under her hands, but she didn't care. He helped her finish and then poured some more before letting go. She trembled as she sipped on her own.

"Where are we?" she asked.

"'Tis a compound Lord Lucien permitted me to keep outside the Arc of True Blood since before its inception." He paused as though hesitant to divulge his secrets. "Few know it exists—only my loyal couriers, generals, and high-ranking officers. There's a small barracks on the far side."

He quieted.

"Will you look at me, my dear?" The lonely sadness in his voice almost pulled her stare to him.

"It's a compound? Out...*outside*—" She blew out a shaky breath.

"With *generals* and *officers*…and your…c-couriers."

She knew who his couriers were. One wasn't alive anymore and the other had taken her place—

"Please look at me."

Hedonistic nerves erupted as he slid the back of his finger down her cheek. She sucked in a sharp breath. He pulled back.

"Is Lady Rainne here?"

"No."

When she remained silent—or, rather, unable to string together a coherent question or thought—he said, "I sleep in this room when I stay here. Consider it yours."

She drew in a shallow breath that blasted out on a burst of energy. The cup and saucer shattered against the glass. Blood spattered and dripped, and the table flew, and she was on top of him, a wild creature, screaming, kicking, clawing.

"You and Lucifer? You and Lucifer! Why would I want this room? Why would I want to look at you? Why?"

Her wings, body, and mind lacked coordination. She crashed into the wall. Iridescent blue feathers erupted from her back as she landed under the full weight of silver bones—a torment that only fueled her rage. She lunged again.

He trapped her in a steely embrace that her wings couldn't break. "Please stop, my dear—"

"You're a traitor!" Tears streamed off her cheeks and blurred his face when she looked at him. "Why should I do anything you ask? You—"

Her legs gave out. He sank with her, even as she punched and shoved at his chest. *"You said you'd never make me choose!"*

She snarled, "I want Alex. *Now!*"

Endymion's aura flinched. Fleeting anger flickered in his eyes. "Sadly, I can only accommodate that request if he's dead."

That stole her breath. And her voice.

"Given recent developments, I was ordered to clip your wings," he revealed delicately, freeing a hand to sweep her hair from her face. "But I gave assurances 'twould not be necessary. The order stands, however, should you become difficult."

"W-why wouldn't I become *difficult?*" she spat. "You handed Rainne right to Lucifer! A-and…you…and…*Salea*—"

"Alas, I am charged with guarding you *and* Rainne. No matter the roles you both play, the Hawkings Protocol is in effect. Do you not see this as a tactical advantage?" He relaxed his arms. Anger simmered in his darkened sea glass orbs, but his aura was shuttered.

"Where is she?"

"Not here."

"Can Lucifer activate her?"

"Not presently."

"Can Paresh?"

His gaze fell for a fraction of a second. The anger blazed brighter when he looked up. "Not presently."

II

ERIC

Orison Crossing, Summer 2006

The humanoid orb that represented Saint Michael, the Archangel, hovered over Grandfather Wisdom and emitted a soft blue glow. His fiery multi-colored eyes somehow locked onto each of them simultaneously.

A teardrop splashed from Alex's cheek onto Eric's chin. The Crimson Commander and Jonathan had tackled him after he realized that Kestrel had pulled Donovan away from the tree. Their fingers mashed muscle and soft tissues into bone, but no physical pain could defeat grief's intangible heartbreak.

His baby and his lover were dead. *Again.*

"You can't kill him, Brother," Jonathan whispered. "*Yet.*"

Alex choked. "Gabriel said it'd be difficult, but I didn't expect this."

"If the angels are protecting *him* now, I don't give a shit what they say!" Eric barked. "*They know where she is, too!*"

Another tear dripped onto his face. Alex clenched his jaw. "She's not gone as long as she has her *Strength* and her *Bridge!*"

"If Gabriel—or Michael—are so damn noble and care so much about this world then they'll tell us! We don't need *that bastard!*" Eric glared up at Saint Michael. "Tell me where she is!"

"That's only an avatar," Alex said quietly. "The Treaty forbids angels from entering the Realm of Man without authorization."

Eric slid through their grips. "That's not an acceptable answer!"

Pain creased Jonathan's brow. "If you keep fighting me, she's going to lose her bridge." He directed Eric's sightline to the bloody stain growing on his shirt.

"Then *you* need to let go." Eric went lax. Alex and Jonathan faltered, and Eric bucked up and broke free. He landed on his feet and leaped over Jonathan to rip Donovan out of Kestrel's grasp.

Eric pulled Donovan forward and rammed their skulls together before jerking him down for a knee to the gut. "*Where is she?*"

Donovan's eyes hardened. "Kill me and *you* kill her."

Eric panted heavily, his fists and teeth clenching against the beast's crazed bloodlust. It roared everywhere at once. Without Paresh's essence, the man and the beast were separating already.

He scruffed Donovan and punched him again and again in a blind rage, unaware of Kestrel and Alex trying to pry him off. Slick with blood, his fist slid off Donovan's broken face and gave Alex a chance to wrench his arm behind his back.

Like a coordinated attack, his psyche conjured Paresh's sun-kissed crown and cheerful smile to remind him that her blood, fresh within him, could fight against the beast—for now. Heat developed in his palm to simulate his baby's kick and the sorrow of that loss punched the beast back into its cage. He threw Donovan at Kestrel.

He'd rarely been one to run from his problems, but he was spiraling worse than he ever had before. Fear *of him* radiated from the Commanders. Jonathan was bent over his reopened injury. Donovan's hearty laugh echoed inside Eric's mind, but the bastard was too banged up to utter a sound.

Staring up at the avatar of Saint Michael, Eric expected his anger to wane. But he didn't feel anything. Not from the orb. Not from the tree. Was Paresh really in there? What if she wasn't? What if Saint Michael had forced Gabriel to let her move on?

The avatar's sight narrowed to Eric. A thin golden ribbon peeled down the trunk from the tallest branch and coiled around Eric's chest. Bathed in warm light, Eric felt comfort and love.

"Paresh?" he whispered.

The ribbon continued weaving a path between Donovan and Kestrel to Jonathan. As it encircled his wound, Eric felt the warmth intensify. The glow brightened. Jonathan straightened with his eyes closed and arms out as though hugging her. The ribbon then looped Alex's ankle and twined up his leg and torso. The tip tapped Alex's forehead and he fell backward—spellbound—landing in the grass.

Alex whispered, "I understand," and the ribbon uncoiled, pausing to hug Jonathan again before returning to Eric and tightening its hold. It slid over his eyes to force them shut and he saw Paresh as he had the night of her arrival home—haloed in bright, fiery light with skin that shimmered like gold and eyes that shined like stars.

Her ethereal arms encircled his neck and tugged him into her calming essence. "My love," she said, her speech slurred and drowsy, "be as strong for me as you can."

Tears trickled down his cheeks.

She kissed each one and pulled back reflecting diamonds on her lips. "They've said it will be especially challenging for you—"

She threaded golden fingers through his hair as her eyes wandered his face sadly. "I'm sorry...I have to go."

Her form began to fade. He panicked, but she cupped his cheek and imbued her essence into him to quell the beast. "Listen to Alex. I love you."

"I love you," he whispered, trying in vain to hold on, but there was nothing to grab.

The golden thread embedded into Grandfather Wisdom's bark from the roots up to the highest peak. Saint Michael's avatar resumed its generalized watch.

No, he rarely ran away, but he'd never been this powerless. She'd entrusted the instructions to Alex. He said nothing as he turned on his heel and walked down the southern trail.

Being strong for her didn't mean he needed to partake in negotiations with the person holding her body hostage. Before his anger could spark again and destroy the gift she'd given him, he returned to memory and re-watched her arrival, returned to their first date, to making love, to the feel of their baby's kick. He breathed in honey and green clover, and stared in awe as she danced with fireflies like a woodland nymph and swirled her finger in the pond for the koi to nip.

As he entered the cottage's dim interior, he gazed at the hearth and recalled how her fingers had climbed the ridges of his abdomen and she'd lifted onto her toes to press her lips against his. He sank onto the Victorian sofa, staring into the darkness, too far gone to hear the voices in the southern clearing. He would commit every moment of the last few weeks to memory.

That was all he had left of her.

III

LUCIEN

Location Unknown, ca. 1849 B.C.

Breeching the village walls in the light of day was a mistake. Humans were fierce when they fought together. Bloody lines crisscrossed the armored scales on his arms and a broken spear stuck out from a seeping hole in his shoulder.

Lucien had reacted on frenzied instinct and eradicated the mob without feeding. He returned to the forest and shoved the spear out through his back. He sought shelter in the trees and healed.

Time passed. Scars remained. Pain lingered. Nature unleashed her cruel fury.

Thunder cracked the sky in twain. Angry clouds spat cold water. Icy rivulets ran over his scales and seeped into crevices. Moisture crawled like worms beneath the surface.

Lucien was agitated and restless, uncomfortable in his skin. He yearned for escape and wandered down the mountain, beyond his hunting grounds, to open plains. The sun rose to its highest peak. He lay on heated dirt and stones to dry the damp.

Relief was fleeting. Rains and snow returned. His skin crawled.

Lucien returned to his forest home. It couldn't protect him from the damp's invasive misery.

He suffered. Alone.

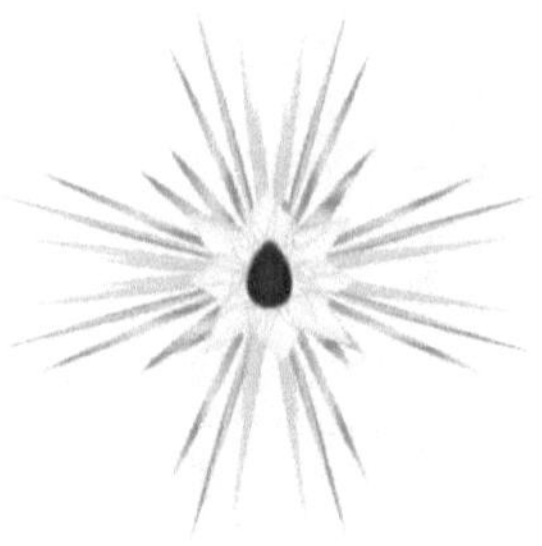

CHAPTER FOUR: FADING LIGHT

I

KESTREL

European Continent, ca. 150 A.D.

Setting the ladle aside, Lior wiped off the sweat beading atop Kestrel's brow. The process was grueling, painful, and slow. Vampires regenerated too quickly for markings with ink or henna. Silver was different.

"Is it too much?" His voice was a balm, gentle and quiet—so unlike his battle cry.

"If we take a break now, I'll need to drink." Her eyes started to roll back. She shook herself awake and focused on the dried mud that had streaked Lior's curls. "Finish the stack. Even if it takes me to black, I'll come back to you—always."

A small cry escaped her mouth as he started carving again. The pain rivaled the first cut into raw skin, but she knew the scrolling vines would loop in perfect arcs and beautifully intricate skeletal leaves.

Silver on its own wasn't enough. The first time he'd carved into her, the channels healed and shoved it out. But holy silver or silver purified in sacred soil led to rejection that her body couldn't completely overcome. New carvings were angry and infected initially, but her skin would eventually burn and heal in an eternal cycle. The constant rawness shaped how she interpreted the sensory changes that came with the wind, spiritual presences, and body heat.

Angelic essences stung. Air carried distinguishable notes about the environment. Bodies varied by emotional state. The vines had associated Lior's touch with the sensual thrill of his fingers and lips on her body—even when it hurt.

They formed a whole in everything they did: killing, altering, suffering, and pleasuring. These torturous sessions allowed for mutual gratification, as well—a reward from Endymion for their successes. They could already detect the enemy's movements, coordinate better assaults, and scout human settlements. They'd grown their army to populate the frontlines with disposable soldiers, thus preserving their dwindling pureblooded compatriots.

They always returned to a scolding from Alexander. While he, too, reaped benefits from their experiments, he bore the brunt of their absences. The Host known as Gabriel had singularly focused on him and constantly lured him dangerously close to the War's front—

"*Ah!*" she shrieked. Lior shoved a human arm into her mouth. Liquid silver raced into her bloodstream. It scorched her veins and struck her heart like a lightning bolt.

"I'm sorry," he said softly, again blotting sweat off her brow. "That was a deep one. Only a little more."

Her eyes bulging, Kestrel was barely conscious. Overheated and shaking uncontrollably, her body wasn't hers to control. She snapped the human's bone and gnashed skin and muscle into putrid slime. The silver cycled and she tensed again. Lior replaced the arm with another and kept working.

As it raced through the chambers of her heart, each lap was more searing than the last. She again snapped the bone and clamped down on her teeth. Lior calmly wedged another arm into her mouth. Her vision tunneled to black. Then she felt nothing at all.

) ❋ (

She awoke to a croaking groan, her own according to the aching rattle in her throat. Her tongue was shriveled and the thirst was nearing madness in her semi-conscious state.

Kneeling at her side, Lior held a human corpse. "They've all entered rigor—the blood is coagulated. I don't think you can get much from the carotid. Maybe the femoral?"

"Cut—" Her throat seized. She forced a swallow that felt like hot sand scraping her throat. "Spl…een."

He dissected the body and perched the organ upon her cracked lips. She moaned as her tongue drifted over his bloody hand. Her teeth sank into the meat and the meager force of her jaw squeezed out every drop. "More."

He studied the body cavity, squeezing at random before procuring another morsel. "Liver with the aorta intact—bite here." He positioned the artery against her tongue.

Her eyes drifted shut. He snapped his fingers in her ear. "Wake up. Drink." It was his battlefield voice, deep and commanding—and sexy. She rather enjoyed that side of him.

The seal wasn't tight enough. More blood escaped down her chin than into her mouth. He held it in place and squeezed. She guzzled like a baby bird too weak to feed itself.

"Next time, don't kill them all." He stood to pick through the remaining bodies. "This one might be better."

He sliced out the spleen. She gummed it to goo and began drifting out again. A hot spark on her new vines jarred her awake. Lior was bent over her abdomen. She stiffened as he dusted her vines with another puff of air.

"You enjoy…this too much," she panted.

"As do you." He grinned mischievously.

"Give me the ladle and help me sit up."

"It's going to hurt."

"It's supposed to."

It wasn't an appetizing meal in the least, but the ladle collected the hemoglobin settling at the torso's lowest points. Lior swapped bodies until they had none left. She needed more, but she was alert enough to sit up unaided and examine his craftsmanship. One spot brushed a hypersensitive nerve—air alone made her jerk involuntarily—but, as usual, Lior's engraving was gorgeous.

"That stack was too much for you." Lior draped her cloak over her shoulders and sat next to her. "We were fortunate to find this place, away from the Host's eyes. Between us, we drained all but the goats, but—"

He pondered the animal pen. "We scared them to death."

"No survivors should make you happy, then. Did the extra silver make it harder in the ground?" She gingerly traced the inflamed, bloody edges across her belly, fascinated by Lior's flawless lines.

Clasping his cloak, he nodded. "It burned more, but when I concentrated, the astral form of its lingering energy was stronger."

He flexed his fingers. "Sequential exposure is also increasing my physical tolerance."

"Hm." She pulled her cloak tighter about her shoulders, hunching to avoid letting it touch her fragile skin. "I'm taking longer to heal. The hosts may overwhelm me when we return—"

A horse whinnied nervously in the distance. Lior's amber eyes flashed to golden black. He grinned, his fangs glistening as they lengthened. His entire affect brightened under the promise of fresh blood.

"No more ladling leftovers, m'lady! Breakfast has arrived." He rose with a dramatic flourish of his cloak and slipped out—an impeccable predator on the prowl.

A wry smile curved Kestrel's lips. She closed her eyes and breathed deeply, pulling and pushing the muscles of her belly. She challenged her brain's interpretation of pain versus pleasure, how it felt good when Lior kissed those swollen lines but burned under her own touch. *Why does it hurt? It's information. Not pain. Focus.*

Each repetition reduced the inflammation and submerged her into a meditative state. The cloak slid between her fingers. The wool scratched a fresh scroll. She winced but held still, narrowing in on the affected nerves. The sensation became an interpretation of proximity—no body heat, no humid organics, no metal, no miasma. *No threat.* The thought cycled like a mantra that attuned her brain.

Lior returned with a hefty male and scrawny child flung over one shoulder and a bulging sack over the other. He dropped everything and scurried over to her, his long fingers dipping beneath the cloak.

Lines creased his forehead. "It melded into the solidifying silver."

"I didn't notice—" Transfixed, she analyzed the sensory readings from his fingers, the metal, the wool, the wound itself.

"Be more careful." He held up a silver-lined red thread. "Endymion expects us back soon—we can't delay more than we already have, and we're out of sacred silver. I'll fix it next time."

She folded her hand over his. "Heat the ladle and smooth it over. It's not too late—I haven't fed enough to heal faster than you work."

He reluctantly returned the ladle to the fire as she poked through the bag, delighted to find silver coins, jewelry, and weapons. "We should detour northeast and bury this. He'd want us to take advantage of being this far off the line."

"I concur." Lior gave her a grim look. "This will hurt more than you think it will."

Pulling her close by the nape, he kissed her, his lips fueling a new fire in her core. He pressed the curved bottom of the red-hot ladle against her side and flicked out a sharp blade, carving branches to catch the melting overflow. Fevered pressure mounted in her head like a blacksmith hammering her skull against an anvil. Empty blackness stole her into its fold once more.

II

RAVEN

Endymion's Compound, Summer 2006

The only light came from the shaft above the manzanita. The blood spatter had dried into crusty lines that dripped down the glass to the shattered tea set. The table was still where it had landed, upending a collection of small silver fragments.

Curiosity rolled her onto her stomach. Suspended by glass pedestals, the exposed pieces, each about an inch in length, formed vaguely familiar, broken loops. She righted the piece that had been knocked over and realized that it looked like Kestrel's—

Endymion entered and latched the door. The scent of blood snaked between them. He set down a bamboo tray with a filled cup and saucer. No pot. No table. No assistance.

She collapsed under the weight of her wings. The white of his robe reflected off the glass. She couldn't allow herself to see the rest of his profile. It hurt too much.

If she tore out her own heart, could he bring her back? He'd argued long ago with Master Jonathan that he could only do so much, but somehow he'd brought himself back—if he'd actually died. Where did the line tip in Death's favor when it came to him? And could she cross it?

A melancholy tendril reached out to her. It felt like the Endymion she'd always known, with an awkward hesitancy. She threw blocking energy into her aura. She refused to be his clay doll ever again.

His reflection knelt near her head. She closed her eyes. Had Alex noticed she was gone yet? How long *had* she been gone? Where was Lady Rainne? They'd want her as secured as she was at the Arc of True Blood—even with the Hawkings Protocol.

"My dear." Endymion's voice was gentler than usual. He didn't sound like a rogue commander with generals, officers, couriers, and a *secret compound*.

She grunted in disgust.

"'Tis not going as expected," he continued, unbroken. "I suspect love has made it harder—"

She scoffed. "Was I supposed to melt into your arms because you're a living, breathing rogue instead of my dead lover? Like my heart doesn't see the difference? You are incapable of love. You aren't even worthy of it."

He quieted a moment. "You truly have no idea what I am capable of or my worth. Your heart knows nothing different of me than what it has always known, and it knows *me*."

"You are a monster. I have an imagination."

"Yes, I am a monster." He lifted her into a sitting position.

Her wings popped open, as they apparently liked to do, and propped her up. She couldn't contain an aching groan. The IV catheter in her arm ran up to a seemingly fresh bag. No wonder she didn't hurt quite as much as she had.

"Drink, my dear," he coaxed, lifting the cup to her lips.

She glared at him through narrowed slits and pursed her lips tightly. But, to her surprise, her mouth opened, and warm blood coated her tongue. When it came to Endymion, her body rarely listened to what she actually wanted—or maybe her mind didn't listen to her body. *Did he wield power over her, after all? Or was it the mix of visceral and physical memory?*

"Perhaps it will be easier if you are sedated, wandering the fantastical dreams formerly seen at the Arc of Celestial Night?"

"Easier for whom?" she asked bitterly. "Your bush is riveting. Don't trouble yourself on my account."

He leaned closer and the spark in his eyes lifted her gaze. "Easier for me, my dear. I tend to enjoy the path I walk, but I'm unexpectedly affected by your pain and it is making this *difficult*."

Fear seized her gut. "Don't put me out. Please."

"You will learn to control your wings and try to escape," he said, his lips almost touching hers. "But you will fail because *I* never fail."

"Everyone has a first time."

"Ah, 'tis true for most." He combed his fingers through her hair. "But you are not capable of delivering that to me. 'Twould be foolish, and, as a Commander, you understand that better than most."

"Ugh," she groaned, rolling her neck. His logic made too much damn sense. She hated that she agreed with him.

"Sedation will prevent foolish endeavors."

"I won't." She swallowed over a crusty lump.

"You won't, *what*, my dear?" he cooed sweetly.

"Try to escape." She met his gaze with earnest eyes. He'd see through a lie immediately. "Please, don't make me live like Salea did for so long. I'd rather die."

He straightened. Her words had landed an intentional blow. "'Tis too painful to see you like this, my dear."

He swept a lock of hair behind her ear and cupped her cheek.

"Love—"

Heat flared in her chest. A tentative hand landed on his chest, drawing in his warmth and pulse. She knew this Endymion.

Suddenly, his entire body went rigid. His gaze narrowed and darkened. "No…you wouldn't *try*." He held her hand firm against his heart and said, "Peto somnus."

His expression was smooth as stone as black waves crashed into her peripheral and swept away all consciousness.

III

LUCIEN

Location Unknown, ca. 1799 B.C.

He crept low, eyes darting, ears focused, mind targeted. Wrapped in furs, he felt the thorny pangs of hunger. Wisps of burning wood enticed his nostrils and made his belly grumble. Human fires smelled good until they added animal carcasses.

He jumped from tree to tree until he reached the tribe's walls—recently capped with sharp stakes. Humans retired to their huts with the sinking sun as groups of men began the night watch, tending fires wrongly viewed as protection from *him*.

He hunted at night for camouflage, not because of their superstitions. Light didn't hurt him and he enjoyed the heat of fire.

The moon was late to rise, giving him many cavernous shadows by which to travel. Hushed voices drew him to a tower of firewood. The air's chemical composition shifted. A young watchman, mostly bare from the waist down and fully erect, leaned into a youthful female's embrace.

Despite only having hair on his head, Lucien's body was similar to the male's—he lacked breasts and had a penis between his legs. He didn't understand the appeal of mammary glands or the strange appendage's role in pleasure. Human sex was a ghastly sight, but pheromones flared off this couple and their hearts pumped hard and fast, promising blood. Their breaths came quick and ragged, their hands grabbing, stripping, and stroking. Drunk on hormones, they exuded a kind of warmth that transcended the sexual act.

Humans called it "love."

Pressure built below his belly and grew into a physical ache that was different from hunger. He tried to rub it away as he would the pain of a hard fall or the discomfort that came with the rain, but as he touched something as stiff as a stake, a dizzying wave of pinpointed pleasure

32

crashed over him. He gasped and the couple froze.

Fright filled the female's gaze as she and her lover peered into the shadows. Lucien lunged and severed the female's vocal box and ankle tendons before sinking his fangs into the male's throat. His aroused body shot sparks into nerves he didn't know existed and the male's hot blood stoked his internal fire.

Panting in a haze of rapture and maddening euphoria, he dropped the watchman and turned to the female, her bloodied face twisted with pain and fright. Grasping her throat, she gurgled and choked as blood streamed into her lungs. He lowered on top of her, flashing his fangs to flood her veins with more delicious adrenaline.

He moaned at the new level her fear added to the night's chemistry and slid his tongue between his teeth and along his lips, barely feeling in control of himself. Every sensory touch seemed to burst from between his legs. He latched onto her throat, eager to drink every drop of their love.

He drained her dry and dropped her body, stumbling backward as pressure built and throbbed so hard he couldn't see straight. Gulping cold air, he staggered into the shadows and fumbled with his furs, grasping hold of his hard appendage and tugging with a frenzied need for release.

His heart seemed to stop. Silence came with a cresting moment of weightless pain before he reached the peak and dropped off the edge, grunting hard and tightening his grip on his pulsing arousal. His heart thundered back to life as he soared into ecstasy's arms.

But that high didn't last long. He'd alerted the night watch. Male voices carried over crackling fires.

Huffing for breath, he leaned his forearm against the woodpile. Sanity slowly returned and his grip loosened. A contented sigh brushed his lips as warmth radiated from his core. His skin had shed its tightness. He felt looser and relaxed.

The skin on his penis was as supple as human skin and pale blue in color—no armor, no scales. As it shrank and returned to normal, the scales and armor returned. He pulled apart the furs covering his chest. The scales there and on his arms were smooth like snakeskin, colored a light bluish-teal that shimmered with iridescence under the moon.

The night watch was getting closer. His skin tightened, darkened, and re-armored. No sign of the couple's intangible warmth remained. He leaped over the wall and returned to his forest home, still a monster alone, incapable and unworthy of the love that humans so freely shared with each other.

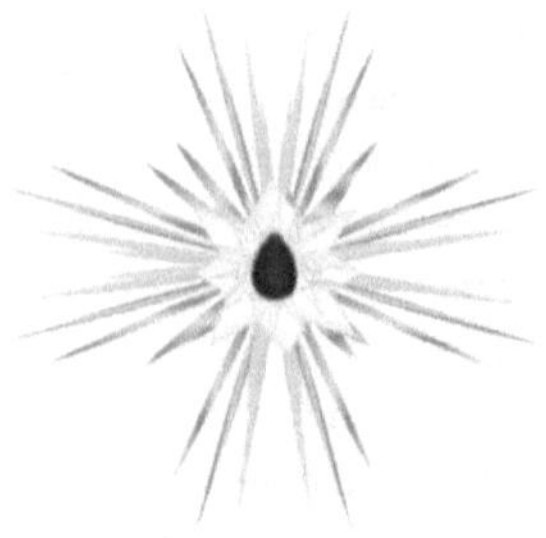

CHAPTER FIVE: A DREAM OF JOY DEPARTED

I

ERIC

Orison Crossing, Summer 2006

The grandfather clock's ticking hammered on his temples. He wiped his face and blew out a nervous breath. The voices in the forest were gone, the negotiations finished. Donovan was officially free to run and hold Eric emotionally hostage.

Grief caged his anger in knots that tightened the more it fought for freedom. Even with her essence inside him, Paresh was dead. Her soul in the tree—dead. Her corpse *somewhere out there*—dead.

A hot tear streaked his cheek. Staring into the blackened hearth, he ground his teeth, trying to bite back reality. Heat burned his chest and his jaw quivered.

How are you gone just like that?

A haggard breath shook loose, and with it came body-heaving sobs. He buried his face in his hands. His shoulders quaked as he hunched over his knees.

Ripped from his arms. Dead.

But she's not, yet. Make him tell you.

The cottage door opened. Eric howled and sprang up. The sofa skidded onto its back as he flew past Jonathan onto the flagstone and into the forest, which blended into the singular shade of midnight. He blew past the tree line, spurred by the scent of cloves and innocent blood.

Footsteps pounded behind him. Branches whipped his cheeks. Twigs snapped under his feet. Rotting trunks were meager obstacles he sailed over on instinct. The voices yelling at him fell on unhearing ears. *He* was close.

What was the point of living life if it wasn't actually living? Paresh would never know freedom. The blood in her veins promised power. She'd always be hunted as a prize—if not by Donovan, then someone else. He knew that well. Jonathan had won *his* prize, after all.

He would force Donovan to talk. They would round up all the rogues. Eliminate *all* threats. Eric wouldn't drag it out again. He'd hesitated with David and Paresh had suffered because of it. No. Donovan didn't deserve to draw another breath. So he wouldn't.

A loping form appeared. Crimson draped the world. Eric lunged.

No! No! It's not right!

The frame was too limber, too thin, too light. He rolled with it and glimpsed a hand clutching white clove-scented candles. Pinning Kestrel onto her back, he curled a monstrous hand around her throat and growled, "*Where is he?*"

Grief and rage reflected in her eyes. "He deserves to die," she spat, flicking her disgusted gaze down at the candles. "I did not partake of this ruse willingly, *my lord*."

The beast roared to tear out her heart. He shoved off with an agonized scream that bordered insanity and charged backward, reaching for Jonathan, but catching Alex when he jumped in the way.

"*You let him go! You let him go and he's got her!*" Eric shrieked into Alex's tearstained face.

Hate lit Alex's engorged orbs. "It's what she wanted!" he cried, panting unevenly. "*But he deserves to die. No one here disputes that!*"

"We'll find her body and destroy him, Brother," Jonathan said firmly even though he sounded nothing like himself. "No matter how long it takes."

"You talk like we have time to spare," Eric snapped. "You're the ones talking about the apocalypse hitting any day. Rogue angels and dark spots falling to Earth. *Even Saint Michael said the world is doomed without her!*"

Protectively covering his abdomen, Jonathan leaned against a tree and shook his head. He didn't touch the hair that fell over his face. His clothes were stained and torn. "We must find her. It's the only way."

Alex hiccupped. "I don't know how long Darkesiel will take to get here, but Donovan said Lucifer needed her alive. If this world hinges on her one way or another, we might have more time than you think."

Eric jerked Alex nose to nose. "I. Don't. Want. More. Time. *I want him talking or dead!*"

Kestrel stood. "Paresh told Alex to distract you. She knew you'd go after Donovan."

He snarled over his shoulder. "Did she also say I'd go after those who aided him?"

"She did." Alex's head bobbed sadly. "This is what she said would happen—*all* of it."

"What do you—" Eric slapped at a sharp pinch in his neck. His fingers slipped over a glass syringe and he glimpsed a tall form.

"Lu…cie…n."

He flailed weakly and fell onto his backside. His vision swam in doubled circles as the foursome became eight and gathered at the edges of slowly encroaching darkness. He couldn't speak.

He didn't know where he was. Where was Paresh? He wanted to see her smile, to hear her voice. He blinked. It was the slowest blink in history. God, he loved her. She made him whole.

The world shifted violently upside down. He was moving through the air. Love made him want to float like that. He wanted to float with Paresh. In love.

He blinked again. Except his eyes didn't open. Invisible barbs rammed into his skin. A vice squeezed his heart. White-hot pain exploded throughout the entirety of his body, but his screams were trapped in his throat. Paresh appeared, glowing like a star, a guiding beacon in the torturous black. She drew him into the warmth of her cradling embrace and he surrendered willingly.

☽ ✳ ☾

ALEXANDER

Alex cringed at the shock that blasted through Eric's aura when he saw Lord Lucien and realized what was happening. Sorrow crested at his back, sparking every nerve to scream, *Run and never stop!*

But he stood firm in his resolve. For *her*, he would do anything. For *her*, he would take any chance, big or small. For *her*, he would protect Eric *and* save her future.

Save him from himself so you can save me. Paresh's voice was the delicate tinkle of a glass bell in his mind. *He can't control it.*

Duty came with composure, but his mind was in chaos. Disgust roiled Alex's stomach. The Crimson Guard would throw life and limb to protect that monster—the most wanted creature in the Realm of Man—from his *victim* who lay in the fiery thrall of box jellyfish venom, among the deadliest and most *excruciating* in the world.

He hated tormenting Eric. Hated that *they* had chosen this method. Hated how helpless he felt. That *he* was a part of this. *Again.* That he'd been with the group that had chased Paresh to a brutal death after she'd come home.

Lord Lucien capped the needle apathetically. The emotional slips of recent days were gone. That stoicism had gotten their nation through the blackest days and nights, but now, more than ever before, Alex wished to see burning resolve, an ember of anger, a hint of sadness, something, *anything*—even his terrifying creature form. Lord Lucien's determination could propel them forward, set the beat of their war drums, energize them into the global search to find what had been so painfully taken. But—

Nothing.

Alex hung his head and wiped his cheeks with the back of his hand. At least he'd had the foresight to add Paresh's blood to the venom to cushion the pain and betrayal.

"How long will that keep him out?" Kestrel asked as Lord Lucien picked up Eric's body.

"We don't know," Jonathan said, slumped against a young oak. "The Chthonic Knights never tested it on either of us—" He gestured at Lord Lucien. "—and the addition of Paresh's blood could backfire and make it wear off faster."

"The Chthonic Knights usually mix it with their liquid silver when they're feeling particularly devious," Alex mumbled. "You'd know better than anyone else, given that Lior invented that delightful torture."

"That's a good idea." Kestrel's black cloak dropped to the forest floor. She closed her eyes and pulled in a deep belly breath to expand her silver vines, focusing her aura and energy on Eric. She rolled her head back and moaned.

"He's…" She grimaced. "Delirious and happy? I think her blood acted as a hallucinogenic while the venom paralyzed him."

"So he might stay out longer." Alex sighed. "It doesn't matter. When he wakes up, we'll have to deal with him. Paresh told me that he doesn't know his own strength—but I think we knew that already—and his beast will rage out of control. Who knows if he'll be able to think straight?"

He quieted a moment. To Kestrel, he said, "You know what to do. Get the rotation going and make sure they don't underestimate Eric. He would've killed them as he was yesterday…so now—"

He tossed a hand up. "He'll go berserk."

"Volunteers only," Jonathan added. "I don't want to waste our best on him—"

"It's not for *him*," Lord Lucien said coldly.

"I know that," Jonathan snapped. "If you hadn't interrupted, I was getting there. They only need to buy time to call for back up."

"I'll call a meeting with Farran, Seneca, and Minerva about intel and recon teams." Kestrel retrieved her cloak. "He can't hide her forever, especially since he needs to deliver vials of Eric's blood at regular intervals to keep her cells from degrading."

"Speaking of—" Lord Lucien glanced at Jonathan.

"I'll get his blood. One way or another. For now, we'll get him away from here. Back to Vermont. Hopefully, he'll be more mindful of his behavior there."

Jonathan shifted his attention to Kestrel. "After your meeting and team deployment, get that human you like and join us."

Surprise rippled through Kestrel's aura. Alex cocked a brow and asked, "You like a human?"

"She—"

"Eric's trustee, Sarah." Jonathan groaned as he stood. He motioned for Lucien to get moving. "She can help him better than we can."

"As you wish, of course, my lord," Kestrel said, tucking her chin.

"Alex?" Jonathan nudged his chin at the Hollow's opening portal.

Alex looked at Kestrel. "You got this?"

She nodded. "It sucks, but Raven would say to have hope, right?"

Alex hesitated at the Hollow's threshold. "Hey, ask Cyp and Heron to look for her."

Lord Lucien's voice filtered through the rolling white haze. "Belay that order. Lucifer has taken her, as well. She is gone to us."

☽ ✳ ☾

ERIC

He was a boy, kicking back in a weedy ditch of prairie switch grasses, cattails, and bright yellow Heliopsis—the false sunflower. Enveloped in summer's golden haze. Crickets chirping. Bugs buzzing his ears. Molding clouds into shapes as they drifted on a lazy breeze through a clear blue sky. Plucking purple clover to suck out its sweet nectar before the bees hogged it all.

He was usually waiting for Dora and the promise of a boiled egg to soothe the ache in his belly. Labor breaks were a rare thing on the Faust farm—especially when expected to cover his drunken father's work alongside his own—but this was the best part of his day.

A young Paresh threw herself down beside him, stirring up scents of earthy, syrupy honey. She rolled onto her side and watched him with her steel-gray eyes, her lips slightly kinked as she held a finger out and a bumblebee landed.

The sun crowned her like an angel and stole his breath. He wanted to stroke her cheek. He jerked his hand back at the sight of the dirt and manure encrusted into his nail beds and under the broken and chipped tips. His calloused hands would surely scrape her soft skin. How could he possibly think of touching her?

She placed her hand on his grimy chest and laid her head in the crook of his sweaty shoulder. He didn't want to sully her with his filth and started to pull back, but suddenly they were older, and the grime disappeared. He cupped her cheek with a clean, smooth hand.

"Is this one of the Elysian Fields?" she asked, nuzzling his palm.

"It could be," he murmured. Slinking down, he kissed her, gently at first, and then hungrier, parting her cushioning lips. She tasted like the nectar from the clover's flowers. "I hope so."

She blinked slowly, again watching him. "You don't want to leave?"

"I want to be where you are," he whispered.

"Then let *them* find me, my love." She closed her eyes and kissed him, pressing her fingers beneath his jaw. "Michael won't let me stay long. He only permitted me this because Lucifer broke one of their celestial rules regarding a former human."

His eyes shot open. Paresh was smiling, but she was pale, deathly so, and her belly——

So much blood. No bump. No fetal heartbeat.

His heart sank into a pit. Wildly grabbing for her, he gathered her close and buried his face into her hair. She smelled like freshly disturbed dirt—like the ground at Molly's funeral, damp with the dew of dawn and tears of mourning.

"N-no!" he cried. "No—you can't go!"

He opened his eyes and saw a bundle of grass in his arms. He was a boy again, in the ditch, waiting for Dora and the boiled egg.

The sound of his own moaning woke him. Through drooping slits, he took in a sunlit parlor, doused in white paint and Depression-era green glass. He blinked and sat up, wincing at his throbbing head.

He shielded his eyes with one hand while the other dropped onto plush velvet. Instantly recognizing the curves of the Victorian era, he scanned the modified highboy, topped with a decanter of port, etched crystal goblets, and a matching crystal platter of savory wafers. Chiffon shears softened the light streaming through a row of windows at his back and a smaller pane on the opposite wall. A glass and wrought iron coffee table sat between him and two high backs, buttoned up in the same forest green as the sofa.

What the…hell?

He tried to stand on spaghetti legs. The trusty sofa caught him. He whimpered and covered his eyes. The brightness was disorienting.

Someone sat beside him and patted his thigh. The scent of blood snaked beneath his nose.

He peered between his fingers and winced again when a wave of throbbing pain knocked him back. "Sarah?"

She placed a highball into his hand and helped him lift it to his mouth. Her expression was concerned and apologetic. "The Smiths thought you might appreciate some *juice*."

The Smiths? The name's familiarity loitered beyond his grasp. He drank and hoped for clarity.

Lowering her voice, Sarah added, "You're in the parlor with external noise blocked to let you rest. H-how…are you?"

He cracked an eye and squinted at her. "Wh-what? Why am I in Vermont? And…and…*juice*? They know——"

"Um, right," she said gently, "but they don't, uh, know that I know, or that the others…"

His stomach churned as reality returned. He chugged the glass and covered his face, huffing into his palms. "No, no, no, no, no——"

"I'm so sorry." Her voice broke. "They're searching *everywhere*."

"*No!*" he yelled, his voice rattling the walls and crystal.

She squeezed his knee and scooted closer. "We have to have faith, right? That this is only temporary?"

He yelled again and stomped his foot, managing to thunder through the floorboards on the ground level. They'd brought him here to contain him, knowing he'd restrain himself in the presence of humans in their home—the Smiths, his innkeepers. Like most who knew his truth, they'd never witnessed his demonic façade.

"Jonathan!" he roared, blindly searching for his Vampiric Star. His pockets were empty. They'd taken everything.

Sarah's grip tightened. "I'm the only one in the house, Eric. It's just us."

The sorrow in her voice finally reached something inside him. His voice broke as he sobbed into his palms. "Please draw the shades. I can't…the sun is too painful."

She patted his leg and moments later, relief came from blackout shades. The parlor doors clicked and the curtains zipped shut. He opened his eyes to a much dimmer room.

Returning to his side, she asked, "How do you feel? They weren't sure about the side effects."

He shook his head. How could he possibly care about himself now?

"They killed our baby, too," Eric whispered hoarsely. "They're both…*both* gone."

"I'm so sorry, Eric." She dabbed at her eyes. "But it's not forever."

She pulled him into an awkward embrace. Grief racked his whole body—shaking and choking, dripping and drooling. She cried softly with him, smoothing her hand over his back and sweeping comforting fingers through his hair.

Eventually, his head emptied of thought and he quieted. On a base level, he was thankful for the thoughtfulness of Sarah's presence and the familiar surroundings. The silence lingered unbroken, and he didn't want it to end. If that moment looped, just for them, in that parlor, the world would turn and they could find Paresh while he hid from his pain. His failures.

"They took her right from my arms." He thrust his head back and Sarah flinched at the *crack* of his skull on the wooden frame. He wiped his face and shook his head—like it'd be that easy to deny his guilt. He'd always fail Paresh. He was her Anointed Strength, but that didn't mean he was strong *for* her—only that his strength belonged to her. She pulled it from him and made it her own. That's why she'd entrusted the instructions to *Alex*.

She knew you'd be a violent mess. He grunted and clenched a fist at his side. He ground his teeth as memories of his father tumbled drunkenly in through a mental door. He understood wanting to hide and wishing for numbing oblivion. But his father had thrown him aside. *I would never do that to our daughter.*

He met Sarah's concerned gaze and covered her hand. She'd hadn't ever seen him like this and hadn't known of the pregnancy. "Thank you." His voice cracked. "This can't be easy for you."

"Don't you worry about me. I'll put my anger to work on finding her and being there for you—always."

The determined gleam in her eyes was disturbing. "What—" He wasn't sure he wanted the answer, but he finished, "do you mean by that?"

She licked her lips. "Just…I'm here for you. I'll get you another drink. Please don't try to stand—the venom attacked your nervous system."

"Venom?" He held onto her hand as she stood. "You mentioned side effects—wha…what did they hit me with?"

"Kestrel said it was a mixture of box jellyfish venom and, um…Paresh's blood." She twisted free of his grasp and made a constrained dash for the exit, closing the doors behind her.

Tears needled his eyes. Anger locked his jaw. His lips trembled into a snarl. He swept his hand over the warm spot Sarah had left behind and thought about Paresh.

She would've loved this house's mismatched style that ran the gamut from cozy wooded cabin to Colonial New England lodge, with Victorian elements mashed with the 1920s and Great Depression. Why had they thought bringing him here was a good idea? Did they really expect him to believe they'd left him alone with Sarah?

He leaned forward on his knees and split his fingers and thumb over his brow. His legs felt stronger, like the paralytic was wearing off, and he was clearheaded enough to see through their lie.

Grinding his teeth, he growled, "I don't care who's out there—if I don't get answers *now*, I'm coming for all of you when this venom wears off—starting with Lucien."

Minutes passed in abnormal silence. Time was a cruel master, isolating him and its passing with his thoughts.

No one came.

Not even Sarah.

They weren't going to let him drink enough to heal. She had given him only enough to soothe his throat. They were stalling, and that riled his anger into a blaze that would destroy anything, and anyone, in its path.

☽ ✺ ☾

KESTREL

Kestrel could hear the dejection in Sarah's footsteps as she plodded up the stairs. The melancholy in her breath as she exhaled past Master Jonathan at the landing. And shared the guilt in the look that passed between Sarah and Alex as Eric yelled beneath them.

"Good luck," Alex whispered.

Sarah locked eyes with Kestrel through the doorway. They were sharing the room at the head of the house, directly above the parlor. Her nervous energy buzzed Kestrel's vines as she shut the door and closed the circuit for the privacy button.

"Now they can't hear us," Kestrel said as Sarah slowly melted onto her. No tears or visible emotion. Just silent need. The familiarity made her silver vines sing. She closed her eyes and easily envisioned Lior in her arms. "You did well. It's for the best."

Sarah let go and looked around uncertainly. She gestured at the bed. "I guess that's the best place?"

She fingered the quilt's patch-worked seams before she sat. "I almost told him." She searched Kestrel's face. "I should have told him."

Sarah reached for Kestrel's waist, nudging her closer and tracing the eternally infantile skin with a touch as soft as Lior's, curling up and around in the same backward fashion and eliciting the same sensual response. A strange tickle crept into Kestrel's heart. Emotions had been hitting hard from the moment she met Sarah only days ago in The Greenery's kitchen.

"Ever since I was a child," Sarah whispered, absently watching her fingers, "I've been enthralled by scrolling patterns—how the tendrils of vines branch off and cling to anything and everything, intertwining and joining things that would otherwise not connect."

The corner of one eye crinkled as she looked up and her hazel orbs sank into Kestrel's. A nostalgic smile quirked her mouth up. "I suppose this is a human thing that you won't understand, but I hated latticing pies. I always made it ten times harder by decorating with pumpkin or squash vines or scrolling morning glories."

She chuckled. "My grandfather would shake his head and say, 'Sarah Berhane Weaverly! You always make it too darn pretty! I hate to cut it, but I love to eat it!'" She laughed at her attempt to mimic his elderly, rasping voice.

Berhane. The name itself strummed Kestrel's vines—it shared the same meaning as *Lior*.

"But then he'd settle back and watch me roll and shape the dough like he could sit there forever in awe of those thin, fragile lines and leaves. He thought I had the patience of a saint to create something so intricate and beautiful."

"Berhane is your middle name?"

Sarah smiled. "Yeah, it's a family name that pops up every other generation or so. It started with my ancestral grandfather, Willy. He was born into slavery, named Berhane by his mother, and then sold and renamed like an animal."

Sarah quieted. "He wasn't allowed anything, not even his own name...but he found freedom with Eric's help. He never found his mother or father, though, so our family starts with him. It's like a legend—direct descendants of Willy's are periodically compelled to give 'Berhane' as the middle name of a child that inevitably grows up to be the next Caretaker. My grandfather, Samuel Berhane, was my predecessor. The compulsion skipped my dad's generation, and it hasn't hit my sister, yet. Hopefully, it won't."

"Are you certain this is what you want? There's no going back." Kestrel caught Sarah's hand and crouched to bring them eye to eye. To eyes that gleamed like Lior's.

My light.

Swallowing hard, Sarah nodded. "I've said my good-byes. Sent my grandfather home to my sister. I don't belong in their world. I never have and I don't want that for anyone else down the line."

Her gaze dropped to her feet, but she seemed to see through them to the man below. A strange twinge thumped Kestrel's heart. "You love Lord Eric."

"More than anyone else in my family. I grew up at his side knowing that I'd be Caretaker one day. There is no backup for me. I...I want to be there for him, always. This is the only way."

She moistened her lips. "I've wanted this for a while, but could never ask him. I knew he couldn't do it, and maybe I was even a little afraid that he wouldn't let me find a way."

She squeezed Kestrel's hand. "But the instant I met you, I knew you could. That we were meant to meet."

"You were so insistent," Kestrel whispered to herself. Her heart was in free fall. She'd thought she finally understood these ravaging emotions, but she'd interpreted everything wrongly.

"I wanted to believe so, as well, but it cannot be for me if you love him," Kestrel said. "Humans love so freely and easily. I wonder if that is enviable or painful."

Sarah's brow furrowed. "What do you mean? I thought—I felt something with you that I've missed with so many others. Didn't you feel it, too? Or is it off because I'm human?"

Kestrel's voice caught in her throat. Her forehead crinkled as she stood and eyed Sarah a moment. Had *she* missed something? She *knew* Lior's soul sat before her, *felt it* deep in her bones. Didn't that mean they were meant to be together? Or had the love locked in his heart died with his body?

"I..." Kestrel ran her hands through her hair. Sarah's energy heated the scrolls looping over her belly. Closing her eyes, she drew a long breath into her lungs and streamed it out slowly between her lips. In her mind, Lior manifested before her. His hands landed on her hips and he leaned in to kiss her with soft, tender lips.

"Say what you feel, what you think, what you want to know," he whispered. "Remember the first time Endymion's aura struck your vines? How much you learned despite the pain? And how you wanted more, to study and hone your skills? How can you learn about love if you close it off?"

His breath was warm in her ear. "Fear does not become you. Speak, ask, and learn through pain. Your light is here, returned to you with love, I promise."

When his lips returned to hers, Kestrel cupped the springy curls at the back of Sarah's head and devoured her mouth in an entirely familiar way. *My Lady Light.*

She slid her fingers along the undersides of Sarah's arms until she could grip her hands. She didn't know why, but letting go seemed to mean losing Lior.

Not Lior—Berhane. Sarah.

Even though she had Lior's soul, Sarah was very much her own person. *More human, but so much like him.*

"I spent centuries training my body and mind to understand what I encounter, but I don't understand love," Kestrel confessed. "How can you kiss me like that when you love Lord Eric?"

A lopsided grin brightened Sarah's countenance. She shifted her weight to one foot, giving her frame a limber appearance that quickened Kestrel's heart. Life had always been cut and dry, black and white. She'd walked the Earth confident in her knowledge and her abilities—even after Salea killed Lior—but love had stolen all of that from her. She hated the uncertainty of it.

"I know I'm just a babe compared to y'all ancient ones," Sarah said, the look in her eyes bringing heat to Kestrel's face. "But there're different kinds of love and I do not love Eric like *that*."

She cupped Kestrel's cheek and kissed her. "See, Eric's family. But you...you're, well, *hot*."

"We were meant to meet," Kestrel whispered.

"I sure hope so, 'cause I don't want to change if I can't be with you. I feel like..." Sarah retreated into thought.

"You're whole for the first time?" Kestrel suggested, leaning in for another kiss. If such a thing was possible, Sarah tasted like moonlight and stardust, and her skin was as smooth as dark silk skimming the nightly breeze.

"Yeah…that." Sarah's kiss grew hungrier, impassioned. "Like I've known you forever."

"I think you have."

Fingers traced Kestrel's vines by muscle memory despite never having touched her. Cushioning lips were as maddeningly gentle and teasing as they'd been for centuries in a younger, mortal body. And a terrifyingly absent aura perfectly locked into place to form a spherical whole for the first time in a century—and Sarah wasn't even a vampire yet.

"Wait." Panting, Kestrel leaned her forehead against Sarah's. "You need all your strength to survive."

A knock at the door interrupted Sarah's response.

Kestrel swore under her breath. She hoped it was Alex, because she couldn't hide her emotions from Master Jonathan.

"Use the button and don't open the door," Sarah said.

Kestrel tapped her head. "You always were the smarter one."

After deactivating the button, she called through the door and was relieved to hear Alex checking in. "We're fine. It's just—"

"Last minute nerves," Sarah yelled. Wide-eyed, she clasped her hands over her mouth. "Oops! I guess I won't need to yell like that anymore, will I?"

In the hallway, Alex chuckled sadly. "Paresh is the same way. I won't rush you, but we do need to check on him again. Soon."

Kestrel shared a somber glance with Sarah.

"I should be the one," Sarah said. "I should tell him."

Shaking her head, Kestrel said, "You wrote the letter. We'll deal with him. Don't worry." To Alex she added, "I'll be out soon."

She didn't reactivate the button to force herself to stay on task. "I'll be here when you wake up. We'll start training right away—Master Jonathan approved my requests. We'll do this together."

Just like we always have.

Sarah nodded and her nerves buzzed the vines again. She leaned back on the bed and arched her throat.

Kestrel smirked and felt a slightly devious crease form beneath her eye. "I can do better than that, but it's going to hurt."

A familiar arrogance spread across Sarah's face. "Ah, it's supposed to, right?"

Kestrel hid her surprise. She'd thought Lior's stronger personality traits might appear once his soul returned to a vampiric body, but now she wondered if his memories might awaken, too. As she leaned over

Sarah, her lips parted and her tongue found its mate, twisting and lapping. She longed to know this woman in ways she'd only ever known Lior. She moaned and buried her fingers into Sarah's hair and delivered the kiss of death.

II

RAVEN

Endymion's Compound, Summer 2006

Rising through sleep's groggy haze, Raven heard Endymion arguing with someone. She couldn't open her eyes.

"…the girl's alteration is underway…addressing my body?"

"Do not concern yourself…dealt with it…will update Sarah when the time…"

The ice in that voice chilled her to the core. She concentrated to hear the voices more clearly and wondered why Lord Lucien was there. Did he know about Lucifer, too? About *her*?

"'Twould not be favorable to try my patience," Endymion warned.

"Neither would forgetting your place, *Third Born*. She's awake. You obviously can't handle her on your own. We should end this."

Endymion snorted. "Do not tell me what I can't do. Return to that pet you love so much——or have you locked him out of the arc, too?"

"Do not spit on love at the moment it's backfired on you. Your command *failed*," Lord Lucien said with biting severity.

Endymion's simmering voice lowered. "She is *one* in an army that always has, and always will, outnumber yours. 'Twas expected. Now go."

Raven steadied her breath and pulse against her spinning mind. She couldn't hide that she was awake, but she could withhold her shock if she was careful. No wonder Endymion never failed. Why would he when they were on the same team, working together?

How convenient that Salea hit the arc when Lord Lucien was absent. No one had questioned it beyond coincidence. But, then again, until now, no one had ever questioned or threatened Lord Lucien other than Eric.

Endymion slipped in and set the latch, as usual. He seemed to linger at the door as though determining what she might have overheard as indecipherable voices filtered in——presumably from his *army*. An army bigger than Lord Lucien's.

How much had the Vampiric Nation fractured? What was going on in the world? She'd begun to think the COMS were smaller than anticipated, but maybe she was wrong. The more she learned, the less she liked. Let him wonder what she'd heard. None of it mattered until she escaped.

"*Peto somnus?*" she yelled, partly to divert his attention, but mostly because she was furious. "I'm not a fucking doll! How did you knock me out?"

Silence.

"I thought me being awake was too painful *for you*," she added, oozing sarcasm, "that I was supposed to wander the dreams we forced on Salea."

"Salea only ever saw nightmares," he said. "As one might under Lucifer's influence during one's formative years."

He was suddenly at her side, his lips against her ear, whispering, "And you said I was the cruel one."

The hairs on her nape bristled. All those times she'd asked "Hawkiel" to pepper visions into Salea's dreams—

"No retort, my dear?" He sounded unusually agitated. "Are you plotting an ill-fated escape?"

"I can't open my eyes thanks to whatever you did to me," she snapped. "You think I can possibly plot and plan with a mind tricked to sleep?"

"Ah, my dear," he whispered, "I believe you can do anything that pops into that head of yours."

Good point, she thought. She rammed her skull into his and her wings blew open as they always did when she sat up. She heard him slam into the far wall. A wisp of a smile crept over her mouth.

He yanked her left primary feather. Pain scorched a direct line to the nerves lining her shoulder blade. Each one felt like a stabbing blade.

She jerked instinctively, screaming as the sensation sliced deeper.

He leaned over her shoulder. "Do not become difficult, my dear. I do not enjoy hurting you and do not wish to clip your wings, but I will do whatever I must."

He let go and the pain dulled to throbbing pinpricks. She drew her legs up and hugged herself, fingers desperately scrabbling over soft scales on her back.

Despite the chill in his voice and the fire in her nerves, the warm caress of his breath woke her body. Tears surged into her eyes as the nerves in her belly sang. This was so messed up.

He ran his fingers down a tingling path to the IV catheter in her arm. His lips alighted upon her earlobe. Butterflies crashed in her stomach. "'Tis a shame, though not surprising, that my clay doll has hardened."

He peeled the tape off her skin, taking great care not to harm her— and making certain she knew it. "I wished to hydrate you and treat you as a queen—"

He removed the catheter with equal care. "But I cannot permit you to heal as long as you choose to test me."

"When…I saw your body, I thought, 'he loved me, he loved me before it was possible, he loved me more than anyone else…'" Her voice broke and she folded tighter into herself. If only the world had swallowed her the day she was born. She'd had the blade *right there*, biting into her breast, ready to stake her heart. She should've died then…but "Hawkiel" had *saved* her…for this.

Endymion cupped her cheek, stroking gently with his thumb. He was tender like the old Endymion and warmed her core to life beneath the butterflies.

But that was the old Endymion.

"Then you introduced me to the rarest plant in the world, Raven's Manzanita, *here* in your *compound*, in your room…and I realized—"

A stone formed in her throat and she was too dehydrated to swallow past it. She tried to massage it lose.

He moved closer. He was facing her—his chest touching her arm, his heart thumping a comforting beat. The scent of lavender enrobed them both.

"It's not love," she croaked at last. "It's obsession. And me—"

A sad laugh dropped off her lips. "I needed a safe space, a place to drop the charades and burdens, but…"

He was close enough to kiss. His breath dusted her cheek.

Tightening her hold on her throat, she shook her head and squeezed tears down her cheeks. "It's not healthy. It's not love. It's dependency. Running away."

She faced him then, nose to nose, lips to lips, and firmly said, "Alex loves me. Alex has always loved me, even before it was possible. Alex loves me more than anyone else. *Alex loves me more than you ever could.*"

His lips moved against hers, turning his words into kisses with a fairy light touch. "My dear, I'm *painfully* aware that I love you—and that you love me—"

His finger swept up her cheek. "Or you would not be crying."

Cradling her nape, his rose petal lips cushioned hers as perfectly as they always had, ripping her open in a new, devastating way. She kissed him back, her body physically responding to him, but her mind—

She knew he knew it, too. Trickling tears turned into a river.

"I am sorry for hurting you," he whispered softly, kissing her cheeks. "'Tis the best I can do to avoid something far worse."

I do not enjoy hurting you.

Why had he said that? He enjoyed everything he did.

"Why aren't I bringing death to the world at Rainne's side as Lucifer desires?"

"You understand so little, young one." He kissed the tip of her nose. "As long as you are here, with me, you will stay the Raven I know and love."

"W-well, he c-can't override the Hawking's Protocol and neither can Paresh. That only leaves me, so good luck with that. Hurt me all you like…it's not happening."

"Hopefully, he won't need you when the time comes." He kissed her crown. "'Tis when you leave my side that you shall succumb to Lucifer's will or fall into madness resisting. Regardless, he shall use you as a tool with no more will of your own than Rainne has."

Raven struggled to suck in a shallow breath. The weight of the silver bones in her wings tipped her off balance as her shoulders sagged. "So if I escape——"

"'Tis the point, child. There is no escape. Stay with me. I wish to trust you." He lightly fingered her hair. "But I know you too well. And you know me, so listen when I say that there is no escaping *Lucifer*."

Despair crushed down with merciless gravity, ramming her flat into trapping darkness. "I can't…I can't *do this*! Let me open my eyes!"

She panicked and lashed out with her fists. As her knuckles punched the white silk and chest she knew so well, that damned crimson stain bloomed in her mind and so, too, did the twin pains of sorrow and betrayal.

"You said you'd kill Donovan for making me cry!" she screamed. "*What are you going to do to yourself?*"

Restraining her fists with a fraction of the required force, he kissed her again and she responded, her heart shrieking angrier than a banshee seeking revenge. She wanted the Endymion she knew, not this stranger. But she also didn't want to be alone and hopeless at the End of Days. "Why can't you fix me? Hold me? Love me more than you hate the world?"

Alex would do all those things, and smile brighter than the sun. Alex would crack jokes, mix his idioms, and act like an idiot for a laugh. He'd never cruelly taunt or tease. He'd never intentionally hurt her——

But he had.

The memory of fighting him in the woods burst open and she felt the tingle of nerve damage caused by the Cataclysm. That was an Alex she'd never known. That Alex had nearly severed her arm——

But he'd been fighting for his life. She might've killed him otherwise. How could people who loved each other act like that?

His heart-broken voice echoed in her mind. *I choose you, Raven, even though you can't choose me.*

And she'd said, *Thank you.*

She wished she'd told him the words he'd wanted to hear—words that were true—and that she had his coin in her pocket to have a piece of him with her. She touched the broken hoops pinned through her ear cartilage, the ones he'd cleft with a precise throw of her daggers.

They'd both hurt each other. They both had unsaid regrets.

The romanticism of love was a lie. All of it was. Every last bit.

She gasped for air and buried her face, sobbing with all her soul.

Alex loved her the most. He didn't know where she was. If she was alive. But he wouldn't stop looking until he found her. And Endymion— maybe even Lord Lucien—would misguide him. Maybe even kill him for it—if he wasn't already dead.

"Alex!" Folding in half between her knees, she screamed, raspy and hoarse, like a mortally wounded animal. She couldn't leave even if he did find her. "*I will never be your queen! And I'll never activate Rainne!*"

"Aw, my dear, Raven." Endymion's fingers moved smoothly through her bob and down her nape. He tucked her head under his chin and folded her to his chest—as though he could possibly comfort her. "You've always been my queen, and you always will be, for only you can be."

An undercurrent of anger flowed beneath his words. "You must understand, young one, that you're mistaken about Paresh. She doesn't need to override the Hawkings Protocol. Her touch alone can unlock *all* of Rainne's restrictions."

Raven shivered in his arms. "What—"

"Alas, Paresh is dead. You are all we have left." He kissed the top of her head. "Now sleep."

"N-no—" Raven started hyperventilating. "P-Paresh is d—"

"Peto somnus."

Black waves swept her into sleep's domain.

III

KESTREL

European Continent near the Swiss Plateau, ca.455 A.D.

Brisk air nipped her exposed skin and silver channels, churning the crisp scents of frosted evergreens into deeper revelations of urine and burning wood. She didn't need to see the smoke. The blood scent of fresh meat was an easy trail to follow.

She tossed the heavy bag over her other shoulder. With a darkening sky that promised more snow, she hoped the humans at the camp had built a shelter. She reached back to pull Lior up, weakened from a longer stint underground. She hated seeing him like this, hobbling at her heels barely upright.

He squeezed her hand and slumped against a scraggly, dead tree. Huffing lightly, he motioned for her to drop their supplies. "It's not far off. Go. I'll follow."

She set the bag down and raced ahead, leaping to the trees before the camp came into view. These humans didn't notice the unnatural silence that came with her presence. With the population shifting away from the Romans, they probably weren't familiar with the area to know any better.

Although silence to any human should serve a swift warning.

She perched on high and observed two men on a freshly cut log, hands outstretched to growing flames, while two others placed fir branches atop a long lean-to shelter, situated for optimal warmth against the wind. Skinned rabbits hung from a branch, their fur stretched and drying on a fallen trunk near the fire.

Only four. And there weren't others around for miles. She wouldn't kill them. Yet. Incapacitation had become their preference, but with so few, she'd need to be extra careful not to injure them in ways that caused bleeding and wasted their only useful resource.

She pulled on leather cording coiled around her waist and whistled, pitching it high with a low dip to distinguish it from a birdcall. All four men jerked to attention. They exchanged looks. Kestrel climbed higher and leaped over their camp into the sharp needles of a spruce. Axe in hand, one man set off to investigate. The other, also armed with an axe, joined the two at the fire.

She dropped from branch to branch, skipping multiple levels, until browned foliage and cold earth cushioned her leather boots. She was a specter in red wool, snapping the spine of the largest man and lassoing the necks of the other two—one with the cording and one with her arm.

Stupidly, the armed man dropped his axe instead of using it against her iron hold. She secured the leather cord in her teeth, kicked the axe up, and threw it at the last man, dropping him with the blunt edge to his brain stem. It risked internal bleeding, but he wouldn't die within their window of need.

The broken man finally loosed his first scream and the other two lost consciousness. She tied them up and gagged the broken man with a rabbit skin. She collected the comatose inquirer and heard Lior limping through the undergrowth, dragging their belongings tree to tree. He collapsed at the camp's threshold. The wind blew his cloak open, revealing his nude, malnourished frame and badly burned skin with visible bone in places.

Kestrel ran to him, throwing an arm under his shoulders to help him get to the clean log. She towed the blubbering gagged man over. "Start with this one. I'll check their water source."

Lior's aura shifted hungrily. His eyes blazed a darkening gold as ivory tips glistened over his lip. He bent at an awkward angle to plunge into the man's carotid artery instead of his jugular vein. Endymion had taught them more about human anatomy. The large man's oxygenated blood would fully restore Lior's strength, and, if the infectious protein didn't kill him, his bones would replenish enough blood for a second meager meal within hours.

Quiet tinkling led her to a small creek. All but a trickle had frozen. She returned to camp and found Lior on his feet, rolling his neck, and stretching his legs and arms. The gagged man was unconscious and draped over a log. A golden brow lifted in question.

"It's small, but it'll do." She rifled through their supplies and pulled out a smaller bag and a pair of fur-lined boots that matched hers. "It'll be a cold rinse, though."

"Then maybe I can keep you conscious this time." He grinned and kissed her. "If I get you too hot, you faint on me."

"Would you have it any other way, My Light?"

"Of course not, m'lady." Swaying with his usual limber confidence, he gagged the unconscious men with the remaining rabbit skins in case they woke up.

Where she prowled, he was a beautiful glider—as light as air. She led him to the creek and shook his cloak out as he bathed. He'd gotten more meticulous about his hands before carving. He soaked his fingers and scrubbed the dirt out from beneath his nails.

He glanced up at the ominous clouds. He could carve as comfortably in the dark as in light, but he'd favor the falling temperatures that came with nightfall to hold off the fever that would inevitably consume her.

He motioned for his cloak with fingers so cold they were almost blue. As he threw it over his shoulders, she began to pull out his clothes, but he stayed her hand.

"I'll dress by the fire. Later." He rinsed his hair once more and swung up, tossing a crystal arc over his back. Freezing rivulets twined down his golden curls.

He grinned and flicked water on her. "Let me stay cold for you."

They reached for each other, intertwining their fingers. "Then I'll burn for you."

"It's the last time." He squeezed gently.

"With twice as much as last time." She squeezed back.

"I recuperated much swifter," Lior said, turning out his arms to reveal healing burns that were hidden beneath sacred soil before his bath. "Perhaps it won't be as bad for you. Try to stay conscious, this time."

She turned for camp and gave him a tug. "I don't wish to steal your fun, so only torture me enough to keep me there."

Flickering light silhouetted the trees ahead. "I'll trench the fire toward the shelter to give you better odds against the wind and incoming weather. As for the humans, I'm not sure how long the comatose one will survive."

Lior snaked an ice-cold arm around her waist, deliberately brushing against every vine he'd carved so far, and laughed softly when she shivered. "His heart is strong and I left plenty in the big one. I will hunt down others, no matter how far away they are, if it comes to that."

She scrutinized him from the corner of her eye. "You're truly healed? And not denying yourself, My Light?"

"I do prefer you conscious," he replied with a devious curve to his lips. He locked their gazes and brought her hand to his lips. "I took only what I needed, but it was enough, I assure you, m'lady. My skin can't lie to you, and I would never."

He slid his arm over her shoulders and she tucked into him, the shock of his cold body blowing her warmth away. She curled her arm around his waist and held him closer. He was still too thin. He'd gone far too long without feeding this time.

"If the silver doesn't enter my bloodstream," she said, "there will be plenty for us both."

He didn't respond. Grunting noises came from their camp.

"They didn't stay out long." She planted a kiss upon his lips. "How long do you think they'll last while you work? I do so hope they enjoy your craft."

"It's my last show. The least I can offer is my best performance." He pricked his tongue on a fang before twisting it over hers, sharing his blood and his uniquely purified taste that she equated with the moon's mystique. "I make no promises for your circulation, however."

"As long as you enjoy yourself, My Light, I shall endure."

He stepped ahead, pulling her along. "Let us get to work, then."

The conscious men groaned muffled pleas as soon as they saw Lior. Their eyes darted from him to their bindings and back, as though it was that difficult to understand their situation. Lior paused at the fire and grinned, revealing his lengthening fangs. The longer and sharper they grew, the wider the men's eyes got until they seemed to comprehend the nightmare that awaited them.

"Ah, any moment…" His darkening pupils focused hard as his aura charged to ensnare them. "And there it is—the death of hope and birth of terror."

Kestrel rested her head on his shoulder. "You and Endymion take far too much interest in these things. Stop playing with them and get to work before the sky opens."

He set his boots and clothes to warm by the fire and readied his tools. She trenched the fire toward the shelter. The men had gathered enough dry material to keep the fire going well into the morning. As long as a spark smoldered somewhere along the line, Lior could keep the fire alive whether it rained or snowed.

Lior pulled their purified silver from the supply bag. She joined him in wiping it clean before rising and tossing her cloak on the log. She stripped off her shirt. Her vines didn't work when covered with heavy, wool tunics. Instead, she'd ripped linen underclothes and knotted them like men's pant legs to secure her breasts and left her abdomen bare.

Not even the fear of death stopped lecherous human males from drooling at the sight of female breasts. Lior's eyes snapped to the men the instant her nakedness changed their fear. He slid his tongue slowly over his fangs, instantly crushing them with renewed terror. Kestrel laughed at his dark enthusiasm, which revealed her fangs for the first time. The men froze and the scent of urine hit the air.

"I wish I could make a man piss himself like that," Lior said, turning his appreciative gaze to her.

"You have your talents; I have mine," Kestrel said, tracing her vines and drawing invisible loops over the virgin skin that awaited Lior's touch.

He shuffled over on his knees and grasped her hips as his mouth chased her fingers, kissing each spot she touched. An audible singe accompanied the slip of his tongue against silver. He tugged her onto her knees and kissed up and beyond the vines, steadily pressing her down until her back met the earth.

"Oh, you must feel *much* better." She cradled his head at her breast with a soft moan. "But are you certain of your strength for pleasure?"

"After twelve months of constant burning by sacred soil and your precious silver?" he mumbled, coiling his tongue around a stiff nipple. "I can't wait to put it inside you and complete you as I have been completed. That first…and then sex."

He stretched up for her lips. "You give me all the strength I need."

"I missed you so much," she whispered palming his curls and kissing him deeply. As they parted, she traced his lips. "So did Endymion."

"Ah. He won't mind a moment more. 'Tis the reward for loyalty." His mouth formed a deep curve and flooded her with desire.

"Carve me up and complete me, My Light, and then bring me to the highest peak of pleasure to celebrate our accomplishment." She arched her back and pressed her belly against his icy body. When she lowered, his skin mirrored hers in burns. "How can you stay cold to ward off my fever if I make you hot now?"

"Oh, I missed you." He groaned against her mouth and his arousal rubbed against her thigh. "You think too logically sometimes, m'lady." He clawed a line of blood across her abdomen and lowered to collect the drops that pooled to the surface.

Without releasing her gaze, he dropped silver coins into the ladle and set it into the fire. He held up the silver chisel he'd taken with him into the dirt with hopes that purifying it might buy him priceless extra seconds against her healing factor. His fingers glided a tantalizing dance over her belly, stopping at each of the three branches he'd left as starting points the last time.

Finally, he dropped his golden gaze. The chisel and a sharpened claw bit into her eternally fresh, scarred skin. Her eyes shot skyward on a sharp inhale, but she would not submit to her screaming nerves. She focused on them, pondering how her brain deciphered pain from pleasure. Why did Lior's fingertips make her skin sing, but not his tools?

Leveling her breathing, she closed her eyes and focused on every cut, every scoop of skin, every channel carved, and the boiling sizzle of liquid silver singeing a river of beauty into her bronzed skin. She reached a trance-like state where she felt only Lior's skilled fingers methodically at work. Her aura rose high above them, taking with it her sight so she could look down and watch him work.

She studied the sensory inputs of his touch, the wind's icy caress, the hum of the trees' tangled roots. She felt the entirety of the Earth, pure and innocent, lava flowing and core revolving, seas churning and winds cycling. She felt the light of the Host and the miasma of the Fallen, tasted bloody battles a continent away—south of the Tropic of Cancer.

The fabric of time ripped apart and lightning struck her astral form. Lior stiffened and looked up. He must've sensed the same disturbance—the sudden appearance of a righteous light morally brighter than the Host.

Lior tapped her shoulder, trying to wake her, but she was no longer attuned to her physical form and he couldn't see her astral spirit. A joyous darkness cleft the Fallen's miasma, parting a pathway to the righteous light—a star dimming by the moment under the mud and blood of the War.

A figure deceptively cloaked with the wings and innocence of the Host targeted the star—a girl, one of *them*, a vampire, shining with sorrow for a life she didn't want. Kestrel could feel the tip of the sword bite into her fingers and sensed Death's ever-looming presence lock onto her light. The star was sympathizing, questioning—no...*mourning*—the loss of a Heavenly Warrior, and aimed to yield her life in contrition.

Kestrel's shock split in twain and struck Endymion's aura. She felt his attention shift, but the Deceiver was moving fast and pulling the whole of her focus as he swept the light away from the sword. Endymion could see what she saw, but he wasn't close enough to intervene. The Deceiver stole the light away, but not before sensing her eyes upon him and blasting her with an immense burst of spiritual energy.

She slammed into her body so hard she jerked up into Lior's chisel. A howl unlike any other raced off her lips as the tool cut her open and liquid silver followed, scorching her innards and branching into veins and arteries. A blinding light exploded and sucked every ounce of oxygen from her lungs. Claws shredded the frozen earth as she arched uncontrollably, desperate to cough or scream, but unable to do either as darkness reveled in her torment and languidly devoured her consciousness.

IV

LUCIEN

Location Unknown, 1713 B.C.

For humans, sex, on its own, didn't mean love. The hormonal makeup was similar, but the chemical composition was intangibly different—heady, thick, and warm. That was the spark he needed—and lacked—in moments of self-pleasure to alter his physique.

Without a companion of his own, he'd never know that warmth firsthand. The sensation wasn't unlike the euphoric adrenaline that came with challenging hunts, but even then, humans were too easy to kill. He never got high enough. He was pathetically reliant on *their* love.

Over time, however, he discovered that he could enter a meditative state after climaxing. Tightly wound muscles relaxed and iridescent snakeskin smoothed into a texture that was closer to human skin. He began to focus more on meditation. The calming energy alone reduced his armor into the coarseness of a lizard's hide. The color was beyond his control, but with softness came paler tones and bluer hues. As long as he could hold onto this calming energy, he could maintain his altered appearance. However, when he lost it, the armor returned.

So, too, did the rainy season, and the plains below the mountain offered no respite when the sun refused to shine. Trapped in a body with too-tight, damp, crawling skin, he massacred an entire village, desperate for capable shelter and the drying heat of their fires. The stench of rotting flesh chased him out long before it alerted the surrounding tribes, but warnings spread rapidly along trade routes and put humans on higher alert for what they called *Waira*—a large, greenish monster that lived on the mountain with an appetite for humans. The tribes evacuated to one location, clutching one another by night and patrolling in armed groups by day.

And yet, it rained. And his skin crawled. He searched the abandoned settlements and discovered a temple or shrine with a circular trench of coal, wax, and tinder. He lit the fire and sat at the center, basking in arid heat. He shoved past his discomfort and fixated on the drumming rain.

He suppressed his desire for companionship, forced out all other wants and musings, and shut down his fear of human mobs. Door after door, he closed everything within him. His scales lost their armor. The fire warmed his skin and dried the crawling damp.

When the rain stopped at last, he eased into feeling other sensory inputs. Dehydration scraping his throat and tanning his tongue like leather. The growl in his starving belly as it gnawed on itself. The blur of the surroundings swimming around him as he tried to stand and stumbled over the Earth's rotation.

He threw his arms out for balance and saw that they were a light teal color and scaled, but smoother than snakeskin. He'd never achieved this much before with only meditation. A sturdy calmness settled in his chest. He emerged into the sun's light comfortable at last with a quiet mind and studied his surroundings with new eyes and ears, not questioning, but rather understanding, calculating, listening, *hunting*.

The heat of day pried deeper into his skin than it'd ever gone. If not for the hunger knotting his gut, he'd stay there, contented in the moment. The air grew viscous with energy that brushed his skin like a bird's feather. He closed his eyes and stretched his arms out, concentrating on the energy. It flowed all about him, stemming from within his body, and fed information to his brain.

He envisioned flesh cushioning his fangs, the explosion of hot blood over his tongue, the warmth of a sated belly. His teeth ached and his stomach grumbled. The energy tugged in one direction. He gave in to the urge to release it and felt it charge with determination, cleaving the air in pursuit of his desires.

A surreal rush skimmed his skin as the blur of the forest raced through his mind. He could smell the coniferous green and sulfuric rock. Hear birdsong and the chatter of wildlife up close. He cracked an eye open. The temple was beside him. He hadn't moved.

The energy—his spirit, he decided—alerted him to a faint, yet undeniably human smell. His spirit soared high for an eagle's view and showed him ant-sized humans chopping firewood, fortifying their protective wall, washing clothes, stirring pots, stripping furs, sharpening spearheads—

Fearless humans doing human things. They'd prepared for him, but they weren't expecting him. The angle pivoted to show him large groups of men hunting and trapping, straying farther from the village than they did within his usual territory.

Men falsely emboldened by assumption and daylight were easy prey. He pursued his spirit's trail, eager to satisfy his hunger and to learn more about this new energy—and its correlation to his smoother skin.

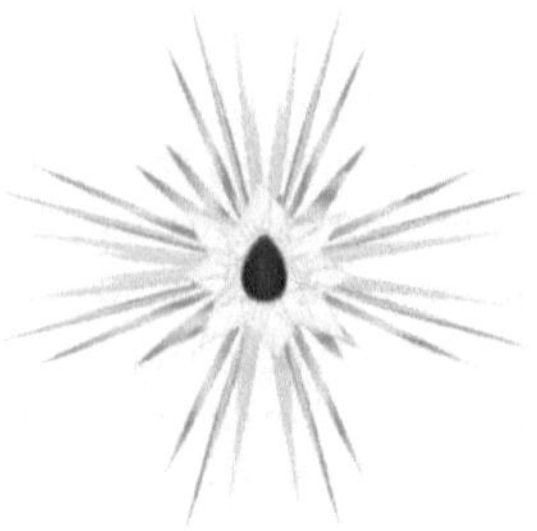

CHAPTER SIX: DEEP INTO THE DARKNESS PEERING

I

ALEXANDER

Green Mountains, Vermont, Summer 2006

Dust motes glittered as the blinds snapped shut. Impatience nipped his ribs like a dog with a bone. Raven treated him like a puppy. Now he was doing it to himself.

Scratching behind his ear, he turned impatiently and faced the Smiths' watchful eyes. He understood Jonathan's reasoning, but wished they weren't there. It seemed like all he did was stand still, a potted plant at the top of the stairs. At least puppies got to go outside and play.

He rolled his neck, keeping the innkeepers in view. They thought Eric's entourage was human. Since Jonathan refused to enlighten them, they'd made breakfast—and not just any breakfast, but a bed and breakfast *breakfast*. The whole shebang with sausage links *and* patties, scrambled eggs by the platefuls, three types of toast—which did not include their almond-crusted French toast, although, that, too, was offered, and, technically, toast—hash browns—shredded and diced—fresh fruit with granola, coffee and a dizzying assortment of teas—decaf and regular, and, *of course*, a pitcher of freshly squeezed orange juice—with the pulp!

And bacon. Oh, *bacon*—the ultimate human obsession. The Smiths surely thought their house smelled wonderful, all those jams and syrups and *bacon*. Alex desperately craved fresh air. The green of the ferns and wispy grasses beyond the glass. Anything but the putrid odors of dead animals cooked to oblivion.

But the worst part? The pineapple and strawberry platter with mango and honey butter drizzle. It drove him nuts—which they also offered, folded into made-to-order pancakes with a ridiculous list of flavored syrups. He'd never even heard of banana syrup, but they had it!

He tapped his forehead, closing his eyes with a sigh, and tried to find his center. Without Raven, he was completely off. He caught a whiff of that cloying fruit and swore she was standing there. In modern terms, her scent was like bubble gum. Easy. But in the days of yore, it was passionflower, sun-ripened strawberry, and pineapple topped with Oriental lilies—the stargazer types, to be precise.

The ache in his chest deepened. He more than missed her. Melting ice clanked in untouched water glasses. He hooked his hand on his neck and gave Mrs. Smith a sheepish look. He couldn't afford to get sidelined by his own sentimental stupidity.

"I guess they're not hungry." His voice squeaked too high. Those bastards upstairs, cowering in their rooms, leaving him alone on the first morning without Paresh. Apparently—as the new VaSH High Commander—dealing with *breakfast* was part of his job.

Mrs. Smith folded her hands in front of her apron and smiled.

Nothing's stopping you from eating, right? he imagined her thinking.

Mentally groaning, he turned back to the freedom beyond the blinds. *Oh, look—white stargazer lilies, right there, growing strong under the window.*

The glass fogged under his sigh. *Damn it, Raven.*

The mists rolling down the mountainside were eerily similar to the movement in Animus Hollow. He shuddered. After the attack, he'd ordered emergency usage only. They'd long thought it was safe, but that clearly wasn't true with Lucifer in play. He was both relieved and irritated that the volunteer hunters "protecting" Donovan hadn't encountered the COMS or gathered any useful intel. His duties as a potted puppy plant meant securing the safety of all the hunters, now.

Another part involved checking on Eric, which he'd protested and was putting off. Eric had tried to kill him. More than once. Seeing *his* face was the last thing Eric needed, especially after being dosed again by Jonathan. If he was awake, he was livid. If he was asleep…well, that'd be a dream come true and reality didn't work that way.

If only they could use a dream regulator to keep Eric off the board. It'd make their jobs much easier, especially when the first delivery of his blood came due. That was three weeks away—and their first opportunity to tail Donovan. Even if he cloaked himself, delivering *that* blood undetected was nearly impossible.

And saying that means he'll pull a successful Houdini, Alex thought. *And don't ask about the regulator——it would dilute his blood with chemicals. It's bad enough that we've tainted it with a toxin.*

The blinds snapped again as he crossed his arms and turned. The Smiths simply watched, their faces sagging with weatherworn wrinkles and happy crinkles encircling their eyes and mouths.

They know what Eric is. He stared back. *They have to suspect, at the very least. Right?*

He smiled wide enough to show off his lengthened canines and raised his eyebrows awkwardly. Surely, he looked like an idiot—why not add that to the puppy moniker? But, ushering them to the correct assumption technically didn't break Jonathan's order.

"Is there something else you might like, dearie?" Mrs. Smith asked, unaffected as she swept a lock of white hair from her face. "Or, perhaps Mr. Ravenscroft would like his morning juice?"

Noooo-ah! Alex kicked his heel out and spun around, his hands fisting in his hair. *He* wouldn't mind a glass of Eric's juice——*wait, no, you can't say it like that, you moron.*

He was back in bizzaro land. *Once a suicidal perverted pirate kidnapper, always a suicidal perverted pirate kidnapper turned potted puppy plant idiot.*

On the laurels of Apollo, he wanted to laugh so badly. The situation was beyond absurd——Lord Lucien as *the creature* and poor Paresh——

Nope. Not going there.

"Uh, you know what? Yeah, I will take him a glass and see if he's feeling better today." Alex smiled again, practically winking his fangs at them, but still they gave away nothing.

As the missus disappeared into the kitchen, the mister cocked his head. "Do you all prefer a *liquid* diet, son?"

Throwing his head back, Alex clapped his hands together as if in grateful prayer. "Yes, yes, yes!" He tiptoed conspiratorially close and whispered, "I couldn't tell you."

"We had our suspicions." He winked. "What about Miss Sarah?"

That damned non-existent itch reared up again. He scratched at it, stumbling over sounds that weren't quite words.

"It's okay, sonny." Mr. Smith patted Alex's spikes. Did he scream puppy vibes to *everyone?*

"We've known Mr. Ravenscroft a long time. Boy, our skin was so smooth back then." He turned out his hands, loose, wrinkled, and mottled with age spots. He laughed softly. "And our hair had color! Back in those days, TV came in black and white, but we lived in full color."

He laughed again and shuffled after his wife. They emerged together with two glasses of *juice* for Alex and began collecting their spread and dishes.

"I'm sorry for wasting your food and your time," Alex said, walking backward into the common room.

"Oh the people here don't waste a thing and we're always good with leftovers." Mrs. Smith placed the water glasses on a tray.

"Yep," added Mr. Smith, pulling out a cart that was hidden in an alcove. "We'll take this downtown and have a good old-fashioned village breakfast."

"You'll need your griddle and pancake batter," reminded Mrs. Smith, pointing a fork.

"My mind hasn't gone that far yet, woman," grumbled Mr. Smith. He winked at Alex again. "We'll get out of your hair and go barter with the neighbors. Don't worry about us. You do you, sonny."

"Thanks." Alex raised the glasses. "Really. I appreciate it."

"Well…" Mr. Smith paused, hesitant. "We've never heard Mr. Ravenscroft as happy as he was when he called in the reservation, so to see him like this…well, we might not know much, but we recognize the heartache of grief. Take care of him."

Alex nodded. "I'm doing everything I can."

"Oh, yes!" Mrs. Smith held up a finger. "I saw Molly's obituary online. Please pass along our condolences."

"I will." Alex offered a half-hearted smile and turned for the parlor. He managed to balance the glasses, enter, and close the French doors without making a sound. Eric was laid out on the green sofa with an arm draped over his eyes.

Alex set the glasses on the coffee table and dropped into the chair closest to Eric's feet since the paralytic wore off the legs last. Given Eric's freakish tendency to recover faster than he should, Alex expected him to pounce at any second, but Lord Lucien had adjusted the doses hoping to compensate for that.

"Are you awake?" Alex whispered.

No answer.

He leaned back and sipped, impressed with the quality. It was fresher than the stock kept at Eido. Had the Smiths freshly squeezed themselves, too?

That thought didn't sit well, but if anyone could pull that kind of loyalty out of someone, it was Eric. And that didn't mean he couldn't enjoy it. He leaned forward on his knees.

"I'm sorry, Eric—I didn't want to do this to you. Any of it," he whispered, lacing his fingers around the glass. "It's not fair. None of it is. I know that, but this is worse than fighting with you."

He kinked his neck and rolled his eyes back against the wet sting of grief. "They should have left you alone and let you tear me apart despite what Paresh wanted. I know she's at peace now, but—"

He clenched his jaw as it started to tremble. "I heard her scream and it was terrifying. She's going to remember everything when she wakes up. I didn't realize until later that Donovan's face was a bloody mess. She turned all of Hell loose on him…but I bet that's what gave Corben the opening to stab her in the back. I'm glad she didn't see it coming."

Tears beaded on his eyelashes. "*Gabriel* saw it, though." The chair's arm creaked in his fist. "That bastard saw that horror and let it happen."

Eric groaned and sluggishly dropped his arm off his eyes. He flinched, because—of course—on top of paralyzing him with a painful toxin, they'd deliberately left him in a bright room. Everything about this came from the Chthonic Knight playbook, and Eric didn't deserve any of it.

Too honorable to be called sadistic, the Knights were experts at vampiric discomfort and torture thanks to Lior, and Alex couldn't wait to hand Donovan over to them. If only Endymion hadn't died. They could take turns killing him. But Endymion was gone. Interred in Lady Rainne's chamber for a reason Lord Lucien hadn't divulged.

"This isn't a nightmare is it?" Eric croaked.

The silver and gold hoops lining Alex's ears jingled as he shook his head. His voice was suddenly gone.

"Please draw the blinds." Eric's leg twitched as he tried to sit up.

Alex dimmed the room without taking his eyes off Eric, who was struggling to rise on wobbly arms. Alex helped to slump him against the padded velvet, but even then, Eric could barely stay upright.

"Here—" Alex tipped the glass on Eric's lips and held it as he took small sips.

"…anks," Eric mumbled.

"Let me know when you want more." Alex pulled the glass away.

"I know…you're loyal…to…J—" He winced with a groan and touched his head. "To Jonathan, but—"

Eric exhaled a grievous sigh. "Please, asking as Paresh's Anointed Strength—don't inject me with that stuff again."

Tears streaked down Eric's cheeks. "It hurts…seeing her again and again—so vibrantly alive and happy. It's a torture worse than reality.

Worse than the venom's pain."

His lips trembled. "B-because I wake up expecting to see her, but she's...she's—"

"Not here," Alex said grimly. "I can only promise that my loyalty belongs to *her*, not to Jonathan."

Eric sucked in a shaky breath. He nudged his chin at the glass and solidly firmed his grip once Alex brought it up. He drank on his own and leaned back with the glass tucked to his chest.

"I keep seeing myself as a boy on the Faust farm. She comes to me like an angel. It's like she's there, but not—"

"Like a spirit."

"Yeah." Eric rubbed his eyes. "She asked you to incapacitate me?"

Alex nodded and gulped from his own glass. "She asked me to save you from yourself. I got the impression that she's anticipating this to drag out."

"It doesn't matter how long it takes. She'll never know freedom. And our—" Grief twisted Eric's already pained façade. "Our...d-daughter? Oh God, they'll always be hunted for their blood—I can't force that on a child...or her."

Alex winced at the desperation in Eric's aura. "I don't want that for her, either, but she deserves a chance to find happiness in the life she's been given—they both do or Gabriel wouldn't have stepped in like he did."

Alex fought hard to keep his own bitterness from seeping into his voice. "I mean, Michael's letting Gabriel keep their souls in stasis, so they must see them in the future. If not in the fibers of light and dark, then in the gray fibers of probability. Michael doesn't act lightly."

Eric closed his eyes.

Alex sipped and saw Eric's foot move slightly.

"It's her decision and she's made it," Eric said at last. "There's too much we don't know, so tell me what we *do* know."

"No developments with Donovan, yet. Lord Lucien said that Lucifer has Raven and denied my request to search for her, so she's...off the board." His chest felt too tight to breathe.

"I don't know what happened to her," Alex said quietly. "If she met with Hawkiel before Lucifer took her or where he is since he has pocket dimensions that we can't access. I don't even know if she's alive. I feel like we're doing nothing right now even though every VaSH hunter is engaged."

"Before she ran off, she kept looking up. Can you see what she saw?"

Alex bobbed his head. "Not as well, but I can see him. He's not any closer than he was."

Fidgeting with his glass, Alex muttered, "I wish she'd told me what she was thinking—it was like she had an epiphany."

Eric finished his *juice*. "Is Sarah still here?"

"Um…" Alex swallowed nervously and inched along the sofa to transition into the side chair. "Yeah…about that—"

Eric's hand clamped down on his knee. Alex howled—more from surprise than the *bone crushing* pain—and his hunter reflexes jerked into Eric's grip, which forced his fist to loosen. The chair screeched against the floor as Alex kicked backward. "What the hell, man?"

"What do you mean '*about that?*'" Eric growled, his eyes darkening and fangs dipping past his lip. "Her blood smells different."

"Hey! It was *her* decision! I had nothing to do with it!" The chair hit the French doors and panic lit a match under Alex's ribs—Eric was trying to stand. "She's in the room right above us—she asked Kestrel to alter her! Oh, hey, actually—"

He pulled a note from his back pocket. Eric's name was scrawled across the front. "Here—she wrote you a letter."

Through cracked slits, Eric spied the offering and grunted. Alex tossed it onto the coffee table. No one had ever scared him like that— eradicating all thought and forcing him to rely on battle instinct. Paresh was no longer the only wonder in his world.

Resting his fingers on his forehead, Eric leaned on his knees and read. The paper crinkled into his fist about halfway through. Alex readied his feet to smash through the doors if Eric lunged.

"Don't you dare think about that, Commander." Icy eyes pierced him over the letter. "Do not damage the Smiths' home."

"I…I was…m-maybe Jonathan would be better for you right now?"

Eric laughed sourly. "When has Jonathan ever been good for me?"

He set the letter down. "Paresh might love him, but she chose you as her knight. Stay put."

"Not to overstep, but you have a bit of an anger control issue that I am *not* equipped to handle." Alex tried to steady his voice, but it came out as a squeaky whine.

"You are too willing to accept punishment. That makes it easy to want to hurt you."

"You don't want to *hurt* me, though!" The emotions inside Alex crested at once. Paresh. Raven. Rainne. Endymion. Donovan. Lucifer. He rose with a teary huff and paced along the far wall.

"Raven's not here to guide me!" Alex cried, throwing his hands up helplessly. "She's the only one who knew what to expect, but I guarantee she never saw half of this coming—and now! Now, it's on me—like I have a clue! But I have to do it. I have to lead the VaSH whether you use me as a punching bag or try to kill me."

Alex shrugged. "You're right. I take every punch because *I believe* that I deserve it. I failed Raven and I failed you. Worst of all—I failed Paresh!"

Alex ruffled his hair and muttered, "Bring her joy. Fuck. What'd that do?" He crossed the room and knelt before Eric. "There's not a cell in this body that doesn't crave to kill Donovan. To dance to his screams as the Chthonic Knights fill his veins with liquid silver. I would give damn near anything for that—"

His gaze locked onto Eric's. "But not *her*."

Jabbing the crumpled note, Alex added, "Sarah made this decision because she wants to help. She's only asking for your blessing. You know what she'll go through. She's scared and doesn't know what to expect. Plus—"

Alex licked his lips. "It's not widely known, yet, but Kestrel asked to train Sarah as her First Officer and Lord Lucien agreed. Sarah will be the only altered human to join the VaSH—*ever*—and she'll be one of the highest ranked officers. It's not going to be easy."

Disbelief rocked Eric's aura. "She's going to be a Wraith Reaper?"

Alex nodded. "Kestrel thinks Sarah harbors the soul that was meant for Lior. He was the Chthonic Knight First Officer until Salea murdered him about a century ago and Farran took his place."

"But...but—Sarah's a chef! A ba-baker! She's never even been in a fight! How could Lucien—"

"Look, Lior was like Kestrel's other half, and if she's right?" Alex interrupted, sitting back on his heels. "I'm not kidding, Eric—Lior was among the best. Lord Lucien trusted him with controversial investigations on a team that I worked with—so if Kestrel's right? This is huge. I mean, she and Sarah will form a perfect whole that can find Paresh *without* Donovan."

Alex kept his worries to himself. What if Lior's soul remembered dying by Salea's hands? That girl had lucked out of so many deathblows that night, and in the end, Alex had saved her after she *cut off Lior's head.*

Eric cleared his throat. "When will I get my legs back? I'd like to see Sarah."

"I don't know, but here—" Alex handed Eric his half-full glass. "Drink this and I'll get you more so you can heal faster."

"You'll actually come back?"

"Yes." Alex hung his head. "Sarah felt bad about that—she really didn't have a choice."

"It's fine. Go do it. Is my room ready upstairs?"

"Yeah. Jonathan's across the hall and I'm next door. Kestrel is staying in Sarah's room. Seneca and Minerva are roaming outside and Cyp and Heron are in the room at the end of the hall."

"What the hell? Why are they all here? They should be with the Elders."

"It's Lord Lucien's order since you were being, eh, *unpredictable*." Alex cringed, but Eric merely lifted an indifferent brow.

"What about Vincent and Betty? It smells like they made a large breakfast. Did no one think to tell them—"

"The Smiths? Well…" That damned non-existent itch reappeared. "I had a thought, but it was denied—"

"By Jonathan, of course—"

"So I coaxed them into connecting the dots on their own."

"How did they react?"

"They didn't." Alex shrugged. "He just…I don't know, he said something about black and white TV and living in color?"

Eric chuckled. "It's a joke—they're old and gray now and TV is in color, but when they met—"

"They were in color and TV was in black and white."

"They were fresh out of high school—newlyweds—when I interviewed them to manage this place. They're in their upper seventies now."

"They seemed okay about breakfast—said they'd take it into the village. Do you know where they keep your *juice*?"

"There's a locked cabinet that opens into a refrigerated panel. There's a blood donation sticker on it. The key's in a magnet holder on the fridge."

"They have an odd sense of humor."

"Gallows humor, yeah," Eric said. "Vincent's father was a mortician and funeral director."

"That explains it," Alex said.

Nostalgia brought a smile to Eric's face. "It gets better—they met after Betty drowned. Vincent was his father's apprentice and Betty was on the slab, in the bag, when she started coughing water up. Vincent was the only one in the room at the time."

"That can't be true—"

"Cross my heart." Eric made the motion. "I didn't care about the other applicants after that. They were perfect. Vincent referred to

Betty as his 'Vampire Wife' during the interview."

Eric paused. "They prove that people enter your life for a reason. And I suppose that gives me faith that you're right about Kestrel and Sarah."

II

WALTER

Orison Crossing, Summer 2006

Voicemail again! Walter clamped his cellphone shut and shoved it into the case on his belt. The station's phone was ringing nonstop with calls about weird blue lights in Sunset Grove. But he couldn't reach Eric or the Smiths.

Gravel crunched under his squad car's tires as it crawled toward the carriage house. He hated going into anything blind, but right now, it seemed like only God knew what he was walking into. Maybe he should have gone to the mansion. He shuddered. With every floor crawling with vampires?

No way in Hell. Not alone.

He parked next to Eric's BMW. His squad's low chassis was the nemesis of his knees and his weight didn't help—with anything, really—but he didn't mind death by donut. It was probably expected anyway—a heart attack lying in wait. Too many cops went that way, but they also ate like crap, and drank and smoked to cope with the stress. He'd seen it in his father. Two packs a day and three fingers of whiskey after a shift. He died two months after retiring—relaxing on the lake in a boat with his pole in the water.

"Kicking back is what kills you," Walter muttered, tugging at his waistband. No sign of blue lights, yet. "I'm good going out with Sarah's pecan pies."

He grabbed his flashlight and set off for the flagstone path. Fiery orange and magenta streaks raced west above the forest, followed by the inky swell of night. The cottage was dark and no one answered his knock.

"Alex? Raven?" Shadows danced with the breeze.

The animals are quiet. Someone's out there. A shiver ran through him as he rounded the cottage and headed for the southern trail. Pops of the sun's color broke through the canopy—but no blue. He didn't expect to get lucky with a natural explanation.

"Hey! Heron! You out there?" he called. "Cyprian?"

He shuddered again and shook it out. "No heebie jeebies, Walter!"

But the heebie jeebies had already latched onto him. Having Eric around was one thing, but not having him? In a town patrolled by vampires? With their ruling body and their rogues? Nope. That was something else entirely. His nerves needed a familiar face.

Branches snapped under his boots as he made his way down the darkening trail. He clicked on the flashlight. The small beam made the darkness even darker. He shuddered again.

"Stop it, stop it, stop it, you old dog," he muttered to himself. *Easier said than done when you know what lurks in the darkness.*

He tried clearing his head with another huff and a little jig. The hunters around the village didn't pose a threat to anyone.

So you think! You couldn't do anything even if they did!

"Okay, we got this!" He straightened his spine, squared his shoulders, and lifted his chin. "Own it and do your job."

He came around a bend to an eerie gold and blue glow on the trees ahead. A cold sweat broke down his back. Nausea tugged at his belly. He unsnapped his gun's holster and crept forward. "Hey! It's Walter! Who's out there?"

He knew to sweep the sides before stepping into the clearing, but all logic fled when he saw Grandfather Wisdom. His jaw dropped and his knees gave out. He fell forward onto his palms, eyes transfixed, and crossed himself despite not being Catholic or overtly religious. "Oh my God."

An illuminated golden stream flowed up to what appeared to be a blue star. It pulsed slightly, emitting short bursts of light before dimming. The golden stream—more like a vein, rather—fluctuated from flashing, tiny white orbs floating within it.

Wiping his mouth, Walter sat back on his heels. "Oh God."

His cop instinct yelled that something was very, very wrong. He noticed that the vein extended out along a gnarled root and down into the ground. He remembered someone mentioning a spiritual nexus here.

He hadn't literally expected that *only God knew*, but—

He fumbled with his phone and dropped it because his hand was shaking so badly. Who was he going to call?

He clicked off the flashlight and dropped it next to his phone.

"Come on!" His voice shook. He felt like he was being watched— he *knew* it. "One of yous gotta be out there! Alex? Raven? Heron? Cyp! *Come on!*"

Silence. Not even a cricket. What other *good* names had he heard? What on Earth would make a tree glow like that?

Nothing natural.

"Okay, uh…Seneca?" he called louder. "Minerva? Look, I don't care who the hell answers me, but Raven's got me in the loop and I need to be looped into this, *right now!*"

Maybe a minute passed. It was probably less. It seemed like forever. The blue light kept drawing his attention and his mind was jumbled, racing in circles and tangoing with crazy conspiracy theories that maybe weren't so crazy. Could it be aliens? Heck if he knew. He had a town full of vampires. *Why not add aliens to the mix?*

He saw reports of triangular lights out of Chicago all the time. Sure—until he heard otherwise, he was sticking with aliens. The creeping knowledge at the back of his mind scared him away from the *holier* possibilities, particularly when he couldn't reach anyone he knew. If he had to contemplate the Devil in Sunset Gro—

A cold hand landed on his shoulder.

"*Oh my God Jesus Lord!*" he yelped, jumping higher than his body was designed to go and landing on his hip when his legs said, *nope*, and crumpled beneath him.

"I did not mean to scare you," said a quiet voice, youthful and feminine, from a figure draped in black at his side. "I am Farran, a new officer under Raven's command, formerly the First Officer of the Chthonic Knights. I know you to be Walter Hodges, trustee to Lord Eric, confidante to my Commander, and the Chief of Police."

"Uh, o-okay." Walter's heart was pounding so hard. He could feel it shaking his ears. That couldn't be good. "All right. Not aliens. The devil you know is better than the one you don't, right?"

The figure tilted its head. "I do not follow your logic. Do you know of another? No devil is good."

"R-right."

Duh, Walter. Don't be a moron when the fan's covered in shit.

Dreading the answer, he nodded at the tree. "What…what is that?"

She knelt beside him and lowered her hood, revealing luminous dark skin, bright eyes that reflected the star, and cropped hair with a silvery shine. "The avatar for Archangel Michael—"

"M-Michael?" Walter inched closer to her. "I-is that a-all?"

"—and the gold ribbon is the life force of Lady Paresh."

Her words rammed like a shockwave that curdled his blood. Wheezing short, tight breaths, he clutched his chest. "Oh God…"

She guided his head down to his knees. His back screamed in protest as he cried, "Ah, ah, ah! I don't bend!"

Where had all the air gone? His lungs burned and his vision blurred.

"P-Paresh's…*w-what?*"

"Apologies, Mr. Walter. Tuck your head below your heart like so—"

She demonstrated and indicated for him to take in a slow breath. He couldn't place her accent. Maybe Caribbean or African? But it had a gentle cadence that helped to calm him enough to follow her prompts and ease the tightness in his chest. Maybe the job would kill him after all.

He eyed the gold ribbon. "Th-that's Paresh?" Maybe it was a trick of his watery eyes, but the golden light seemed to pulse brighter at her name. "What…happened to her?"

"I am not yet certain. I know only her soul is there and the Crimson Commander has scattered hunters across the planet to find her body."

"Cuh-Crimson…that's…Alex. Where is he? Where's Raven? Eric?" Walter tried to sit up, but flickering lights rushed his visual field and he started to sway. Farran shoved his head down again.

"Stay level and keep breathing to avoid syncope," she said. "But do not worry. Should you lose consciousness, I'll take you to the Hawthorne Mansion."

"N-no, no. No!" He didn't want to meet the Elders while he was conscious, and the fact that she saw that as a safe place over a hospital or Eric's house was petrifying. Where were they all?

His tears dripped to the Earth like rain. "Please…just tell me what happened—what you know. Are the others okay? Is the Devil here? Oh my God…it's the end of the world isn't it?"

"Breathe, Mr. Walter." She touched a metal sliver on her jaw and said something in a language he couldn't identify. He only understood, "*Alexander.*"

"The High Commander and his elite hunters are in Vermont. Lord Eric is sedated, unharmed."

"Why is he *sedated?*" Walter demanded, wiping his eyes as frustration briefly deflated his fear. He jabbed a finger at the tree. "*What happened to that girl? What the hell is going on?*"

"I don't know." Farran nodded at the blue star. "Michael's presence has rattled the few who know he's here—he acts only by direction of *The Word*. During the Great Holy War, he only entered battle to fight our creator directly, but now he *and* Archangel Gabriel watch over Lady Paresh. The situation is quite dire."

Walter couldn't speak if he wanted to. He wasn't even sure he was still in his body. Or alive. Or awake. Jonathan's voice rang through his mind like a bell tolling for the dead—his comment about God being on his side—and he really wanted Farran to stop talking, because she wasn't making it sound any better. But he needed to know. Cops got the dirty details whether they wanted to or not.

"Doom will befall the world if we don't find her," Farran whispered. She paused and touched the metal sliver again. "High Commander Alexander is asking why you are here?"

"We, uh, got reports of weird blue lights in the forest," Walter said robotically, eyes glued on the *Archangel's* avatar.

She responded in the same foreign tongue and touched the metal with finality. "Our perimeter watch will keep humans away."

"Oh God, don't hurt anyone." Walter groaned, bending over again. The contents of his stomach wanted to come up this time. It didn't matter if he went to the mansion. *They were everywhere.* "Why not aliens?"

She gave him a puzzled looked, but then touched his shoulder with her icy hand. "Do not worry. As a former Chthonic Knight, I know that we possess many non-lethal repellants that are as harmless to humans as peppermint oil is to a mouse."

Nope, it was coming up. On his hands and knees, he scurried to the tree line and vomited. His stomach cramped under the heaving force. He wiped his mouth and fell onto his side, uncomfortably aware of the star at his back.

He knew where he stood on the Thin Blue Line and how important— and precariously balanced—that position was. But did *they* have a line drawn in blood? Was that Treaty of theirs enough to stop them at "repellants" for humans equated with rodents? Especially when—

"Oh God, Paresh is really dead," he whispered.

"If we don't find her body, yes."

Walter squeezed his eyes shut and rubbed his forehead. The last time he felt this sick was when Eric told him what really happened here after Paresh came home. "So is this like…that night…when the Devil stabbed her? Eric's blood—is that why he's sedated?"

He felt Farran's energy shift before her gaze bore into him, pricking every inch of his skin. Goose bumps popped up in places that never saw the light of day.

"Those details are confidential. Be less forthcoming with the privileged knowledge you have."

Her words shattered like ice water on his spine. His stomach seized again. He lurched into the brush as bile surged up his throat.

The needles disappeared as the huntress refocused on the blue star. "*Rumors*, however, say that his beast is beyond control and he is a danger to himself and us."

Blood splattered in Walter's mind, forming dark pools beneath a materializing body with a golden hilt buried in her chest. Eric's dark eyes flashed dangerously and the scene shifted to his law office where his chair slammed into the built-in bookshelves and his angry roar vibrated the walls. Walter hadn't cowered then. He'd stupidly fought back like death by vampire, *with a vampire,* was a normal argument.

Eric's philanthropy and friendship had lulled him into a safe zone. He would have relentlessly argued against Eric ever physically harming anyone—

But she's scared of him, he realized. More images scrolled across the marquee of his mind. Alex squirming, Raven's slight trepidation, Donovan shifting to best behavior the instant Eric stepped into the room. They were *all* scared of him and it had never occurred to Walter that Eric deserved to be feared. But after losing Paresh *again*—

He pushed himself up on his hands and knees. Sorrow shredded his soul to confetti as he gazed upon the golden vein. "Oh honey— Paresh—I'm sorry."

He sat up, wiping his hands on his khaki pants. "What can I do?"

"Nothing." Farran's attention jabbed him again. "Cimex Drones haven't picked up useful chatter about *her*, although we did discover a few rogues hiding amongst us."

Walter blanched. "And?"

An unsettling smile lit a dark gleam in her eyes. "They've been terminated."

"B-but…couldn't they help find Paresh?"

Farran's expression flattened. "Only one priority target carries that information."

A stone sank into Walter's empty stomach. "Not him…"

Farran's long eyelashes fluttered as her stare darted to him and back up to the avatar. The stone multiplied.

"Oh God…Eric." Walter huffed and scratched the top of his head.

Farran's eyes suddenly glittered and her God-awful smile widened. "I imagine our new lord will enjoy tearing that one apart with his bare hands."

Walter shot her a horrified look.

She released an excited sigh. "The rumors about Lord Eric are exceptional! The hunters here *that* night got to witness him cross the beast's line. He was depleted, exhausted, and yet, still! He charged the leader of the Fallen Host without hesitation."

She nudged her chin at the avatar. "Only Archangel Michael has ever battled him so fiercely."

"O…kay," Walter said, gasping and shrinking inwardly. On top of bloodthirsty vampires, *no aliens*, and Paresh's soul trapped in a tree, there was *that*. He was never "putting the fear of God" into anyone ever again. Knowing the stark truth of reality transcended fear. At a moment like this, the avatar of Saint Michael the Archangel should be comforting.

But it wasn't.

It was unequivocally terrifying.

III

ERIC

Green Mountains, Vermont, Summer 2006

Eric's feet thudded into the risers and the banister creaked as he struggled to pull himself up the stairs. Behind him, Jonathan grumbled about his refusal for assistance and Alex was silent.

"Your humans here are quite old," Jonathan said, skirting past Eric as they came upon the landing. "Perhaps they have a walker?"

Eric planted his feet and managed to stand. "You are dumber than I thought possible."

He glared at Jonathan and took a tentative step, his entire ability to stay upright dependent on the railing. Jonathan stayed at his shoulder. Alex was a few steps off his heel.

"You know I'm going to fight you on that on principle alone, but I can't fathom where it's coming from now."

"*Look at me!*" he roared. "How many times did you shoot me up with that stuff? If I'm that much of a threat, then I sure as hell should be an asset in a time of crisis! What if we're attacked? How can I protect myself or Sarah?"

He shoved Jonathan aside and tipped off balance. Alex caught him before he fell over the railing. "The fucking irony!"

Eric huffed, got his bearing, and waved Alex off. "I refuse to be a liability that hurts someone close to me and yet here we are."

Jonathan's jaw bulged and guilt swam in his eyes. There wasn't a thing he could say to change the situation, so he didn't even try. Disgusted, Eric motioned for Alex. He ducked under Eric's arm and helped him into Sarah's room.

They entered without knocking and startled Kestrel. She jumped up from the bedside, where she'd been hugging Sarah's arm.

Eric muttered an apology and nodded at the velvet chair beside the bed. Alex got him situated and Eric leaned forward on his knees. The beaded sweat on Sarah's brow was concerning. She was deathly pale, too—the normally apricot blush to her dark skin was an ashen gray.

"How long should this take?" he asked, motioning for Kestrel to return to her spot. She threw uncertain eyes at Jonathan first.

"Oh for the love of…" Eric groaned and pointed at the door. "Why can't something go the way I say without your approval? Get out. You, too, Alex. Give us a moment."

Kestrel stiffly knelt on the floor. "I meant no offense—"

"No one ever does," Eric interrupted with an inpatient wave. "Millennia of archaic traditions undone in a night—I get it." He raised his brow. "How long?"

"If they survive the protein, usually a few weeks." Kestrel held Sarah's hand. "If they die, it's usually in the first few days."

"How high is her fever?" Eric pulled a tissue from the nightstand and patted Sarah's forehead. He gently nudged wayward brown curls with his knuckle. "I remember waking up with a cold cloth on my face. I felt tired, like I'd been laboring for a long time."

"She's hovering under a hundred and three," Kestrel replied, her expression softening at Eric's kindness. "It's a little higher than I'd like, but not within range to cause damage, yet."

Eric licked his lips. "And if you cool her down?"

"It'll slow the process and make the fight harder to survive. She'll get chills soon, but if I cover her, it will interfere with the fever. It has to run its course, for better or worse. Until she's stable, she must stay right here, as is."

"She didn't need to do this for me," Eric whispered, guilt tugging at his soul. He wished he'd ended their tradition when he learned about Sammy, but his mother had insisted that "Berhane" had visited her in dreams foretelling of the boy she would birth—that he'd live long and well, and honor the family legacy with pride. There'd been no way to know the gender that long ago, so when she had a boy, she took the dream as a sign.

"I wanted to send her to culinary schools in Europe. She's so stubborn—determined to do what she was *meant* to do, but she deserves to live her own life, free of servitude to me. Alex said she'll train as your First Officer?"

Kestrel nodded.

Eric sighed. Sarah had outlined her perfectly reasonable logic in her letter. He could let go of the anger at her decision, but he refused to let her devote an eternal life to him. "My first order to you lasts for the rest of her life: she is never to serve me *in any official capacity*. No security detail, no kneeling, no titles—nothing. She is my family."

"That is one reason my request was permitted."

He clenched his jaw. "I know about the other reason—that she wants to find Paresh, and that the two of you together may be able to do that—"

His throat hardened. "And that's fine. I hope it works. Just make her happy—let her enjoy things. It's her life. Not mine. I will forever hold her dear in my heart. She is always welcome to visit or contact me—no restrictions."

"As you command, my lord," Kestrel said, tucking her chin. "I understand your wishes, truly."

She smoothed her hand over the vines etched around her navel. "Your aura burns strong, *here*, and translates your desires for her happiness. They match what she wants for you—a life of joy and love."

He smiled softly. "Will you tell me about Lior? Molly always said Sarah had an old soul. Who would've thought…how old?"

"Lior and I, and many others, were created in 40 A.D. He died in 1888." Sorrow cast a shadow over her visage.

"That's not long ago; it must feel like a fresh loss. I'm sorry."

"He was My Light." The bed dimpled as Kestrel leaned over and affectionately crisscrossed Sarah's arm with her fingertips. "Now *she'll* be My Light. She's not him, not exactly. The elements are there, but she's very much her own person, too. I want to know her and get back the time I lost with him."

Kestrel's fragile joy ruptured his grief as he remembered the incredulous feeling that hit him when he saw Paresh's face the night of her arrival. Fear and joy had collided, and he'd been so scared that reality was playing a figment before his eyes, an illusory trick of a dream long-held in her absence.

"Reuniting with your soul mate can feel too good to be true," Eric said. The nostalgic shift in his mood seemed to disturb Kestrel. She was rubbing her belly again. "Am I hurting you?"

She tried to swap surprise for uncertainty and averted her gaze when she failed. "It's intense and powerful, strong, and sharp as steel, vibrating at the same frequency as my purified silver. But, no, it doesn't hurt."

"It's unintentional." He grabbed the back of his neck, feeling awkward in his need to explain without saying too much. "It's a side effect of being the Sacred Vessel's Anointed Strength—shielding energy that I need to learn how to channel. It's been manifesting my emotions into my aura and lashing out unchecked."

That was an understatement. He'd choked both Alex and Raven prior to—and during—the COMS mansion invasion, but hadn't known anything was amiss until Jonathan asked him about it. Lucien later suggested that Paresh's blood made his aura stronger and the baby's growing essence amplified it beyond restraint. With them gone, he expected that untamed power to dissipate, but it hadn't, and now he had the beast to contend with, as well.

"Long ago," Kestrel began hesitantly, "Lior carved these into me and I honed my skills specifically to track energy on that—*the celestial*—vibrational frequency. May I?"

She motioned to touch his chest. When he consented, she grabbed Sarah's fingers and completed the connection by pressing her palm over Eric's heart. The huntress closed her eyes and rolled her neck back, pulling in deep belly breaths and relaxing as she exhaled.

Warmth gathered beneath her hand, and he felt her pulse slow and gradually level out to match the strong and steady beat he could hear coming from Sarah. For a long while, he focused on that fusion of sound and sensation, and stared out the dormer windows at the mists rolling down the mountain. The sun angled in and glazed the white plaster walls and hand-hewn colonial furniture a cheery shade of yellow. A maple leaf tapped the far window and prompted his gaze to slip briefly to Sarah.

He returned to watching the mists and listened to the *thump, thump* of her heart and the *tap, tap* of the maple leaf.

Thump, thump.

Tap, tap.

Something was off.

Thump, thump.

Tap, tap.

The button was active—no sound in or out.

Thump, thump.

Tap, tap.

Kestrel's eyes snapped open. Sluggish, as though entranced, she crossed the room and tapped the glass in tune with the leaf.

Thump, thump.

Tap, tap.

Kestrel's words slurred drowsily. "Did'ju'no treeessss talk thru' thar rootssss o'er distance?"

Tap. Tap.

Eric's skin crawled. There was an old wives' tale about opening a window to release a trapped spirit after someone died. He grabbed Sarah's wrist. Her pulse was unchanged.

He sniffed for an electrical odor. Nothing.

"Mm-hm…I's *hhher*…hummin' thru' m'vines." She swayed with Sarah's heartbeat and the leaf's tapping. "I's like—"

She collapsed. Kestrel's pulse disappeared. The tapping stopped.

Eric bolted up on legs that weren't there to support him. He dragged himself over to Kestrel, forcing his toes to push off the floorboards for extra traction. With his ear against her chest, he heard faint, slow pumping.

"Kestrel?" He lightly slapped her cheeks.

A croaking sound rattled in her throat.

"Come on, wake up!" he yelled. "Kestrel!"

The groan evolved as air whooshed into her lungs. Her chest expanded and she sat up gulping for air.

"That's never—" She glanced at Sarah and back to him. "I was floating in a…in a black void. It felt like a tree. Familiar, like Grandfather Wisdom."

Eric felt the blood drain from his face.

Kestrel shook her head as though to clear it. "She didn't mean to— she wanted to check on you, but wasn't supposed to be here."

"It was Paresh?" Eric lifted onto an elbow and eyed the leaf silently moving beyond the window.

Kestrel nodded and offered her hand. They worked together to sit against the wall. "She disappeared like lightning—it's like she took my soul with her. Then there was a bright flash. I think her angels kicked me out—I've been hit like that before."

She studied the window. "I don't think they'll let it happen again."

Eric swept his fingers over his eyes. "How—"

He couldn't clear the catch in his throat. He touched the blue floral wallpaper over his shoulder, wishing he could feel her.

"She wanted your attention without attracting theirs." Kestrel leaned her head back. "That girl's got some scary power."

Absently tracing her silver vines, she whispered, "I felt her desires. Her sorrow for your pain. And her love—the strongest love I've ever encountered."

Eric closed his eyes and pictured Paresh dancing with fireflies. "I need to get back to her. I need a drink. I need to heal."

"I have coolers." Kestrel pointed at the chests tucked under the dormer windows. "I was ordered not to give you blood, but you—"

"Bring a cooler over," Eric demanded. "That's *my* order."

"As you command, my lord," Kestrel said with a small smirk, tilting her head. She retrieved the cooler and sat back down beside him. "No stemware yet."

He grabbed a blood bag and twisted off the cap that sealed the outlet port. "I don't need anything fancy."

Kestrel watched him drink with an expression of fascination. He gave her a questioning look.

"Sarah loves you," she said. "But what I felt from her is different from what I felt with Paresh."

He drained the bag. "There seems to be a learning curve for the different types of love. Think of a human family—I'm like Sarah's favorite uncle, but you're her lover, like Paresh is mine."

Kestrel cocked her head in thought. "I wonder what Lior would've felt toward you. Had he not died, you wouldn't be family, but I imagine he'd be enthralled. Coming from Master Jonathan's lineage, you aren't the same as us. You'd be a...curiosity."

Eric traded the empty bag for a fresh one and gestured at Sarah. "She can tell you when she wakes up, right? She and Lior are one if she has his soul."

He opened the outlet port. "The body is but a vessel, after all."

Contemplating Sarah, Kestrel said, "Then Lior loves you, too."

Eric expected jealousy to radiate off Kestrel, but she was focused on understanding the emotion that had struck so hard and so fast, more pensive and logical than the others.

"Remember to account for life experience. Sarah may love me, but if Lior hadn't died, she wouldn't have his soul. She might not even exist as the person we know—this is the path her soul took to find its life mate. To get back to *you*."

Kestrel hummed thoughtfully.

"Paresh's soul was withheld from her at birth," Eric confessed quietly, "as part of your Servator prophecy. Without it, she wouldn't have lived at all. She was stillborn. Empty."

Kestrel's brow dipped as she integrated that into her thoughts. "Why do you suppose Lior's soul didn't die with his body?"

"Who's to say? What about that silver embedded in your body? You altered your physiology. Did he, as well? Was it enough to sway his standing with Gabriel?"

"Maybe. Lior used sacred soil as a type of sensory deprivation—

he'd starve the existing senses to develop new ones like astral sight and an increased tolerance to holy light or objects. I suppose we're in league with the anomalies created with divine intervention, like Endymion, Alex, and Raven—forces for good?"

Eric finished his second pint and held up the empty bag. "Thank you for this."

He stood with ease and stretched high onto his toes, touching the pitched ceiling with his fingertips. "And thank you for the message. I'll take it as a sign that what you're hoping to do might just work."

IV

LUCIEN

Location Unknown, ca. 1446 B.C.

His skin never dulled to a human earthen hue. It had paled to the color of the sky, however. The light of day patterned the outlines of his scales in a darker color that shimmered like silver under the moon.

The tribes had adjusted to living in the *Waira*'s territory. They continued to believe in safety under the sun and tightened security by night, training wary eyes on traders and travelers who requested entry to their sanctums.

His first attempt at blending in failed before it began. He hadn't accounted for his height being twice that of most humans or that the bladed tips of his ears flashed as a warning beacon in the light. Screams rang out the instant they spotted him. They mobilized a response to an armed human threat, making them easy prey. But, he chose to slip out before they cried, "*Waira!*"

Neither fear nor anger filled him—only that growing and pervading sense of empty loneliness. Humans were social creatures who succeeded most when working cooperatively. He envied that unity.

He'd waited a moon cycle to try again. He covered himself head to toe in fur and slouched as low as possible. His spirit gathered about him like a shield as he brazenly followed the day hunters through the gate. He ducked into hiding until the sun sank into the world of sleep.

The tribe's elder and leader resided in the central hut. He got the first choice of meat and drink, both of which affected the nutritional quality of human blood. With few exceptions, males made for a more robust meal than females, and children weren't worth the energy. Until now, Lucien had relied on outlying dwellings, but, as part of their adaptation to his presence, humans had transformed outer

81

buildings into storehouses filled with corded pottery and food stores. So, too, had they adjusted how they tasked their hunters and gatherers seeking food from the *Waira's* forest—the tribes often sent groups that walked with their backs together to safeguard themselves at all times.

Try as they might, they were incapable of evading an apex predator. He enjoyed so little in his solitary existence, but their attempts at thwarting him provided opportunities to hone his skills and adapt. He had learned much about his spirit companion and was beginning to wonder if it somehow shielded him from sight.

They hadn't noticed him at all when he walked through the gate.

☽ ✳ ☾

"*Waira! Waira!*" The high-pitched scream pierced the sleeping village.

The night watch reacted swiftly. They attacked with rocks and spears that easily bruised and pierced his tender skin. He clawed through the shafts of three spears sticking out from his chest before leaping to the roofs and bounding over the wall into the forest.

But they didn't give up this time. They knew where he lived, and he'd crossed a line. Angry voices chased his retreat.

His heart thundered into his throat with each hard-hitting footfall. He ran wildly, whipped by low branches and bleeding badly. A splotchy trail of bright red highlighted his escape.

If the moon were high, they'd be hunting him on his turf and he'd have the advantage. But, he'd chosen a moonless night and they had torches. It was difficult to focus his vision in constantly shifting light and dark.

He'd underestimated the human sense of community and need for leadership. Emboldened by his attack on their elder and how easily they'd forced him to flee, they united in their purpose to *hunt him*— organized in numbers that posed a real threat to his existence. The instinct to escape was surprisingly stronger than the urge to turn and fight. The Morning Star had engraved in him a compulsion that would not permit him to accept death. He ripped the spear blades from his flesh and threw them over his shoulder. Each landed with a human death peal.

He eyed the branches high above. *They'll set the wood ablaze if it means killing the Waira.*

The forest wore the color of blood and his lack of focus was hardening his skin, slowing him into awkward, lurching movements. He'd gotten too used to being comfortable in his altered body.

He needed to get off the ground. He had to risk it. Pulling his spirit in tight, he leapt, reaching high and connecting with a solid branch. The mob gained time and space in those crucial seconds, and seesawing leaves betrayed his escape. They touched their torches to the dry tinder of the forest floor.

The fire spread quickly. Rising smoke clogged his lungs. He faltered, missing a branch, and tripped on the landing, but managed to keep his feet on the ground, kicking up dust and dead undergrowth. The mob pursued, screaming his location and chanting for his death.

Instinct pushed him harder. He jumped up to shake a large branch and then veered perpendicular to his escape path. He blended into the darkness and dove over a fallen trunk, crawling to the wide girth of its broken stump and pressing his back against its rotting bark.

Smoke burned his lungs and his wounds seeped as they healed. The yelling drew closer. They'd seen his diversion and lit new fires. He closed his eyes and inhaled deeply through his nose, and counted the seconds to exhale, calming both his breathing and his heart.

Calm. And breathe. Calm. And breathe. He envisioned the layers of his protective spirit binding him, reflecting his surroundings, and camouflaging his presence from the human eye.

The yelling and chanting got louder as the mob got closer, and the roaring blaze was burning hot on his softening skin. Still, he hid in the darkness behind his eyelids. *Calm. And breathe.*

The villagers charged down his original path. Fire licked the stump at his back and singed his hair and skin. The unease of hunter becoming prey nipped sharply at his ribs. Once they passed him, he maneuvered through the undergrowth and outpaced the fire in the opposite direction until he reached trees that overlooked the village's far side. He jumped to a high perch and studied the women and children left behind with little protection. Their confidence was their ignorance.

Dark smoke plumes rose above the opposing canopy. The mob's voices were distant. They wouldn't hear the screams. He launched over the wall and sped through the settlement, slicing throats and spearing bodies as an unseen ghost of death incarnate, felling guards, children, mothers, sisters, elders. He didn't drink a single drop. They were helpless against a predator they couldn't see.

Let them bear witness. Lucien blew through the gate, splintering it beyond repair as a vengeful omen to the mob. He would return. He would *eradicate* them, too.

☽ ❉ ☾

A sliver of moon hung low over the smoking forest as humid, stagnant air drowned the fires. Cries and sobs echoed within the village walls. The *Waira* had rendered his judgment.

Men blamed each other and fought. Others wailed and drank. Most worked together to collect the bodies and dig a mass grave. They would not challenge him. As with the villages before, these survivors planned to relocate.

Lucien had other plans.

Enveloped by his spirit, he strolled through the fractured gate, unseen by the few watchmen who stood alert, spears in hand and straw padding their chests. He ripped their throats open first.

They collapsed in a line, spurting blood, unable to scream. The others froze, horrified. Energy tensed the very air as their pulses quickened and adrenaline amped their fear. The eerie stillness broke a man who dropped to his knees and pled for his life. Some ran. Others rallied into a protective circle.

Lucien sailed into the center at their backs and unpeeled his spirit's layers. Gooseflesh raised the hairs on their napes. Reluctant, fearful eyes crept over their shoulders and saw the *Waira*, fully armored and truly monstrous.

Lucien bared his fangs and spun in place, severing their spines with a single claw. Momentum hooked them together in a circular bloom of blood. They cried in pain and for mercy, knowing it might take days for them to die.

Lucien left them to scout the four remaining men. They were cowering against the back wall, trapped by their own protections. He pointed to the one with the strongest heart. The man quaked where he stood, too terrified to utter a sound or move as Lucien latched onto his back and tore into his throat. He trained his engorged eyes on the others as he feasted and then dropped the corpse at his feet.

With blood dripping from his chin, he glanced victoriously down his nose at the survivors and turned his back to them. One attacked. Lucien snapped his neck. The other two huddled together, crying as they begged for their lives.

Lucien left the village of the dead. Those humans would tell the tale of the monster who lived in the forest—a forest smoldering to ash by their hands. A monster doomed to live alone.

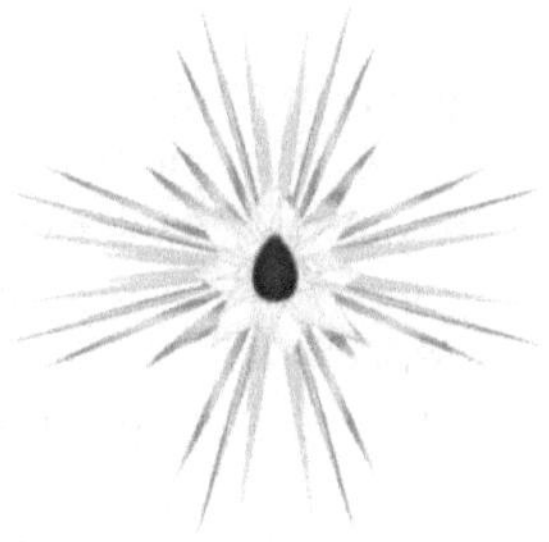

Chapter Seven: Evil Things Enrobed in Sorrow

I

ERIC

Green Mountains, Vermont, Summer 2006

No one was sticking that damn needle into him again. He wanted to ram it into Lucien's neck and watch him writhe. The loss of sensation in his legs added a hollow feeling to his usually firm footing as he closed Sarah's door behind him.

Jonathan jogged up the stairs and wisely remained silent under Eric's glare. "Where are my phone and Vampiric Star?"

"In your room."

Eric threw up a blocking hand when Jonathan moved to follow him. "If you test me, it will not be the thrill you're expecting. Send in Alex."

Jonathan stayed on his heels all the way to his door. Eric whirled around and threw him by the lapels down the hall. Where he might've normally restrained himself and gone into his room, he chased after Jonathan and callously punched his wounded side. Moaning, Jonathan curled into a ball and spat up globs of blood.

Saliva slid down Eric's fangs. "I. Am. Not. Playing. With you. Or Lucien. *If I even see him——*"

"Hey! Hey!" Alex dragged Eric away and scowled at the crimson stain on Jonathan's white shirt.

Eric snarled through gritted teeth. "See me after you tend to him."

He managed not to slam his door. He heard Alex order Heron and Cyprian to take care of Jonathan and then approach his room. But Alex hesitated to knock.

"Come in already," Eric snapped. "And put up a button."

Alex did as asked, watching with questioning eyes as Eric opened drawers in the dresser and nightstands, and ducked into the closet. Eric threw a red v-neck t-shirt and a pair of jeans at Alex. "Change."

He returned to the closet and came out in a blue t-shirt and jeans. Under Alex's wary attention, he collected his keys, wallet, watch, phone, and Vampiric Star.

"I'm not going to attack you. Relax and change." Eric clasped his watch and slid his glasses onto his nose. "We're going to Sunset Grove. Kestrel told me about Walter and the blue lights. You might want to mention stuff like that sooner going forward."

"W-we can't just leave!" Alex protested in his squeaky voice. It grated on Eric's already raw nerves.

The beast's rage blasted beyond the bars of its cage and its howl pillaged Eric from within like a raging wildfire. Its power swelled and surged as volatile as dynamite. Eric glared at the floor, tracing the wood grain with his eyes, back and forth, winding and twisting, desperate to control the thing inside him that clawed for release.

Faster than his own awareness, he was in Alex's face, speaking so gutturally low that it scared even him. "Paresh is dead. Donovan's *protected*. Raven is missing. Sarah is…"

Eric huffed and clenched his jaw. "Not Sarah."

He ripped Alex's Vampiric Star off his uniform. "Walter's floundering on his own in a town full of vampires under the watch of a *literal* and *very visible archangel*. I will go with or without you, so choose. I will not ask again."

Alex sobered. "Thank you for the consideration."

"It's not for you," Eric growled, shoving the pin at him. "You're the only one I can tolerate and I'm well aware that I'm not thinking clearly. I'm sure a *neurotoxin* leaves lasting effects in that regard."

Fidgeting uncomfortably, Alex said, "Um, well, t-to be more forthcoming, Farran was with Walter. She contacted me after he appeared in the forest yelling every name he could think of. I ordered her to keep him company."

Eric pinched the bridge of his nose. "*You what?*"

"It seemed better than leaving him alone in the dark." Alex scratched at his ear. "He didn't know what happened after we left, and everyone he knows is here or…gone."

Muttering angrily under his breath, Eric ran fisted knuckles through his hair. "Did she tell him about Paresh?"

"She doesn't know what happened exactly, so he only got the gist…" His voice faltered as Eric turned.

"Does 'the gist' include information about our daughter?"

"No!" Alex pressed an earnest hand to his chest. "I would never endanger her like that. Neither of them! Walter doesn't even know she was pregnant!"

Eric locked onto Alex's honest green eyes and sucked in quelling breaths. The beast's talons speared his heart and squeezed as he grabbed his sunglasses off the nightstand.

He turned away and conjured the memory of Alex and Paresh dancing, the sun spotlighting her bright grin and the yellow fabric stretched over her growing belly. She'd been so happy. Her last truly joyous memory before—

No.

Gabriel had told Alex to bring her joy and he had. Her final happiest moment was with Alex. Not him. As he tried to convince himself that he was okay with that, the beast shook with laughter and taunted that he'd lost his purpose in life. How was anything going to be "okay" ever again?

"No daft idiot routine with me," Eric said in a strained voice as Alex hurriedly changed. "I want the Crimson Commander."

Alex held his hands up in concession. "You have him, I swear."

Animus Hollow's white mouth split open.

"Was Farran a good pick to pair with Walter?" Eric asked. "He's not exactly comfortable with the situation."

"He's done well with Heron and Master Jonathan, and he's fond of Raven. He's been fine hanging with the deadliest of the deadliest."

"But I was there. And now I'm *not*." He stared deliberately to ram his point home.

Alex's countenance blanked as understanding dawned. "Oh, no. No. She was not the best pick. Uh, we should go."

Alex entered the Hollow first to check for oddities before motioning an all clear. Eric stepped into the soundless haze and each rolling wave amplified his anxiety that a shadow would suddenly attack. Panic crawled into his lungs, squeezing and flexing, its urgency closing around his throat and insisting that he *get out!*

When the exit appeared, he lunged into a world of green and sucked down humid summer air. Planting his hands on his hips, he bent over and closed his eyes, willing control to return. If the beast broke free now, he'd be a danger to Walter. They'd use that venom again and he couldn't bear the thought of reentering dreams haunted by Paresh and his childhood.

Alex waited behind him, dutifully quiet and alert. Eric's stomach plunged as he kicked at the twigs under his feet. The surrounding forest and unnatural silence of it all brought reality crashing down much harder than it had in Vermont. Perhaps they'd made a decent decision in taking him there.

His feet took him south, though he wasn't mentally aware that he'd moved at all until Grandfather Wisdom came into view. A blurry swell burned his eyes. The beast retreated as he approached the tree, cowering and whimpering in a corner. His throat seized and turned each breath into a laboriously painful act.

He couldn't look away from Paresh's golden ribbon, even as he felt the stare of Saint Michael's avatar drill into him. The glowing light called for his touch. The course bark was warmed only by the sun—not by Paresh's essence. It was devoid of feeling. Like it was empty.

"I'm sorry I failed you," he whispered, lifting his fingers, kissing them, and pressing them back. "I love you, always."

Defeat weighed his shoulders down as he dropped his hand to his side. She'd felt safe in his arms. The arms not strong enough to keep her from being ripped away. He stared at his feet feeling strangely pointless in his reason for being. *Anointed Strength.* He scoffed at himself. He couldn't count a single time that he'd saved her.

And he wasn't even strong enough to control himself without her.

Alex lightly clapped him on the back. "Let's go, huh?"

Eric sighed and lifted an exhausted gaze. When was the last time he'd felt this tired? "Is my car still here?"

"Yeah," Alex said, his eyes mournfully drifting over the tree. "But we shouldn't advertise your presence in town."

He pointed to his wrist to indicate Eric's watch. "We added some tech to your watches. You can cloak with them until Master Jonathan helps you learn how to do it with your aura."

"I'm not slinking around my hometown." Eric trudged toward the southern trail. "Who's going to see me that's worth worrying about?"

"*Everyone.*" Alex kept pace with Eric. "The hunters especially."

"They can see me now."

"And word will get to the Elders or Lord Luc—"

"Don't say it!" Eric shoved Alex hard and took off. The beast's wrath was already rising to the surface. It rammed the bars of its cage and an internal fire exploded. Eric snarled and launched himself off the path, colliding with a massive tree that splintered under his fists.

"Let Lucien find out!" he screamed in a monstrous voice. "Let him come after me again! *I will rip him to pieces!*"

Alex chased after him and pulled the Cataclysm from his belt. Eric shot a deadly glare at him. Alex held his hands up. "No—it's not that. Here—"

The mechanism at the base of the hilt opened and a small silicon vial slid out. Alex offered it to him. "Drink this."

As Eric panted and seethed, Alex added, "Look, I promised no more venom. It's exactly what I gave you in your car the other day. Like it or not, you'll need these until we find her. Lord Lu—*He's* stopped distributing her blood to avoid a shortage."

Eric felt himself go pale. "How long does he expect this to take?"

Shoving his sunglasses to the top of his head, Alex sadly said, "We hope only a matter of weeks, but it could take years. As long as you and Jonathan live."

"Years." Eric staggered backward, the battered tree catching him as his fist closed around the vial. He popped the top and swallowed the contents. Paresh's blood calmed the uncontrollable rage and merged his warring halves. He slumped with relief, having already forgotten how good it felt to be *whole*. "Thanks."

"Of course." Alex shrugged. "Thank you for not attacking me."

Eric whispered, "*I* didn't want to hurt you…but I would have."

"Hey, I can't say I get it, but I know *you*. And you're a decent man."

They travelled in silence to the cottage's clearing and emerged into the sun's radiance and a gentle breeze that rustled the leaves.

"It feels abandoned," Eric said.

"It's been like this ever since."

"She's not here to counteract the auras of the hunters." Eric stepped onto the flagstone. Entering the cottage would only do more damage at this point. He turned toward the carriage house. "How many are here?"

"I actually don't know. The Chthonic Knights took over for the Crimson Guard. Nallura left a small crew at Eido. Everyone else is here or searching and hunting. I've only been getting broad updates in Vermont so I could focus on you."

"Then while I'm with Walter, check in with Nallura and get the details you're missing. I want you apprised of the smallest happenings." Eric pulled out the remote for his car. "And find out what the hell Farran said to Walter."

The everyday familiarity of driving felt odd as he steered down the lane. "What happens if you run out of Paresh's blood?"

"I think *he* and Jonathan extended some of the supply with theirs, but—" Alex shook his head and gave Eric an "it's not good" look.

Eric nodded to himself. "Okay, then."

At the police station, Alex accompanied Eric into Walter's office to take Animus Hollow to the Hawthorne Mansion with plans to return cloaked so they'd be seen leaving together. The lawman was lost in thought behind his desk. Dark circles anchored his eyes and his coffee mug reeked of whiskey. Eric closed the door quietly, gestured for Alex to go, and activated the button over the door.

"Hey," Eric called softly. Walter bristled in his chair. There was something new in his eyes—fright. What the hell had that huntress said to him?

"It's okay," Eric said, hands up, open. "It's just me. I sent Alex to the mansion. The others are in Vermont and don't know I'm gone."

Walter chugged the remnants of his mug. "Do...b-but...he, eh—"

He whimpered and buried his face in his palms. Eric gingerly pulled a chair back from the desk and sat. "Hey—take your time."

Walter slapped his desk and kicked his chair into the wall. His eyes were feral and bloodshot. "D-do you...G-God kn-*knows!*"

He bolted up and paced behind his desk. "*He* only acts by God's direction. I-I mean...it's in the *Bible* for crying out loud! *They wrote it in the Bible and now he's here!*"

Bewildered, Eric motioned for Walter to calm down. "Breathe, Walter. Walter! Breathe."

The Chief finally looked up, but Eric wasn't sure what he really saw. At least he followed Eric's prompts and visibly calmed.

"What are you talking about?" Eric asked. "What did Farran say?"

Walter's eyes widened as he shook his head. "No! I looked it up. Did you know the Archangel Michael is the only one listed in the Bible? And he only says four words. *Four.* That's it."

He held up four fingers for emphasis and then grabbed his head. "And he only acts under God's specific direction! Do you realize what that means? *Do you? Cos' I do! And I'm freaking out!*"

Panic blazed in his eyes as he finally focused on Eric and recognized him. He backed into the wall. "Ohh, noo..."

Eric waved defensive hands. "Walter—I'm not going to hurt you; you don't need to be afraid of me."

"*They're* afraid of you. They're *all* afraid of you!"

Genuine confusion burned a hole in Eric's chest. They'd broken Walter. He should've been here. If they hadn't taken him to Vermont,

Walter wouldn't be a rambling lunatic. He needed to bring Walter back from whatever edge he'd gone over.

"You aren't afraid of me, though," Eric said, catching Walter's eye.

"Oh no! No, no, no you don't! You can't make me just *think* that with your voodoo!" He shut his eyes and started hyperventilating.

What the hell happened to you?

Eric's jaw dropped as he sat back at a complete loss. He needed to try something else. He gently cleared his throat.

"Say, do you remember when Andrew did that ride along with you for class credit? You swore up and down that he'd never drive your squad car, but then he bribed your boss and forced you into it?" Eric laughed softly.

Walter's eyes cleared a bit. "Huh?"

"Remember what you did?"

"I pulled him over every single time I saw his car for an entire year! He was such a brat for doing that!"

"You didn't just pull him over—you practically stalked him any time he left the house!" Eric gave him an easy smile.

Walter plopped down into his chair. "He deserved it, though, every bit of it. Made the department good money that year."

"Did you know all those fines almost kept him from getting his license to practice law?" Eric laughed—softly—again. "The Senator stepped in and framed it as a teachable prank. He was able to clear it up so Andrew could get his license without causing trouble for you."

Walter looked up. "I didn't know that. I never thought about how those tickets would affect his future—"

"Oh no," Eric said with a dismissive wave, "don't worry about that. It was funny and it flustered Andrew. It was definitely a teachable moment."

Eric and Walter chuckled and fell silent.

Eric lowered his gaze.

"You know I'd never, *ever*, hurt you, right?" Eric asked gently. "And I'd never *brainwash* you—ever."

Walter stared at his mug and nodded. "I know."

"Things are a bit tense. Scary right now."

"Understatement."

"Yeah," Eric whispered.

"Can I ask what happened?" Tears glistened in Walter's eyes.

Eric shrugged somewhat helplessly. "I'm not sure, myself. Donovan is involved. They drugged me so I wouldn't kill him."

Walter paled. "*That's* why they drugged you?"

"They think I don't know my own strength, that I don't see the way they look at me—and I didn't at first, but—"

Eric licked his lips. "I do now. You're right: they are afraid of me."

He leaned forward. "But they're killers. *They* have a reason to fear me. You don't, Walter. You never have and never will. I will always stand between you and danger any chance I get. I promise you."

Walter nodded, his head lowering in regret. "Sorry for freaking out."

"If there was ever a time—"

"It'd be now, I suppose." Walter stared at his mug with disgust and buried it in a drawer. "I don't usually—"

"I know, Old Friend."

"I mean…if she'd given me context, I never would've—"

"It's okay, Walter." Eric rubbed his forehead. "Even I'm not all that clearheaded, right now."

Walter picked nervously at his thumbnail. "How did she die?"

Eric blew the breath from his lungs, tipping his head back as tears swelled. "I don't know. I was holding her in my arms—"

Eric swallowed hard. "And then she was gone. It—" He pulled his glasses off and wiped at the sting in his eyes. "God…maybe thirty minutes later she was dead."

Walter was grievously quiet, his head bowed. "Donovan?"

Running his tongue along his teeth, Eric shook his head again. "It was someone else. She wasn't supposed to die. But *he* stole her body."

"That's why Farran said there's only one priority target."

"The COMS and the VaSH are both searching for her. They had no choice other than to protect him and hope he leads us to her."

"You know, this whole knocking you out thing is making a lot more sense. They definitely have a reason to be afraid of you."

"I would have killed him on the spot, Walter. I swear I would have—hell, I tried." Eric wiped his face. "Gabriel or Michael, I don't know which, let Paresh's spirit out and she told Alex to do it."

"P-Paresh told Alex to *knock you out?*"

Eric could only nod.

"And he did it?"

"It was a group effort—bait and ambush. They didn't let me stay conscious long and didn't give me enough nourishment to heal from the toxin's effects until today."

"Hence, they don't know you're here."

"Exactly." Eric scooted to the edge of his seat. Walter looked tired and wary, but the fear was gone. "How much bad news do you want at once?"

Walter sat back in disbelief. "Good God, how much do you have?"

Wiping his face again, Eric stared at a spot on the desk and streamed his breath between his lips. "Sarah sent Sammy to live with her sister."

"Wasn't she also going to stay with her sister until things calmed down here?"

"She…" Eric tousled his hair. "She made a decision while I was out."

Walter paled, again. "No…"

Eric couldn't bring himself to look Walter in the eye. He faced the door and sighed.

Walter slumped forward dejectedly, his arms hanging loosely between his legs. "Son of a bitch."

"I had no idea," Eric whispered. "None at all."

"Are you sure she wanted it? They didn't just—"

"She wrote a letter and confessed that she'd dreamt about it as far back as she can remember, like it was her true calling. She wants to find Paresh, and as Fate would have it, she's uniquely skilled to do just that."

"H-how?"

Eric looked at the ceiling and tossed his hands up. "Divine intervention."

"Seems to be going around," Walter mumbled.

"Yeah…about that…I'd just learned that Paresh was pregnant."

"P-pregnant? How did that happen?"

Eric tipped his hands. "Divine intervention is the best we came up with. Hardly anyone else knows. Our daughter's soul is in stasis with her." He clenched his jaw.

"They, uh—" Eric coughed to clear the catch in his throat. "They killed the baby first."

"Oh hell." Walter retrieved his mug and the whiskey bottle.

"And on the other side," Eric said delicately, "Raven is missing—"

Walter's hand worked his balding head as he filled the mug to the brim with a trembling hand. Amber liquid dribbled down his chin as he gulped.

"And, a cursed angel might be about to usher in a premature apocalypse—but we don't know when."

Inhaling mid-sip, Walter violently choked. He grabbed his garbage can and hugged it between his knees, retching in between coughs.

In the putrid, verbal silence that followed, Walter's heart hammered against Eric's eardrums. He wished he could say things couldn't get worse, but at least he hadn't said that *Lucifer* had Raven.

Eric jumped up as a white portal appeared in the corner. He was about to charge when he saw Alex's crown of golden spikes.

His eyes narrowing, Eric asked, "I thought there were only two entrances here."

"Lord Lucien intercepted me when I exited in the orchard—didn't want anyone to know we're here." Alex sucked his teeth and gestured at the Hollow. "Apparently he can open these at will, like the Host could during the War."

"You didn't know he could do that?" Eric asked.

Alex shook his head. "There's no reason I would know. We didn't have access to the Hollow before the Treaty."

Alex nudged his chin at Walter. "Eh, he most assuredly does not look all right."

Walter hadn't even glanced up. Alex leaned over the desk and patted him on the back.

"Walter, man, I'm sorry about Farran. She was the only one who thought to contact me and, in the thick of it, I thought it'd be better to have someone with you than not. But I should've talked to you myself."

"He's not okay," Eric said too lowly for Walter to hear. "I want Heron and Cyprian here for him—as protection and liaisons—until we return when Sarah can travel."

Alex held up his hands. "Don't kill the messenger, but I bet Lord Lucien will fight you on returning here. Only you and Jonathan can resurrect Paresh, and I'm the only one left who can see the dark spot's movement. Without Raven and Endymion, that's all we have as warning."

Eric laced his fingers on top of his head. "Jonathan will back me up. If he doesn't, he'll need to help Lucien stop me."

"Wow, you can really feel it, can't you?" Walter asked quietly. "Her absence? I hadn't noticed until now. The way she calmed a room just by being there. It's so—"

"Empty," Alex finished sadly. "Yeah, it really is."

II

KESTREL
____

Scandinavia, European Continent, 920 A.D.

In the land of ice and snow, the farthest north they'd yet travelled, Kestrel and Lior journeyed through inhospitable conditions to deliver Endymion's second scroll to Raven, the leader of the rebellion and the "light" who'd been swallowed by the Deceiver. Icy wind needled Kestrel's face as she plunged into another knee-high snowbank. Lior

94

seemingly lifted upon the air and effortlessly took his next step, yet sank all the same.

They'd ignorantly expected heavily forested mountains rather than rocky plateaus and blustery gusts and had bypassed merchants in the coastal towns who sold skis and snowshoes. A faint gray ribbon billowed from a cluster of trees to the northwest. She pointed and Lior nodded. A detour wouldn't delay them anymore than the weather already had. This far inland, trade routes, and therefore humans, were scarce. The camp's smoke was a welcome sight on several fronts. He moved the pouch holding the wax-sealed scroll to protect it at his back. The wind whipped harder at his cloak and furs as he turned toward the distant tree line. She fell in line behind him.

The first scroll had challenged them to find Raven on their own. After a detestably cramped voyage across the English Channel, smothered in human fear, they'd located her party's angelic trail on the Isle of Wight. They eventually found it again on the mainland and followed it to a remote encampment on the Scottish coast. Lior was tasked to look beyond the Deceiver's illusory innocence, but Raven had been alone when they delivered Endymion's directions to cross the icy waters of the North Sea to the Kingdom of Norway.

The thick copse of evergreens cut the wind's intensity as they drew closer. They encircled a troupe of explorers. Exhaustion and the promise of warm blood drove them to attack like the savages they hated to resemble.

They drank their fill, dried their boots by the fire, and warmed their frosty cheeks. They scavenged furs and wooden skis, and rested by the quiet crackle of dying embers. Lior hugged her close and kissed the back of her hand.

"M'lady," he murmured.

"My Light." She leaned against his shoulder. When they touched, their abilities worked in tandem. The holy light emitted by Raven and her companions burst onto the horizon like a sunrise. "Do you see it?"

He nodded. "The Deceiver's power must be immense to be seen this far away."

"It's brighter than any I've seen in battle. Don't let him see you."

"Don't let him see your vines." Lior drifted into thought. "I know I've seen a light that bright before."

Lior kissed each of her fingers. "Come, we can make up a half day of travel with these skis, but not if we dawdle."

"Mm," Kestrel moaned lightly, "parts of human life are enviable. This peace, the quiet, being alone with you—"

He tipped her chin and kissed her. "We have that now, m'lady."

"Only if we don't leave."

"But we are leaving."

"Then we don't have it."

He purred against her lips, "Consider it a taste?"

"I want more than a taste."

"As do I."

Reluctantly parting, they retrieved their boots, laced them tight, and bundled the explorers' furs with theirs before fastening their cloaks. The thicket's protection didn't last long. They reemerged into the full rage of the blistering storm, but with the sturdy oak skis, they made better time than Lior predicted. The storm cleared as the temperatures plummeted. They crossed the delineating line for the Arctic region, noteworthy for the comforting darkness of Polar Night.

Haunting ribbons of ethereal light swam above patchy clouds. She gaped in absolute awe of their majesty. They rippled in vibrant purples, blues, and greens like gossamer fragments of stardust.

As she stretched a hand to the heavens, Lior parted her cloak to expose her belly and she gasped at the sensation of tiny pins striking the silver vines. Lior nestled against her from behind and tucked his chin to her shoulder. "What do you feel?"

"It's amazing." Closing her eyes, she saw the ghostly lights flicker behind her eyelids. "They're particles…they sting and tickle, but when they strike, I can see the lights. What do you see?"

He drew in a breath and leaned his head against hers. "I see waves radiating from the Earth that catch your 'particles' in an arcing web." He sounded like he was smiling. "Surely this energy can be harnessed and reproduced—we could do so much with it."

Kestrel curled her hand through Lior's hair. "It feels…*electric*. I don't know how else to describe it."

She opened her eyes. "Do you think that's where the Host live?"

Lior shook his head. "It's not the same energy."

"But the beauty of it?"

"It's still not the same, m'lady." Lior was smiling again. "But it is quite beautiful."

"My Light…" she whispered.

"Ah, should I be jealous? Will these replace me?"

"Oh hush, nothing could ever replace you."

They fell into a comfortable silence, astounded as they watched and felt the celestial veils flow until the clouds filled in. Relaxed and at peace, Kestrel held Lior's hand and led him toward the other glow—their target. They weren't too far off, now.

They pulled their hoods down to shroud their faces. Lior gave her the scroll's pouch and veered off on his own as she closed in on a small shelter, constructed of logs with a roof and stone chimney. It sat beneath a ledge of protective rocks in a pocket of evergreens. Raven rested on a log, staring at the clouds, looking more youthful than most of their kind with shiny, chestnut hair braided down her back. Across her lap lay a young, sleeping girl with black hair. She was draped by a crimson cloak.

The Deceiver was up on the ledge with his back to her, but he knew she was there. He speared Kestrel with a gaze that burned hotter than the light of the Heavenly Host. She cried out and alarmed Raven, who stood to investigate. Neither seemed to notice Lior's hidden presence.

"Are you Endymion's courier?" Raven asked, shielded by her aura and a red cloak. Guarded strength dwelled within her vivid blue eyes.

Kestrel skillfully parted her cloak as she reached for the scroll to sneak Raven's essence into her silver. It was spirited and smart—with a fiery wit that had undeniably attracted Endymion.

Raven accepted the delivery and broke the wax seal. Endymion was directing her east into the Russian territories in case he couldn't hold the line. A shift in Raven's aura drew the Deceiver's attention and gave Kestrel and Lior an opening to retreat unseen.

☽ ✳ ☾

They raced home and skirted the eastern edge of the War's stalled frontline near the northern European border. Winter in the warpath's scorched wake was chilly, but mild by comparison to the Arctic. The castle Endymion had commandeered blended into the bleak gray sky. Vampires that Endymion had smuggled off the battleground lived here.

They snuck through a crack in the wall and ducked into the courtyard's shadows. They emerged from a blind spot, chins up and cloaks snapping on the wind. Small signs of life were returning to the blackened earth. Endymion had taken to nurturing seeds from the region's purple flowers. Somehow, despite the temperature, small, leafy stems sprouted as pockets of bright green against death's background. She sidestepped his tiny babies and trod through the interior gate.

Endymion met them in the large hall. He studied them through lowered lashes before moving closer to investigate, first sniffing Lior and then her.

"The Deceiver was with her this time," Kestrel reported. "He sensed me, but not—"

"Me," Lior finished. "He wears an illusion of light that mimics the Host we see in battle, but his core is filled with the blackest darkness of the Fallen."

Endymion mulled the report with interest. He pursed his lips and touched a silver vine on Kestrel's belly. He sank to his knees, moaning against her skin.

"There she is," he cooed, tracing the vine lightly with his tongue. The silver hissed on his flesh. "Your experiments retained her essence again."

To Lior he asked, "The Deceiver's true face?"

"The imprint is similar to that of the Second Born's with darker hair, but his light prevented me from seeing clearly."

Endymion's eyes narrowed. He grunted and drew a line in blood beneath the vine he was licking. "This section."

Kestrel nodded to Lior. He gouged her skin deeply and snapped the metal in two places before ripping it out. He knelt beside their commander and nuzzled the gory wound as he placed the piece onto Endymion's palm.

"Ah, my dear Raven!" Endymion kissed the piece and burned his lips. He stood and dismissed them with a flick of his wrist. "Take a few days. Repair, replenish, revel. Then we return to battle and pull more of our soldiers off the field. We must maintain the line's position. The First Born has been apprised."

"As you wish," Kestrel said, curling her fingers through Lior's hair as his mouth moved over her bloodied belly. "Forge or bedchamber, My Light?"

"Mm." Lior murmured unintelligibly against her skin. Her vines absorbed the hum in his throat, the caress of his lips, and the warmth of his breath. Heat sparked deep in her core.

Grabbing his chin, Kestrel forced him to stand and hungrily took command of his mouth. Parting, she said, "Forge first—repair and replenish. Then we revel in comfort and get back to work."

"As you wish, m'lady."

Lior twirled her by the hand. She pulled him to her side and draped his arm over her shoulder. They still had much to do, but only a mission or two separated the time that Raven would return with them.

The end was coming.

III

LUCIEN

Northwest Coast of Asia Minor, ca. 1194 B.C.

Humans had forged killing into an art form. Too bored to enjoy their wonderful planet, they invented more weapons, sought more power and land, and built bigger armies to kill, torture, and punish. Sometimes they hunted each other simply to visit death upon another.

They'd nullified what little purpose he'd found in his existence. He was bored and devoid of motivation to do more than feed. Death did not deliver to him the same joy it did to humans. The need for blood was an inconvenience, a pang in his belly that woke him when he'd rather hibernate.

After the villagers burned his home, he vowed never to attack the lords of the land again. He avoided human politics and crossed seas and lakes, grassy flatlands and drowning valleys, and steep hills and snow-capped mountains, feeding on humans of all colors—color mattered so little when what they ate determined their nutritional value.

He'd discovered murals and statues depicting monsters and dragons, and sought to find these creatures along his trek. Tales of scaled gorgons with a stone-turning gaze and snakes for hair had attracted him here, a region of color and culture where the sun reigned high on bright days and the moon ruled black starry nights until dawn broke the veil between.

Long ago, those tiny twinkling prisms had enthralled him. Humans called them gods. His creator called them "Watchers." The Morning Star rarely came to him, but he had once claimed the existence of a single, nameless god, whom Lucien had assumed was the Sun, as Earth's star—until he learned the story of Eos, the embodiment of Dawn, the Light Bringer, and supposed mother of the Morning Star. Surely, his creator would not refer to his mother as nameless?

Perhaps *Eos* was a human-born name that the Morning Star refused to use. After all, humans claimed a great many gods beyond the Sun—known as Helios or Apollo here—and called them different names based on a variety of attributes, only to castoff them off, renaming and changing them, or creating stories of punishment by new gods.

In the Far East, near the construction of a great wall—where images of teal-colored dragons fueled fantasies of finding others like him—he'd heard stories of Lei Gong and Raijin, gods with the ability to throw lightning. Here, humans believed in gods with the same power, yet their names were Zeus, Set, and Jupiter.

Were these different gods or the same god with many names? Or maybe the nameless god threw lightning to manifest its presence to humans who then chose to give it a name? If there were other gods, did they fight amongst each other to throw bolts? Did they war in the heavens as humans warred on Earth? Did the gods live in a hierarchy of classes based on wealth, skin color, and belief?

So many gods. So many names. So little proof.

Centuries of musing had delivered a startling clarity that left a void in its wake. The nameless god must exist, for his creator existed, and, without him, *he* would not exist. But the others? False gods. Mere excuses—stars or not.

"Gods" granted humans permission to drink fermented fruits into oblivion and enter orgies or rages, to turn upon each other in wrath or love—there was no difference anymore—if there ever had been. His world had been too small for too long. He'd known nothing of the planet beyond his mountain, his trees, his villages. They'd worshipped nature and he'd had no reason to doubt them—they knew of a monster named *Waira*, and it was him, but they had given him that name, not his creator.

Now they were one and the same: reasons to murder and wage war. Having gods granted humans freedom from liability—their personal responsibility—for, in their stories, gods often behaved poorly, and so humans, desiring to become gods themselves, mimicked them and molded them to fit their beliefs and needs.

All but the nameless god—maybe *Eos*—were lost on him. Skin color, class, beliefs didn't matter. Humans were animals of identical natures, salivating for an excuse that delivered meaning to meaningless lives.

But not their wars. Their violence bore him necessary fruit and a healthy harvest. They no longer called him *Waira*, but they'd still cry, "Monster!" upon first sight, and elevate him as a creation of the gods— some great creature sent to punish taboo acts. Humans rejoiced in stories of heroes who slay such monsters—like the gorgons—to prove their might, and he refused to fall prey to an angry mob again.

He lay on his side in lush green grasses and propped his head on his palm. The wind carried the salty scent of the coast and the cries of gulls fleeing from his aura. No amount of admiration had brought him closer to the natural world, called Gaea here. Few creatures tolerated his presence. He had once yearned to stroke the warm bodies his furs had adorned in the wintry forests of the Far East.

Alas, he'd never know the sensation of a rabbit's heart beating beneath his fingers. Just as he'd never catch the rainbows of night's light above or touch the silver celestial orb known as Selene until humans invented Artemis.

No. He knew the stars were Watchers created by the nameless god and he'd watched the chariot-less moon rise and fall countless nights. Other earth-bound wonderments had died long ago. The humans who called him a monster were pathetic creatures ruined by love, jealousy, and greed, living lives as empty as his own, but too stubborn to stop searching for purpose—in that vein, they were creatively persistent.

From his perch, the wooden horse looked tiny, no larger than a child's toy. But the beating hearts within its creaking belly belied a strategy of lies and sabotage. All to claim ownership of a woman coveted for her beauty alone and done in the name of a war goddess that didn't exist— the same goddess equated with the moon, who had replaced Eos' sister and fallen in love with the hunter of night only to kill him and send him into the stars. For that preposterous, interchangeable goddess, they were willing to kill and die, to destroy a city and go to war.

No human's beauty was worth scorching a path of death. How did they not see the wonder of the natural world after they had given it a name? Did the nameless god not wish it, so? Was that why *he'd* been created? To celebrate and honor the biological world that rejected him while the plague of humanity wiped itself off the planet? If so, the nameless god had failed. Humans replicated faster than they died.

The toy horse soldiered on. The city gates opened. The promise of blood didn't drive him down the hill—as it should. His gaze lifted to the white-capped swells of the sea and the tropical green of the far shore. He blinked slowly, the currents forming a new image each time.

He drifted into a dreamless sleep. War cries woke him later. Clanging swords and hungry flames nipped at the night sky from inside the city walls. Chaos screeched and black smoke plumed. The Watchers watched through a clear sky that would deliver no salvation to the burning city. They were performing for their goddess of the war moon, real or not.

He rolled onto his back and crossed his hands over his chest, contemplating the cloudless sky. The Morning Star had built him for war—he had the power and stealth—but, if he'd been given the ability to throw lightning as easily as the false gods, cities like Troy and destructive humans who coveted beautiful women would no longer stain Gaea's natural splendor. If he could throw lightning, no human would blemish the Earth ever again.

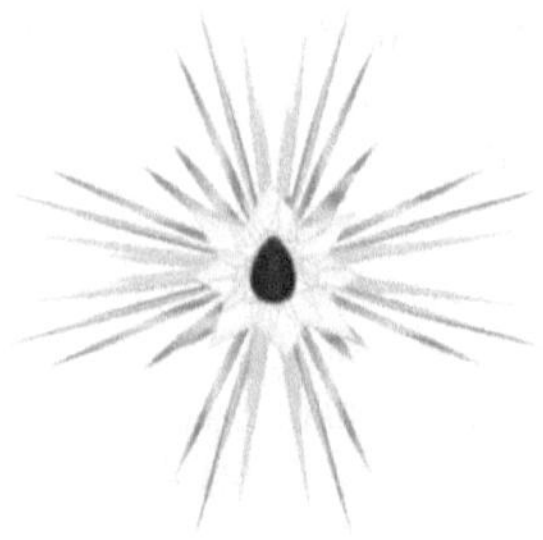

CHAPTER EIGHT: OF THE SOUL OF SORROW LADEN

I

RAVEN

Endymion's Compound, Summer 2006

Her eyes were open. Whatever Endymion had hit her with had worn off, but she'd been deeply out. Someone had cleaned up the blood and broken tea set. Her stinging joints and cramping muscles ached to stretch, but she knew if she moved, she'd lose the steady hold on her pulse and breathing she'd managed to keep as consciousness returned. Endymion had yet to notice that she was awake and she wasn't keen on maintaining the status quo.

And yet, she'd failed to think of a way to change it. She'd memorized every detail of that damn manzanita—same with the silver fragments, down to the slants of the broken edges and the dimples in the rounded curves. Her mind insisted on working against her. What little she knew of the situation outside kept creeping into her thoughts.

Paresh is dead.

She didn't believe him. He'd been dead, too. So had she—maybe more than once given the countless beatings she'd taken by Master Jonathan while "training."

No. No. Keep the blood pressure down.

She focused on the flowers—light as snow with a blush of color—and then closed her eyes and concentrated on the afterimage in the darkness. She held her breathing steady and relaxed every muscle from the top of her head to the tips of her toes—the best she could, at least. The image began to turn in slow circles and the pressure gradually lowered.

Paresh. Rainne. Salea. Endymion. Donovan. Hawkiel. Lucifer. Darkesiel. *Lord Lucien.*

The justice in her heart had never reacted to Lord Lucien. She'd always had his favor. He'd always treated her differently.

Return to that pet you love so much, Endymion had said.

But Master Jonathan hadn't treated her differently. Not until she'd *earned* his respect. What did that mean?

He must not know that Endymion's alive, Raven thought. *But why wouldn't Lord Lucien tell him?*

Master Jonathan was Lucifer's favorite—everyone knew that. Lucifer, himself, had said as much the night he killed Paresh and Eric.

But they didn't really die. No one really dies, do they? That wasn't right.

I'm going to die. She knew that. She'd known it the moment "Hawkiel" marked her.

And Molly had died. It'd been Donovan's fault even though Master Jonathan had stabbed her. No—he couldn't know the truth about Endymion. Master Jonathan had found his penitent heart.

So Eric doesn't know either. And likely not Alex.

Which rounded out the limited few who even had a reason to think Endymion was dead. The majority of the Vampiric Nation knew nothing of Salea's invasion at the Arc of True Blood. If Raven couldn't change her circumstances, she needed to find a way to take herself and Rainne off the board before Salea or Lucifer—

"I am certain it's Lior's soul. Her alteration has accelerated." Kestrel's voice filtered clearly through the door.

By now, nothing should surprise her. Kestrel was one of Endymion's loyal couriers and—as with the majority—should have no inclination that Endymion was alive while secretly playing dead.

But, surprised she was, and not only by Kestrel's presence at the compound. Why was she talking about Lior? And who'd been altered? What was going on out there?

"At the rate by which you have synced, one might assume she'll awaken with his sight intact," Endymion replied.

"That would require less searching time, my lord." Kestrel's voice was dutiful—like reporting to an Elder, outside the Arc of True Blood, in an undisclosed compound was a totally natural, *normal* thing to do. "If his soul doesn't awaken with True Blood muscle memory, training will cause delays."

"What of the hurdle?"

"Lord Eric has given his blessing. He only wants her happiness."

"Then keep her happy," Endymion said. "Neither of you ever had trouble in that regard."

There was an expectant pause before Kestrel asked, "Have you gotten news on Raven's whereabouts? We can search for her light, too."

"Sadly, no, and she is likely lost to us. Lord Lucien would not have granted your requests if he did not expect your position with the Wraith Reapers to become permanent. We *need* Paresh."

"*I'm here!*" Raven tried to scream. Her voice was a mere scratch on air, but enough to force Endymion's hand. He quickly dismissed Kestrel.

"*Why?*" she screeched into the futon as he entered the room. She pounded the pillow with her fist. "*Why are you doing this?*"

He hesitated at the door. She felt his aura moving around him in restraint. In between the layers, she sensed impatience and disturbance.

"It's torture. *Cruel torture!* Lord Lucien and Kestrel...*you!*"

"So you *did* hear us, my dear? You're getting better at evading detection." He knelt and stroked her hair.

"Is Lior really alive, too?" she croaked. "Working with Salea? How many of you are there?"

His aura leaked a spiteful energy. "The night of Lior's death, Salea stole one of my greatest assets—a mistake Kestrel shall rectify when the moment presents itself. However, for now, your girl is hiding off the board—likely dragging Lucifer around by the ear or experimenting on herself again after that *fool* shot her with another silver bullet."

Raven's blood ran cold. "She attacked Alex? Is he..." No. She couldn't say it. Couldn't think it.

Endymion's hand froze. "If all hope were lost, would you stop fighting me?"

A sad chuckle seesawed down. "Asking the leader of a rebellion to cease resisting? 'Tis an answer in itself and I am not so cruel as to deny you. The Crimson Commander is as steadfast as ever."

Raven exhaled in relief. The world was a better place with Alex in it. She couldn't imagine it otherwise. "You lied to Kestrel even though she can sense my light. Do you pay for loyalty in lies?"

"I trend toward honesty, as you know, my dear—"

She snorted. "You literally took custody of me from the Prince of Lies, you fucking liar!"

The layer of impatience cycled through his aura. "Careful words are easier to track than lies. I can shield you from her sight—she needs to focus on her task as Commander without distraction. 'Tis likely Alexander shall receive eldership, should this situation last much longer."

Raven swallowed the bitter hurt at Kestrel's fast-tracked promotion. Was *anyone* looking for her? Likely not with Lord Lucien able to issue unquestionable orders. "And why, exactly, is this situation lasting?" she spat. "Wasn't Lucifer supposed to break the board?"

"One would think he'd account for Salea's unpredictable nature and Corben's arrogance, thereby foreseeing Paresh's death; however, he didn't, and a certain snake stole and hid her body." His anger slithered unrestrained. "I would rip his heart out——"

Raven laughed. It was a pitiful squeak, but her acidic joy was genuine. "*Donovan* left Lucifer stuck without a move? Bloody stars, he's just another piece on the board! Lucifer can't break it. Karmic irony is such a bitch. I hope you never find her."

"Lying is beneath you, my dear."

"Says the lying traitor holding me against my will."

"A will you should be grateful is your own. Not many have that luxury." His voice broke over her like shards of frozen glass.

Something within Endymion had fundamentally changed. She'd never seen him stressed or angry, and he was far beyond both. She hesitated to push him further, afraid of what he'd do or reveal. If he couldn't get her to comply, what measures would he take? Alex was the only way to break her. Would he go that far?

He stood suddenly and left, slamming the door, his aura churning with more emotion that she'd ever felt at once. He returned a short while later with a fresh tea set and cold blood bags. His aura was composed and restrained. Perhaps he also wondered how far he would go.

This time he forced visual contact, kneeling between her and the atrium wall. He offered his hand. She accepted wordlessly, studying his emotionless face. He wasn't as capable at affecting apathy as Lord Lucien. Sorrow and anger warred deep within his pupils. Things were not going well for Endymion *or* Lucifer. She'd take that as a good sign.

She was weaker than she thought. Her wings barely propped her up, and Endymion had to tip her chin and hold the cup at her lips. She sipped slowly, melting as warm liquid coated shriveled membranes.

"The Crimson Commander put a security detail on that snake to protect him from the COMS—and Eric," Endymion revealed with a dangerously dark edge to his voice. "By holding Paresh's body hostage, he has ensured that *no one* may move against him."

Raven sipped again with an appreciative moan. Donovan was a smart rat. He'd hidden under her nose for centuries and could probably drag this stalemate into eternity. But would Paresh's body last—

"Wait…why protect him from Eric?"

"'Twould appear that, despite her wishes, he'd rather see her resting in peace than hunted for the rest of her life."

"He is selfless and would rather live alone with a broken heart than hurt his one true love." Raven shot the words straight into Endymion's blackened heart.

His gaze hardened as he tipped the cup. "'Tis selfish to make that choice knowing she yearns to live."

"You're one to talk. Lucifer will only use her to unlock Rainne and destroy the world. I'd rather kill Donovan, too. She'll find peace."

The grievous darkness reappeared. "That disappoints me, my dear. Your mouth speaks words your heart would never allow. An innocent life hangs in the balance."

"Against the survival of billions of innocents. You think my heart can't weigh? She's already dead."

He pursed his lips and tipped the cup. She drank. He inserted a new IV catheter into a vein, connected a blood bag, and hung it on the rack. She shivered as chilled blood looped through her fingers and up her arm.

"If the people closest to her are willing to kill him, your plotting is doomed to fail, isn't it?" Raven asked.

"Alexander will not permit it," he said with a slight spark in his eyes. "She chose him as her knight. He is too loyal for sentiment."

He sat back and visibly relaxed. "An interesting contradiction for one known to be so emotional."

"That's love," Raven said with a hateful flick of her eyes.

"Do you not love her, as well?" he challenged. "Love does not guarantee life or death. Loyalty outweighs love."

"Were you not loyal to me?" she whispered. "Did you not give yourself to me?"

"Can you lay claim to me without knowing who I truly am?" he asked. "Would you claim me now? You were willing to fight Lucien over my remains."

She ground her jaw. But…her teeth didn't connect. She wilted into Endymion's arms.

"Wha' didja…" She glanced at the teetering IV line. "No…"

"You must stay asleep, my dear. It is too much to bear—*a cruel torture*." He kissed her on the lips. She tried to protest, knowing he'd say those dreaded words and then the sleep regulator in the IV would keep her out until he wanted her awake.

"I am yours eternally, my dear," he whispered as he lowered her onto her side. He kissed her once more. Her eyelids were too heavy to open. She was already halfway to dreamland when those words, *Peto somnus*, crashed over her like waves on a stormy night.

II

ERIC
____

Green Mountains, Vermont, Summer 2006

The feathery tips of switch grass tickled his cheek. A warm breeze ruffled his hair. The sun heated his face through a cloudless sky. He popped off a head of purple clover and plucked out a tube of nectar. Buzzing flower flies lapped at his sticky fingers. They looked like little bees, but they were harmless and he didn't mind sharing.

He sat up and looked at his hands. He was an adult. All around was nothing but prairie—tall grass, milkweed, false sunflower—no fields or farm buildings. The air was fresh, lacking the strong odors of cattle and chickens from his boyhood days.

"No," he whispered, swiveling his neck. She would appear soon, and that meant this was another dream—a moment that never existed— and he'd awaken alone.

The breeze intensified, teasing his nose with syrupy sweet notes. He closed his eyes as soft caresses swept up his cheekbone and a light voice hummed in his ear.

"I miss you so much," he whispered. The sting in his eyes matched the deep ache in his heart. He fell back, crickets chirping, grasses sighing, and sun smiling. "So, so much, my love."

Delicate fingers smudged his tears. Her scent of honey and clover draped over him as warmth appeared and she nestled comfortably against him—a perfect fit.

His lips trembled. He couldn't bring himself to open his eyes.

"If this was an Elysian Field, it'd be perfect since you're here." She snuggled closer, tugging on his arm to stretch up and kiss him. "I miss you, too."

He peered through watery slits at her silhouette's untamed crown. He pulled her by the nape and kissed her again, reveling in the sensation of her lips on his. Her skin was smooth as satin, her hair like spun silk, her frame thin and delicate as he pulled her into his embrace.

She was vibrant. Alive.

107

He held her close, tucking her head beneath his chin, her ear above his heart. He drew in breaths of her shampoo, clean and floral, reminding him of bees and clover patterned with white chevrons. Wavy strands of her hair tickled his face. The wish to pause the moment into forever hardened the ache in his chest.

He couldn't let go. Not this time. Not ever.

But she wasn't really there. His arms collapsed to his chest, her warmth erased, her scent gone. He covered his eyes and cried.

This would never be an Elysian Field.

It was Hell.

His eyes flew open to moonlight streaking over the Victorian curves of the highboy and vanity. White sheers flapped like ghosts as the crisp air of the Green Mountains filtered in through the open pane.

The floorboards creaked as he rose from bed. He stared at his lonely reflection—hair ruffled, chest bare, lounge pants wrinkled. He didn't recognize that sad man. Grabbing his Vampiric Star from the nightstand, he opened Animus Hollow.

Sunset Grove's prickly forest floor greeted his bare feet. As the Hollow closed behind him, the suffocating silence told him that he wasn't alone in the practical sense. He swung his gaze up toward Grandfather Wisdom's clearing. Patches of light shaded the darkness.

Burning moisture surged into his eyes. He bolted into a run, not toward anything, but away. From pain. Grief. Anger. Love.

From her.

He charged through the undergrowth as though he could outpace his sorrow. He couldn't hide from any of those things. No one could. He'd learned that a half century ago.

Emerging from the forest, he was vaguely aware of a faint electrical odor, but pressed on into head high stalks of corn. He raced out into shorter soybean rows and ran until sharp tips of gravel bit into his feet at the Cemetery of Eternal Hope.

He paused at the crumbling brick pillar that once supported a gate guarded by hawthorn trees. The faint electrical odor registered again.

"Leave me alone," he ordered in a low tone that hid the catch in his throat. "Clear the area."

The cloaked hunters retreated.

Molly's granite headstone gleamed with the newer graves at the back. He wasn't here for her.

A few rows in, he stood before an aged marble obelisk on a stone plinth. An engraved lamb lay beneath a weeping willow. Beneath were words he would always know by heart:

Wife of Eric Ravenscroft, Lucinda Marie
Died November 4, 1864
Aged twenty-five years, four months, and thirteen days.
Infant son, Darien Christopher
Died November 4, 1864.
The golden gates did open, a gentle voice said 'Come,'
And with farewells unspoken, they calmly entered home.

His wife and son, dead and buried in the ground.
His soul mate and daughter suspended in a tree.
And an empty grave.
He stared at the standard issue Civil War memorial:

E. Ravenscroft, Sgt Co I, 10th IL Cal.

So many times he'd thought he should be there, in that dank earth, at rest beside his wife and child. Countless nights he'd come to her— to them—knowing they were gone. But now that he could stand beside his love and daughter, who had a chance to return, he'd run away. Back to the past. To the pain he knew. Not the heartache he refused to face.

The marble was pitted and darkened with age and spotted with lichen, coarse under his finger as he traced the lamb etching. He tried to remember Lucinda, but couldn't see her, only the monochrome gray on a stone that was white by day. She was inanimate now. He'd let her go.

An owl hooted in the distance and the surrounding fields rustled. Organic compounds in the wind spoke of crop growth and rain to come. There were no auras or essences or angels. No spiritual nexuses or hazy portals. It was only him, alone, with ghosts of his past who had found peace. Not him, alone, with the radiant souls of his future who longed for life.

Dew seeped into his pants as he sat against his headstone. He dug his fingertips into the earth and let his eyes drift over tall elms and oaks to the gloomy heavens.

"People say that when you lose someone you love, they live on in your memories—like that somehow weakens grief's weight." He firmed his fingers in the dirt. "But it's not a comfort when you wake from memory and lose that person all over again. They're *right there*...and then they aren't."

He unsteadily sucked down warm air. "But then memory turns into fantasy on the wings of Divine intervention, and you open your eyes and you're alone with a memory that never existed."

Tears dripped down his cheeks. "That's the cruelest of all."

Guilt hollowed his chest. "I should be there, with her, with *them*," he whispered, "but it's quieter here. I feel better *here*."

You've found peace, my love. But she'll never find peace. Not in this life.

☽ ✳ ☾

ALEX

The slam of his door hitting the wall jolted Alex awake. He jumped out of bed as Jonathan stormed into his room, eyes dark and glowering, hair wild and furious.

"Eric's gone!" His pupils dilated with fear. "*Why were you asleep?*"

"Kestrel asked to switch shifts last night—said Sarah was doing well and I needed a break."

Alex shouldered past Jonathan. "Some of us *need* to sleep, you know."

Eric's wallet, keys, and phone were in his room. Alex slapped the doorjamb in frustration and pointed at the nightstand with Jonathan's breath breaking down his neck. "Damn it! He promised—look, he took his Star. I'll go get him."

"If he went after Donovan—"

"We'd know." Alex returned to his room and got into his uniform.

"But not if he killed them all," Jonathan insisted, trailing Alex like a shadow. "They—"

Alex gave him a pointed stare. "We'd know."

Kestrel appeared in his doorway as Alex propped a booted foot on the ottoman and jerked the laces tight. He eyed Jonathan. "Where would *you* go if you couldn't sleep?"

Jonathan leaned against the wall and crossed his arms. "Excluding Donovan, I'd go to Pare. To be with her."

Alex snapped his fingers. "Yep."

He laced his other boot and opened Animus Hollow. "I'll bring him back. Kestrel, you're in command."

"Yes, sir," she said, submitting furtive glances at Jonathan. "I didn't hear a thing last night."

Jonathan sighed miserably, clearly stung by Alex's newfound footing with Eric. "He trusts you more than me."

"We ambushed him," Alex said, circling a finger to indicate all of them. "Would you trust any of us? He *tolerates* me."

He entered the Hollow and stepped out into Sunset Grove. Pressing another prong on his Vampiric Star confirmed that Eric's energy signature had landed here. But it led away from the forest.

He called Nallura on his communicator. "Any of your hunters report seeing Eric last night?"

She reported an affirmative with the details. Alex cloaked and ran. His heart hammered at the uncertainty of what he'd find. He uncloaked for the last mile and crept in silence, using fields and trees for cover.

At the cemetery, he pulled his aura in tight and padded through the grass to peek between the arborvitae. Slumped against an old gravestone, Eric dozed with his chin tucked and his arms crossed. Alex cursed internally. Eric was next to his wife's grave.

He noticed a change in Eric's breathing the instant he entered. Sitting across from him, Alex softly said, "I'm surprised you're not with Paresh. Master Jonathan was frantic—thought you might've murdered my hunters and Donovan."

"I'm tempted," Eric mumbled, his tired eyes glinting with awareness before closing again. "Old ghosts are more comforting."

"Do you..." Alex scratched his neck. "After all this time, do you still miss Lucinda?"

Eric shook his head.

"She found peace after I rescued Willy." Eric tilted his head back. "She was there that night. She stopped me. It was the last earthly deed she did—giving me a choice."

Eric's eyelids drooped. "Succumbing to the beast. Or retaining my humanity. She saved my soul."

Alex kicked his legs out. "And now?"

"Same choice, I suppose. Different stakes."

"And?" Alex prodded.

"Your hunters are in danger." His crystalline gaze shot right through Alex. "Or will be. At some point."

"Why didn't you go to Grandfather Wisdom?"

"I can't...be where *he* was, where he brokered his deal." Eric quieted. "No—I can't face her. She enters my dreams and another piece of my control slips away. I wake and she's gone. Every time. I expect to see her everywhere. But not here."

Alex was speechless. Songbirds celebrated the dawn and the crest of fiery orange over the horizon. A cardinal landed on the tip of Lucinda's obelisk.

"Hey, what's that adage about cardinals carrying the souls of the dead? Something about letting you know you aren't alone?" Alex nodded at the scarlet bird. "The fact that he's this close must be a sign."

"How'd you find me? The hunters tell you?"

"After I asked. You know, I think Master Jonathan is scared of losing you, too. He seems…stoic about all this, but I saw beyond his façade this morning. He's a mess."

"I should've gone to her," Eric wiped his face. "I can't…I just—"

"Hey." Alex knocked his boot against Eric's bare foot. "I get it. Honestly, I do. If it was Raven, I'd be the same way. I wish I knew where she was. Or if she's alive. Something. I'm not all that good on my own without her. She just disappeared."

"You'd be at her side if you knew where she was." Eric's gaze burned through him again. "I am going to kill him, Alex. I can feel it. She'll always be hunted. Never free—"

"She's a caged bird," Alex said softly, "and she knows it. She insisted that caged birds can be happy and sing beautiful songs. It's her choice."

Eric shook his head. "I can't do it."

Alex stood and offered his hand. "I'll help you, okay? Trust me."

Eric hesitantly accepted, only it wasn't for assistance. The world violently flipped and Alex hit the ground hard on his gut with Eric on his back, wrenching his arm and tapping the tip of a razor sharp claw at his jugular.

"And what if I kill you to get to him?" Eric asked quietly. "We both know that's the reality."

"True, but would she ever forgive that?" Alex asked sadly. "Would Lucinda? After stopping you in the Confederate camp? I don't believe you'd belittle their feelings like that."

Eric's grip loosened. He shoved off Alex's back and dropped into the grass, throwing his arm over his eyes.

Rolling over and lifting onto his elbows, Alex faced Eric. "I *will* help you. I promise. You won't kill him until it's time."

Dropping his arm, Eric stared at Lucinda's headstone. He released his aura and Alex cringed at the intensity of his despair.

Eric looked over at Molly's grave. "I'm losing everyone I love."

"You haven't lost Paresh, yet. Or Walter. Or Sarah. Come on—why don't we go back, eh? Check on Sarah? Kestrel said she's doing better than expected."

Eric blinked slowly. "I won't ever see her here, huh."

"She made her choice because she loves you. Same with Molly." Alex stood and hoisted Eric up. His eyes misted as his thoughts turned to Raven. Maybe he understood Eric's grief better than he thought—but it'd been padded by the luxury of knowing it was coming. "Love is painful and forces hard choices, but we should all be free to make those choices for ourselves."

III

LUCIEN

South Africa, ca. 1000 B.C.

A bright flash ripped apart the fabric of time. The Morning Star appeared, barefoot and stately in pristine robes that rippled in the still air. Three pairs of virginal white wings flourished from his back. A holy flame burned brightly within his unblinking stare and innocence glowed like a crown above his brow. In his arms, lay the body of a man.

Lucien cocked his head. Not a man, exactly—a creature, like him, but of humanoid appearance. The face matched the Morning Star's, but the hair was a rich, fiery red instead of straight, glossy black.

"He is for you—a companion, a subordinate, a gift," his creator, announced, musically and painfully shrill. "Call him Jonathan."

The Morning Star tossed Jonathan into Lucien's arms, added two red garments, and returned to the void. The seam of time sealed with another brilliant flash.

He lay Jonathan on the sun-heated sand and traced the outline of his face. He was beautiful—the first beautiful thing he'd admired outside of Gaea's natural world. Every part perfectly chiseled, angled, and smoothed like the marble statues in Athens. Except he was real.

Flesh.

Bone.

Blood.

He brushed the garments aside and stroked Jonathan's muscled chest and arms, the defined ridges over his belly, the v-shaped skin and muscles between his hips, his thighs and calves, his ankles and toes. He was pale like fairer-colored humans, without scales or armor, and his ears were round. Parting his lips, Lucien found lengthened teeth shorter than his, with a different curvature—as though to extend and retract.

Something stirred deep within him, like snakes writhing and twisting in the pit of his stomach. The pulse beneath his fingers was strong, the skin supple, the body firm—he didn't want to stop touching him, exploring, discovering. Jonathan wasn't human. And he wasn't prey.

He's a companion, a subordinate, a gift…

Lucien sat back, welcoming the baking heat on his scales, and visually followed the lines of Jonathan's body, memorizing each in vivid detail. He envisioned muscles tensing and coiling in movement, lunging, and hunting—Jonathan was shaped differently and would blend with humans easily. Yet, he'd move like Lucien, a predator.

He watched the slight rise and fall of Jonathan's chest as the moon chased the sun. Tall clouds loomed on the horizon. The Morning Star had caught him journeying north from the continent's southern tip. He had barely outpaced those clouds—omens of heavy rains and oppressive humidity.

The humans in this landlocked region were dark skinned and nomadic in nature, rarely clothed or sheltered. They moved easily among tufty grass and trees with bulbous trunks, trailing roaming herds from one resource to the next. They lived off the land much differently than he'd witnessed in Athens. The rain came so little in the dry season that they built simple rain shields or tiny grass huts around water holes, but this village's water source had withered. Its people had moved on, leaving behind huts in various stages of disrepair. None would keep him dry.

The air's water content inched up and triggered that uncomfortable crawling sensation that made him want to peel off his skin. He squeezed through a hut's small entry and hunched over his knees, folding his arms and tucking his head to fit without destroying the roof. As a soft rain began to fall, small droplets slipped through the woven grass.

The intensity grew, splashing and pooling around Jonathan. It pitted the sand, shredded dilapidated huts, and churned dirt into mud. Soon, it was a heavy white curtain and Lucien was nearly soaked, but he far preferred a leaky shelter to the torture of wet needles—

Jonathan sat up, the beginnings of a smile playing over his mouth as he faced the sky. He leaned back on his hands, his hair streaming like kelp in a swift current. The torrent splashed off his cheekbones and forehead, and raced rivers over the curves of his lips and his arms and chest. His lungs expanded and fell as he breathed deeply and evenly.

Contentment radiated from his aura, rippling greater with each hammering drop as though mirroring ripples on a pond's surface. Rolling his neck, Jonathan grinned wider and flashed the white of his teeth—an expression of pure joy at his first tactile sensation.

He kicked his legs out and dug into the sand, flexing his fingers and body in accordance with the rain's beat, a rhythm Lucien had never before noticed. Jonathan's bliss enveloped him and made him yearn to sit out there like that, showered with sky kisses. Each drop was a lick of a new awakening—warm splashes jerked nerves to attention and delivered sensory pleasure in place of stabbing misery. A beautiful hum caressed Jonathan's skin, lighting his cells and tingling in his palms and the soles of his feet—the whole of his being sang of life.

The torrent slowed. The curtain thinned. Jonathan stilled. Droplets pooled into the grooves of his muscles and trickled down the length of his slender form, opening his nerves anew to the atmosphere's barest caress. The sweet perfume of honeysuckle blossoms lifted above a mixture of earthy vanilla and virgin pheromones as water ran down the slope of his abdomen into the creases of his thighs where his body fully stirred with excitement.

Lucien felt every bit of this pleasure, this awakening. His own heart quickened to match Jonathan's; his lungs expanded faster and deeper with longing. Carnal pressure built and grew in need of release.

Jonathan cracked an eye. His amber irises flashed brilliance with flecks of gold and glossy obsidian, fully aware that he was filling Lucien with his pleasure. His voice was as luscious and smooth as silk.

"I am Lucifer's Second Born." He swiveled to face Lucien, sitting upright and butterflying his legs so that his heels touched. "Designed to kill the Children of God with you."

Not ready to relinquish this newly discovered melody, Lucien tried to linger on Jonathan's beauty and the painful pleasure burning deep within him, but his mind had already latched onto that word, that name, *the name*: God.

The Second Born knew the name of the nameless god—the father of humanity. It was plain, neutral, simple. If there was only one, perhaps a proper name was unnecessary. Perhaps the once nameless god preferred discretion to avoid becoming an excuse. Such a god would meld into the background as camouflage, innocuous and innocent, a mysterious force behind the fabric of time.

His creator, the Morning Star—or Lucifer, as Jonathan had called him—had already told Jonathan more than he'd ever told *him*. Lucien had learned everything in his life from three words etched into his brain, but Jonathan came with a name and knowledge.

Why would the father of humanity create a star to create an underdeveloped monster? Why did he create humans if he wanted them to die? Had the once nameless god created the Morning Star specifically to kill humans? Why create humans at all? Or a star to kill them? Why—

His skin prickled. Jonathan trapped his gaze. The rain stopped. Jonathan raised an eyebrow. "First Born?"

Lucien tilted his head. Curious. No one had spoken *to* him before. "I suppose, yes."

Jonathan tilted his head, too—an innocent imitation even as the fire of knowledge burned in his eyes, a fire not given to Lucien. The musings stacking in Lucien's mind threatened to pull him away from reality—he'd been alone for so long. This had to be a dream.

"I was created for you," Jonathan said, continuing his study from a skewed vantage.

Lucien crawled out into humid air scented thickly of mud and hot grass. He knelt beyond the roof's drip line and glanced at the soaked bundle of red wool. Jonathan's eyes followed. He sifted the two garments between his hands.

"Aegis cloaks to aid us in our quest." He dipped his chin in reverence. "I am a gift. Yours, until the end of time."

Jonathan. Gift.

Aegis. Protection.

Humans had prayed and celebrated at Delphi—dancing to music and drinking wine for graces and protection that their gods never delivered. *He'd* done nothing of the sort, and yet the Morning Star had delivered protection—a garment, a shield—and Jonathan—a gift, a companion.

A predator—a weapon.

Jonathan stood, his muscles etching lines into his calves and thighs as he approached with a cloak in each hand. He knelt before Lucien and dipped his chin again. Closing his eyes, he offered a cloak.

Grimacing at the dripping garment, Lucien said, "Leave it. The sun will rise soon and bring the heat of day to dry it, albeit briefly at this time of year—"

He cupped Jonathan's cheek and gently caressed his lips with his thumb, nudging them apart. Jonathan's eyes burned into his as he opened himself for examination. The skin around Jonathan's mouth was soft—no scales, no lines—and his teeth...

"Show me your fangs," Lucien said.

Jonathan's pupils dilated with an arc of gold and the whites filled thoroughly with thick, engorged red veins. The hinge of his jaw elongated, and his teeth descended into his mouth, one sharp tip drawing blood from Lucien's thumb. Jonathan curled his tongue around it, stroking and sucking lightly. In his predatory eyes, Lucien saw a great lust for more than blood.

Companion. Lucien's heart skipped a beat or two, or more—he wasn't quite sure, not under that golden-black gaze.

Jonathan studied him a moment longer. He tossed the cloaks aside and crawled closer, his hair dripping a dark path. "I am yours. You may do whatever you please."

Lucien's eyes dropped to faint cracks in the supple temptation of Jonathan's mouth. "You're dehydrated and need to feed."

He grinned. "I am starving."

Lucien made a thoughtful noise and dropped his hand. "Humans are sparse here in the rainy season. We must travel."

Jonathan licked his lips, doggedly eyeing Lucien's mouth.

"That can wait," Lucien said, swallowing his own disappointment. He stood. "Nutrients for a hungry body cannot."

Darting up quickly, Jonathan tottered and purposefully caught himself on Lucien's chest. He kissed Lucien, tentatively at first, but then pressed against him, probing, ravenous, impassioned. He straightened with a pleasured moan, panting lightly. "I needed a taste— of you—first."

Lucien touched his lips, shocked at the delight and desire coursing into his core. Gone were the writhing snakes, replaced with fluttery wings that beat relentlessly and drove his pulse up. His heart quivered uncomfortably, and his breaths came quicker and heavier. He reached for Jonathan and noticed his scales had softened to a smooth semblance of skin with a subtle violet tinge.

Clouds on the horizon warned of longer rains to come. He needed to stay ahead of the weather. But...Jonathan had so thoroughly consumed his thoughts that he hadn't noticed the irritating damp seeping between his scales. It wasn't better or worse than usual, but somehow, Jonathan's presence made it tolerable.

Sucking down a calming breath, he rubbed his arm and avoided Jonathan's gaze, mentally searching for his center. He'd existed for a thousand years. Time was on his side. "You were born to kill, so come. Let's find you a worthy hunt."

Jonathan's blackened eyes glinted with bloodlust. Lucien nodded at the cloaks and began walking north. As Jonathan hurriedly swept the garments into his arms and followed, Lucien focused his mind away from physical need and returned to the once constant echo that had gone silent long ago: *Eradicate*.

The "whys" of the nameless god didn't matter. Through a broken cloud cover, the Watchers watched him walk the same Earth he'd always walked. The Morning Star hadn't changed the reason, or lack thereof, for his existence.

Lucien spied Jonathan through lowered lashes as he faced a sky that sparkled in patches. Wondrous awe consumed his expression as he studied every new thing and turned in the occasional circle to take it all in. Lucien had never felt such infantile fascination, but the grandeur of life pulsed vibrantly from Jonathan's aura into his. He knew then that their lives were forever entwined.

He was no longer alone.

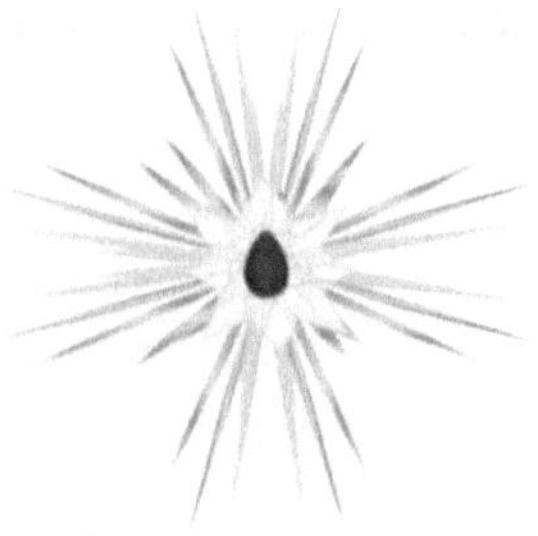

Chapter Nine: The Anatomy of Renaissance and Ruin

I

SARAH

Green Mountains, Vermont, Summer 2006

Rhythmic swishing eased her consciousness into waking. She floated at the precipice for a time, not quite ready to meet her new life, yet. But the part of her that had lived before swam up from the depths with eager insistence. She cracked an eye open and cringed. The cold, electric blue of dawn reflected as blurry radiance off the white of everything.

She shielded her eyes as her vision adjusted. Through the dormer windows, the mountain's vapors refracted the sun's early light into rainbowed shards that glittered over verdant treetops. The constant underflow and swirling motions were mesmerizing, lifting, dissipating, swelling, and sinking all at once.

Beyond the beat of her heart, it was silent. No birdsong. No voices. No creaking or popping. The button had even muted the maple branch tapping the far window.

The drag of her skin on the cotton sheets scraped her eardrums. The mattress's springs squeaked loudly as she sat up. She steadied her breathing to dampen the *whoosh* of her ballooning lungs. She'd expected to feel hung over, and the light and sound sensitivity—and the dry gumminess in her mouth—was certainly close.

Stabbing pain came with the luminance of the insanely lit room. She must've woken earlier than Kestrel expected or the blinds would've been drawn. The rustic blues, reds, and aged ivory of the Colonial style quilt were dark and absorbent, and therefore gentler on her eyes. The pain began to fade.

Individual wooden fibers in the floorboards seemed to tense under her toes as she stood and felt herself teetering off balance. It wasn't the same as the spin of dizziness or vertigo's violent tilt. It was…a delicate listing, like a boat on a bobbing lake. Her first steps were wobbly as she scurried to the vanity bench and pulled her feet up, tucking her hands under her soles. She contemplated the floor and wondered about the electrical voltage running through the house, but the sensation traveled up the bench's legs and into the seat as a vibrational hum. She suddenly felt wound up, reflexive and responsive with a new buoyancy.

The mirror gleamed as though seeking her attention. She'd seen too many movies as a child where vampires didn't have reflections. Of course, Kestrel had promised that wasn't true and—logically—she knew Eric had one. But still she wasn't sure if she'd recognize herself. She had someone else's soul inside of her. Wouldn't it expect to see *him*?

She swiveled on the bench and planted her feet. The reflection in the mirror…was her reflection. She touched her forehead, cheeks, and chin, fluffed her hair, and grinned the same grin. But…it wasn't *all* the same.

She leaned for a closer look at the glimmering flecks of gold in her hazel irises and the new bronzed blush to her light umber skin. She stretched out a spiral of hair that shimmered like polished copper and burnt bronze. She bared her teeth, whiter and brighter than ever, but otherwise no longer or sharper.

Sitting back with a troubled huff, she closed her eyes to think and saw a faint glow. It disappeared when she opened her eyes, but it had come from the top right drawer.

Her brow creased as she looked inside and found only a blue velvet lining. She blinked and glimpsed the glow again. The ability to see with her eyes closed was familiar.

She closed them again. The glow firmed into a circular outline. Under the lining, she found a necklace with a crucifix pendant. She saw it as clearly as she would with open eyes and even recognized it.

It'd been a gift from her grandfather at her baptism as a young girl. She was wearing it when Kestrel bit her. The way it radiated its own aura, pure and definitively holy, felt right, but not quite *right* enough— like it should be stronger.

This must be Lior's sight. She clasped the closure at her nape.

Feelings of need and desperation that weren't entirely hers alone swirled into an excited frenzy as Kestrel opened the door. Warmth streamed back to her as her aura embraced Kestrel and age-old nostalgia and relief swelled within Sarah's chest. An easy smile lifted her cheeks.

Kestrel looked at Sarah like she was too good to be true. She dashed over and threw her arms around Sarah's neck, resting her chin on her shoulder. Sarah swept her fingers through Kestrel's glossy black and gold hair, closed her eyes, and swayed in place. Contented in the moment with clarity, conviction, and confidence, she murmured, "M'lady."

"My Lady Light."

Their hands found each other and interlaced, tightening and relaxing. Kestrel's aura cascaded over Sarah with the viscosity of rich molasses and took her into memories of The Greenery's kitchen. A pot of soup boiled on the stove, the handle of a stainless steel ladle clinging to the side. The pot morphed into a flaming pit, but the ladle remained, holding melting silver. Aching delight bloomed at her core as she recalled the heat of Kestrel's fevered body and the bite of winter air on her naked skin. Then she was back in the kitchen with boiling soup steaming her face as the scent of tart apples and cinnamon wafted from cooling racks.

Every bit of the pride she'd taken from her desserts and soups perfectly matched the emotions Lior had felt while carving Kestrel's scrolls. His care was *her* care—the work, the detail, the ritual. Love enhanced it a hundred fold.

As Kestrel held her, Sarah's memories synced with those embedded into Lior's soul. She'd worried that he might erase her, but his soul was her soul. The experiences of her previous life flooded in on a tide of melancholy and sorrow.

Curved blades flashed against a swollen black sky. Pain exploded in her chest with the crack of breaking bones. The scent of rancid, *metallic* blood rushed up her nose and then she was in free fall, tumbling backward in a horrifyingly slow moment that denoted defeat. She crashed hard into London's cold damp. There was no air. Only crushing agony and despair as a silver arc limned overhead—

Sarah instinctively pulled the dagger sheathed under Kestrel's forearm, dodging and throwing in the same instant. The blade sank into the far wall. Jumping against the vanity, she clutched her chest, winded and frantic, swinging her gaze wildly as decorative perfume bottles shattered on the floor. "*Where is she?*"

"Oh, My Light." Kestrel knelt on the bench and cradled Sarah's head at her breast. "You remember."

"I..." The sensation of movement returned under Sarah's feet. "I need to sit—"

The dual blades flashed again. "Raven's Deathscythe," Sarah whispered with an involuntary shudder. "I can't catch my breath."

Clawing her throat, Sarah panted heavily. "What…is this?"

Kestrel grabbed Sarah's hands. "It's your final memory."

"It's a nightmare! What happened to him?"

"*You*," Kestrel said, trapping her gaze, "were murdered by Salea. Beheaded."

Sarah stammered for words. Silvery blue silk flew through her mind as part of a calculated plan that had gone horribly wrong. "B-but…my chest. I can't breathe."

"She crushed your lungs first," Kestrel whispered. "She was faster than any of us anticipated, and Raven—"

A lengthy pause stretched between them. Sarah was locked into a loop with those blades—hearing her ribs shatter, smelling the blood, feeling the slam. "What did Raven do?"

"Nothing. Alex shot Salea in the head."

"Mission accomplished, at least," Sarah said bitterly.

"No—no, it wasn't."

Sarah squared her shoulders and pulled her spine straight as a weighted stone formed in her gut. "One doesn't walk away from an exploding silver bullet to the head."

Surprise lit Kestrel's countenance. "Unless one shares the blood of the Deceiver and uses silver to alter one's body. How did you—"

"Is she still alive?" Sarah interrupted. Her control was spiraling deep into the Earth's axis as it rotated beneath her feet. The color of blood drenched her visual field and an ache spread along her cheekbones, building behind her canines. "How could Lord Endymion permit such an atrocity? *Why didn't he kill her himself?*"

"Sarah? Sarah!" Kestrel flicked nervous eyes at the open door. She squeezed Sarah's hands. "Don't talk about *him*!" she hissed through clenched teeth.

Conflicting emotions were at battle and Sarah didn't recognize either one. "I swear there's a beast inside me that's about to explode."

Kestrel's eyes widened. "But that's…it cannot be! You're the first new true…va-vampire since…that is you have a soul! You shouldn't have a beast!"

Clenching her jaw, Sarah silently pleaded for help as anger ran circles through her aura. Kestrel quickly shut the door to close the button's open circuit and grabbed a blood bag. She emptied it into a chalice along with the contents of a tiny vial—only large enough for a few drops. "Drink this!"

She guided the chalice into Sarah's hands and up to her mouth, not giving her a chance to hesitate. The viscous liquid was thick and cool. The pressure eased. Control returned in jagged waves. Her lungs expanded.

"How are you now?" Kestrel asked, lips drawn nervously.

"Better." Sarah finished drinking. "What was that?"

"Turn around."

Sarah gawked at crimson veins that throbbed in her eyes around a sliver of gold iris and bottomless black pupils. Her jaw's hinge had stretched at least an inch or two, and her bloodstained…*fangs*—

She touched the tip of her tongue to one and sliced into her flesh. Long and sharp, her fangs curved slightly outward to clear her bottom lip. She lifted a finger to investigate and was distracted by dagger-like claws.

Kestrel sat on the bench. "I wonder if this happened because your soul was locked away when you died. Maybe that was you passing the judgment of the Second New Age?"

Old and new memories collided. Paresh and Eric—the Servator. The prophecy that had been a far-off dream in her previous life had finally arrived. "Why can't we talk about Lord Endymion? And why is Salea alive?"

"It's complicated. He faked his death at Salea's hands, but most of the Nation has no clue and Lord Lucien wants to keep it that way. It's easier for us to avoid slipping up if we just don't talk about him. It's confusing as hell, but I've kept him updated on your situation and he's looking forward to seeing you."

"It doesn't sound like he's changed, at all. And Salea?"

Kestrel shrugged uncertainly. "The bullet didn't kill her. Alex suggested rehabilitation at the Arc of Celestial Night."

"*After she cut off my head?*" Sarah enunciated and clipped each word.

"Yes."

"Raven did nothing?"

"Salea likely would've died in her arms if not for Alex."

Sarah sat back in thought. "Why did Lord Endymion agree?"

Kestrel shook her head. "I don't know. I took your body to Eido. Raven and Alex reported to the Elders."

"Who knows that we know he's alive?"

"Only Lord Lucien and the Knights at the compound."

"Not Master Jonathan?"

Kestrel's voice dropped. "Our lord's view of the Second Born remains unchanged."

"Leverage, of course." Through the mirror, Sarah watched the thick mists roll down the mountain. Her vision and teeth returned to normal, and her nails shrank. She pulled in a stiff breath.

"In this body—in this life—I can't accept being disposable," she whispered at last. "Things were different then—I was different then—I get it. But I am not expendable. I will not accept that now. I will not bow to someone who cares so little for my life."

"I was so empty without you, My Light." Kestrel draped her arms around Sarah's neck.

"I'm sorry, m'lady."

"Do not be. We have roles to play. Salea will be ours to kill, soon."

Sarah covered Kestrel's hands with hers. "My memories will continue to sync and we'll train—*play our roles*. But first, I want to check on Eric and let him know I'm good."

"He sat with you for long hours every day."

A tender love swelled within Sarah's chest. "That sounds very much like him. He's a better gentleman than I ever was."

"I draw no comparisons, My Lady Light, but he cares for you, like you cared for me when I ailed."

"You're wrong. His care is driven by love. I never loved you—" She kissed a path from Kestrel's wrist to the tips of her fingers. "Until now—heart and soul, m'lady."

☽ ❋ ☾

KESTREL

The parlor's cuckoo clock chimed noon when she and Sarah finally emerged from the white room. Lior's rail-straight posture and swagger seemed to add an extra inch to her height. Alex was wilting at his post atop the stairs when Sarah offered an adorably bashful smile in sharp contrast to the awareness she exuded.

The Crimson Commander straightened and shared a look of confirmation with Kestrel. He grinned and crossed his arms.

"You look well rested," he said to Sarah, leaning back and propping a foot against the wall. "You'll start training tomorrow."

"I look forward to it, High Commander," Sarah replied with a respectful nod, her eyes shining golden mischief. "I don't expect it to take long. Chefs are pretty good with blades."

Alex laughed. "Let me rephrase then. Welcome back and welcome to the Wraith Reapers."

"Ah!" Sarah feigned disappointment. "Always a First Officer and never a Commander?"

"Every bride needs a bridesmaid." Alex nudged his head down the hall. "Eric's in his room."

Sarah's aura shifted nervously. Alex gently added, "He'll be happy to see you up and moving."

"Where's Master Jonathan?" Kestrel asked.

"Shockingly," Alex said, "playing chess with Mr. Smith."

Her expression must have conveyed what she couldn't say because he bent over laughing. "Yeah, with a human—I know, right? But Eric taught that old man, so he's vexingly tough."

"Even for Master Jonathan?"

Alex winked. "Oh yeah. I should probably go umpire or something, but I watched Lords Ceallach and Satiereon sit on one move for six hours. I'm chessed out." He wiped his hands free of it.

"We'll check on them." Kestrel glanced at Sarah. Her mix of fresh wonderment and old knowledge swirled within her aura like puzzle pieces that couldn't connect just yet. "We need to report to Master Jonathan anyway—after she visits with Eric."

"Take your time," Alex said, sobering. "You know what Eric wants—"

Kestrel nodded. "I will honor his wishes until the end of my days."

"Don't sound so apocalyptic, especially now!" His voice squeaked as he scratched behind his ear.

He'd been doing that more since Raven's disappearance. Kestrel gestured for Sarah to go on ahead. "No word yet on Raven?"

"Lord Lucien won't approve my search requests." The muscles in his arms pulled taut as he shook his head. "I can't just accept that she's gone. Paresh and Raven within minutes of each other? No way. If Lucifer really has her, then he needs her, and she's going to fight like hell to escape. I should be looking for her."

"If *Lucifer* has her, we can't rescue her—no matter how many hunters you take."

Alex drummed his fingers impatiently, withdrawing into himself and gnawing the inside of his cheek.

"But," Kestrel said in a softer tone, "just because we cannot go *now*, doesn't mean we can't ever go. Toss that coin of yours and plan it out. Maybe we'll get lucky and see her light."

The hinge of his jaw bulged a few times before he dug into his pocket. "Nothing's the same without her."

Kestrel glanced at Sarah. "I know exactly how you feel."

Alex nodded absently, walking the coin over his knuckles. "I suppose you do. What does she remember?"

"Salea swinging the Deathscythe."

"Damn." Alex's voice was barely audible. "I can't imagine—she must hate me."

"Why?" Sarah asked from down the hall. "You took the shot."

"I saved her."

"Pity yourself all you want, but we can safely assume that a silver bullet is little more than a scratch to her," Kestrel said.

A shockwave rammed through Alex's aura. "What do you mean?"

"Look at how she modified herself—silver is like magic to her—it's not toxic," Sarah said. "Without staking her, I doubt she would've died. I don't think anything made with silver can kill her."

"But I——" Alex sagged against the wall. "I shot her twice on the Isle of Wight. One went through, but the other landed."

"Then Sarah has a fresh trail to follow so we can give her a proper hello," Kestrel said through a falsely sweet smile.

Alex bobbed his head. "I'm glad you got him back."

"If you truly mean that, then focus on getting Raven back, too, instead of missing her. We'll check on Master Jonathan when we're finished."

"Hey, hold up." Alex pulled Kestrel over and dropped his voice. "Do you still have Lior's Vampiric Star?"

Shock crept over Kestrel's vines. Alex seized on her hesitation.

"Yes, I know—I've known the whole time."

Kestrel's blood ran cold. No one should have known that it wasn't incinerated with his body. She'd swiped it to make reporting to Lord Endymion a tiny bit easier. How did Alex——

"Look, it's fine. If I had the same opportunity, I would've kept Raven's. I'm sentimental, too. I'd want to keep a piece of her with me." He blew air over his lip. "While you're training at Eido, I'll pop up to recode it for her."

"Of-of course," Kestrel replied.

Alex gave her an odd look. "Why'd you think I'd care? You do know me, right?" He ducked and glanced around dramatically. "I'm still here—I think. Or am I the one who's gone, and this is all a dream in Raven's mind?" He waved his fingers to match his ghostly voice.

Touching her fingers to her forehead, Kestrel refocused and found her center. For once, Alex was truly as clueless as he acted and had no idea she'd been using it. "Unlike Raven, I won't cater to your eccentricities. I'll have the star for you at Eido. Please excuse me; I have a job to do."

He straightened and gestured down the hall. "Good luck, Commander."

She nodded and joined Sarah. The nervous ripple in her aura was stronger now. Kestrel rapped on the door before Sarah could object.

When Eric greeted them, Sarah's cheeks flushed bright pink. He didn't say a word—just hugged her tight. Sarah visibly relaxed and returned his embrace, resting her head on his shoulder.

Eric's smile didn't touch his hollowed cheeks or haunted eyes. "Welcome back to the world of the living."

"Mr. Ravenscroft!" Sarah ushered him to the bed and made him sit. "Molly would have a heart attack looking at you now!"

She shot an alarmed look at Kestrel. "Please get him something!"

"No, no." He waved off the request and gathered Sarah's hands in his. "I'm so relieved that you made it. I've lost too many friends already."

Sarah froze in horror. "Did something happen to Walter?"

"No—he's fine. I didn't mean..." His gaze trailed with his words. He blinked and shook his head as though to clear it. "Never mind. How do you feel?"

"Great, honestly."

He patted the spot beside him and Sarah sat. Kestrel leaned against the wall. "She came through better than anyone I've ever seen."

"And...Lior?" Eric asked cautiously.

"My older memories are coming back," Sarah said. "In fact, part of me wants to say that I'm honored to meet you even though I've known you my whole life."

He nudged her chin up and watched the light sparkle in her irises. This time his eyes crinkled when he smiled. "I suppose there's a part of you that I look forward to meeting, as well. But, for the *you* that I do know: Sammy is proud of you. I talked with him this morning."

She blushed again. "Aw shucks, Mr. Ravenscroft, you're going all sweet on me now."

"Please, call me Eric." He sighed and clasped his hands in his lap. "Everything's different now."

"You're right. Like you not taking care of yourself! You look terrible!"

"It's worse than I feel. Don't worry—Alex is mother-henning me." He swept his fingers over tired eyes. To Kestrel, he asked, "Are you staying the night?"

Kestrel nodded. "We'll head to the Arc of Mourning Eidolons in the morning."

"Then we have a final night to be Eric and Sarah," he said. "Have a drink with me later?"

Sarah's expression darkened with concern. "Only if you get some rest. Technically, I'm older than you."

He chuckled. "And *you* need to respect your Arch Elders."

Sarah straightened. "Hm, I suppose, in more ways than one, I'm not used to having more than one Arch Elder."

"I have every faith that you'll be a natural at this whole thing." Eric pinched the bridge of his nose.

Kestrel's vines drooped under his fatigue.

"To be honest, I didn't know what to think when I read your letter," he added, "but your happiness is all I've ever wanted for you, and now I know—I can see—that you were born for this."

He patted her knee. "Stay true to yourself and you'll demolish your goals. I know you will."

"I set my family free." Sarah smiled brightly. "That's one down."

He patted her knee again. "I would never give back any of the time I've spent with your family, but I wish they'd never started the Caretaker Tradition in the first place. I didn't rescue Willy from enslavement to gain a valet."

"We know that," Sarah said quietly. "He wanted to show his gratitude and it was important to us to keep that alive. We've never seen it like that, I promise. We're family."

"And we will be for eternity." His eyes drifted as he absently rubbed his forehead. "I'm a bit tired—I think I will lie down. We'll have a drink later?"

Sarah's expression was troubled, but she nodded. "Of course."

He smiled weakly at Kestrel. "Thank you for giving me hope. I'll rest up, we'll have a drink, you'll train and find Paresh, and then—"

"You'll be whole again," Kestrel finished, locking onto Sarah's eyes and seeing Lior's fierce determination.

II

ERIC

Green Mountains, Vermont, Summer 2006

Eric rolled onto his back. The moon threw angular silver patches through the windows. An hour ago, Mr. Smith had tapped on his door and invited him down for warm "cider" under the stars. He'd promise to join them at nightfall.

He sighed and sat up, wiping his face as he contemplated the en suite. He should freshen up for Sarah. He didn't know when he'd see her again. Maybe a hot shower would soothe the venom's persistent ache in his joints, too.

Later, freshly steamed with wet hair combed back, he pulled on a soft black t-shirt and drawstring flannel pants and jogged down the stairs. Each hit hammered pins and needles into his feet, but he was mobile at least. He passed the welcome desk and paused at the screen door.

The sky was clear, robbing the mountains of their blanketing mists. Paper lanterns and citronella candles transformed the yard into a cozy, magical place. Sarah and Kestrel huddled together on a picnic bench. Alex sat in the tire swing that hung from an ancient oak, swaying back and forth. Jonathan sat on an overturned barrel, hunched over a folding tray opposite Mr. Smith. Seneca and Minerva weren't visible, and Heron and Cyprian had gone back to Orison Crossing to be with Walter.

Mrs. Smith appeared behind him with a nudge and a smile, shoving a mug of "cider" into his hands and leading him outside. He asked why they continued the charade and she simply winked. She squeezed his arm and joined Kestrel and Sarah at the table to watch her husband beat Jonathan at chess…again.

Jonathan gave a questioning glance as he passed by and Eric tossed a dismissive hand. "I'm okay. Play your game."

He sipped from his mug, thankful for the warmth soothing his throat. Heating blood without destroying the nutritional value was difficult, but the Smiths had learned how to do it on their own—they enjoyed the challenge of keeping up appearances at morning breakfast. Mrs. Smith cheered for her husband when Jonathan finally made his move.

Fireflies flickered in the grasses and wildflowers that buffered the house from the mountainous copse. A knot lodged in Eric's throat.

Alex muttered, "Paresh would love it. She'd be out there dancing like a Bohemian fairy."

Eric drank and nodded, feeling the grim set of his lips pull his weary eyes down.

Alex kicked off a worn patch of grass. A faint whoosh blew at Eric's neck. He turned slowly, taking in a scene that looked deceptively normal and peaceful—a night like many others the Smiths had hosted. Usually, there'd be platters of baked muffins or streusel cookies, too. The air cooled at night despite retaining the humidity that came by day.

Faraway owls hooted, Kestrel and Sarah murmured, and Mr. Smith grunted every time Mrs. Smith cheered. The lighting reminded him of The Greenery's greenhouse, so he cast his eyes to the stars instead. With elevation and less pollution, the sky bloomed almost as vast and bright as it had when he was a kid before there were cars or electricity.

He returned to the stoop and sat, determined to watch Mr. Smith claim Jonathan's king, but his gaze drifted to the mountains across the road and sank into the richly dense forest, invitingly soft and cushioning with its velvety darkness. If he'd been at home, he'd go for a run.

Goosebumps trickled down his legs and shot stinging pain into his heels. He tapped the mug and ground his teeth. He wouldn't be running anywhere anytime soon. He stood sharply and circled the table. Sarah squeezed his hand and pulled him down next to her. Moisture stung the back of his eyes.

Orbs of chartreuse light blinked across the meadow. Paresh materialized in his mind's eye, fingertips gliding over the tips of the tallest grasses. She smiled wide, threw her arm ups, and danced in circles. Fireflies completed her choreography with glowing wakes of magic and fairy dust.

Sarah squeezed his hand again. He nodded absently and set his mug down. He rose and waded into the empty sea of grass and flowers to dance with his memory. Facing the stars, he held his arms out and turned slowly, stirring up scents of pollen, moss, and ferns. The breeze cooled the tears that streaked his cheeks. The world was like a fairytale when Paresh was in it.

But she wasn't there.

He drifted to a stop. His arms dropped to his sides. The others were watching him—their collective stare burned into his back. Tears dripped onto his t-shirt. He fell to his hands and knees and rolled onto his back. The stars blurred under a hot, liquid haze as he kicked his legs out. If Paresh was with him, her palm would be over his heart. But she wasn't there. She wouldn't be there when the others retired for the night. Or when dawn cracked the horizon for the sun to rise. He didn't think she'd ever be there again.

☽ ❈ ☾

The screen door slammed. Seconds later, Alex plopped down beside him, sunglasses wedged between his blond spikes. The rising sun cast an amber glow upon the mountain mist.

"Hanging in?" Alex asked.

Not trusting his vocal cords, Eric only nodded.

"We're ready to go whenever." Alex leaned back on his palms. "I wanted to make sure you're actually *ready* ready to go before we leave. Jonathan packed up your room, so you don't have anything to worry about here."

Eric's anxiety ballooned under his ribs. "Being ready or not doesn't change anything."

"Do you want to say good-bye to the Smiths or Sarah? She wants to see you before she leaves, but insisted there's no pressure." Alex knocked his sunglasses down as the sun rose higher. "Her memories as Lior might be coming back, but she's still a young woman—I mean…she's nervous. I think seeing you would reassure her."

Pangs of guilt stabbed through his shell of grief. He didn't want to say good-bye to anyone. He didn't want to go back to his empty house. He didn't want to move a muscle. But he also didn't want to be treated like a delicate flower that would break in the wind. He sat up with a heavy sigh.

"Okay?" Alex held his hands up.

"Okay."

Alex's throat bobbed under a hard swallow. He busied himself with dusting weeds and grass off Eric's shirt.

Another pang stabbed Eric's heart. "Hey…I'm sorry about Raven."

Alex froze. They sat in silence another minute before the silver and gold hoops lining Alex's ears jingled as he shook his head. He patted Eric on the shoulder and stood. Sighing to himself, Eric got up and followed him into the house.

Mrs. Smith met them in the foyer. He embraced her and whispered words of gratitude. She pulled him closer before letting go. The others were gathered on the second floor landing.

Sarah came down first, trailed by Kestrel, Jonathan, and Mr. Smith. Already uniformed and booted in the militaristic black of the Wraith Reapers, Sarah floated into his arms. Eric hugged her, welcoming the feel of her frizzy curls on his cheek.

"It'll take some time to get used to seeing this new look on you," he said. "But you're going to be fine. I believe in you."

She tightened her hold on him with bruising new strength. Paresh hadn't exhibited an increase like this—her physicality had hardly changed at all.

"We'll find her," Sarah said. "I promise."

They parted and Kestrel approached. She shook his hand.

"Take care of her." Eric nodded at Sarah.

Kestrel smiled. "We'll take care of each other."

She pressed a prong on her Vampiric Star. The Smiths gasped in unison as the white portal appeared. Kestrel offered a reverent tilt of her head to Eric, Jonathan, and Alex. "My Lords, High Commander."

"Update Nallura and Landor, and stay at Eido," Alex said.

As they disappeared into Animus Hollow, the Smiths shared a look. Alex shifted his weight from one foot to the other. "Sorry about that," he said. "It's the way we travel—she should have done that outside."

"It's fine," Mr. Smith said, stepping off the stairs to slide his arm over his wife's shoulders. "There's a lot in this world that we don't know and we're good with that. We already know more than most."

He extended a hand to Jonathan, who hesitated briefly before accepting. "It was nice to beat, eh, *meet* you." Mr. Smith grinned mischievously. Mrs. Smith elbowed him in the ribs.

"And he looks forward to future rematches," she said. She smiled sadly at Eric. "I look forward to meeting your future missus. Come back, won't you?"

"Of course." Eric shook Mr. Smith's hand. "Thank you for being so hospitable to everyone. I didn't intend to drop a crisis and strangers on your doorstep."

"Well, it's your doorstep, so don't trouble yourself over it," he replied with a grunt. "It was nice getting to know your extended family—especially your brother."

The lump in his throat replicated as a stone in his stomach. Eric simply nodded and motioned for Alex to open Animus Hollow again. Alex cocked his eyebrows and pointed at the door with both index fingers. Jonathan hit the prong on his Star.

"Thank you both. It was a pleasure." Jonathan swatted Alex to go ahead of him.

"Yeah, it's peaceful here. Real nice." Alex tossed up Raven's two-fingered salute and disappeared with Jonathan.

The innkeepers patted Eric on the back as he contemplated the white haze. "It's not good-bye forever, just for now," Mr. Smith said, quietly.

Eric stepped into the dimensional divide. The exit in Sunset Grove opened, but he couldn't move. The sun hadn't yet risen here. Jonathan and Alex stood on the path beyond, and an unnatural silence governed the forest in the half-light. Jonathan's eyes burned into Eric. Alex walked south toward Grandfather Wisdom. The thought of being with Paresh without being with her filled his feet with lead. And yet he took that dreaded step out.

Jonathan tucked his hands in his pockets. "Come on, Brother. Let's watch the sunrise with Pare."

He lumbered behind Jonathan, who slowed his pace to stay close as though fearing Eric might disappear, too. Soon, the path yawned with rising light and Eric's breath caught at the back of his throat.

He couldn't do this. Not again. He'd look at the tree and see her bloodied and lifeless, pinned to the trunk by daggers like a collected butterfly. And then she'd be bloody and weakened, assaulted and sobbing into Raven's neck on his couch. Next, the eight-year-old girl, bloody and alone, crying for him with her parents dead in the front seat.

"No, no, no," he whispered, covering his eyes. "No. Please. No."

Jonathan ushered him forward by the elbow. He was further gone into memory, seeing her for the first time, covered in the blood of birth, silent and still, handed off to be hidden in the shadows—surrounded by death from her first moment of existence.

The clearing was empty of her essence. The tree stood grand and majestic under Saint Michael's avatar, washed a fiery shade of persimmon in the dawning light. The ribbon of gold glittered as tiny orbs floated within. She appeared in his mind, embraced in wings of brilliant light, suspended in a black void—asleep and at peace.

What happened when they found her? How would she die the next time? What about their daughter, already part of this violent pattern? How would *she* die the next time? Would she even survive childhood? Or grow up? Why doom them with resurrection in the face of a coming Apocalypse?

Guilt and grief took turns chomping off greedy chunks of his heart and soul. He shook as tears swelled and deeply rooted anger mounted. It scared him—the fury that explosively flared when Alex and Jonathan closed in on his sides—so he turned and ran.

He hit the path hard and swiftly arrived at the other clearing, where the cottage sat, windows dark, interior empty, and the clock ticking meaningless seconds. He stared at it, dumbfounded, not wanting to go in, but needing to hide from the forest. Somehow, he found his keys and got inside without really knowing how.

No one was waiting for him.

He walked down the hall in a trance. The master suite's doorknob was cold in his hand. He smelled her everywhere—clover, honey, innocence. On that bed, they'd conceived their daughter. Her heartbeat thumped in his ears. He felt her fetal kick and the curvature of Paresh's expanding womb.

They hadn't even given her a name.

He slammed the door in his face and pounded on it. The wood's grain vibrated under screams he didn't recognize. Paresh's ghostly fingers tiptoed up his chest, her arms curled up his back, her tongue parted his lips.

Darkness swallowed her whole. A smirking mouth cracked and golden eyes flashed—framed in dark curls that formed apart from the shadows. They reeked of clove oil. The door shattered under Eric's fists. Crimson shaded the world and air rushed over his fangs as he ran for the door and stormed outside.

He'd rip Donovan's spine out through his throat.

Alex and Jonathan stood on the path ahead, wary, but determined. Eric charged like a feral beast. Steel arms hooked under his shoulders. Eric's momentum almost took them with him, but they worked together to sweep him off his feet and drag him back inside. They pinned him against the carpet and said nothing as he howled and fought to escape.

They remained like that, their eyes solemnly pointed ahead, burning with the same desire, the same rage, but resolute in their vows to protect Paresh from anyone who endangered her survival.

And that included him.

III

LUCIEN
____

Egypt, ca. 950 B.C.

Under the guise of meditating, Lucien admired Jonathan's perfect silhouette at the tiny window. A gusty wind slapped the papyrus reed covering. He turned away with a bored sigh and scanned the mud brick walls and dirt floor, his nose wrinkling in disgust. He glanced at Lucien with narrowing eyes.

Sliding his tongue over a fang, he fidgeted with the linen cloth wrapped around his waist. He leaned against the wall to stay out of view before drawing his cloak about his shoulders. The cloak itself would draw more attention than its vibrant color. The humans here considered wool impure.

Odd how their superstitions change from one region to the next.

"Must we always go after the poor?" Jonathan dropped another bored sigh and panned his hand across the single room. "This place doesn't even offer a stool to sit upon so I don't soil my shendyt."

134

"The richer the human, the more noticeable the kill," Lucien replied in monotone. "You need shelter from the sun——"

"But farmers who stink of animals live in better structures than this!" Jonathan crossed his arms.

"Then go kill a farmer. Most of the villagers have made their daily journey to the Nile. The village is largely empty." Lucien inhaled deeply through his nose. "We can travel to a different shelter mostly unnoticed."

"*You* can travel unnoticed. *This*," he said, picking at the cloak, "will draw attention to me."

"Your flesh can blend in. Go without it. Walk fast to reduce the sun blisters." Lucien peered through his lashes and internally smiled at Jonathan's incredulous expression. "Or, wait until nightfall and preserve your beautiful skin."

Pouting, Jonathan swung his face toward the covered window. "Farmers don't have proper mattresses," he said. "The merchants and wealthy——"

"Are too prominent. We'd have one night at most before the absence is reported and investigated."

"Great, so it'd work as bait for our prey. Why don't we ever bring them to us?"

Waira! Waira! The screams of a five-hundred-year-old memory opened Lucien's eyes. Out of habit, he pressed the heel of his palm into his shoulder. On damp days, it still ached. "Humans in large numbers are dangerous, especially with weapons and seeking revenge for a fallen leader."

"We've walked plenty of battlefields without problem."

"Oh, to be young and ignorant of injury," Lucien muttered. "There, we are specters, not monsters to hunt and kill."

"But we are! Or should be!" Barefoot, Jonathan padded over and squatted in front of Lucien. He wore a devious grin. "I want the luxury I deserve and you want safety. We can have both if we kill the landowner and enthrall the slaves."

"And the corpses? In this heat?" Lucien raised a dismissive hand.

Jonathan smirked. "They mummify their dead—this heat with a body in the ground?"

Jonathan's natural lines of ethereal beauty too easily distracted Lucien. His gaze dropped to Jonathan's mesmerizing ivory smile and his belly quivered.

"No human will hurt you again," Jonathan said in quiet earnest. "I will tear through any who dares to try."

When Lucien remained silent, Jonathan asked, "After all this time, aren't you tired of sleeping in trees and swapping shelters day after day? We are gods of death—like Anubis and Osiris! We can take anything we desire and make them beg at our feet."

"Because you desire a mattress?" Lucien scoffed. "You sleep less than I do."

Jonathan flashed another devilish grin. "Not for sleep—"

"Sex?"

Jonathan's splendid visage drew closer as he licked his lips. "Comfortable sex."

He pushed Lucien back and pressed his luscious lips against his mouth. The quivering dipped lower and built into pressure between Lucien's legs.

"You hate the rain and I can't tolerate the sun," Jonathan whispered against Lucien's mouth, kissing him between words. "Must we always be uncomfortable? I want you. On a proper bed."

The warmth dusting his lips scattered all of Lucien's thoughts into the fire filling his belly—and Jonathan knew it. His golden and black eyes glittered.

"A sturdy roof to block the rain. An in-house fire to banish the damp. And I!" Jonathan kissed him. "I will shred any mob that rises! We'll cultivate our own village and live as kings."

"That's not why we are here," Lucien whispered. "I do not seek to rule."

"Nor do I, but we aren't here merely to survive, either." Jonathan's eyes darkened. He crept forward, forcing Lucien down onto his elbows. "This village is peaceful, but look at the region—that foreigner seized the throne and other villages are revolting. They're only *beginning* to fight—"

"We are not killing the King."

"Oh, to be old and ignorant of strategy." Jonathan hovered over him. "It's not about the King; it's in their numbers! They enjoy killing each other and they're angry—so let them tear each other apart."

"I've never stayed in a place this populous."

Jonathan lifted his brow expectantly. "I am yours to use at will, you recluse. I won't even need to enthrall them all. They'll do whatever I say!"

Doubt seeped over Lucien's face. "These humans are more organized, smarter, and better armed than the tribal mobs that hunted me."

"Always with the age. Tsk." Jonathan exhaled against Lucien's lips. He trailed a finger down Lucien's chest. "You've never let me out to play on my own. Set me loose tonight."

Before Lucien could retreat into thought, Jonathan lapped at his tongue, teasing him but not kissing him. "Do it…"

He licked and kissed a trail down Lucien's chest and belly. Jonathan hesitated between Lucien's legs and blew a caressing breath over his naval. "Say yes, and I'll make you comfortable in your skin, right now."

"You say that like I've ever said no to you," Lucien said, panting lightly.

Jonathan puffed delicately over Lucien's skin as his hands glided up his inner thighs. "Say it…"

Jonathan fluttered his lashes innocently and traced a line across Lucien's belly with his tongue. He began to loosen his shendyt.

Lucien moaned his answer and pulled Jonathan up for another kiss. He intended to enjoy the afternoon thoroughly—and, in truth only to himself, the thought of an in-house fire *was* enticing. He'd let Jonathan have his fun.

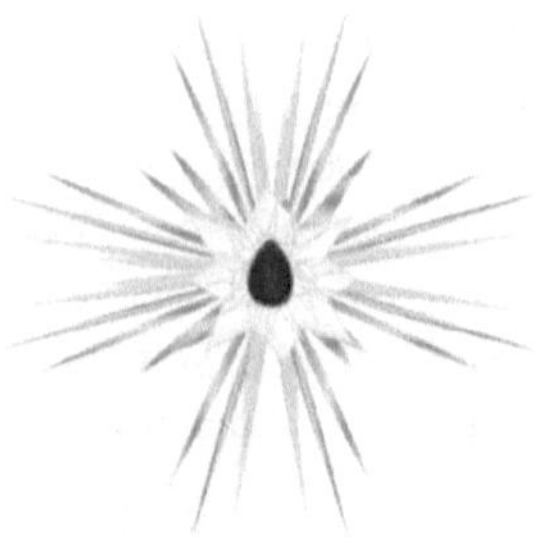

Chapter Ten: Loneliness Unbroken

I

KESTREL

Arc of Mourning Eidolons, Spring 2007

Kestrel was relieved that Sarah seemed instantly at home in the Chthonic Knights' headquarters. The arc of technology buzzed with portals, checkpoints, gliding beltways, and platforms the same as it had in Lior's day. And though she expected Eido to rebel at an altered human as First Officer, Lior's former squad mates recognized him in Sarah's aura. Seeing them again unlocked recognition in Sarah, as well, and they resumed their relationships as though Lior's death was a mere blip.

While the remaining Wraith Reapers, Chavnia and Jocathian, awaited eldership, they sparred with their replacements, Farran and Orn, and Kestrel spoke with Alex about honoring Raven's wish to keep Walter informed. He offered Cyprian and Heron as ambassadors under her command and sent them up as she re-trained Sarah, whose once human body managed to inherit Lior's vampiric muscle memory.

Months had passed since then and the squad was running final sparring matches and full-force drills. Kestrel decided to set Master Jonathan's prized elite against Sarah as a final test of skill. Even at its reduced capacity, the arc bounced with excitement as every hunter gathered to watch the bout. Lior's expertise had made him a valuable asset to the Chthonic Knights, but his battle skills would've placed him at the top of Master Jonathan's pack.

The trio chose their weapons. Cyprian and Heron split up and attacked in unison. Lighter on her feet and better balanced, with a

138

feminine agility that polished Lior's already smooth grace, Sarah swiftly and ruthlessly took them down armed only with a cloak and training staff. Had it been a real battle, she would've killed them both with a single deathblow.

"Sorry it took so long." Sarah winked. "I'm not used to the handicap of fighting with a weapon."

Cyprian and Heron groaned in good humor. Of course, they wanted a rematch since they'd never lost that fast, but Kestrel was satisfied and her squad was officially functioning at twice its original size. It was finally time for her and Sarah to depart for Rome. The holy light of Vatican City would be the first new challenge for their collective sight.

Animus Hollow took them to the Celestial Landing Point deep beneath that special hill, a cavern created by the Heavenly Host's arrival on Earth during the Great Holy War. The only CLP underground discovered by humans was revered as sacred and, while they didn't know why, they maintained an eternal flame in a lantern suspended from the ceiling. In centuries past, they tended to wicks and oil daily, but the modern flame burned blue from a retrofitted gas line.

Kestrel motioned for Sarah to begin. Beneath the lantern, she turned in a slow circle, studying every crack and bulging stone. After one full turn, she closed her eyes and reversed direction. Her brow crinkled and she stepped aside, motioning for Kestrel to look. Sarah flattened her palm against a wall.

Kestrel stretched her arms out, palms up, and dipped her head back with her eyes shut. Far beyond the cavern's roof, the city above shone blinding white, as expected. But...

Stagnant air suffocated her skin. Her vines begged to shrivel into hiding. Only the flame carried a *faint* signature of holy essence. She shared a look with Sarah.

"The CLPs are supposed to be hallowed ground," Sarah said, dropping her hand, "but this darkness——"

"Resembles that night in London," Kestrel whispered. "Salea and Lucifer together again?"

Sarah touched another wall. "Common denominator, simplest answer."

"But Salea's essence is angelic. This isn't."

"The walls smell like sulfur." Sarah rubbed sediment between her fingers. "Same as the docks."

"Was he here all this time?" Kestrel approached the only door, sealed by humans from the other side. "Even when Raven trailed Donovan here?"

Sarah touched the south wall and recoiled. Closing her eyes, she tapped her finger against the air. "There—it's an entrance to a pocket dimension. I can barely see it—tunneled in blackness with a faint light at the end."

Kestrel touched the same spot and scanned it with her aura. A blueprint formed in her mind. She saw the larger cavern and its anchor to the Realm of Man—the sealed door—but the space outside, which should have been limestone and the Earth itself, was endless, beyond time and the fabric of reality. A sea of black surrounded a tunnel that connected to a dim cavity, but the darkness wasn't empty. It shifted with creepy shadows.

She backed into Sarah, her voice shaking. "It's his army—there are hundreds, thousands of them. This place barely exists in this realm anymore."

Skin contact with Sarah made the sensations more vile and barbed. Kestrel felt those creatures crawling all over her, not just along her vines. "It's pure evil."

Looking through her closed-eye sight, Sarah said, "The eternal flame and the blessings on the seal are the only remaining anchors. They aren't enough to hold them back."

She faced the south wall. "I can see that light better. It fills the chamber—strong enough to block the tunnel."

"What is it, though? The miasma is too sinister for me to get through."

Tilting her head in concentration, Sarah pursed her lips. "It's…angelic. But then, why is it—"

"Surrounded by demons?" Kestrel asked. "It's like he's eroding the Host's leftover presence—"

"—to use it as a gate to cross over." Sarah pressed the prong on her Vampiric Star for Animus Hollow. "Paresh was never here. We need to check the others quickly."

"*He* was at Hawkiel's CLP," Kestrel said, "but I didn't sense anything else."

"You weren't looking for more at the time." Sarah gestured at the wall. "I didn't see that tunnel until I looked harder and that makes me wonder how bad the others are."

The surface CLPs were all fine, but the Hollow erected barriers to the remaining underground points. Lucifer had gained three entry points for his legion, and if the eternal flame—or that angelic presence—under Vatican City disappeared, he'd gain another.

They needed to report this to Alex. But first, Kestrel wanted Sarah to reconnect with Lord Endymion.

The Great Holy War's original CLP was a subterranean cave in South Africa that Lord Lucien had asked Gabriel to bequeath to Endymion in the Treaty. She and Lior, as Endymion's trusted warriors, knew he'd erased it from vampiric memory, and because access to his compound came only through Animus Hollow, no one else knew it was a former CLP or where it was. In the earliest days of the Vampiric Nation, Lord Lucien had housed Lady Rainne there, a risk given the site's accessibility to Lucifer, but he'd had no better option with her cell under construction at the Arc of True Blood.

The destination's encryption within their Stars bounced their energy signatures elsewhere before dropping them into a pitch-black room that was similar to Snowblood Square. All entrants began here and gained admission only with Lord Endymion's authorization. He must have felt them coming because he met them there but lingered in the darkness. Kestrel wouldn't have known had Sarah not squeezed her hand to show her what she was seeing—a residual angelic essence that hovered within his aura. Unlike the usual white or gold, it was a lustrous azure and deep, rich scarlet. It burned with a too-familiar moral justice.

Kestrel forced herself to breathe. He'd lied to her about Raven.

Worse, he's kept her hidden from you.

A dim, sourceless glow bloomed around them as Lord Endymion came forward to study Sarah. Apprehension evolved into recognition and his mouth loosened into a smile. He clapped his hands together. "Ah, 'tis welcome, this nostalgia! 'Tis good to make your re-acquaintance, My Light."

"And yours, as well, my lord." Sarah dropped to one knee and nodded reverently, followed by Kestrel.

"Success on the search?" he asked, his countenance gleaming with expectance.

"The opposite, unfortunately," Kestrel said. "No trace of Paresh, but—"

"We discovered entry points for Lucifer's forces," Sarah said. "He's contaminating the underground CLPs—"

"—and has three completely under his influence." Kestrel rose.

Lord Endymion's eyes narrowed. "What, exactly, did you see?"

"We only gained access in Rome—" Sarah began.

"—which is barely tethered to the Realm of Man," Kestrel said. "The dimensional space beyond is swarming with demons."

"It's like that night in London—the cavern walls reeked of sulfur."

"Salea?" Lord Endymion asked cautiously.

"We saw an angelic presence beyond the walls that wasn't hers. The only light—" Kestrel gestured to Sarah.

"—that we recognized belonged to the lantern."

"This presence…" He drifted into thought. "Could it be the real Hawkiel?"

She and Sarah glanced at each other.

Kestrel started, "We've never seen his—"

"Or this light before," Sarah finished.

He withdrew again and muttered, "It's a trap—if Hawkiel chooses to leave, they'll follow him out."

Sarah squeezed her hand again and Kestrel acknowledged by squeezing back. Their lord hadn't meant to say that aloud, but the meaning was clear. Regardless of how it *appeared*, Lucifer already had four entry points. They knew little about the real Hawkiel, only that Gabriel had confirmed his curse and that a premature apocalypse *would* come when one of the twins made a choice.

"I haven't been outside—what of the dark spot?" he asked.

"Until we find and recover Raven," Kestrel said, not surprised when her lord betrayed nothing. "Alex can only speculate. He can't see Darkesiel as well as she can."

"But, at the rate Darkesiel is traveling, he'll likely arrive on Earth in about thirteen years, maybe more." Sarah stroked Kestrel's palm with a deliberate finger—a signal to watch closely. "Have your Knights learned anything about Raven? Perhaps we can trace—"

"No, nothing." He seemed distracted, but they wouldn't fall for that and he knew it. His expression hardened. "You are only responsible for finding Paresh. Stay on mission."

"Our scope is narrowed to finding her, yes," Sarah said, pushing him further, "but within these troubling discoveries lays the potential for finding Raven—or, as you suggested, Hawkiel. If we can see his light, *we can see hers.*"

The grim set of his mouth finally betrayed the emotions hidden within his aura. Kestrel answered Sarah's finger stroke with one of her own—they had to let it go. He'd met them there deliberately to keep Sarah out of the compound. He could shield Raven's essence from Kestrel's silver vines, but not Lior's sight.

Kestrel didn't know what this meant. If Raven *was* there, then Lord Lucien knew it, too—Lord Endymion shared the smallest morsels of information with him, the result of a deal struck before the Great Holy War began. If she and Sarah trusted one, they trusted the other, and they'd been loyal to Lord Endymion from the beginning. She had to believe there was a just reason for his lies—likely tied to Lucifer revealing himself to Raven on Marblehead Island and Lord Lucien's order to keep Lord Endymion's survival a secret from the others.

Loyalty firmed her resolve, but she wilted inside for Alex. Even *if* Raven was here, she *had* lost a lot of blood that night. It wasn't like she could tell him Raven was okay—she didn't know that for sure. And she'd never break Lord Endymion's confidence.

"We shall continue our search, my lord," Kestrel said. "The world's fate depends on us."

"It's good to see you again." Sarah smiled and dipped her head. "I am delighted to be back in your service."

He opened the Hollow. "Do not report back until you've found the Sacred Vessel. We cannot move forward without her."

II

ERIC

Orison Crossing, Winter 2007

...and I want to come home. Please come and get
me. I don't understand what I did wrong...

Penned by a scared little girl, those words—once bolded in ink and pencil, and now smudged and faded with time, handling, and tears— were his last tangible link to Paresh. He'd slept with Lucinda's letters beneath his pillow during the Civil War. He kept these closer. Released from evidence by the FBI, these small pieces of Paresh, their crisp, folded edges already crumbling into powdery, worn seams, fit into his pocket.

It was another listless night in a year of empty days. He barely went through the motions anymore. If not for the others, he wouldn't have hired replacements for Molly and Sarah, or packed up his office and transitioned into a silent partner at his firm. Alex and Sarah took over The Greenery and handpicked a human trustee to lead a new management team and head chef.

The Elders chose to stay at the Hawthorne Mansion—not that Lucien would've let them return to the Arc of True Blood—and they'd begun to form a relationship with the villagers. A mixed crew of heralds, trustees, and local specialists restored the buildings, and cared for the grounds and orchard. The town, of course, believed he and

Paresh had retired there to seek privacy after the ordeal with her uncle. Walter had tried, once, to ask about protections for the human staff, but Eric had wanted no part of it—Alex and Jonathan knew the wrath they'd face if harm befell a single person. And he welcomed any excuse to unleash it.

His nerves frayed quicker than his patience when he'd performed his duties as Arch Elder to lift True Blood Elders to Eternal Blood Elders, and to bestow eldership upon Jocathian, Chavnia, and Alex. Lucien had refused to fill Endymion's seat—the final opening—or to release his body for cremation. Alex—granted more freedom in a hybrid position that preserved his status as VaSH High Commander—must've noticed Eric unraveling.

He'd gotten Eric away from Lucien and back to the cottage, where he suggested using the remaining casements from the Arc of Celestial Night to build a dome over Grandfather Wisdom—wisely pointing out that it'd ease the strain on Walter. The Chthonic Knights still encountered villagers whose curiosity outweighed their fear of Sunset Grove's haunting presence and mystery lights.

They'd all handily proven that they didn't need him. He wished he could say the same—that his fluctuating mental state didn't warrant visits from Alex and Jonathan beyond the need to pull his blood for Donovan—

Donovan…

—or to tranquilize the beast with Paresh's blood, as they had that afternoon. But without her essence, they left behind a shell of a man who didn't know how to exist.

Fresh blood might energize his body, but his mind couldn't survive that much clarity. When Paresh disappeared as a girl, he'd run to the cottage and through the woods, but now the ghosts of memory chased him away from both.

Eric released the letter before it disintegrated in his fist. The ghosts of memory were strong tonight and dredged up Joshua—one of many better left buried. Images flew across his mind so fast that Eric didn't bother with shoes. Frozen ground bit into his toes and icy wind nipped his face.

Fitting.

It'd been the same that cold night in 1935—another attempt to escape his guilt. He'd thought he'd been hopeless and beyond redemption then, but he'd been too emotional. It wasn't truly hopeless without the genuine emptiness of living an existence that meant nothing and tossed him like trash into despair's endless void.

The guilt he'd felt from killing Joshua was more like shame enrobed in the thrill of a kill that he'd repeat without hesitation. But this…*this* guilt was failure intertwined with irreconcilable grief. He'd successfully protected awful men. Where had that power been when he'd needed it for *her*?

What is the point of having people to protect if you have nothing to protect them from?

It was Jonathan. He'd kept Eric sharp, on his toes, aware. Without Jonathan, he would've failed them, too. Maybe because of Jonathan's repentance, Eric had failed. *But*…his failure was still *his* failure.

He ran past the cemetery's crumbling brick column. Joshua faded when Eric stopped at his family's plot. He traced his wife's name, as he had many nights before, and carved out a new spot of lichen with his fingernail. The marble needed so much care from the elements, unlike Molly's headstone.

Yet another loved one dead at Jonathan's hand.

A merciful death.

He hadn't been there to save her, either, and Jonathan hadn't made it in time. Donovan had stolen everything from him, but it seemed like it always circled back to Jonathan. His brother was at the center of his orbit—his sun—no matter what he did.

He felt Molly's grave trying to tug him out of the void. But he couldn't let her help him when her sacrifice meant nothing in the end. Her granite marker was hard and unyielding, not soft and fragile like Paresh's letters, and her presence loomed as an eternally unspoken accusation. Somewhere deep—unfathomably so—inside, he knew Molly didn't blame him, but her forgiveness was pointless. He'd always blame himself.

He sank into the snow covering his empty grave and stared at his last name on both stones for so long that they began to blur together. He imagined Paresh's name there. Paresh Ravenscroft sounded nice—right.

But changing her name would end the Hawthorne legacy. He laughed bitterly to himself. The Hawthorne legacy was already dead.

He folded his hands behind his head and rolled onto his back. A light streaked across the sky. The Geminid Meteor Shower had yet to peak, but it was a moonless night. Maybe he'd get a decent view. Stargazing nostalgia pulled him up onto his elbows and sent him back to the nights on the hill with Jonathan. He sighed.

Back to Jonathan.

Those days had been simpler in so many ways. Most homes hadn't had electricity and cars were luxurious toys for the wealthy. Elizabeth Hawthorne had happily partied at Nathaniel's side—she'd had no reason to think of suicide yet. It was before Jonathan's first deception, before he'd shown Eric his inner monster. Eric hadn't known any better and had innocently watched the stars and chatted with Jonathan like he was the brother he'd never had.

Another meteor streaked. The kind voice of his mother—long forgotten—urged him to make a wish. Then she began to sing *Twinkle, Twinkle Little Star*. He couldn't place the memory. He didn't remember her ever wearing a silk nightgown or his mattress being that comfortable or having such thick bedding. He tried to hold onto it, to see past the fuzzy boundaries where toys lined shelves and a carved armoire stood guard between tall windows—

"Twinkle, twinkle, little *star*...how I wonder *where* you are." That chord, sung in a masculine voice, *did not* belong in the natural world.

Fear pulled Eric's eyes down to Earth, to a figure shimmering into the visible spectrum across from him. Eric scrambled to sit up—or so he thought. His movements were slow and frustratingly calm—his body irrationally paralyzed by fright.

Six pairs of wings flickered transparently at the being's back, discernible from their surroundings only by their movement. The bottom two enveloped his legs, covered with jogging pants, and slid over his feet, and the top two collapsed to his neck and crept up to cover his...face...

His *identical* face. He wore the same black t-shirt as Eric. He was a mirror image. Dread clenched the air from Eric's lungs.

The angel stared at him with the same widening eyes and confusion that knotted Eric's visage. His mouth gaped slightly and slowly twisted into a sinuous shape as flames of hellish orange snapped to life in his electric blue eyes.

Eric's aura instinctively threw up a barrier and packed him in protective layers. The angel's grin widened, but it didn't reach far. He was too intense and too focused for any sort of joyous expression, sardonic or not.

"The *stars* are so beautiful, aren't they?" the angel asked, his pupils enlarging as they dove into Eric's in search of his soul. He sucked his teeth and shrugged. "I didn't think it'd work on you, but you never know until you try, right?"

"Who are you?" they asked in unison. The angel copied Eric's movements, even his jerky flinch as the scent of sulfur streamed into his aura. Eric's heart jolted into a gallop.

"Lucifer…" they whispered in shocked unison.

"Luc…i…f…" He matched Eric perfectly.

Alarms blared throughout his body, but he was trapped—no, *rapt*—by his own face. Cold air stung his eyes as he huffed for oxygen that wasn't coming. Pressure built within his head. He tried to blink to clear his mind. There was too much there. Too many questions. Accusations. Voices. Memories. It was worse than going blank.

"Interesting, isn't it?" Lucifer asked at last. "One's image?"

Eric barely managed to swallow. *Lucifer* blurred into a runny mess as protective tears surged against the elements.

"Aw, you weren't expecting this, huh?" Lucifer circled his face with his finger. "Last time I was a hot redhead. Oh! Speaking of the importance of image and redheads…Jonathan seems to be on your mind tonight."

His flames flared brighter. "I chose to bestow my likeness upon him as an insult to Father—to put perfection into humanoid form. He didn't care, clearly. But it did catch Lucien's attention in an unexpected way—so I have to wonder…is that why Father chose to *recycle* my image onto you? I mean, at least I gave Jonathan his own look. *He* simply baited Jonathan with a reproduction, not caring *how* you caught his eye, only that you *did*."

He tilted his head back, glancing down his nose and smiling as Eric tilted his, too. "Lucien and Jonathan obviously have daddy issues. But, you're an anomaly I can't explain."

He snapped his fingers. Images of people cycled through Eric's mind. He'd killed each one of them. They clicked through like a slideshow and stopped in a cold Virginia forest. Confederate soldiers in nightdress encircled him, mangled and bloody, open mouths unleashing horrid screams of agony and death.

Scuttling backward, Eric rammed into his headstone. *"No, no, no!"*

The soldiers crumbled into ash that drifted off on a heated gust. In their place stood a little boy in his pajamas, his eyes bulging in horror. A fully demonic version of Jonathan patted his hair, grinning at the boy's mother, Elizabeth, her cracked skull spilling blood on the concrete.

The boy's face aged into the adult version of Joshua that had chased Eric here in the first place. His expression twisted with insanity and terror as flames licked the surrounding darkness. Smoke poured in from the nursery. A door slammed—as it had in reality—but Eric wasn't on the other side. This wasn't his memory.

Jonathan smirked monstrously, flaunting his needle-tipped fangs and cackling at Joshua's panicked screams. The smoke was almost too thick to see through. Joshua tugged on the broken door in vain. He tried to leverage his foot against the frame and to shoulder through the solid wood. His screams turned into choked cries. He glanced at Lily's body, ravaged by the fire hungrily consuming the bed. His gaze landed on Jonathan.

"Help—" Joshua staggered toward him, gagging, barely conscious. Jonathan sneered and shoved Joshua into the inferno. The roar swallowed his tortured screeching as he writhed and burned like tinder. Jonathan glanced at Eric—or rather, the jammed door—with a satisfied smile. He kicked through the plaster wall, effortlessly escaping a nightmarish death.

"No, no, no," Eric whispered. His face. His memories. *Jonathan's* memories? Of course, the Devil would fight this way—psychological warfare. Erosion of the self through sin.

But Eric had saved Daniel that night. His head cleared. "I atoned for Joshua's death and I was forgiven."

"By whom, exactly?" Lucifer smirked and threw his arms up. "He made you in *my* image, not *His*. You are just as doomed to fail *her* as I am doomed to lose the final battle with Michael. The thing is, only one of us believes it's true."

His expression wasn't one Eric had ever worn. No—it was a smug, arrogant *Jonathan* face that Eric wanted to punch. He clutched the cross he wore around his neck—his proof of forgiveness. "Is that why you've resorted to cheating? Showing me Jonathan's memory because you know the guilt is gone from mine?"

"The guilt that chased you here, you mean?" Lucifer snickered. "But, sure, ohh yesss…please, let's talk about guilt, shall we? Who do you think ripped *her* out of your arms?" Wickedly confident, Lucifer crept forward on his hands and knees. "Salea can do wondrous things in Animus Hollow that most can't, but she's not strong enough to face you head on—and not that stupid. So, it wasn't her…although, she did rip your daught—"

Eric's claws were tearing through Lucifer's shoulders before he knew what was happening. Monstrous howls raced along rows of headstones. Lucifer hurled his middle wings open to brace and the transparency changed to virginal white. The flames in his eyes blazed with light. He yanked Eric to his chest and launched into the air.

"My *pride* doesn't permit the loss of hope!" Lucifer yelled. "And hope *always* has a chance to change the path. Certainties are taboo in the natural order."

An image of a girl formed in Eric's mind. Red fruit bounced from the folds of her skirt as she ran toward a woman who triumphantly held up a fish. The woman was Raven, in what looked like medieval peasantry garb, with long brown hair. But the emotions weren't his. Social pleasantry hid layers of forced emptiness and disgust. *That* was how Lucifer had tried to bury his hope.

"It took a few centuries to realize it, but that was the moment my Little One tipped Karma's scales in my favor. Not even I could have anticipated Salea's true potential and the unexpected result of an altered vampire feeding solely on *me*."

Lucifer stopped climbing and flapped his massive wings to hover above patchwork fields of gray and black. "Salea is smart and cunning— more than Raven knows. She is the temptress who will bring down the Vampiric Nation and all of humanity with it. I needed them to broker peace, and now they're going to shatter it and destroy the trust that they think they earned."

Lucifer tightened his embrace. Eric's ribs creaked and snapped. He desperately speared the skin and muscles that connected Lucifer's wings to his back. The vice-like hold loosened enough for a trickle of air to enter, but Eric's chest felt like an inferno. He slashed through the connective membranes and tore into the thick musculature that flexed with each flap.

Lucifer emitted a shrill, inhuman noise, and the Elysian Fields swarmed around Eric. Alone under a radiant sun, Eric saw yellow flowers in every direction until the breeze blew golden hair into his visual field.

"Heliopsis, the false sunflower." She plucked a stem and twirled it under her nose. Her smile lit his world. "It's named for Helios, the Sun, brother to Selene, the Moon, and Eos, the Dawn. Butterflies love it."

She bit her lip and tucked her hair behind her ear. "It's tempting to kill Lucifer, isn't it?"

"It's tempting," he echoed in a trance.

"That's kind of what he does, isn't it?" She threaded the flower into her hair and hummed into the wind. "Which makes it a choice. Remember that, my love."

Fear hooked into his spine. "Did something happen? Are you really here? Are you...dead?"

"No. Yes. And, not yet." She smiled into a warm gust that lifted her off her toes. She waved sadly as she and the field blew away like dandelion seeds into the moonless night.

Cold orbs of electric blue bored into his eyes. Eric was nose to nose with Lucifer—and he was livid.

"...because the blunt truth is that I may have a habit of falling, but I also have wings. How far can *you* fly? Perhaps you should join your beloved—"

The sky flashed bright white. Saint Michael's avatar phased through the casements and rose high above Sunset Grove. It spotlighted Lucifer like a lighthouse's beam.

"Always intervening. Always with the *rules*." Lucifer scoffed. Slowly descending, he glared at the avatar and snidely yelled, "Where did I go too far, *Brother*? Did you think I'd try to kill him, *again*? Or reveal where she—"

Lucifer grinned. A spark lit his pupils as they sank into Eric's widening gaze. "Ohh! Right. Oops. My bad."

The wintry air bit deep into Eric's bones as Paresh's smile appeared in his mind. Why had she rushed in so suddenly like that? What had Lucifer said while he was gone?

"Where...?" Eric whispered. "Where she *what?*"

Licking his lips, Lucifer tapped Eric's nose and sang in a discordant voice, "Rules are rules, and this is your stop!"

He dropped Eric fifteen feet off the ground. Rolling into his landing, Eric grunted and darted up, but Lucifer was gone.

"Why did you send her?" he cried at the avatar. "Why did you intervene?"

Alex stormed through the bushes and rushed to Eric's side. Saint Michael's avatar dropped out of sight.

"What happened?" Alex asked, panting. "The hunters reported screaming, and then *Michael*, well, *did that*." He pointed at the empty sky.

"He...he knows where she is," Eric said hollowly. A meteor streaked as a tear ran down his cheek. "And I think she does, too."

"Michael?" Alex cautiously asked, taking a step back.

"N-no. P-Paresh...and *Lucifer*." Another tear dropped. "She came to me before Saint Michael stopped him—"

His mouth continued moving without a voice. Disbelief collided with sorrow as the beast's wrath simmered low in his gut. Alex seemed to be at a similar loss for words, his aura churning with confusion and alarm.

"*Lucifer* was here?" Alex asked at last, his voice squeaking.

Eric nodded.

"And *he* knows..." Alex's voice faltered.

"He looks like me." Eric whispered. "Identical—I look *exactly* like the Devil. No wonder—my whole life has...just—"

A car skidded to a stop on the driveway. Jonathan hopped out and ran over. Eric's eyes instantly locked onto to his and the beast howled. He flew at Jonathan, seething with frothy saliva as he twisted the lapels of his brother's suit into his fists.

"It's you! Everything always comes back to you!" Eric slammed Jonathan against the car. *"Because you have his face, I look exactly like him!"*

Slapping at Eric's grip, Jonathan stammered, "Wh-what are you talking about?"

Eric felt his control racing away and he wasn't sure he cared. Paresh's visit...her blood...they weren't enough. He stared into Jonathan's bewildered eyes and fought against the beast, but it was *his* face. Jonathan's face. The Devil's face. The face he saw every day in the mirror. Most of his life, he'd been haunted by a demon that looked so similar they could pass for brothers, and now, he was the Devil's twin—purposely created that way *by God.*

He exhaled a jagged breath and closed his eyes. He threw Jonathan aside and punched the rear window, shattering the glass and shrieking through a convergence of emotions he couldn't decipher. They packed energy and hit hard.

"You know what it is?" Eric asked, his teeth chattering. "Like ripping my heart out but leaving the beat behind to remind me that it's gone."

He was vaguely aware that Jonathan had yet to rise and that Alex was deliberately hovering out of his sightline. In his mind, he tried to visualize Paresh and convince himself to run before those emotions reached the beast. Lucifer's electric blue eyes drilled into him, and he realized that the angel and devil sitting on his shoulders were one and the same. Lucifer had been with him since birth.

He landed on top of Jonathan, tearing at his face and screaming, *"You knew it, didn't you? All along!"*

A heavy weight landed on his back, forcing him down against Jonathan's chest. "Eric! *Stop!*" Alex cried.

Eric growled and gnashed at Jonathan's throat. Jonathan blocked and shoved him back. Blinded by deep, bloody gashes, Jonathan synced his aura with Alex's. Together, they managed to restrain Eric against the rocky driveway.

Eric screeched and fought like a wild animal. He was no longer capable of coherent thought. Somewhere in the recesses of shrinking logic, he could only watch in helpless horror.

☽ ✳ ☾

JONATHAN

He was tired of this. Not sleeping enough. Not drinking enough. Working too much. And now his eyes howled in burning agony, increasing more and more as nerves and connective tissue regenerated.

"*What the hell was that, Alex?*" White spots rapidly popped into his blindness with the stabbing pain of an ice pick.

"H-he said Lucifer was here." Alex's voice was low. Exhausted.

"In *his* body or as a possession?" Jonathan firmed his grip on Eric's arm. If he continued to fight in this uncontrolled rage, he'd get free and kill them both.

Alex seemed to have the same thought. "Should you call Lord You-Know-Who?"

"He won't come—especially if Lucifer was here." Jonathan sighed and rolled his neck. He wished this nightmare would end. "Tell me what happened."

"I honestly don't know. I only got here a minute ahead of you. He was amped up, raving about Paresh and Lucifer knowing where she's buried, and Michael not letting them tell him." He paused for breath. "Right before you pulled up, he said that Lucifer looked like him and started to say something about his life."

Jonathan's heart sank. Confessions and penitence aside, *he'd* been the main source of Eric's misery.

"*You* and Eric look alike," Alex hesitantly started. "What if it's true? D-do you know? Does Eric look like him? Or was it an illusion to screw with him?"

Jonathan shook his head. "I've never seen Lucifer in his own body. Only Lucien—"

"Don't say—oh shit!" Alex yelled as Eric growled at Lucien's name and his muscles bulged beneath them. "Come on! Call *him*! We can't do this alone."

"No." Jonathan pressed his knee between Eric's shoulder blades. "If it's true, then Lu...*he*—had to know—he *had to*. About both of us. If Eric sees him, this'll only get worse."

Jonathan nodded at the car. "I have venom—"

"But we can't get to it!" Alex pressed his full weight onto Eric's legs. "I swear on Apollo's laurels—if he gets up, I'm grabbing you and running."

"Just…*wait*. Give me a second to think." How was he supposed to deal with Lucifer *and* Eric?

"We. Don't. Have a second," Alex grunted.

"Fine!" Jonathan huffed in frustration. "Do you have another vial?"

"I haven't restocked since we saw him this afternoon. H-he was fine. I didn't need—"

"It's not like we saw this coming! Here—" Jonathan bit a chunk of meat from his palm and shoved the bloody wound into Eric's mouth. "I've been sneaking in a few drops of her blood to keep going—this should calm him down, at least a little. I swear, sometimes I wish I still had you at my beck and call."

"Because I'm not busy enough overseeing every aspect of VaSH operations as High Commander, *on top of* my new duties as a True Blood Elder?" Alex groaned. "Look—sorry—I know what you meant. The Elders are a handful and you're doing the job of three Arch Elders."

Eric formed a seal on Jonathan's palm and began to stop fighting them. They didn't let up a bit, though. He was too good at launching surprise attacks.

"What does it all mean?" Jonathan whispered in earnest as fatigue weighed on his shoulders. "Lucifer coming here? Eric looking like him…and me? And *Paresh* knows…?"

"Why would Michael stop either of them from revealing where she's buried?" Alex asked. "And when did Eric see her to learn that?"

Jonathan shrugged. "The night they died, Paresh knew that we could bring Eric back, but was forbidden from telling us. We had to figure it out on our own; it was part of the prophecy—our choice to accept salvation."

"Well, that makes sense for Paresh, but does that mean Lucifer has to play by the same rules? Why would he do that? He started the Great Holy War!"

Gritting through a new blast of piercing white spots, Jonathan shook his head and eased off his knee. "Maybe there are ramifications that even Lucifer doesn't want to risk. Or maybe they're forcefully prevented from saying what they can't say."

"Or, maybe old Gabe and Michael are holding her soul as ransom to keep Lucifer quiet," Alex said bitterly. "They know he needs her alive and they don't want celestials interfering in the Realm of Man—yet."

Fear was an icy drizzle that raised Jonathan's flesh. "What do you mean by that?"

"Plain and simple—Paresh is no good to Lucifer if she's dead. So if he breaks the rules, they send her *up*," Alex said with a tangible depth of sadness. "It's part of *our* test, not theirs, so it's up to us to succeed or fail. *We* must do this on our own."

Jonathan wished he could dispute that logic, but he'd fought in the War and knew better. It sounded colder than it was, but the borderline between realms was not to be crossed. Lucifer was walking a fine line and pulling strings, but he hadn't broken the rules. Whatever he stood to lose was equally weighted to the fate of a world dangling over an apocalyptic edge—and that didn't bode well for anyone's survival, vampire or not.

III

ALEX

South of the Tropic of Cancer, Africa 5th Century A.D.

The metallic clash of the sword was sharp, but not nearly as brutal as its bite. Crimson light flooded the battlefield as Alex charged. The blade struck again, slicing clean through his thigh and scraping the bone. A beastly sound erupted from his mouth. The hilt dug into his skin. He pinched his claws into a penetrating spear and connected. The winged body fell limp against him.

He staggered backward. The Host's body thudded lifelessly. With a hefty groan, he pulled the blade from his flesh and angrily pinned the angel into the gore-slicked mud.

Wiping sweat from his brow, he panted and slunk away, keenly watching for danger at every turn. The sounds of war were growing faint. He was losing feeling in his leg.

"Steady on." A strong arm enveloped his torso. "I wouldn't envy a face full of that muck."

Another arm, smaller, but no less powerful, came around the other side. "He hit the femoral."

Alex sagged between them. "Where were you?"

"It took longer this time." Lior was matter-of-fact as he deflected an inbound strike that Kestrel then parried. She yanked the sword from its Host by the blade and speared it through the heart— another winged enemy down. Lior scavenged a shield and the pair dragged Alex to safety behind the front line.

"Why are you directly engaged?" Kestrel ripped off a piece of a dead Host's robe and tied it around Alex's leg to staunch the blood

flow. "You're so exhausted that you aren't healing."

"They found a weak pocket… were dividing and driving the line back," Alex huffed as his head lolled and black stars shot through his vision. He swayed on his good leg. Kestrel and Lior firmed their hold.

"Get your head even with your heart and raise that leg." Lior stabilized the injury as Kestrel eased Alex into the putrid slime.

"We apologize for our delayed return," she said, dutifully presenting the new stretch of raw, blistered skin that gleamed with purified silver.

"It'd better…" His vision blinked to black. A hard slap roused him. "…be worth it. Endymion gives you too much freedom."

"We understand the importance of our roles," Lior said under his breath. "We won't let you die as long as you keep your head about you and stop rushing to the front line like that."

"Rushing in?" Alex growled, glaring through one eye as blood dripped into the other. "It's war! Stop deserting your posts!"

They shared an unreadable look. "It will happen again," Lior started, and Kestrel finished, "But it won't be for nothing—we will stop their advance."

"We need to stop the bleeding," Lior said, surveying the fledglings clashing with the Host. "Our blood is toxic now; you can't drink from us."

He vanished in a flash and returned holding the winged body of a fresh kill. He pressed the side of its neck into Alex's fangs. "Here, the carotid will supply you with more energy."

Kestrel tightened the tourniquet. "We shall uphold our vow to you, Alexander. You are becoming increasing vital in Endymion's predictions for our future as the War progresses."

Lior nodded in reverence beyond them, at someone Alex couldn't see but knew was Endymion. "We were only a step ahead of him. He watches you when we are gone."

Alex tried to sit up, but the deadweight of the Host's wings kept him down. "He shouldn't need to watch me; I have an army of my own to command instead of picking up your slack!"

They shared another one of their irritating glances. They were like mind-reading incestuous siblings. Alex huffed and blew blood bubbles over his face.

"There's been a new development," Kestrel said, wiping Alex's forehead clean with her arm. "Endymion has plotted the likely scenario and thinks he can bridge it to a desirable outcome."

Alex shook his head. That didn't make sense. "As far as we know, only Gabriel can pull the Threads of Time."

Lior grinned. His eyes flashed golden black. "Your divine intervention is protection, which means you have a future beyond this war. Endymion has tethered us to you as much as we are tethered to him."

"Worry not," Kestrel added, checking his wound and heaving with relief. "We shall protect the future that he seeks. Trust us."

☽ ✻ ☾

Alex woke doused in sweat in a pitch-black room and rubbed at the phantom pain in his thigh. A whopping 1500 years later, in the winter of 2010, and that day still haunted him. He used to wonder why, but gave up after deciding that Fate was like Charon, and, like many of the dead wishing to cross into Hades, he couldn't afford the payment to let go. The brutality of that battle. Gabriel baiting him to a frontline ambush. He was trapped like a wraith on the banks of the River Styx, doomed eternally to remember being stuck there, barely able to defend himself by the time Kestrel and Lior had arrived. He should have died.

But those two were right about his future. Raven's birth had been the "development" and Hawkiel had already branded her. And then *he'd* been the first true blood she'd met, not Endymion. All of the threads of time, the red strings of fate, the blood and the death…and a slow burn apocalypse—

Trust us.

He shook his head. Like it was that easy. All that work they'd done to themselves. *For nothing*. Four years in and the modern pairing of Kestrel and Sarah only reported worsening news about the Fallen Host's grip on the world, too blinded by the souls bound inside Grandfather Wisdom to see anything in a multi-state radius. In death, Paresh's soul glowed as brightly as a star, but her body didn't shine at all.

He sighed. At least they hadn't given up. They'd shifted focus to tracing the essence of Eric's blood once handed off to Donovan. It hadn't worked yet, though, and with Endymion dead, Alex could only wonder about the future he'd predicted and what *his* supposedly "vital" role truly was.

Beside him, Jonathan was asleep for once. Alex hadn't anticipated that this would become a long term—or permanent—arrangement, and still wasn't used to sharing a bed, but the steady rhythm of Jonathan's breathing indicated he was really out. They'd been pushing themselves so hard…he couldn't believe they'd fallen asleep *at night.*

It had to be after midnight. Eric didn't keep a clock in his bedroom—and this would always be his room, where he and Paresh had laughed and made love. This room, this house, would never be his or Jonathan's. When they found Paresh, she and Eric would return here and make this *their home* again. He had to believe that to keep moving forward.

He kneaded the back of his neck and slipped out from beneath the sheet. He grabbed his boxers, silently swept out the door, and padded barefoot down the cold granite hallway. He paused at the kitchen, hopping into his underwear and thinking about grabbing a drink, but the scent of blood would awaken Jonathan. He could wait. Jonathan needed the rest. Alex moved on to the atrium.

Fat snowflakes filled the overcast night, cascading in thickening sheets that shrouded the distance in a darkening gray film. Snow covered the angled glass overhead and blanketed at least three inches of the surrounding fields.

Rattan fibers creaked as Alex sat on the loveseat and stretched his legs over the ottoman. In such insulating weather, the room was peacefully ambient, the humidifiers humming and heating ducts rattling faintly.

He ground the heel of his palm into his leg. He'd been stabbed before and after that attack, but only that injury stung when he dreamed about it. He settled back with a sigh, absently zigzagging his fingers through his hair. Eric's conservatory was his fairytale escape, where he could think and calm his frustrations amid tropical palms and canes, birds of paradise, and umbrella trees.

Their silhouettes towered over the plants hidden beneath their guard. The muted night and white snow added a velvety depth to their living shadows.

He wound a fern frond around his fingers. Some time ago, a lone cricket had moved in. Its solo performance was a welcome contrast to the silence that had descended upon Orison Crossing. The villagers talked amongst themselves about odd behavior in their pets. Dogs didn't bark and panicked on walks. Cats didn't go outside. Hamsters hid in their cages. Parakeets stopped talking.

Walter had begged him to do *anything* possible. Pulling hunters from residential areas and deploying Cimex Drones had helped. But that'd meant adding members to the surveillance team, the equivalent of desk duty. Seneca fielded complaints, but Alex had finally lost his temper and ordered a mandatory rotation for every hunter stationed in Orison Crossing, regardless of squad. After he stepped away and returned to "normal Alex programming," he dangled bonus free time for every shift "worked" as an incentive.

He groaned and mashed his palm into his eye. This was their *life*, their purpose—not just their jobs. He hated making them feel like bogged down worker bees, but he also resented that they felt that way to begin with. They were all in crisis mode.

"Raven," he whispered softly, ruffling his hair for her, "I need you to tell me what to do more now than ever. Time's no longer on our side."

Kestrel and Sarah's latest report had come from the detail assigned to Donovan. They'd documented small changes in his appearance: fine lines creasing his forehead, eyes, and mouth. It was proof that confirmed what had been seen in others: the non-repentant were aging.

But that gave the hunters an advantage, and it also revealed that not all of the non-repentant were rogues and not all rogues were COMS, but all known rogues showed the same signs. He had to wonder if that meant Salea would age, too, and how she'd change since she'd been altered so young. She could probably walk right by him and he wouldn't know it. That definitely made him glad he could trust Kestrel and Sarah. They'd *feel* her. But they hadn't found her either. Or Lucifer, for that matter—likely waiting for Paresh's body to surface, under the *rules*, or waiting for Darkesiel to land.

Alex scratched behind his ear. He'd become more self-conscious about it since Sarah began teasing him. He interlaced his fingers behind his head.

"If I looked in the mirror and literally saw that I'm one day closer to mortal death, what would I do? What do you think, Raven?" he asked, sighing as he tried to sink into that mindset. "Would I find a sudden, *genuine* willingness to seek redemption? Or would I say screw it and give in to repressed urges?"

The recent uptick in rogue activity gave him his answer. The Wraith Reapers were too bogged down to take a break. In the morning, he'd order Seneca to create a division within the Crimson Guard for Kestrel to command as temporary back up.

That left him with Eric.

"Arg. Noooo!" He rolled his head along the back of the love seat and groaned into his palms. He dreaded the days he had to check on Eric with a capital "Deimos." He mostly went alone now. Jonathan was either too busy or too triggering, and it was impossible to know what version of Eric they'd get.

"Everything's fucked up, Raven." He groaned again. "You see what happens when you leave me alone? The world goes to hell. That's what. Lord Lucien won't even come out of the Arc of True Blood!"

And that was a sad truth. He'd locked down the arc after Endymion's death. Alex assumed Jonathan stayed in contact with him, but the Second Born hadn't returned to the arc in years—no one had. One of the last times Alex had seen Lord Lucien was when he'd been trapped in his monstrous creature-esque form.

He shook off the memory before it materialized—one nightmare was enough—and instead heard the tinkling peal of Paresh's laugh. It was light-hearted, yet nervous—also from that visit with Lord Lucien. It'd been the first laugh he'd heard after she revealed her pregnancy. His jaw tensed. Apparently, one nightmare *wasn't* enough. He couldn't comprehend Eric's willingness to give up on her so easily. Today, he'd make Eric make him understand.

☽ ❋ ☾

The skies cleared after daybreak. Five inches of undisturbed snow sparkled across the cottage clearing. Forecasted winds would gust it into drifts measurable by feet later, but for now, it was serene and beautiful. He imagined the dainty swirls Paresh would leave behind prancing through it trailed by ice crystals that glittered like fairy fire in the sun's light—

No. Any other day—maybe. Not today.

He didn't bother with keys or knocking. The handle turned easily. He stepped into the dim interior, shaking his head at the letters strewn across the dining table and living room. Most were in tatters and had formed a layer of white dust upon every surface.

He shut the door and peered over the sofa. Eric wasn't on the floor, which meant he was in the bedroom—on the floor.

Great.

A check of the fridge confirmed that Eric hadn't touched his blood supply. Leaning on the counter, Alex sighed and hung his head, drumming up dust with his fingers. Maybe he should wait until Jonathan finished the meeting at the mansion, just in case.

But he couldn't get answers with Jonathan there.

The counter creaked as he reluctantly straightened. The grandfather clock ticked in tune with his steps down the hall. Faint light filtered through the door at the end, cracked ajar. He peered in, seeing the quilt undisturbed, the surfaces untouched, the layer of dust on the floor evenly uniform.

He hated going in there. Paresh's brushes, perfume, and cosmetics waited for her atop the vanity, teasing her presence and her scent, yet not delivering either. Worse, he hated handling what had become of what she'd left behind. Grinding his teeth, he pushed the door open and left dark footprints on the hardwood planks. He passed Eric's side of the bed to Paresh's, where she'd slept before it all went to hell—before *he'd* chased her to her death.

Eric blames himself, but none of us are innocent.

Eric lay on the floor, hair dull and brittle, bare frame hollowed from hunger, and jogging pants loose and coated with a fine layer of white dust. Alex kicked the sole of Eric's foot.

"What would Paresh think if she saw you?"

No response.

"The fridge is full. Of course you know that since you haven't bothered to open it," Alex continued, as though to himself—might as well be, he supposed. "I'll call the heralds to clean—"

Eric's empty gaze rolled up. "Don't touch the letters," he croaked.

"You care more about those pieces of paper than the girl who wrote them!" Alex didn't try to hide his anger—he couldn't if he wanted to, honestly. He kicked Eric's foot again, harder. "Stop living in the past!"

Silence. And an icy glare.

"How can you just cast her aside like this? You want her to move on after dying a violent and traumatic death? They ripped the baby from her womb and *then* stabbed her through the heart while *Donovan* h—"

He didn't see Eric move.

Oh shit—

But that was definitely Eric's fist crushing his windpipe.

Well, at least he's up.

Eric rammed him into the wall and cracked the plaster. "How can you ask me to bring her back from that? *Huh?* You're the one who pointed out how terrible that'd be the day after she died!"

Eric faltered a step back. "To live with that memory, you said? *You know* she couldn't even come back *here* after her *first* violent and traumatic death! It's a curse! And now you want me to force that on her? *Both of those memories!* For the rest of her next life? *Until it happens again!* Because it *will* happen again, *and you know it!*"

He threw Alex at the chaise and staggered to a bedpost. "How can you expect me to protect her when they took her straight from my arms? I will only ever fail her—break every promise I've ever made. I…I'm not her Strength. I'm not her *anything*. I'm just a devil in disguise…and not a good one at that."

Rubbing his throat, Alex stretched his jaw and shot back, "This isn't about you! You can't—"

"No, it's not," Eric growled, swinging forward on the post and jabbing a finger in Alex's face. "It's about *her*. You want to bring her back so that history can repeat itself. She will always, *always*, be a target. Violence and trauma—that's what you worried about then, but it's what you want for her now. That's the sentence she gets if you bring her back."

"You are such a son of a bitch," Alex growled. He charged Eric and knocked him off his feet, kneeling on his chest the instant he landed. Dust bloomed about them.

"*She wants to come back!*" Alex screamed, his fist slamming into Eric's cheek. "*That's. What. She. Wants. How can you ignore that?*"

His other fist connected. "Do you think she doesn't see you doing this to yourself? *You know she's watching.* She's always been stronger than anyone's been willing to see." Alex threw an arm across teary eyes. "Even Gabriel doubted her."

"*If* she's actually watching—*if* I'm actually seeing her in my dreams—why doesn't she tell me where she is? She knows! Do you think she'd actually tell me to let her go?" Eric's burst of energy must have been a one off. He could barely lift his arms.

"Of course I do!" Alex yelled. "She gave me the instructions to protect you from yourself because she knew—shit, *somehow* she *knew* that you wouldn't be *strong enough* to do what needed to be done."

Eric's eyes darkened. A menacing growl rumbled deep in his throat. The tips of his fangs appeared over his lip. Alex bolted for the kitchen and grabbed a blood bag. He ran into Eric in the hall, barely dodging his lunge or his fists. He shoved the bag into Eric's mouth and used his momentum to sweep his legs. They fell together, Alex bracing Eric's shoulder and squeezing the bag to force blood down his throat.

"I'm sick of doing this with you!" Alex yelled. "She wants to live! She *wants* to live!"

He didn't let Eric reply. He squeezed harder. The bag would burst, but he didn't care.

"We all owe it to her to respect her wishes. You talk about violence and trauma when she *knows* what she'll come back to! She knows! Probably better than any of us since she lived through it! She's a survivor!"

His tears dripped into Eric's eyes. "She knows, Eric. And she's made her choice. And you really need to deal with that, because if this is about her, and not you, you'd respect her decision."

Freeing the arm wedged under Eric's back, Alex straddled his chest. "This is about you—it's your insecurity, your failures…your *face*. You never go to the tree! Because *you* can't stand to see her gold ribbon. It's all *you*. What you want. What you can or can't handle."

He sniffled. "But she breaks out to see you. You *are* seeing her. Kestrel told me what happened in Vermont—that tapping tree branch and the black void? Can you honestly dismiss that? On top of every other time she's come to you? Do you have any idea how much energy it takes to fight *an angel*? Because *I do*."

He pulled a syringe from his pocket and held it up for Eric to see. It was mostly clear with a streak of crimson—venom laced with Paresh's blood. "Because that's what she does any time you're incapacitated. She uses your thinning consciousness to her advantage and escapes every single hold *both* of those angels have on her soul. Even if it only means she gets a second with you—she fights them. *And you want to let her die*."

He bit the cap off and spit it out. "I can't understand or forgive that. And if she dies for real, I'll never forgive you."

Eric's eyes widened in terror as Alex jammed the needle into his chest. "Yeah, I know this is torture. But right now, you deserve it. Say hi to Paresh for me."

IV

LUCIEN

The Far East, ca. 370 B.C.

Anchored against the Yellow River Valley's mountainous horizon, a bloody mist hung above infantry and cavalry troops numbering in the hundreds of thousands. A writhing mass of screams, violence, and death, they'd abandoned all measure of civility and the rules of war alike.

Auburn hair streaked like fire under the setting sun. Jonathan's gleeful smile terrified men far more than his engorged eyes or blood-caked nudity—an advantageous camouflage that he loathed, but used to prevent sun blisters. He crushed a soldier's face with his own crossbow and shot an arrow between the linked plates of another's armor. Jonathan was fascinated by the variety of ways humans killed each other, and the longer this conflict lasted, the more inventive and ruthless they became, refining weapons, armor, tools, and so on. Like starving locusts, they razed fields of crops and whole villages. Villagers not recruited for the State's military fled before the battles reached their boundaries. They'd lose it all regardless of the outcome.

Lucien sat atop a pillaged storehouse, its roof sturdy and high enough for a decent view. The Yellow River churned at his back, its sallow color maintained by swift currents that were untamable when the rains came. He'd seen the banks overrun and alter its course in his previous travels. If not for the clear weather and Jonathan's unabashed joy, Lucien would've moved on quickly, but once set loose, Jonathan had delivered on his promises. He was free to revel in his element now.

Lucien locked eyes with him and nodded before turning his attention to the strips of red silk and coiled thread in his lap. As they traveled the eastern trading routes from Egypt, they'd perfected cloaking and hypnotizing their way into enjoying a wealthier lifestyle. Lucien had spied upon many happenings within the palaces from elaborate tea ceremonies to women embroidering extravagant silks in cramped workrooms. Pulling fabric taut, they slipped needles in and out, creating intricate knots and striking patterns like an entwining magic.

On the trade route between the Kunlun Shan and Tien Shan mountain ridges, Lucien had found and secretly tucked the fabric and thread within his traveling pouch. He rubbed his thumb and forefinger together, pale blue and wondrously soft and smooth like Jonathan's skin, rid of scales and the plaguing damp at last. The crawling sensation still came with the rain, but he didn't know if it was real or an enduring specter of sensation. Regardless, Jonathan's companionship had changed his life and he wished to bestow upon him a gift of appreciation.

By itself, the silk was too delicate for Jonathan's rigorous activities. He was too restless and too bloodthirsty to sit still for long. He knew well not to kill clan leaders or advisors, lest he lose his comfortable bedding, cleansing baths, and luxurious silk robes. Lucien indulged him as long as no human eye turned upon them—in that, they'd come to understand each other and their roles. Jonathan never tested him, and, since he'd proven his strategic skills in Egypt, he'd earned Lucien's trust.

Of course, Lucien could kill Jonathan easily if warranted. His skillset was vastly superior, but he hid the extent. He enjoyed Jonathan's beauty and confidence too much to risk their relationship over an unnecessary power play. Jonathan already sulked at not being able to alter his skin—he was stuck with cells that degraded in the sunlight.

Jonathan's fiery hair flared from the center of a violent horde. He was flouncing about more than usual today. A third army must've joined the skirmish. Neither of them required much sleep, so Jonathan frequently outlasted the battles—and they could go for months at a time. He particularly relished the fresh energy that new soldiers infused into an exhausted campaign.

The nerves in Lucien's belly quivered. His gift wouldn't change Jonathan's life. It was a mere token, small and insignificant, with only thought and effort behind it, nothing more. Perhaps he should've focused on something more practical.

On the trade routes, carved jade and glittering jewels had caught Jonathan's eye despite having no use for them. He'd enthralled a handful of merchants to move their wares and money into deep, unexplored caves for safekeeping, and taken bejeweled golden clasps for their cloaks. That brought the embroidering women to Lucien's mind—their skills embellished their leader's façade and bolstered his comfort. Jonathan took that same pride in his appearance. This was a start. Lucien could choose practicality next time.

He successfully threaded the eye of the needle. When they'd arrived here, he'd willingly stalled their journey to his homeland farther east when the warring states provided ample distraction for Jonathan. Lucien took the opportunity to practice in private. He'd needed it— better finger dexterity did not equal skill.

He stacked the silk strips, ran a central line of evenly spaced temporary stitches, and looped thread along one edge, checking Jonathan's proximity on occasion. He notched the ends and tended to the other side. Another group surrounded Jonathan and fell limp all at once. His efficiency at killing without even touching his prey made Lucien smile.

Along the trade routes, across steppes, deserts, hills, and mountains, they'd experimented with wielding their auras as weapons of fear, with stopping hearts and suffocating lungs. Jonathan delighted in the ease of spooking thieves' horses and camels to throw their riders with bone crushingly fatal results—a lofty thrill came with killing by presence alone, even to Lucien.

He finished the decorative edging, pulled the temporary line from the lower quarter, and began chaining a leaf pattern anchored by link stitches. The delicate embroidery added stability to the layers without increasing the ribbon's bulk. He placed the final stitch and secured the thread so that no knots betrayed one side from the other. He turned the ribbon in his hands and tied it around his finger, testing its hold. Jonathan could wear it into battle to keep his hair out of his eyes.

He loosed a low whistle. Jonathan emerged from the fray and took a running leap into the river. Surfacing with an exhilarated *whoop*, he swam against the current and scrubbed blood from his face and body. Lucien dropped to the ground and added wood to the fire. He'd wait until Jonathan's hair was dry.

He lifted the hood of his cloak and raced to a campsite between them and the battlefield where he plucked two meaty soldiers from the heavy infantry. Tired men made for a meager drink, but size usually compensated with a few extra nutrients. He struck them at the base of their skulls and carried them to the empty village. They weren't dead and wouldn't regain consciousness, which gave him more time to enjoy Jonathan and their meal together.

Jonathan came ashore and walked along the bank shaking out his legs and arms, and wringing his hair. He kept his distance to avoid getting water on Lucien as he stretched his hands to the fire. Lucien dipped a cloth into a clean washbasin and dabbed behind Jonathan's ear. Looking up in surprise, Jonathan covered Lucien's wet hand, moving with it as the cloth slid down his neck.

"Stay in tonight," Lucien murmured, dropping the cloth to trail his fingers along Jonathan's shoulder.

A contented sigh brushed Lucien's skin as Jonathan's body stirred to life. Jonathan took the cloth and stood as though to kiss him, but he wouldn't touch Lucien until he was clean—that was an idiosyncrasy all his own. He grabbed a large earthen jar filled with drinking water and squatted at the washbasin. It wasn't the same as a palatial tub or even close to the bathhouses in Greece, but Lucien knew Jonathan wouldn't be happy until he washed his hair and rinsed off the river's sedimentary film.

"You were having more fun this time." Lucien stepped clear of the splash zone. "I don't think you killed a man the same way twice—groups withstanding, of course."

"It's invigorating! I can stretch my arms and legs in every direction and draw blood. You should join me more often!" He tossed the dirty water and refilled. "The armies are tiring. I don't expect them to last much longer. If they don't kill each other—and I don't kill them—they'll die of exhaustion. Someone's going to retreat soon."

"Surely, such easy kills get boring for you."

"A kill is a kill; it's what I do best." Jonathan paused and smirked mischievously. "Well, not the only thing I do best."

Lucien let his agreement speak through his admiration. A relaxed smile turned up Jonathan's mouth as he squeezed the cloth and it ran clear. He twisted his hair and it, too, dripped clear. He suggestively approached Lucien. "And they may be tiring, but I'm not."

"Tempting, as always." Lucien lightly dragged a fingertip down Jonathan's throat to his navel and nodded at their meal. "But first…I grabbed a few of your new friends for dinner. And I—"

Jonathan's smile stiffened. "I should have brought them—"

Lucien held out his hand. "Worry is unbecoming and unnecessary. I…have a gift…for you."

"A gift? For me? Why?"

"I wish to give you something."

Jonathan clasped Lucien's hands. "Then I am eternally grateful and cannot wait to receive it."

"When your hair is dry."

Confusion scrunched Jonathan's features, but he said nothing further and threw his cloak over his shoulders. Lucien selected his dinner first and Jonathan dragged his as close to the fire as he could without singeing his hair. Afterward, he tossed the bodies in the river and returned the fire, finger combing his hair until it was dry.

Jonathan's face lit up expectantly as Lucien knelt behind him. Cushioning his nerves with his aura, Lucien pulled the ribbon from his sleeve and threaded his fingers through Jonathan's auburn locks.

"May I see it first?" Jonathan asked.

Lucien displayed it over the back of his hand. Jonathan gasped and traced the crimson tonal pattern. "It's beautiful. Did you make it?"

"I did."

"Ah!" Jonathan eagerly examined the intricate loops and chains, and turned it front and back as though trying to determine which was which. "It's…it's beautiful."

"Yes, so you've said." Lucien didn't hide the humor in his voice at Jonathan's childlike wonderment. "May I?"

Jonathan bit his lip and nodded. Lucien gathered Jonathan's hair at his nape and centered the ribbon, tying it into a square knot so the pattern flowed with his hair.

Stroking it, Jonathan said, "I can't stop smiling."

"It suits you well."

Jonathan faced him. "I'll wear it into the fight tomorrow. Will you join me?"

"It's your element—" Lucien tipped his chin up and leaned in. "But when do I ever say no to you?"

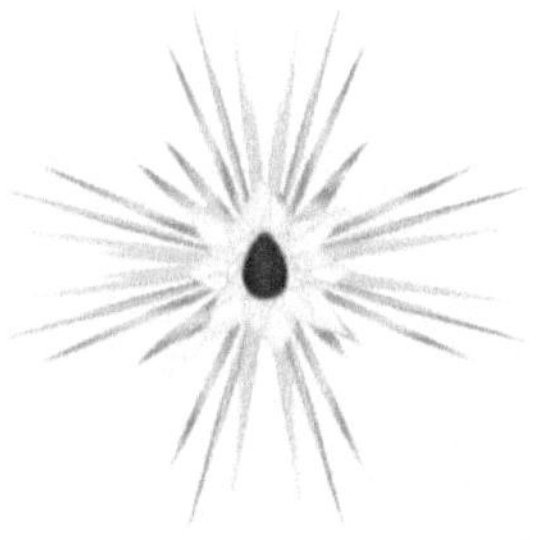

Chapter Eleven: Seems of Demon Dreams

I

ERIC

Orison Crossing, Winter 2010

Flagstones at the hearth's ledge scraped his skin through his t-shirt as he fisted a crumbling letter at his chest and folded in on himself on the living room floor. Through the window, the winter moon hung low over the bare canopy, not quite full, and the forest's silence was maddeningly deafening, as it always was.

He felt like a wisp of a broken man, a deficient thing carved with holes. He no longer read the words because they were etched onto his hollowed heart, and he could no longer stand to look upon himself, to see the face of evil incarnate, a face designed to lure a demon into his life, a life of waiting…just waiting…for news that never came. And never would—and somehow, regardless of his wish for her to find peace at rest, knowing that she'd never return enflamed the beast's explosive rage.

He knew it was there, but he'd numbed himself to the feeling. Sometimes he tried to restrain it, but Alex dosing him with venom a month back had splintered something in his mind. He and the beast had forged an unspoken truce, and so the beast itself waited, as well, for a moment long overdue—a moment Eric promised to deliver.

A quick knock preceded the metallic scraping of the key in the deadbolt. A blast of wintry air, sharply scented of seasoned maple wood, blew in with Jonathan and Alex, scattering the letters and stirring up vortices of papery dust.

Alex stepped over him to refresh the exhausted log stack. Looking from the letters to the moon, Jonathan removed his gloves and tucked them into silk-lined pockets. His tailored cashmere and lamb's wool coat brushed Eric's legs. Alex swept ash from the dead fire pit, kindled a new fire, and tossed his coat—red, of course, a bright contrast to Jonathan's tan—into the corner rocking chair before assisting Jonathan from his and dutifully hanging it behind the door.

Great. They're staying. Eric barely blinked. The fire crackled and popped, exuding cocooning warmth even as the moon tried to mock him, whispering that he didn't deserve the attention they gave him. He merely stared back. The moon clearly didn't understand the concept of mockery.

Alex perched on the hearth with nervous energy boomeranging through his aura. On the sofa, Jonathan moistened his lips. Eric closed his eyes, wishing they'd leave—the beast's internal fire was alive and too healthy for anyone's good tonight.

And he didn't care.

"Why don't you come home with us?" Jonathan asked quietly.

When was the last time he'd sounded like that? Rather…when was the last time he'd seen *Jonathan*? Why was *he* there? Alex usually came alone. Jonathan's aura connected with Alex's—a prompt.

"I visit the plants in your atrium every day. They're mostly doing well, but an orchid has stopped blooming." Alex's voice was calm.

Oh. It's that time of the month.

An irritated edge cleft Jonathan's aura. Alex's shirt rustled—likely a shrugged response. They'd gotten better at these silent discussions. Eric's pupils dilated and narrowed to focus on the treetops. Of course, Alex noticed—and misinterpreted the meaning. They really needed to leave.

"A cricket's moved in, too. Sounds like a lonely little thing, but it's nice to hear *something*," Alex said softly, "really anything—it's like Mother Nature's clawing her way back."

Eric sprang up and threw Alex against the stones, cracking the wall. Jonathan jerked Eric backward and hurled him into the sofa before he could lunge again.

"*Mother Nature?*" Eric shrieked, his voice shredded and unrecognizably monstrous.

"You're dehydrated, Brother." Jonathan restrained Eric with an iron grip on his shoulders and a crushing knee in his groin. "If you're going to yell at us, at least wait until your throat is no longer so sorely dry."

"You want me to go *home?*" Eric glared at Jonathan. "Are your heralds too scared to check on me *here?*"

"Everyone's too scared to check on you here," Alex muttered, rubbing his shoulders. He sat at Andrew's roll top desk and leaned forward on his knees. A blood bag and a syringe were in his hands.

"You were out of firewood." Jonathan nudged his chin at the kitchen. "And I bet your fridge is full…as usual."

He held his hand out. Alex hesitantly gave him the syringe. "Are you sure you want to do this first?"

"I want to see how dehydrated he is before I check his supplies." Jonathan returned Eric's glare with a look of warning. Lightly fingering his forearm, Jonathan located a withered vein and inserted the syringe. A slow drudge of dark blood appeared as he pulled the stopper.

Anger curled over Jonathan's mouth and crinkled his brow. "She'd hate what you're doing to yourself."

"She's. Not. Here," Eric growled.

Jonathan removed the syringe and said to Alex, "Connect the IV." In the kitchen, he threw the refrigerator open, cursed, and slammed it shut.

"If you won't feed yourself, I'll force it into you!" Jonathan yelled.

Eric jerked to stand, but Alex set a firm hand on his shoulder. His green eyes were stern, tired, and miserable. "Please don't fight me this time—*for her*."

"Isn't that what you're good at?" Eric snapped at Jonathan, his entire body tensing tighter than steel springs. "Forcing it into whoever doesn't want it?"

"What the hell are you—" Jonathan cracked his knuckles and sucked in a strained breath. "I don't want to go where you are right now."

"Well, as long as you don't want to," Eric retorted. "Keep your heralds away from me."

"They work in all of the Elders' residences except yours." Alex threaded the IV catheter and started the blood drip. "It's what they do, you know."

"How much?" Eric demanded, eyeing the blood bag.

"Only a few drops, I promise." Alex lightly firmed his grip on Eric's arm—an assurance. "The supply is holding. Trust me."

"I don't have much of a choice." Eric rested his head against the sofa's wooden frame. Fewer drops of Paresh's blood calmed the fire without plunging him into the torturous Elysian Fields. He couldn't face her again, not when he was forced to waste away like this. The last time had been so cruel. He'd had so much time with her. She'd danced through fields of yellow Heliopsis with the butterflies and he'd danced with her and laughed—he'd felt it, the genuine joy of it, like it was real. Like she was there, a memory in the making, and he'd been the man he recognized—the man she loved.

But he'd woken to the ruthless cruelty of life without her, weakened by the toxin, with pins and needles stabbing his nerves, forced to realize that none of that had happened. None of it was true. And she wasn't there even though his heart screamed that she was. It had screamed for days in denial. And he'd cried from sorrow and the pain of it all—mentally and physically aching more than a tortured soul should ever have to ache. Alone. In the dark. In the bed where he'd touched her so intimately—

The heralds rushed in on another frigid gust. Faceless shadows in black scurried about, cleaning and restocking. Eric had half-expected Jonathan to drag him home. He must have given up—this time, at least.

Moisture leaked into the corners of his eyes. He ground his jaw. His breaths grew shaky.

"Do you need a few more drops?" Alex swapped the empty bag with a fresh one. "Can you control it?"

"No. And no."

"If you can't control it, then you're coming home, one way or another," Jonathan warned. Alex's aura tensed with wary anticipation.

"Do you ever stop to think about *why* I starve the beast?" Eric growled, focusing hard on Alex before looking at Jonathan over his shoulder. "Care to spar, *Brother?*"

Jonathan's shoulders sagged. "I never thought I'd tire of fighting you, but I'd rather not."

"I have the venom," Alex said in a low voice.

"Of course you do. I'm sure you're looking forward to using it again, too," Eric spat.

The heralds stopped moving. Jonathan's aura hardened into a shell. Alex kept downward pressure on Eric's shoulder.

"I'm sorry for that," Alex whispered.

Eric's attention snapped to him. "How's Donovan? Enjoying a good hot soak? Laughing it up with his entourage? Relaxing under the starry sky knowing he's untouchable?"

Alex flinched. "No hunter enjoys any part of that assignment, I assure you."

"Hold out your arm," Jonathan ordered, holding a new syringe.

"Yes, do please gift him a vial of my blood on top of the best security in the world." Eric slapped Jonathan across the face. "The hot springs must be nice this time of year. I bet the Crimson Guard isn't complaining about *that.*"

The hinge of Alex's jaw bulged. He took a moment to center himself and pulled a vial of Paresh's blood from his shirt pocket.

"Don't you dare," Eric snarled. "I will tear out your throat."

Jonathan finished collecting his blood and carefully placed the syringe onto a warm pack to hold the temperature. "Kestrel's taking it this time."

"Why?" Eric asked. "Sarah, too?"

With a chin nudge, Alex dismissed the heralds. "She and Sarah think the scent and steam will help them feel out her residual energy on him before and after they give him your blood."

"Hopefully that gives them a lead on where he goes after he loses his detail," Jonathan said. "We'll see the moment of delivery as a flash in Grandfather Wisdom's golden stream."

Eric took in a deep breath. The first time he'd seen that renewal of Paresh's spirit, his heart had dropped. It wasn't just her body decaying. She deserved better than this.

The beast howled, trapped in an unlocked cage by starvation. But now that fresh blood—enhanced by the Sacred Vessel—was flowing, the beast was pacing. It only needed a little more blood and little more patience. Eric knew where to go, now.

The second bag was nearly empty. The beast eagerly stood at the threshold. Eric latched the door and locked it with a silent promise. The beast stilled, for the moment.

Eric surveyed his brother and the Crimson Commander through hooded eyes. Jonathan's injury had finally healed beyond danger territory, but Eric's repeated assaults had turned it into a constant vulnerability. Alex's only weakness was his duty to protect the syringe of Eric's blood and the precious the vial. Eric drew in another deep breath. It seeped out between his lips. The air recoiled from building tension.

"Please don't," Alex whispered without looking up.

Eric was already moving, gut punching Jonathan and lashing his heel at Alex. Glass shattered under his foot and Jonathan fell to his knees coughing up blood. Paresh's blood blossomed on Alex's shirt as he fumbled with the warming packs to grab the venom. Pressing Jonathan's Vampiric Star, Eric opened Animus Hollow and kicked Jonathan inside, and then deflected Alex in after him. Eric removed the IV line and disappeared into his own Hollow portal.

Donovan was a creature of habit who favored one hot spring resort on the Japanese island of Hokkaido. It was more modern than the one Eric knew Jonathan preferred, but most of the resorts had similar layouts depending on the terrain. Luckily for him, and stupidly for

Donovan, the Hollow exited directly onto the grounds, but the instant he stepped out, Paresh's blood scent would hit the air and alert Donovan. He had to be quick.

A faint electrical odor mingled within the strong sulfuric atmosphere of the springs. Binding himself within his aura, Eric ran unseen along a tall wooden fence and heard Donovan's telltale moan. His internal fire flared and the beast screamed for blood. He leaped upon a steep rocky ledge and got eyes on Donovan—seemingly alone and stretched out in the water. The hunters couldn't use electric weapons against Eric without hitting their detail. Perfect.

The beast rattled its cage and pried at the bars. Eric released his aura and jumped. Donovan saw him a fraction of a second before he landed and managed to dodge. Ghostly splashes sounded as three cloaked hunters leaped at Eric from behind.

Time slowed to crawl as Eric drew a breath down his throat and let the lock slide open. The beast hungrily took control, easily shrugging the hunters off and shredding Donovan's chest like cloth. Shrieking in pain, Donovan lashed wildly at Eric's face. Blood poured into his eyes, but his fist was already slamming into Donovan's cheeks and nose. He didn't need to see to make contact.

Invisible hands tried desperately to pull him off. Eric was too far gone—deafened to the beast's roars and blinded to its violent bloodlust. Saliva ran torrents off his chin as he savagely tore into Donovan and ripped off flesh in fistfuls. Eric roughly grabbed again and caught something unseen—a throat. He snarled and squeezed. The body dropped with a large splash. Eric tried again, this time catching a fistful of Donovan's hair. Chunks audibly ripped from his scalp as he clawed for escape.

Eric swept Donovan's feet and jumped on him, forcing him under the water. More hands futilely attempted to pull him off. His elbow connected and shattered a nose. An arm was trapped across his torso. He twisted and snapped the bones. The hunters dove under and pushed up from below, gaining enough traction to bring a gasping Donovan to the surface. Eric screamed an unnatural sound and hooked his claws into Donovan's neck.

Too late, he felt Alex's enraged presence at his back. The needle punctured his carotid artery, and the mixture of box jellyfish venom and Paresh's blood squeezed his brain like a vice. Alex rendered him unconscious in the one agonizing second he'd needed to slit Donovan's throat for good.

☽ ❋ ☾

ALEX

Panting for breath, he held Eric's head above water. The entire spring was the color of blood—and not just because he was seeing red. Large flaps of skin and strips of connective tissue bobbed in the current. Clumps of wavy brown hair twirled in circles.

Seneca was going to yell. A lot.

"Uncloak!" Alex barked.

Charon materialized, huffing through his mouth with blood gushing from his crushed nose. He looked dazed but had enough bearing to dip his chin. His short dark hair was plastered to his head. "My lord—"

"Commander is fine—just...catch your breath, damn it." Alex managed not to snap, but patted the air impatiently. Deep gashes marred Charon's face and neck. "You need medical clearance. The others?"

Charon hit another unseen wrist switch, and Taryn appeared, propped against him, unconscious with blood oozing from her mouth and her broken arm. Donovan surfaced, moaning through swollen lips, his cheeks smashed in, and an eye socket shattered. His jaw was broken, again, and Eric had torn off large chunks of his flesh. He was barely alive and at risk of bleeding to death.

Dread chomped down on Alex's ribs. "Where's Urien?"

Charon shook his head. "Lord Eric got him."

Alex touched his brow and exhaled slowly. He tapped the communicator and opened a channel to Kestrel. "Both of you report to my location, directly."

Next, he called Seneca, now the Commander of the Crimson Guard with Minerva as Co-Commander and First Officer. "Seneca...you need to join me—bring additional officers. We have a casualty."

Through clenched teeth, he added, "Not the one we'd welcome."

He slapped Donovan on the back of the head and kicked him under the water. "*You are a fucking waste of air! I should let him kill you! Curse you like Prometheus to suffer eternally without a chance of salvation!*"

Seneca tapped Alex's shoulder. He got in one more kick before grunting and slicking his hair back. "I know, I know...but...*fuck!*"

She firmed her hand and trained her eye on Donovan, staying at Alex's side as portals opened and closed, and hunters appeared and disappeared. Kestrel and Sarah arrived first and took Donovan into custody. Together with Charon and Taryn, they left for Eido. Meanwhile, Valerian and Lenore arrived with Minerva, and fished for

Urien's body. When they uncloaked him, his neck was pulp and his head was missing.

"Another member of the pack, down," Seneca snapped, flicking disgusted eyes at Eric. "He's already cost us Raven and Rowan, and he nearly killed the pack leader last time. How many more must I waste on that traitor?"

"I swear on the Daughter of Night, I'm about to lose my shit. *None of this is on him.*" Shrugging her hand off, Alex pulled Eric to the rocky ledge. "It's on Donovan and the COMS. Find Urien's head. Clean up and do damage control."

"As you wish…*High* Commander."

"Watch your tone," Alex warned. "No one likes this situation. If it wasn't so sensitive—"

"Yeah, you'd have the Vespers here to do their job instead of us, got it." She waved him off. "Take him. We've got this."

"I try *very* hard not to overstep with *your* squad," Alex said in a simmering, quiet voice. "Some might say I give you special treatment in that regard."

"But they don't because you aren't putting *their* hunters in jeopardy."

"Look." Alex forced a calmer tone. "The Crimson Guard's in good hands—I hope you know I truly believe that."

Seneca lifted her chin. "That doesn't stop them from looking to you when you're present."

"That won't last forever." He sighed and looked over the hellish scene. "And neither will this."

"Fair enough." Seneca crossed her arms. "So once this is all over, who takes over as VaSH High Commander?"

"Huh?"

"Aren't you expected to retire as a full time Elder?"

Alex threw his hands up. "Look, I don't even know if the world is going to survive whatever *this* actually is. I honestly hadn't planned on giving up any of my Commander titles—"

He held up a silencing finger before she could interrupt. "But, I always intended for you to take the Guard. I might still be the 'Crimson Commander,' but the squad is yours. I don't want it back."

"You'd have to pry it out of my hands anyway."

Alex thumped his heart. "Those are the words of a true Commander."

Seneca smirked. "You're not going to cry are you? I don't have Raven's patience to deal with you."

"I know," he said quietly.

"Sorry." Seneca awkwardly patted his head. "I miss her, too."

"We've all lost something in this mess." He jumped onto the rocks and pulled Eric out of the water. "He's going to be a handful when he wakes up—and Jonathan's going to…get moody…with the pack taking another loss. He wants me to reinstate Heron as pack leader, but the Wraith Reapers can't spare—"

"Hey," Minerva called as she surfaced on the far side, "I found his head."

"How do you clean blood from a hot spring?" Seneca asked, hopping up next to Alex. She squeezed bloody water from her blond ponytail.

"Down for maintenance? Let nature do the work?" Alex asked.

"I'll assign a watch until the biological trace is gone." Seneca nudged her chin at Eric. "Really, you should go. I'll take it from here and check for any incidental human witnesses."

"There shouldn't be any with Donovan here, but you never know." Alex's head bobbed. "Kestrel has Eric's blood. Fingers crossed that it works this time."

"And that Lord Eric didn't damage him too badly to delay delivery. He would've decapitated him if you hadn't gotten here when you did."

"The medical attention Donovan needs is going to destroy the scent and steam Kestrel was hoping to use," Minerva said. "*He's* wrecked the whole operation. It's not going to work."

"*Damn it.*" Alex fisted his hair.

"This can't happen again," Seneca said lowly.

"It shouldn't have happened at all." Alex hoisted Eric over his shoulder. "And it sucks. He's the victim, but gets the most punishment and blame."

Alex grunted. "Eric doesn't deserve it, but he didn't do himself any favors by pulling this again. We'll have to tighten our monitoring."

"Hey—we both know he's the only one left who can go berserk with a legitimate reason to stay that way." Seneca clenched her jaw. "I hate say this, but *when* it happens again, call me immediately and we'll get on it, too—more damage control and back up. Just…code word *Ravenscroft*. We shouldn't have dismissed the first time as a one off."

"Too bad the Arc of Celestial Night is gone," Minerva said. "He'd be far easier to handle if he was asleep."

Alex forced his spine to stay upright. He wanted badly to sag in defeat. So many *shoulda, coulda, wouldas*. Too many missed opportunities to avoid catastrophe altogether.

"Raven would have prepped for the first time," he said. The usual pang struck deeper and twisted sharper. "Maybe she'd even dig a regulator out of Eido's storage and do just that, but I can't do that to him."

To Seneca he said, "Do me a favor?"

"Of course."

"Act as my proxy at Eido and call a meeting for tomorrow evening. Commanders and First Officers. We need to compare notes."

"You want someone to dust off the High Commander's office?" Seneca attempted a playful jab, but they'd never had a casual relationship, so it was just…*weird*. "You haven't been there in years."

"Tell you what." Alex lifted his hand to scratch his ear, but stopped under her scrutiny. Sarah had her watching him now, too. "You use it."

"But—Kestrel? Shouldn't she be your number two? It was you and Raven, after all."

"Right, because of seniority, not position. You're my number two when I get to choose. Kestrel is my number two when I need her clearance levels."

She paused in thought. "Why *did* Raven break rank with Kestrel?"

"And this is where that clearance comes in—that's classified." Alex tipped the rim of an imaginary hat. "It's end of the world type stuff, you know—don't take it personally."

II

ALEX

Orison Crossing, Early Autumn 2021

The earliest violets of sunrise crested over a canopy that would soon glow with fiery autumnal color. The casements cleared to transparency with daylight, although the static charge of the anchor points remained visible.

Tipping his usual nod to Michael's avatar, Alex patted Grandfather Wisdom's trunk like an old friend. Paresh's golden stream was thin and frail. It had started dimming years back, but it was deteriorating quicker now.

"Morning Pare," he said softly. "I'm here. I don't know how many sunrises we've got left together."

He gingerly touched the stream. The orbs sluggishly lit up under his finger. She was still there. For now.

"Jonathan will try to come by tonight before the casements go dark." The orbs dulled as he lifted his finger.

"I'm so sorry, Pare." Regret swelled within his chest and stung his eyes. "I wish we'd found you. We should have. Everything seemed to stack against us."

He blinked his eyes clear and sniffled. "I wish they'd tell us where you are. Or let you out to say goodbye. Something. *Anything*."

He leaned his forehead against the coarse bark. Blazing light rose over the tree's eastern side, burying him in its mammoth shadow. He dug his fingers into the grooves.

"I love you so much, Pare. Please, please feel it. Don't drift away." Tears splashed dark spots onto the roots. "So much has gone wrong with this world. I don't even know if you'd want to come back to this, but—"

His throat clenched. *I won't stop searching. I promise. And we'll check on Eric today. I'm…I'm afraid of what we'll find. I always am.*

Splinters stabbed his fingers as he crumpled and sobbed into his free hand. It'd been fifteen years since Donovan hid her body, and somewhere in there, the bastard had stopped delivering Eric's blood. The timing likely correlated with her stream's degradation and when Donovan's aging hit an unexplained plateau.

They theorized that he'd started drinking the blood instead, but they couldn't risk not giving it to him. They tried injecting it into Grandfather Wisdom directly, given that the tree itself craved Eric's blood, and sure enough, it grew faster and shone with vibrant majesty—but nothing had changed for Paresh.

No one could deny the power in Eric's blood. It'd given life to a stillborn infant. It'd resurrected Paresh after a dagger to the heart. And until that selfish prick started drinking it to stop aging, it had kept Paresh's physical cells from decomposing even if it hadn't done a thing for her spirit. If Donovan had stopped upholding his end of their fucked up bargain, then he deserved every ounce of hell the Chthonic Knights would inflict. His security detail would soon become his wardens.

Alex gulped air by the lungful and twisted on his feet to sit amongst the roots as magenta softly faded into the blue of dawn's veil overhead. He perched his sunglasses on his nose.

The world had gone to Hell. The Red Horseman had pulled the one meaningful thread that held society together and unraveled it at a wicked pace to reach a prize beyond war. The War Horse sought out the Black Horseman, and together they ignited tensions along peaceful borders and in the backyards of ordinary people, while droughts, fires, floods, winds, and pests destroyed forests, crops, and habitats—human, animal, and vampire. They'd been arrogant to think the Horsemen wouldn't affect the Vampiric Nation.

He tipped his head back. Anxiety always nipped at his heels. If he stopped for even a moment, it crunched on him extra hard—like now.

He felt it, marching like ants in spiraling rows around his heart, their spiny feet digging in, multiplying and growing heavier. They blew into hummingbirds buzzing to escape his claustrophobic ribcage—only there was no escape, nowhere to fly, nowhere to go.

He shoved his palms under his sunglasses and counted to himself in the darkness. *One. Two.*

Gigantic craters in Siberia. Permafrost melt. The ground giving way beneath the Arc of Ebony Stars. Some had escaped into Animus Hollow. Most were impaled on the broken, jagged beams of their home—an arc that had been anchored into the Arctic Circle for more than a millennium.

Three. Four.

Four arcs down. The Arc of Celestial Night—gone. The Arc of True Blood—locked. The Arc of Ebony Stars—evacuated. The Arc of Mourning Eidolons—restricted.

Five. Six.

The remaining Asian-based arcs—evacuated until the Silent Vespers evaluated the terrain. The Vampire Shadow Hounds—overtasked and overworked with aging rogues. A third of their population moving into human society, irritated by inconvenience and growing impatience, waiting for arcs to be cleared or reinforced.

Seven. Eight.

A High Council not working so great. Lord Lucien—a recluse at the top of the world. Eric—lost to madness and grief. Jonathan— struggling to hold stressed Elders into unified governance.

Nine. Ten.

The White and Pale Riders had appeared—joining forces to usher in the Romanized year of MMXX. The Realm of Man stopped in an instant, and the veil hiding signs of the Biblical Apocalypse lifted from every human eye.

Alex half-laughed. The ants marched on and the hummingbirds flitted like crazy to get out, get out, out, *out!* He wished he didn't know how truly dire the situation was. That Kestrel and Sarah hadn't confirmed Lucifer's erosion of the barriers between Hell and the earthly plane at nearly every Celestial Landing Point.

The sun was a bright yellow ball in a giant blue sky now. Deeply entrenched in Grandfather Wisdom's shadow, he tossed his sunglasses into the grass and ran both hands through his hair. He tucked his head between his knees.

Breathe…just breathe…in, out, in, out.

It was bad. But there were silver linings that might matter if they survived *the end*, because in a year that shut the world down with a virus, delivered murder hornets, rocketed *Perseverance* off to Mars, and released actual UFO footage from the Pentagon, no one cared that vampires existed. The people in Orison Crossing waved it off as another oddity in the worst year of their lives—but they'd also been coexisting peacefully for more than a decade, whether they knew it or not. Hunters had stopped cloaking years ago and many used their immunity to the virus as an opportunity for outreach—to get to know the residents and ease their isolation and anxiety.

True bloods and altered vampires alike took that inspiration and found ways to help around the globe—they couldn't go home until the Vespers finished their assessments, and the Vampiric Nation had collectively envied the lives of men. It was hardly fair for them to wait a thousand years for the Second New Age to arrive only to sit back and watch the entire world die.

Alex had seized on the power of positive thinking and used Michael's avatar and Gabriel's presence in Sunset Grove to shape an avenue of hope within the Nation. It was the only thing helping him maintain what little order remained in the ranks—and he needed it more than most—

In, two, three, four. Out, two, three, four. In...

—because he knew it was going to get much, *much* worse. The sky had been darkening for some time as Darkesiel sped closer to Earth. As he'd blocked the light of more and more stars, the world's scientists had taken notice. But religious leaders had failed to quote the Book of Revelations—because the stars were supposed to fall like figs, not disappear.

He sucked in a deeper breath and held it. Hawkiel's premature apocalypse didn't play by The Book's rules. Only one star was falling—a massive black spot that no human had ever knowingly observed. In a world panicked into fatigue and fatigued into panic, Alex used the Nation's influence to point astronomers to the dimming of Tabby's Star and the possibility that the Milky Way had entered an ancient cosmic debris cloud.

His lungs were going to burst. He exhaled and plucked at the grass. After all *that*, he still had no idea what was going to happen when Darkesiel landed. No one had witnessed an angel falling to Earth—not even Lord Lucien—*not that anyone could ask him*. Would Darkesiel's entry destroy the planet? Leave a crater? Would he seesaw like a feather? Not only did no one know—no one knew if it even mattered. If stopping him meant stopping the Horsemen, or if they even *could* stop him—without Raven.

The ants stalled and started carving. Ugly tears burned his eyes and snot streamed from his nose. "Just when Poseidon said it was safe to go back into the water," he whined softly, hanging his arms over his knees.

He willed his mind to find a quiet place that matched Sunset Grove's haunting silence. Nothing made a sound. The air was stagnant. The ants and hummingbirds calmed and his heart resumed its normal programming. A simple thought popped into his head: maybe they'd let her out if he asked.

"Gabe…Michael…whoever—please let me talk to her," he begged, "please don't let her fade away. Restore her, help us—I want to do the right thing. I want to save her…and the world."

Snot dripped off his upper lip. "Please…"

He almost turned, confident that—in the light of day, even in the shade—Paresh's flowing essence would look sparkling and healthy, but he knew the sickly reality. And he had yet to check on Eric, who was probably half-dead. He choked out a sputtering sob and bawled into his hands, his shoulders shaking as he begged the angels to do something—anything—but knowing they wouldn't do either.

III

ERIC

Orison Crossing, Early Autumn 2021

Flat on his back, he listened to his heart clunk. Through the window, a crescent blur hovered in a persimmon smear. He'd lost track of the days—or weeks? Maybe years? Every day, he promised himself he'd go see Paresh. If he made it out the door, he'd stare at the southern trail. That's as close as he ever got. He always ended up on his empty grave, talking to Lucinda.

Maybe she heard him, maybe not. He liked to think she'd found peace long ago, but talking to her was his only catharsis.

A low noise rattled his eardrums. His eyelids fluttered and he realized he was groaning. Today—or maybe it'd been last week—he'd thought he'd try only walking to the trail. But he hadn't made it to the door. He hadn't gotten off the floor.

His head lolled left. That was Paresh's side of the bed. He envisioned the porcelain curvature of her neck under the moon's caress. Her soft skin beneath his fingers. Her girly laughs blossoming into womanly moans.

Hard boards dug into the dehydrated skin and bones of his back, but who was he to complain about a little discomfort after how many years of failure? After the fourth time, or maybe fifth…or was it more? His lungs fought against gravity to pull in a hollow sounding breath. It didn't matter—whichever time it was, it'd been the last—he'd failed to kill him. Every time he attacked Donovan, he only succeeded in killing or maiming the VaSH hunters.

He blinked. The moon was lower. Had he drifted off? It shouldn't take much longer.

For a while there, *they* strictly monitored his diet. No risks. No chances. No attacks. He was lucky they left him alone in the cottage. Each bag came with at least one drop of Paresh's blood to keep him sane.

They'd stopped pulling his blood to give to Donovan. Instead, they gave him *Jonathan's*, as her Bridge. Something about it not giving Donovan the same benefit—and he was smugly happy at that.

But he hated the way Alex held him down while Jonathan bit him. He bet Jonathan enjoyed it, though. Plunging him into an abyss of concentrated pleasure that he fought with every ounce of his being. He'd always hated it, but it was so much worse now. Again and again. Unable to stop it or to say *no*.

He never thought he'd regret not dying at Poison Spring. But he did. This wasn't living. He yearned for death.

The moon swirled a moment, as though rolling on tears, but his eyes were too dry to blink without scraping. Maybe he was hallucinating. Or maybe the moon was dancing.

A screen lit up beside his head. Squinting, he made out Sarah's contact picture. The low noise came again, gravelly and tattered. She texted him almost every day to lift his spirit—but it was really a reminder of her failure, because even though Kestrel said they only needed one chance, that one chance never came. And it never would—even the COMS seemed to understand that.

Hell. Lucifer knew where Paresh was. But he hadn't made a move, even as the VaSH hunted the COMS down one by one. If any remained, they were hiding. That snake was showing too many signs of aging and was slowing down, no longer so quick on his feet. Apparently, aging vampires were as prone to sudden death as humans. Eric didn't need to try to so hard. Donovan would die, thanks to Father Time.

The bedroom door swung open. Jonathan appeared, impeccably

dressed in a dark gray suit with matching fedora, hands on his hips and scowl on his face. Alex wouldn't be far behind. They'd stopped bringing the heralds after he tore one apart in a fit of beastly insanity. He wished they'd waited a few more hours.

"It's the usual drill with the fridge," Alex said from down the hall. "He hasn't had a single one."

"He has a death wish." Jonathan kicked the sole of his foot—he thought. He couldn't feel it. "Right? You want to go home to Lucinda where you belong and abandon Paresh, *again*, thinking she'll rest in peace without you?"

Alex came in scoffing. "You'd honestly rather reunite with your wife in death than with your soul mate in life?"

They had it wrong. He didn't want Lucinda. He wanted the one he didn't deserve, and he loathed the thought of leaving her alone with angels that held her captive in a tree. They should be together—he belonged with his family. Going to them should've been the easy answer all along, but it wasn't that simple.

"Can you talk?" Alex squatted to pinch his cheek and shook his head at Jonathan. "*Damn it*. It's not rebounding at all. I'm not sure if he can even hear us."

"His heart hasn't stopped, yet. He can hear us." Jonathan handed off the all too familiar tubing for IV catheterization. Alex cursed under his breath as he tried and failed to find a vein that worked. He pulled a vial from his shirt pocket and popped off the rubber top.

No! Eric tried to scream, which only gave Alex a slightly gaping mouth in which to pour the vial.

As the Fields closed in, Jonathan said, "Give him another," and ushered in two heralds.

Eric tried to plead with Alex, but he wouldn't look at him. He flooded desperation into his aura. Alex shook his head and withdrew another vial.

The heralds began packing his clothes and Jonathan disappeared. Eric drifted away from Alex and rushed into a euphoric haze swimming with cattail grasses, Heliopsis, and a bright, cheery ball in the center of the sky. Paresh knocked shoulders with him, giggling as she tucked a wild strand behind her ear.

"No…" The wind carried off his croaking moan. Paresh's smiling gray eyes sparkled brighter than the cosmos. He reached for her cheek, desperately yearning to vanish with her forever.

"I hate doing this to you, man." Alex's quiet voice filtered down from the heavens.

"I love you!" Paresh smiled wide and laughed. "I'm glad I get to see you in the Elysian Fields. It's been so long, though."

She tapped his nose. "I can't wait until we're reunited."

He couldn't speak. He couldn't feel her skin as she nuzzled his palm with her cheek.

She closed her eyes, bit her lip, and pulled in a long, deep breath. "I can't smell your cologne. I miss it."

Cupping his face, she dotted his lips with a kiss. "I miss you, my love." Her voice turned somber and secretive. "If you give up, I will never see you again. You mustn't do this to yourself."

Tears burned his eyes hotter than acid. "I'm so-sorry," he choked out, "so, so, so-sorry."

"It seems like he's talking to her." Alex's voice came from above, far, far away, like a god's. "I've never seen him do this before."

"He was trying to kill himself." Jonathan's anger slipped through like radio static. "I wouldn't be surprised if she snuck out again to reach him."

"He's in bad shape. They might've let her out."

"Well, he won't go to see *her*—"

"He doesn't need to worry about losing Lucinda," Alex said. "She's already gone."

"Which is exactly why he should go to Paresh instead." Jonathan's voice oozed disgust. "He doesn't even know her thread is splintering."

"Huh?" Eric tried to swim back to reality, but Paresh held his face steady on her.

"Hey my love, I'm over here. I don't get to see you much, you know." She playfully shoved his shoulder. "Pay more attention to me while I'm here."

"I'm sorry for not visiting." He glanced from her to the sky. "What…what do they mean?"

"It's okay." She nervously picked at her nails as the wind tossed her hair. "I understand that it's painful. Don't feel bad. I know where your heart is. And I know why you really starve yourself."

"I'm selfish." He tried to brush his hands through her hair, but he couldn't feel them. "I'm sorry…would you feel me if I did come?"

"Yeah, but I understand why you go there instead. It's okay. It's better." She sniffled.

He felt a rod slam into his heart. "Oh honey, I'm so…all this time…"

He gathered her into his arms and kissed her crown, her cheeks, her lips—he hoped. She'd never cried in the Fields before. "I'm so sorry. If only I'd known—"

Moisture swelled in her eyes. "I couldn't tell you…there are rules, you know, like last time."

"You couldn't tell Lucien what to do," Eric said, kissing her hands— he hoped. "But that was different—"

Pursing her lips, she shook her head. "But it's not…this is the world's fate—I can't—"

She whispered, "Maybe? I'm not supposed to, but…but, um, my body is *decaying*."

She sniffled again and rolled her eyes across the sky. "I wish…"

He brushed tears from her cheeks and tried to swallow over the lump in his throat. How could he have done this to her?

She glanced around nervously. Her voice quivered with panic. "I wish I was there with you. I miss you so much. I don't want to die—"

Suddenly, she was gone and he was hurtled away from the Fields so violently that his physical body bounced. Alex shrieked and jumped onto the bed.

"*What the…?*" Clutching his chest, Alex came back down. "Fuck all the wraiths on the River Styx, man!"

Eric clawed at Alex's leg, trying to pull himself up. "They took her away! *She's dying!*"

He rubbed a fist into his eye. "Those bastards took her and know where she is, *but they won't let her tell me!*"

"Jonathan! Um…*Jonathan!*" Alex threw his full weight onto Eric.

"I'm not fighting you!" Eric yelled, desperately trying to get his eyes to focus. "I need to go!"

Jonathan's shined leather Oxfords gleamed in his corner vision and his summery scent of honeysuckle nectar whooshed over him. The tall grasses and bright sun flashed in his mind. The Fields were empty now—they'd always be empty. They wouldn't let her come back, ever.

"*No!*" Eric screeched, shoving against Alex's chest. An IV was taped to his arm. "She's not there anymore! She broke the rules! *You don't understand!*"

"Do you have it?" Jonathan demanded.

"*No! No! Don't you dare! She broke the rules!*" Eric accidentally scratched Alex's face, leaving streaks of red behind. "*Please!*"

Dripping blood, Alex held Eric's arms and pleaded. "I really don't want to! Calm down!"

"*They know where she is!*" Eric screeched, fighting with every ounce of strength he had. Jonathan took over holding his arms and Alex slid down to control his legs. "*They're keeping her from me while her body rots in an unmarked grave! Let. Me. Go!*"

Jonathan slammed a thick syringe into his chest and depressed the plunger. An electric jolt squeezed every muscle and burned every nerve. The grasses swayed at his cheek, scraping skin off with each pass as puffs of searing wind burned his face. Pollen scratched his eyes like broken glass and his consciousness jerked him into a ditch of nails.

He howled in pain, convulsing and arching, repeatedly driving sharpened tips into his skin. Fire erupted along his arms and legs. Explosive pressure built within his head. He screamed, but no sound came out. When the crushing black finally came, he begged it to take him swiftly, but it crawled inch by inch, denying its mercy. This was no longer the Elysian Fields—it was Hell.

☽ ❋ ☾

"What did you do to him?" Sarah's voice shook with anger as light footsteps raced to his side. He wasn't on the floor—it was cushioning, more like a matt—

Damn it. He was in his bed. And it smelled like Jonathan and Alex.

"He didn't give us a choice!" Alex cried. "You think I *wanted* to do that to him? That was straight venom, not a mix! We could have killed him in his condition!"

"Which he would've welcomed. He was incoherent and too unstable," Jonathan said tightly. "Do not stretch your privilege as his friend by disrespecting your Commanders, First Officer."

"I will stretch whatever I see fit, *Master Jonathan*, because he is *family* and family *always* comes first!"

"Sar—" Eric tried to swallow. His throat wouldn't cooperate. He couldn't move. The blackness began to break apart. Grass whipped his cheeks. "Sa-Sarah?"

A warm hand slipped into his and squeezed firmly. Oh God, it burned so badly. "Thank God!"

"Don't…thank…*Him*." Eric's eyes rolled back against sandpaper eyelids.

"Don't you ever say that," she said, both snapping and pleading. She jerked his hand to her bosom. "He sent those angels to watch over her. They're doing a job, just like the rest of us. You wouldn't blame Walter if it was him and you know it."

"If Walter was your god," Jonathan muttered, "we'd all be dead."

"Hey-hey, don't fight to wake up. Let it come naturally," Sarah coaxed. His hand slipped free and landed heavily on his chest. As he moaned in agony, she leaned over him to whisper, "If you don't have the strength left to keep walking, *you know who does*."

Alex sighed. "We've given him two vials and five liters. His organs were shutting down when we found him. I'm surprised he's alive."

"It is good, then, that you arrived when you did, High Commander," Kestrel said. She was near the door. Eric hadn't noticed her presence.

"I hope he stays conscious longer," Sarah said, crushing his hand in her powerful grip. "If she really did appear to him, it'd make more sense out of what we felt."

Bright flashes zapped and sizzled behind Eric's eyelids. "What?" he croaked. "What…happp—"

Sarah squeezed his hand tighter. He groaned. "Don't exert yourself. We felt a…a…"

"Ping," Kestrel finished. "But it came from nearby, likely from her soul and not her body."

"Well, wait," Alex said. "Wait, wait, wait."

The calming black lulled Eric to return.

Alex snapped his fingers. "What if Donovan hid her body *here*?"

"Like in town?" Jonathan stood. Eric hadn't realized he'd been sitting beside him. "No way. Someone would've seen him that night."

"He wasn't wearing his cloak when he came back," Alex said. "He could've moved her without anyone noticing. He was covered in her blood, so it was already in the air, and…and after…afterward, her soul in the tree—"

"Would've masked her *fresh* body's essence!" Sarah interrupted.

"Exactly!" Alex said. "It's possible, right? We didn't know then what we do now and we weren't exactly thinking clearly."

"What if he left her in the forest?" Sarah asked. "*He* didn't need to cloak—if he cloaked *her*, he could've left her anywhere."

"And moved her easily," Jonathan said quietly. "We have hunters everywhere—there's no reason I'd find the scent odd—was he wearing his wrist switch?"

"I don't remember," Alex said.

"But wouldn't her body decay faster above ground?" Sarah asked.

"He teased me about digging," Kestrel said sourly. "For all we know, he might've buried her later. Or stashed her someplace arid for natural preservation."

"She sai—" Eric groaned. "She's die—decay…ing."

"Her thread is splintering, too," Jonathan said. "It has been for some time now.”

“My blood’s not enough.” Eric struggled to open his eyes and failed. “I swear I will murder you if you dose me again.”

“If you weren’t so hell bent on killing everyone in your path, it wouldn’t be necessary!” Jonathan snapped, shoving Eric’s limp legs aside to sit on the bed again. “You’ve wanted to let her die from the beginning. Why do you care now?”

“It’s a little different when you see her crying and scared. She was panicking when they ripped her away from me!” Eric fired back in a raspy voice. “Fucking angels…always taking her away from me. Damn it, I need a drink!”

“Donovan stopped giving her your blood,” Alex revealed. “The pack thought they saw his aging stop—”

“He’s drinking the blood to save his skin instead of giving it to her,” Jonathan interrupted.

“*That’s* why you’re biting me?” Eric demanded. “Why is he even alive? *Why?*”

“What if he only drinks some and gives her the rest?” Sarah asked.

“We couldn’t risk dooming her all together,” Kestrel said. “But he’s less interested in Master Jonathan’s blood.”

“Can you use that ‘ping’ to calibrate your sight to distinguish between her aura in the tree and any essence that might linger in her body?” Alex asked.

“We’ve never detected her body,” Kestrel said, “but her light is dim enough that we could investigate everything beyond that clearing.”

“If we focus on Grandfather Wisdom, we can push our sight out,” Sarah said. “And if we can see the Sunset Grove Parish—”

“—or the cemetery—” Kestrel’s voice was closer. “We’ll start a grid. Clear the forest first and work our way out.”

“And Donovan?” Eric growled.

“The Chthonic Knights would love to play with him,” Alex said. “Right, Sarah?”

“Oh, indeed.” She leaned over Eric to kiss his forehead. “You get better. Keep your faith that this will work out in the end, okay?”

He blew out a shaky breath. “Find her. Sh-she’s terrified.”

Sarah and Kestrel’s presences disappeared and Alex’s moved closer. “Is that what happened?” he demanded. “She told you?”

Eric nodded again. The pain he’d seen in her eyes…heard in her voice…

He was on his back, so his tears pooled in his ears. “And they took her away for it."

"You weren't fighting us," Jonathan whispered under his breath.

"I haven't given you any reason to think otherwise," Eric said, sniffling as his voice caught. "It was horrible, Jonathan. I've never been more afraid for her."

"I'm going to go see her right now," Alex said.

"She…" Eric huffed and tried to control his voice, but it was as broken as he was. "Sh-sh-she said, uh, that she could…she'd feel me…if…"

Jonathan stood and swore again.

Alex took his spot, sitting on the bed beside Eric. "I've gone to see her almost every day. I know it's not the same, but at least she wasn't alone."

"That's not it," Jonathan said before Eric could reply. "I have his blood in me—I'm her Bridge—and lately I haven't—"

"You berated me for not going to see her?" Eric asked. "But you weren't going—"

"No!" Jonathan flew back over. "It's not the same! I wasn't *avoiding* her—I was holding our Nation together! I went every chance I got!"

"Those have just been infrequent lately," Alex added. "And besides, Jonathan isn't *you*—it's not *his blood* she needs—it's *you*."

"Look, I'm sick of fighting," Jonathan said. "You have no idea what's been going on in the world—we need to pull it together. So are we going blame each other or—"

"No—" The fear and sorrow in Paresh's eyes looped through Eric's mind. "From here on—it's about her. I want to see her whether I can open my eyes or not. Let's go."

IV

LUCIEN

Foothills of Mount Fuji, Japan, ca. 200 B.C.

"I don't understand your insistence on doing this," Jonathan whined, dragging his feet up the hillside. "Biting them is so much easier and you can see the mountain from the village."

"The humans here have changed much since I left." Lucien paused beneath a blooming cherry tree and nodded across the lake at the majestically capped mountain. "But they still hold that sacred, and I lived there for half my life wanting little more than to understand why I existed and to coexist with nature."

He cupped a delicate pink blossom. "I haven't achieved either."

He set a bamboo tray on the ground and folded his legs beneath him. The ceremony of tea drinking was a recent arrival here. He couldn't partake in its traditional form, but he'd found a ritual that enhanced his meditation. Jonathan leaned against the trunk and alternated between staring across the lake and watching him.

Placing drinking bowls beside each other, Lucien said, "The tribes were smaller and lived in domes built directly on the ground. The settlements nearest me established fenced perimeters—"

"To keep *you* out?" Jonathan scoffed and crossed his arms. "I bet that didn't work out so well for them."

"They looked to superstition and found false safety in the daylight. They fought for survival and lost." Lucien patted the grass beside him. "Join me."

As Jonathan sat, Lucien smashed stones together to spark a fire in a wide, shallow bowl. "But I also lost. So, I started to walk."

He set a kettle into the fire. Jonathan gave him a questioning look. "It mustn't boil and can only sit at the desired temperature for a few seconds."

At Jonathan's unchanged visage, Lucien added, "When you go off to hunt, I learn new skills—like the one that led to your gift."

Jonathan absently touched his ribbon. "So, this—" He glanced at the kettle and bowls. "—is special, too?"

Lucien nodded. "Our village isn't like the others—the men there traveled the same trade route as us and formed those dwellings on the hillside as outliers to avoid attention."

"But they farm and fish like the other villages."

"They also brought new techniques and beliefs, call themselves monks and brothers, work quietly, and meditate—"

"Without women." Jonathan's mouth gaped. "I hadn't noticed."

"You don't stay long before you head out."

"There's not much here. They bicker about annoying, miniscule things. But there is a thrumming undercurrent like the one on the mainland—war is coming. I won't stay bored for long."

Lucien hid his disappointment and pulled the kettle from the fire. He poured water into the bottom quarter of the drinking vessels. Steam gently puffed off the surface. Human tea ceremonies used bamboo ladles and caddies, and poetic movements, but he could only mimic that grace. He hoped meditation might tame Jonathan's bloodlust and give them more downtime together.

"The people here revere nature," he said, "and fears of the *Waira* kept many away from my territories in the forest—"

"Do you want to live in trees again?"

A small smile tugged on Lucien's lips at the horror on Jonathan's face. "Not at all. I was quite relieved to see structures upgraded to wooden foundations with beam posts and sturdy, thatched roofs that block the rain."

He returned the kettle to the dying fire and lifted the large kettle. Fresh blood poured from the spout into the hot water. Though it was unnecessary, and he needed to be careful not to break the cells, he enjoyed incorporating the whisk. He stirred gently to mix the water and blood and handed a bowl to Jonathan. He took up the other. They nodded to each other and sipped.

His smile widened at Jonathan's appreciative moan. Though diluted, blood warmer than the typical human body temperature settled in the belly with a comforting weight. Jonathan finished his bowl and set it upon the tray, nudging it to Lucien for more.

Lucien arched a brow. "I thought it was easier to bite them?"

Jonathan's gaze drifted from Lucien's kettle to the mountain's reflection in the lake. He sighed contentedly and touched his ribbon again. "This is peaceful. Special."

"Indeed." Lucien invited Jonathan to drink from his refilled bowl. "The benefit of not killing the men we live with…they have no reason to fear or kill us. I simply puncture a vein with my finger and fill the pot—"

"They would kill you if they saw your face," Jonathan said.

"Perhaps." Lucien sipped and gazed upon the mountain. "Enthralling them removes that threat. The cloak does the rest."

He finished his bowl. "I like to meditate after drinking. Join me?"

Jonathan shook his head. "But I'll stay and not interrupt if you hunt with me tonight—I…I miss our hunts together."

"I suppose returning here awoke something of the old days in me," Lucien said. "Perhaps I'm seeking to find now what I could not find then."

"This seems to be a start," Jonathan said with a jealous bite to his voice. "Those men and that mountain get more attention from you than I do."

He cupped Jonathan's cheek. "I do not seek to coexist with them— only you, but we've learned that coexisting makes our lives more…*comfortable*."

Jonathan grinned. "Come with me tonight. We can travel as far you like and decimate whole villages—bring war a step closer through fear. Pit them against each other."

Jonathan could easily recreate the chaos of the warring states they'd left behind. If violence came to the region, the peace in his village would not survive.

Jonathan sat cross-legged with his feet bouncing under his knees. Lucien had to acknowledge a truth he'd tried hard to suppress: he and Jonathan excelled in different elements.

"Lucifer gave you a purpose," Lucien began reluctantly, "but I am still searching for mine. I carry wrath, to be sure, but I do not find as much thrill where you thrive."

"But we are gods of death," Jonathan said. "We glide through battle together—that's our purpose."

"I was not given a purpose. I was not given knowledge. I was thrust into this world and left to learn on my own." Lucien swept his hand over the tray and up to the mountain. "This is where I found peace, and peace enabled me to transform myself from a tortured, armored monster into the being I am today. Yet I am incomplete."

Jonathan sat quietly with that awhile. Lucien closed his eyes and began his meditative breathing, inhaling deeply through his nose and expanding his belly, and exhaling steadily out through his mouth as his belly deflated. His aura relaxed and streamed in cleansing air.

Jonathan didn't move or interrupt him. When Lucien opened his eyes, the moon was rising over the mountain's snowcap.

"How long do you intend to stay here?" Jonathan asked quietly.

"I hadn't thought about leaving. This is my home."

Jonathan's jaw clenched. The veins in his eyes began to bulge. "How can you admit our differences, yet settle here knowing I am tethered to you? Do you not care that I am bored and restless? That my joints ache from inactivity? That I'm *sleeping* more because of it?"

"Meditating—"

"Does *nothing* for me!" Jonathan exploded, leaping up and ripping off a flowering branch to bat at the tea set and tray. "I am a beast! You are a beast! We are meant to be beasts together, not play house among the humans we should destroy!"

Lucien quelled the anger stirring in his gut. The rage in Jonathan's aura prickled his skin He pulled his aura in protectively.

Jonathan growled at Lucien's silence. "I want to go back to the wars of the mainland! They have mountains and...*tea*. You can pretend to be human there."

"I do not desire to be human," Lucien said. "And I don't care for *those* mountains—*this* mountain was my home for six hundred years! You've never lived in one place long enough to understand what that means!"

Wild savagery gleamed in the blackness of Jonathan's eyes. He growled again and ran down the hill, thrashing bushes and trees with his lengthened claws. His disgusted, animalistic screeches and screams echoed throughout the night. Warning flame signals popped up from village to village.

"Spread your wrath beyond nearby villages that will seek retribution!" Lucien warned lowly as cries of "*Waira!*" echoed within his mind. Jonathan's regional assessment was correct—civil war was coming, and his strategic bloodlust would spur frenzied battles that would rival the warring states *he'd* sought to leave behind.

But, more than that, Lucien knew that Jonathan's restless nature, coupled with envy and rage would turn his episodes of blind bloodlust closer to home, and none of those monks would survive. Their deaths might even plunge their neighbors into power grabs under the guise of revenge—regardless of the *Waira's* return. The old stories told them how they'd forced him to flee—that they'd set the wood aflame. They'd do it again. He picked at the broken pottery—shards of the life he wanted, but would never have—and chased after Jonathan.

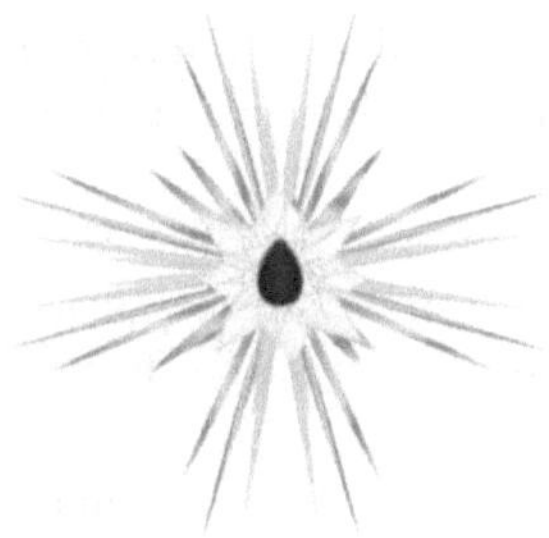

Chapter Twelve: Stars by Day; Stars by Night

I

ERIC

Orison Crossing, Autumn 2021

He was still a man divided, but the day seemed hopeful—like something big was going to happen. The sun had yet to rise when he parked at the carriage house and the air was crisp with renewed purpose. But fifteen years of despair and a straight dose of venom weren't so easily overcome.

The cottage was dark. Empty. The southern trail seemed impossibly far away. Blood infusions had flushed the toxin, but the effects were there in the tingling that shot up his feet and into his legs, and in the vast web of synapses that fired throughout his body with each tug of his jumpy nerves. He ran his hands through his hair and tried to shake it off.

Nope. That wasn't enough. He had to force it.

He set off into a jog. Up the flagstone, around the cottage, across the clearing's back half to the trail. There, he stopped. He closed his eyes, saw the fear in Paresh's eyes, and bolstered his resolve. He crossed the tree line and fell into an old rhythm. The beat of his feet on the forest floor was same as it'd been when he'd run during the ten years Paresh was missing. He'd faced her then; he could do it again.

The glow from Grandfather Wisdom illuminated the trail's mouth, and Eric saw Alex kneeling before Paresh's golden ribbon—fractured and sickly as it was. His heart broke into even smaller pieces at the sight of the tiny lights that languidly moved beneath Alex's fingers. They perked up when Alex cast a sideways glance at him.

Eric held his hands up. "I didn't mean to interrupt. I didn't hear you leave this morning."

"You were conked out on the sofa." Alex lifted his face to the higher—thinner—reaches of the stream. He had yet to look Eric in the eye. "I didn't think—man, Kestrel said she wanted to observe you by 'day' so I thought—"

He tousled his spikes and stood. "You should be here. I'll go."

"Stay." Eric backed onto the trail. "I'm the interloper. Be with her now. I'll be here all day."

Alex dropped to his knees. The lights bounced to life under his palm. "She's happy you're here. Come on over—there's room."

"Are you sure, Alex?" Eric asked. "I have so many amends to make—"

"Stop. This is her time."

"Yeah." Eric joined Alex, afraid to touch the stream, but lured by warmth. The full length of it flashed when he made contact.

"Wow," Alex whispered. The mood within his aura soured, directed at Eric, contempt that he knew he deserved.

All the time he'd wasted wallowing…he should have been here—with her, for her. "I'm so sorry, Paresh."

"Alex?" Emerging from the thick brush of the western edge, Kestrel asked, "Why are you here?"

He glared over his shoulder. "I watch the sunrise with her like every day."

"But I thought you knew—"

"That we were on watch today." Sarah was a silhouette at home with the forest's darkest secrets.

Alex stood and waved. "Look, I'm gonna go. You guys do your thing—I have a ton to catch up on anyway. Good luck. Bye, Pare."

Guilt pinched Eric, but before he could stop Alex, the orbs brightened beneath his palm. Sarah whooped under her breath.

"Did you see that?" she asked Kestrel.

"And felt it. They won't let her out again," Kestrel replied, "but they're letting her interact more than they have recently."

"It looks like you should be able to feel her, Eric," Sarah said.

"My hand is warm, but…I don't feel *her*—I feel drawn by…comfort?"

"Is that what you felt in the Elysian Fields?" Sarah asked.

Envisioning the sunny ditch and Paresh at his side, he said, "Yes."

"Oh!" Kestrel yelped in surprise. "My vines! It's like she's sending energy pulses, but I don't want to ask and risk them shutting her off."

The holy flame burning in Saint Michael's eyes left no doubt, whatsoever, that he was aware of every happening in that clearing. Eric nudged his chin up. "Whatever she's doing, he's permitting it."

He stroked the stream. "Hey honey. Hi baby." At the catch in his voice, the lights stirred into a frenzy. "I wish I knew her name."

The warmth pulled back and rammed his hand—like a kick. He chuckled quietly. "We never got to talk about it, did we? Lucinda chose Darien's name after my mother's father, and we only considered our mothers for a girl."

"Don't stop," Kestrel whispered.

Eric pulled a tissue from his pocket and wiped his nose. "But, Victoria and Collette are a bit old-fashioned, right?"

The orbs rippled upward. "Celeste, huh? It's perfect, honey."

"How did you…?" Kestrel asked. "Is she talking to you?"

"No, that's not it," he said with a smile.

"You're connected." Sarah touched Kestrel's lower back as she stepped into the clearing.

"Yeah, we get that," Kestrel said.

"I need a Sarah and Eric moment," Sarah said, running over to hug him. "Your baby's name is Celeste! That's so exciting!"

He gave her a gentle squeeze. "Thanks, Sarah. It means a lot to me that you've done all that you have. I know I haven't—"

"Hey," Kestrel interrupted, "like Alex said—this is her time."

Sarah closed her eyes and stroked the light. Eric swore he felt Paresh's essence sweep through him.

"Your connection to her is so strong," Sarah whispered, lifting her hand. "And her presence is even stronger with you here."

"Gabriel adores her. I bet he's pulling every trick he can think of to help us. The fibers of probability are likely moving closer to the fibers of light and dark…they probably don't look great."

Kestrel grunted. "Focus!"

Eric sputtered out a genuine laugh and the lights flickered in harmony. "That was such a Raven moment. God, everything felt normal just then."

Sarah patted him on the back and returned to Kestrel's side. "It was very much a Raven thing. I guess you learned a few things from the Commander while I was gone?"

Kestrel rolled her eyes. "You were not gone that long, My Light."

They retreated into the shadows and Sarah teased, "It must be Walter's influence, then, m'lady. Does he also call you Vampire Hunter?"

"No, it's not, and no, he doesn't." Kestrel pushed Sarah, who impishly shoved her back.

"Mr. Ravenscroft, talk to her and be with her, and we'll keep watch—no one else is within range, so say whatever you want."

"Thanks, Sarah." Eric squatted and gnawed the inside of his cheek. The orbs flickered. "Talking to you was always easy...like I'd known you forever, but now...I feel—no, I *know* I've let you down. And I know this is your time, but it's also our time, right?"

The light winked in agreement. "So, I won't...I won't do 'what ifs,' okay? Because once I start, I won't stop."

He wiped his nose again. "I wasn't strong for you—I don't deserve to be called your Anointed Strength. But I want to do better. To *be* better."

The light struck his palm with the heat of skin-to-skin contact as though she was standing there, holding his hand. "Paresh, you are so much stronger than I am," he said, swallowing over a lump. "I was such a coward, giving up on you, on our little girl...on myself. I've never gone to such dark places before—"

His breath shuddered as he collapsed against the tree, holding onto her light as a life raft in his sea of guilt, his shoulders quaking as he wept deeply from his soul. "I wish you could put your arms around me—I need you—and I hate myself for it. *You're* the victim, the one in danger—*you* need me and I'm still not strong enough."

Fifteen years in the darkness, fighting the beast and his grief...he was a fool to think he could change after one night of revelation—that he could forgive himself and be the man she needed. The man she deserved. The man that put her first, but he wasn't sure if that man would ever exist again.

☽ ❋ ☾

Constant reminders of life *before* had turned the cottage into a prison. Itching to get out, Eric paced a moonlit swath of rose-colored carpet, amped up and ready for the signal. Kestrel said their collective sight worked best at night and she wanted him at the cemetery to avoid contaminating their grid.

He crossed to the dining table and rested his fingertips lightly upon the surface. Through the window, the forest's inky depths laughed at his self-loathing, emboldened by the rising pale moon.

Doubt's vice squeezed his heart. He ground his teeth. The table groaned. Glossed wooden fibers stretched and snapped. He heard, "Go!" and bolted outside, his heels pounding the flagstone path.

The ghosts weren't gone either. Tonight it was Nathaniel, who'd cast his wife aside as a forgotten *thing* after she bore him a son. He'd stolen her life, her vibrancy, her freedom, and run wild at parties, sleeping with other women only to spiral into inexplicable madness after Elizabeth's suicide. How could a man who beat, abandoned, and cheated on his wife suffer such grief? Nathaniel would've killed Elizabeth had she not killed herself.

But that was it, wasn't it? Nathaniel hadn't loved her. He'd loved *controlling* her and she'd stolen that power from him by dictating the terms of her death. Was *he* any different? After not honoring Paresh's wishes in death?

He ran hard all the way to the Cemetery of Eternal Hope, past its crumbling pillar, and didn't stop until he saw Lucinda's name. So jittery with anticipation, he rambled incoherently until the jumbled mess in his head untangled and he quieted.

The marker's pitted marble, as a reminder of time's passage, hit him more severely than usual. Not only did everything age, everything decomposed.

What would Paresh look like when they found her? How much had she decayed? Would she heal? Had she aged? Had he done irreparable damage to her by not doing anything?

If he hadn't accepted Jonathan's offer—if he'd died on the battlefield that day—he wouldn't be sitting on an empty grave. A vampiric legacy wouldn't have upended the Hawthorne family's trajectory. Paresh wouldn't exist in a tree after enduring trauma upon trauma and three deaths.

You said no 'what ifs.' His words. Her voice.

Sighing in frustration, he rolled his shoulders and tried to relax. This thought cycle had to stop. Rolling his gaze up to the stars, he glimpsed a flash of neon pink. His heart jumped.

"Raven?" He focused on the collapsing brick column and the fingers creeping over its broken mortar.

A tentative sliver of pink hair appeared, followed by a rounded cheek and a nervous, darkened eye. One fang hooked her lower lip as she slipped into full view and clasped her hands behind her back, her gaze studious and her aura as alert as a doe studying a hunter.

She gnawed her lip and drew blood. "I...I didn't mean t-to spy. I've just...wanted to meet you for s-so long." The girl grinned uncomfortably, her stare dropping and then rising hopefully.

"Who are you?" Eric asked. The girl physically looked older than Raven and was slightly taller, on the lanky, skinny side of thin, unnaturally pale from once-human skin, with the aura of an awkward teenager. She looked familiar, but the girl in his mind was younger, maybe half the age of her appearance, but he couldn't place her or the memory. "I thought you were—"

"Raven?" She twisted a finger through her hair. "I knew her as a child…I mean, I'm like a fan girl, I suppose? Once human, like you, but totally enamored by her. She was just the coolest and then she disappeared."

The girl took a step forward and stopped as though expecting a reaction. She shrugged and flicked her hair. "So I bleached out the black and did this kind of as a way to remember her? I guess? If that makes sense?"

"You've never walked on holy ground as a vampire, have you?" Eric had noticed that her first step beyond the entrance was nearly identical to Jonathan's at the church for Molly's reception. "It won't hurt you."

"Y-yeah." She forced another step. "But, well, we're supposed to live by the old rules, right? I really didn't mean to disturb you, I…" She half-turned. "I should go."

"How long did you know Raven?" Eric coaxed her to face him and take another step.

Blood trickled down her chin. He didn't recognize the scent. It was…unique and oddly metallic for a vampire.

"A-all my life, really. But she hardly knew I was around for most of it—maybe like one of those 'admiring from afar' kind of deals?"

She quickly waved her hands. "N-not like a crush though! I mean, that's fine and all—well except maybe for stalkers? But…I…I guess I wanted to be like her when I 'grew up' except that, well, I'm a vampire, so…"

Eric grinned in spite of himself. "No growing up?"

The girl nervously dug the toe of a platform boot into the grass. She must have been altered in her mid-to-late twenties, although she dressed and acted much younger in a denim short skirt and a white halter-top with rainbow suspenders and thigh-high striped socks.

"Is your appearance a way of honoring Raven?" Eric asked. She put him at ease in much the same way as Raven had. Her aura, despite her nerves, lacked the scarring that true bloods carried from fighting in the

Great Holy War—although, he didn't know if that was unusual for an altered vampire. He hadn't met many former humans.

"Um, my name's S…" She wiped her chin with the back of her hand. "Bad habit. Um, Seren—it means 'Star.' And it's just the hair. I can't imagine Raven wearing something like this! But I…recently learned that I want to enjoy each day and rainbows help me see the world through different eyes."

"Carpe diem?"

"Quam minimum credula postero!" She swung down into a laughing bow. "You can't ever count on tomorrow—I suppose that's ironic for a vampire."

"It's not a bad way to live at the best of times, but it's especially pertinent now." He sighed and glanced up at the stars.

Seren continued her slow advance. Keeping his gaze high seemed to give her more freedom to fight her nerves. He had to admit this was a nice change—someone actually wanted to be near him. That made him wonder who was watching him, and, by proxy, Seren—unless she was the one watching him.

He threw a deliberate look that stopped her dead. "Are you a VaSH hunter?"

She cocked her head. "Human-born vampires can't be VaSH hunters—" She made a thoughtful noise and tilted her head to the other side. "Well, except for that lady First Officer with the Wraith Reapers, but she got special permission or something. I'm not really clear on it. Raven's not there anymore, so I don't pay attention."

"I didn't mean to scare you," Eric said apologetically. "I've always got eyes on me. I thought maybe they were trying something new."

"Oh…" Seren turned in a circle. "So…someone's watching me, right now? One of the VaSH?" Her hands flew to her cheeks. "Oh, I'd die if Raven saw me right now!"

"How'd you know I'd be here?" He let his gaze settle into her bones. The reminders of Raven's absence were riling up the beast. Their truce had ended long ago and he couldn't control its impatience swelling in his chest. He should've asked Alex—

"Um, well—" She blew a burst of air over her upper lip and dug her fang deeper into the lower one. "Y-you're something of an urban legend, you know? And, well, like a cat—I was curious. There's been such an upheaval—no matter the secrets and shushing, one ripple in the Nation grows bigger the farther out it goes."

"Okay, I get that. But how'd you find me *here*? And do you realize how dangerous this is?" He looked at his hands and imagined the blood that should be there. "I've killed VaSH hunters. The Commanders are scared of me. The Elders, too, if I'm honest, which I shouldn't be."

"Oh." She studied the grass, her boot tip swiveling a crescent patch. "It's well-known that Master Jonathan likes this village. Lesser so about all the——"

She dropped her voice and whispered past the back of her hand. "*Secret stuff.*"

Kinking her neck, she finished, "Also, I saw you run out of the forest."

"Do we need to back up to the stalker part?"

Her eyes rolled skyward. "Well…maybe a teensy bit? But not in a creepy way, at all, I promise. I only recently figured it out and found what I was looking for." She held her hands up. "It's like meeting Big Foot or the Mothman or something."

"They'd be more interesting, I'm sure." He sniffed and scrutinized the cemetery. The electrical odor of a VaSH cloaking mechanism was getting closer.

"Whoever's out there," he said in a deep voice, "you are hereby bound to confidentiality of what you've witnessed here and are relieved of all duties. I don't care who you are, you are no longer a VaSH hunter. Report to the High Commander with orders for a civilian downgrade. He's lucky I'm not sending a body back."

Seren's aura and body went rigid. "Um…"

Eric draped an arm over his knee and pinched the bridge of his nose. The odor was gone. "You're fine. I'm just…tired."

"I-I really shouldn't have bothered——" She took a step back.

"Look, honestly, this is the first normal conversation I've had in more than a decade," he said, tossing his hand up. "It's nice, so don't apologize. You didn't do anything wrong."

He sighed and hung his hand off his nape. "I come out here to clear my head, but it never works. I'm stuck in a loop of self-destruction."

He gestured at her and chuckled. "But you, you're all rainbow-y and bright-y. How can that not lift a spirit?"

"Can I…" Blood trickled from her lip. "Come back, then?"

"I can't promise I won't hurt you," Eric warned.

"I'm smart enough to use my judgment." She nodded and threw up a peace sign before jogging back to the entrance. "I'll see you again, Mr. Ravenscroft!"

"Wait——"

"What the hell?" Alex demanded, charging through the arborvitae at the end of the row. "What was that all about? I didn't put anyone on you tonight!"

"Then they shouldn't have the job anyway, so what's the problem?" Eric demanded.

Alex ruffled his spikes. "You're not the only one the VaSH follows, you know! Donovan slipped his damn detail and they thought he came here."

"Well he didn't. Otherwise he'd be dead and I'd be much happier."

"Of course, 'much happier' equates with more murder-y." Alex snorted.

"In his case, yes," Eric replied tightly. Warning flared from his aura as the pit in his chest turned into a squeezing cage. "Do you disagree?"

Alex held out a hand. "Look, man, I don't want to fight tonight, 'kay? Can you rescind your order so I can get him back on Donovan?"

"Sure." Eric said through clenched teeth. "Give me a vial. This area is off limits. You need to leave now."

"Yeah, noted," Alex said, tossing a silicon tube from his pocket and tapping his Vampiric Star. "It was an honest mistake. Believe me, no one in their right mind wants to be anywhere near you."

☽ ✳ ☾

Cold morning dew soaked his shirt as the sun yawned over the arborvitae. Cracking his neck and stretching, he admonished himself for chasing Alex off instead of asking for help.

"You need to walk away from the dark places, Eric," he muttered. "Make amends. Don't make it worse."

Already late, he used Animus Hollow to get to Sunset Grove. Kestrel waved him over to where she and Sarah stood in the tree's looming shadow. "Say good morning. Our report can wait."

"Did Alex come today?" Eric asked.

Sarah shook her head.

Eric sighed. "I'm sorry, Paresh. God, I'm going to be apologizing for a long time. I don't want to rob you of your mornings with him. But, he's not happy with me."

He kissed his fingers and pressed them to her fading light. The particles flashed. "But, I'm here—good morning, my love."

A line of orbs imitated a digitized backflip and cheering crowd. It was amazing to watch. And overwhelming. His heart leaped into his throat.

"And Celeste, of course! Daddy missed you, too." Talking to his daughter felt both foreign and natural. "I can't wait to meet you, sweetheart."

Heat ignited beneath his palm. "I don't know where to begin to make up for my failures, Paresh," he whispered. "It's like the past fifteen years were a dream. I was just—"

He shook his head. "I'm anxious about being here. I feel like I'm stealing you from Alex. You chose him; he should be here when he wants—"

"To ease your mind, he didn't *not* come because of you," Sarah said softly. "There was a development last night—"

"Right, I saw him—"

"So he's with *that* detail right now," Kestrel said.

Eric eyed the tree. "We spent so much time sheltering you instead of including you." He faced Kestrel and Sarah. "I can't keep hiding things from her, and, really, she probably knows anyway. And I...I need Alex's help—I can't control the beast. Even last night, *it* wanted to attack him, but *I* didn't."

Turning back to Grandfather Wisdom, he said, "You're my only world right now, but...Donovan escaped. Alex is on it."

The orbs flashed.

"And I..." He licked his lips. "I'm torn again—man or beast, but not both, and the beast is so strong...without you, it is so much stronger than my heart."

He leaned his forehead against the ribbon. "Without you, I am incomplete. Please come back to me, my love. It's not fair to ask, I know. It's selfish, but I need you to save me from the darkness."

A tear dripped off his cheek and splashed a root, and the entire ribbon glowed white. More tears landed and the frayed edges began to heal. "Keep fighting, Paresh—you are strong, so strong—"

Kestrel's hand landed on his right shoulder and Sarah's on his left. They touched the tree and instantly flooded him with Paresh's protective love. Her essence enveloped him like a cozy blanket on a cool night.

"Her absence may have been hard on us out here," Kestrel started.

"But she was meant to be in there all this time," Sarah finished.

"Gabriel told Alex that her mind was too young—" Eric said.

"But that is no longer true." Sarah squeezed his shoulder. "She—and your daughter—"

"Have grown under Gabriel's watch." Kestrel squeezed his other shoulder. "Your daughter will be born with that advantage, as well."

"Everything that has happened *here*," Sarah began.

"Was meant to be." Kestrel glanced up. "Michael was sent to ensure no manipulation from the Fallen Host before the time came."

"That's why...when Lucif—" Wrathful electric blue eyes flashed in Eric's mind. He saw bouncing red fruits from Lucifer's memory and then his angry face—the same as his. Did Paresh know that he looked like the Devil?

Her essence snuggled closer. He could feel her arms around him and her hair tickling his cheek, could smell her honey and clover scent dancing in delightful circles. He was missing something—

"Does that mean you're going to find her?"

Kestrel's grin spread to Sarah's lips as they nodded in unison. "We'll do this again tomorrow, but that should give us enough."

"We could see bright spots at the Sunset Grove Parish and the cemetery," Sarah said. "Tonight, we hope to pinpoint you at the cemetery and other small targets, and then fine tune it."

"Her essence spreads through the tree roots," Kestrel added. "That's why her light was so bright for so long. But now, we can sense—"

"And see—"

"Those roots and where they flow underground."

"You're going to find her," Eric whispered.

"We're going to find her," they replied.

☽ ✳ ☾

Seren was waiting for him at the crumbling column, hands clasped behind her back and eyes darting nervously. Her hair sprouted from short pigtails, and she wore an off the shoulder rainbow striped sweater and torn jeans with the same platform boots.

She smiled as he approached. "Forget I'm here. I didn't mean to beat you—just over eager."

"The early bird gets the worm," Eric said as he crossed the gate's threshold. He gestured for her to join him. "Please—"

She anxiously gnawed her lip. "I should wait, give you time—"

He waved a dismissive hand. "The VaSH isn't watching me here, if that's what you're worried about."

She jerked up straight. "Oh, no...um, I know how to stay out their way. I don't mind their surveillance—"

"Well, I do."

When she didn't move, he asked, "Are you frightened of me?"

Her fingers twisted and interlocked in impossible configurations as she contemplated the cloudy night sky. "Inherently? Yes. But logically?

No—at least, n-not right now." She held her hands out. "But I totally get how dangerous you are. I don't mean to be disrespectful."

He sighed. It might've been a partial laugh. "You're not. Please—" He gestured at the gravestones. "They don't talk back. Conversation is good for the soul."

"O-okay." She scurried to his side and tugged her sleeves over her fists. Only her thumbs and silver nail polish were visible as she sat cross-legged on Lucinda's grave. The furtive glances she stole at him were similar to the ones Paresh had shot at him on their first date.

He sat on his grave. "You'd think I'd be used to this by now."

She glanced at the badge shaped indentation in his marker. "It must be nice to be remembered by a family that mourned for you, though."

"You weren't?"

Her lips didn't quite smile. "No marker for me or my family. I…" Her fang pierced her lower lip. "I don't know what happened to their bodies— I never saw them. And…well, I don't remember my given name."

"How old are you?"

"I-I don't know. Old? Way before the Black Death decimated Europe." She tried to pass off a laugh and stole another glance at him. She seemed terribly uncomfortable in her skin, plucking at the grass and chewing her lip raw.

"Are you okay?" he asked, suddenly wondering what life would be like for his daughter. "I don't mind listening if you'd like to talk."

"I guess I wonder why people want to live forever? I mean, who actually chooses this life? It just seems like people evolve backwards."

"You were forced into it," Eric said, the realization knocking him mentally back. "During the War?"

Sucking her lip into her mouth, she nursed the bloody wound and shrugged. "It was common back then. You know, let the lesser copies get slaughtered instead. But I didn't fight…"

She looked up through her lashes. "You really look exactly like *him*," she whispered—an admission that she seemingly needed to process.

Entranced, she reached for his face, but the spell broke and she blew a heavy sigh over her upper lip. "This weather, the gloom—it gets to me. I hardly think about it anymore. I mean…life these days? It's like sorcery compared to the world I was born into."

"Humanity has made advancement upon advancement. It seems like they went from the automobile to putting a man on the moon in the blink of an eye." Wagging his phone, he added, "And now we carry the entire world in our pockets."

"What do you—" She squared her shoulders and then hunched under another heavy sigh. "W-what do you think it'll be like for *her* when she wakes up? Alive with all this technology and moving into a future of tech? Her experience is entirely different—this stuff has always been around for her."

Shredded grass stained her fingers green. "Not that anyone's experience is at all like hers. I get that."

"No…it's not," Eric whispered. "For so long, I wanted her to find peace and rest. She doesn't deserve all this…trauma."

His shoulders sagged, too. "I didn't give her a choice. I forced her into this life."

"I didn't know that," Seren replied quietly, again studying him through hooded eyes. "Not that I should, I guess, but I feel bad."

"Me, too." Eric folded his hands in his lap. "The thing is I know she wants to live. That she's accepted all that's happened. And that maybe it was even *supposed* to happen—but I couldn't accept it. And I know that's not fair. I abandoned her despite knowing her wishes and I can't ever take that back."

"How do you know she wants to live?" Seren's expression was troubled. "I thought those angels had her locked down."

Eric smiled to himself. "She's tenacious and finds ways to slip out to check on me. She's so much stronger than I am."

"She loves you," Seren whispered. "If I had known love, maybe I would've been able to accept my life."

"You can love now," Eric said. "Don't give up."

"If the man I looked up to had been like you, everything would've been different…happier. Your daughter is lucky."

Eric's internal alarm rang. "How do you know about her?"

She dug into her lip. "Don't be mad…I…"

Ducking her head and sighing, she hurried out, "I watched you today at the tree—I was curious, too curious, I know and-and I'm sorry for overstepping. But you're just *so nice* and *so gentlemanly*—very unlike *him* and I just…I just had to see *more*."

She peered up anxiously. He didn't like being spied on, but he couldn't be mad at her either. What had she lived through to look that scared all the time? Were others in the Nation like this? He'd only met hunters and Elders.

"Promise no more spying, okay?" Eric said. "I'm surprised the others didn't see you."

A corner of her lips turned up. "I know how to stay out of their way. I didn't want to interrupt you. I swear, I didn't mean any harm, I promise."

"I believe you," Eric said, patting the air earnestly. "But if you're out there sneaking around undetected, then others probably are, too, and that means they'll bring in more security."

"But you're so powerful," she said. "And *everyone* is scared of you. Why do you need security?"

"I suppose for the same reasons Jonathan and Lucien have security."

"N-no…" She tugged her pigtails and closed her eyes. "No—you're stronger than them. You're stronger than *him*. They just don't know it…yet."

"Well…" Eric thought through his battles with Jonathan over the years. "He's come close to winning a few times, but I guess I've won our physical fights—maybe not the mental battles, so much, though."

Seren looked confused, but didn't ask for clarification. "So…since you know what I heard, um, when do you think they'll find her? I figured you'd want to tell Lucinda."

"Maybe I did," Eric started slowly, "but I don't think she's here, which means she already knows."

"Wouldn't she be jealous? I think I'd be jealous."

"She'd want me to be happy. We had our time." Eric stroked Lucinda's stone. "She cared about others above herself—she was a kind woman."

"Hm…and your time with Paresh is eternal, so you can always be together," Seren said, drifting into thought. "That's quite enviable, I must admit."

☽ ✳ ☾

It was the final morning. Eric hesitated on the path, not wanting to disturb Alex's moment at the base of Grandfather Wisdom. Alex beckoned over his shoulder. "Damn it, stop doing that. Just come over."

Alex glanced up the partially healed ribbon, his watery eyes red and swollen. "I can't believe it."

"Hey, Alex," Eric started, "her time, my time, your time—it's all *our* time and I know I have *so much* to atone for. I can only start by saying I'm sorry for everything I've done and haven't done."

Alex nodded, but wouldn't look at him. "I appreciate that. But let's talk about it another time, okay?"

"Okay." Eric patted him on the back. He stroked the gold ribbon. It was warm and emanated joy. "Good morning my loves."

Alex gasped. "I can feel her! Them!"

"She's getting stronger." Eric glanced at the western tree line. His watchers weren't there. "Did Kestrel tell you what happened yesterday?"

Alex shook his head.

"Paresh communicated through them. I think she doesn't want you to blame yourself because she said she was meant to be here——"

The orbs beneath their hands jumped with excitement.

"——so that her young mind could catch up to the power in her body, and I think that's why Saint Michael stopped Lucifer when he attacked me, and why Gabriel told you to bring her joy."

"He didn't want her to break," Alex realized. He wiped his nose on the back of his hand. "It still sucks. I will never forget her scream. I wish I'd gotten a cleaner shot at Salea."

The light pulsed under Alex's hand. He smiled sadly. "Sorry——I love you, too, Pare. I'll get over it, in time, I promise."

"Did you find Donovan?" Eric asked.

Alex gawked at him.

"I'm done hiding," Eric said. "You were right——we should have told her everything. I'm done with running from my feelings and fears. How can we form a whole with secrets between us?"

Alex threw both arms around him and squashed him into a hug. "This doesn't mean I forgive you."

Laughing softly, Eric said, "I know, but I'll take it."

Paresh's warmth traveled up his arm to Alex. He seemed to melt under her essence and broke down sobbing against Eric's shoulder. Eric held him with one arm until Alex straightened and pulled a folded tissue from his pocket.

He dabbed his eyes and blew his nose. "She really has grown in there."

"She told me that our daughter's name is Celeste. According to the Internet, it means 'Star,'" Eric said, grinning up at Saint Michael.

An awed smile lit Alex's face. "Celeste, huh?" The orbs danced happily as he stroked the ribbon. "Hello little bean! Raven said I'd be the best nanny to you. I can't wait to prove her right."

He sobered. "Uh, yeah, back to you-know-who——we found him. He's at the Arc of Mourning Eidolons and no one's letting him out this time. He's strapped into agony, and I promise you it's way worse than what we put you through."

New tears swelled with the bitterness in his voice. He wiped them away. "The Knights welcome your visit at any time. Jonathan deferred the first one to you."

Eric studied the ribbon and the orbs floating within. Seren's words filtered through his mind.

…nice and gentlemanly…

"I don't want to waste another second on him." The orbs warmed under his finger. "You guys get him for me…*for us.* I need restraint. Seeing him will only move me backward."

Alex nodded and softly said, "Good-bye," to Paresh.

Eric caught his arm. "Before you go, I—"

"I still need time," Alex said.

"No, I mean, yeah, I understand, but that's not it." Eric ducked down to get Alex to look at him. Sadness and anger swirled in his green orbs. "For so long, I could either starve the beast or let it overpower me, and now…I feel a measure of control while I'm here with her, but it's not enough. I need help, Alex, and I think you're the only one who can do it."

"The vials aren't enough?" he asked.

"They're working better now that she's stronger," Eric said, "but, no, they aren't."

Alex nodded in thought. "I don't have any on me, but I'll think of something, okay?"

"Thank you," Eric said. "And I know that doesn't mean you've forgiven me either."

"Maybe that'll come when you can forgive yourself." He shrugged. "Or when she forgives you…but I doubt she ever blamed you in the first place."

☽ ✳ ☾

He was sitting on Lucinda's grave, staring at his last name when Seren's pink bob appeared in his peripheral vision. She approached with less nervousness, dressed in star-patterned leggings and a t-shirt bearing a moon with a rainbow halo. Her white canvas high tops were patched with duct tape and safety pins and doodled with marker ink. She plopped down beside him and tossed a hand up in greeting.

"What happened?" he asked, nudging her chin up. Her lip was bloody and swollen.

Her eyes widened at his touch. "I was thinking."

"About what?"

"I've lived my whole life—well, almost my whole life—one way, but now I'm wondering about what could have been or if it's really too late to change it."

"We can't control or change our pasts," Eric said, "only how we use them to shape our futures. God knows I'm going through that myself right now. Alex tried to beat it into me for years and now I need to reconcile with it to move forward."

"Alex?"

Tossing his hand up in a random gesture, he clarified, "I don't know how you address him. Crimson Commander? Lord Alex? High Commander?"

"No...I-I know who he is." She fidgeted with beads pinned to her shoe. "I just...thought you were closer to Jon...Master Jonathan."

"Well, we do look alike, as you said, but things have been, well, strained between us for a long time."

"That's not who—" The pin came loose and jabbed under her nail. She tucked her finger into her mouth.

"He's my brother and always will be, but " Eric sighed. "Paresh asked Alex to watch over her, and he extended that to me so Jonathan and I wouldn't kill each other."

Surprise crinkled Seren's features. Her mouth moved to form a question but he swatted it off.

"Never mind that," he said. "Back then, Alex told me I wasn't thinking about what Paresh wanted. That I was being selfish, that it was all about me and not about her, and he was right. My relationship with Jonathan will work itself out eventually. I need to deal with my own shortcomings first."

He gestured at Lucinda's headstone. "I came here instead of facing reality. It's like...talking about letting her die gave me permission to hide from my guilt."

Tapping his head, he continued, "But it lives here and it knows. It was all a farce. No one gave Paresh a choice to live, not when she was born or when she was killed, and we smothered her with protection when her life went wrong instead of empowering her. I thought if she found peace at rest, that I could release this guilt because I wouldn't—couldn't—ever fail her again."

He wiped his face with his palm. "I am a terrible man for saying that—for *ever* believing that."

"So what?" Seren snapped cynically. "In your grief you blamed yourself? You tried protecting yourself from a harsh reality under grief's umbrella? And that makes you selfish? Because *Alex* says so?"

She scoffed. "It's hard for me to trust anything Alex says when he never once tried to look for Raven. All it comes down to is you not behaving within their expectations."

Her tone caught Eric by surprise. "You clearly don't like Alex. He was forbidden from looking for her."

"That wouldn't have stopped you. Or her, if the situation had been reversed."

"When Paresh went missing as a little girl, I never stopped looking," he said. "But this time? I never even started."

"She wasn't the only who was traumatized, you know," Seren said sourly, her brow furrowing deeper. "You both died traumatic and violent deaths, and sure, you got a choice the first time, but not the second time, and you came back into a world that not only wanted you dead but also feared you. And instead of focusing on yourself *then*, you poured all your energy into her and her suffering, feeling helpless and blaming yourself for it."

"How do you——"

Intertwining and folding her fingers, Seren smiled sadly. "I'm old like that ancient lot——I know things." She shrugged. "Nothing about this seemed right, like something was missing. Or like *you* were missing something——permission to process *your* trauma, *your* grief, *your* life."

Pink strands draped her face in shadow. "It's a human thing. *Alex* can't understand that because he was never human. He likes to play with human ideas like rehabilitation, but he doesn't really understand it. None of *them* ever had to suffer loss alone. They've never dealt with trauma the way we have. They don't know that it never goes away, regardless of the blood in our veins."

"True bloods never had a choice, either," Eric said. "They were unnatural creatures born to fight a war in which they had no stake."

"Stop rationalizing it! God! This is getting harder by the freaking day!" she cried, slapping her thighs. "They got a choice and they took it or they wouldn't be here now! You focus on you! What do *you* want?"

"Paresh." Her name fell quietly off his lips. "To be happy with Paresh."

"Then *find her* and do it!" Seren stood with a frustrated huff. "Life will throw obstacles at you, but you need to determine how they affect you. Stop feeding your guilt! Find her so you can jump those hurdles together before it's too late!"

II

LUCIEN

____

Foothills of Mount Fuji, Japan, ca. 36 A.D.

The veil of reality split into a dark void. A humanoid being, fair of skin and hair, wearing Lucifer's signature crimson cloak, strolled out brimming with alarming awareness. Lucifer lingered at the borderline, shrouded in blackness with only the fury in his flaming eyes visible. A voice slithered forth, betraying effort and pain.

"Endymion—Lucien."

Endymion's tongue slicked lips that quirked up on one side. Arrogance anchored his eyes, serene and pale yellowish-green, into the face he angled down at Lucien. As their gazes locked, Lucien's skin bristled.

The void shuttered, leaving a sizzling crack behind. Endymion let his gaze sink into Lucien like he savored such strangely rigid silence.

Through narrowing slits, Lucien studied Endymion's appearance and noted how eerily similar it was to his own. A stone formed in his gut. If Lucifer had given *him* humanoid coloring and appearance, he'd be looking at his reflection. Bitterness shrunk the walls of his heart. All those centuries of suffering—

He snarled and hurled his aura at Endymion.

The imitation swatted it off with a flick of his wrist. "Now, now," he cooed, "'twould be of benefit to listen first. I am not as powerless as you think."

"Then speak."

Endymion's unnervingly crooked smile told Lucien, *not yet...you can wait.* He didn't speak again until Lucien met his gaze.

"Ah! 'Tis polite to look at the one speaking, is it not?" Endymion asked, diverting his attention to the majestic mountain.

"Then speak to become worthy of my attention."

Endymion's grin widened. "Ah, 'twould appear you think I need your approval? 'Tis the other way around. Your, ah, *pet*, caught the attention of *someone upstairs*, so to speak. Apparently, the slaughter of monks in cold blood did not go unnoticed. Lucifer was thrown to Earth for it, and since he lives here now, he desires to claim dominion."

The stone sank uncomfortably low. "Lucifer created Jonathan with a strong bloodlust. Isn't that what he wanted?"

Endymion's focus hardened. "He was to be led by you, not left to fester into a blind beast that lacks control. It's put me into a position I rather dislike."

"How have you even existed long enough to dislike anything?" Lucien growled.

"Lucifer is building an army—my army, to be precise—a legion of walking wrath to fight his war and turn the Children of God against the

Host ordered to protect them."

The very air seemed to slap Lucien in the face. "Lucifer's war? Wrath? Your army?"

"Oh, to be clear, you are Lucifer's shining achievement, and he is…proud…of the other one." His eyes glittered. "You and your pet command great power—of which, he made sacrifices to endow me with specific abilities."

"Then you are an underling seeking a power play like a pitiful human." The disdain in Lucien's voice barely veiled the underlying threat. "I have listened. Now I—"

"Ah, no," Endymion interrupted, "listen now or learn later."

He bent at the waist to whisper, "I will thoroughly humiliate you if you choose to learn later."

Lucien slapped him away, glaring up and growling deeper. "Then. Speak."

Endymion's smile finally spread evenly over his face. "The creations in my army are lesser beings than either of you, the First and Second Born, and of me. Lucifer calls them vampires and I am their King, linked mind to mind. They cannot defy me."

He hooked his tongue on a fang. The scent of blood snaked between them and over the rising stench from the village down the hill. "My army may lack your strength and otherworldly abilities, but they will be quite formidable foes should you, or Jonathan, become difficult."

Lucien couldn't hold back his incredulous expression. "You're threatening me?"

"You are nearly equal to our creator," Endymion said smoothly. "'Twould be foolish to threaten you. We'd destroy each other—I am equal to you in many ways, but…no, no. 'Tis the truth of the matter—Lucifer is at war with his brothers, and he created me to command his army."

He wagged his finger between them. "We all share a thirst for blood; however, you and the Second Born are not vampires—in this sense. And therefore, you are not part of my army."

"Then why am I listening to you?" Lucien waved him off. "Go about your war."

"We are…cousins, if you will, and his war is your war."

"I won't interfere with your command and Jonathan will enjoy a new challenge. I am not well-suited to engage his energetic needs at suitable levels."

"Yes. 'Tis the problem."

"Do explain. I am losing patience. There is no army to protect you now and I will kill you if you don't get to the point."

Endymion's grin widened, displaying his teeth and lifting his eyes. "Ah! 'Tis what I've yearned to see! Perfect!"

As Lucien's jaw clenched and bulged, Endymion sat beside him and conspiratorially lowered his voice. "They don't know I am their King and I don't want them to know. Given all that Lucifer told me, you are born to rule. I merely wish to enjoy this life."

Lucien's eyes narrowed further. "First you threaten me and then you confess to being a coward who refuses his title?"

Endymion scoffed. "I am not a fool or forfeiting my throne—I will hold onto my power, but instill in them a base fear of you that will keep them in line. They will never truly be yours—I am merely appointing a proxy."

The claws on Lucien's right hand lengthened to daggers. He turned toward Endymion.

"Ah, don't be difficult," Endymion warned. "I shall also instill in them a base fear of your companion. But as proof of my power? Lucifer will soon present a biological weapon capable of annihilating life on this planet. She has no will of her own, but I will gift her the ability to choose which orders she obeys from the Second Born."

He closed his eyes and mimicked Lucien's meditative state. Endymion's aura moved away from them and into the sizzling crack. His eyes opened and the crooked grin returned.

"It is all done," Endymion said triumphantly. "All who enter this world shall fear and respect the power you and your pet wield, and when Blood Rainne Pathos enters this world, she will obey your every command."

"And Jonathan?"

"She shall choose. 'Twill be the only freedom she'll ever know."

Lucien's eyes drifted over the mountain without seeing it. The prickling anger was gone and the sinking stone had lightened. His home was destroyed—again —and his heart was hollow and cold.

Endymion inched closer. In the lowest, quietest voice possible, he said, "As a gesture of good faith, I offer you this, which you may use at your discretion: Lucifer's father intervened in my creation without his knowledge. I have yet to determine what that means for me, but it certainly rings of sabotage, you agree?"

Lucien nodded.

"Then we have an understanding? Equal footing between us while I play the loyal Third Born? No one else knows."

Lucien's chest rose and sank under a heavy sigh. "Jonathan receives the same reverence you show me."

Endymion smiled. "Anything you wish, of course."

"He will find you beautiful," Lucien whispered. Endymion's unnerving appearance would have a lasting effect on Jonathan. His sole companion of a thousand years had just become a pawn in Lucifer's game, and Endymion's ultimatum would last eternally. They were deadlocked.

"I look forward to enjoying whatever path I walk in this life under your command," Endymion said. "'Twould be foolish not to. I am quite…*energetic*…myself."

"You will keep me apprised of what you learn about yourself and this world. What you know, I shall know."

"Yes."

"You will obey Jonathan as you do me."

"Yes."

"You will lift the restrictions on the biological weapon."

"No. And because you pushed, I will never lift that restriction."

Lucien ground his jaw. "You shall never lie to me or ever hold power over me. You and I are eternal allies based on mutually assured destruction. No ultimatums or threats."

"Yes."

"Then tell me about this war and army I shall command."

"In time." He drew Lucien's thumb into his mouth, nicked it on a fang, and knelt before him. "Claim me as one of your clan and I shall be your subordinate until the day you lift your mark."

Lucien subverted his gaze between the blood on his skin and the vampire's reverence. Though uncertain of the whys of it all, he pressed his thumb to Endymion's forehead. "And now?"

Endymion swept into a respectful bow and his aura streamed back to the sizzling crack. It ripped open into a rolling haze of pure white. "Now, you retrieve the Second Born and we go to Africa. War awaits."

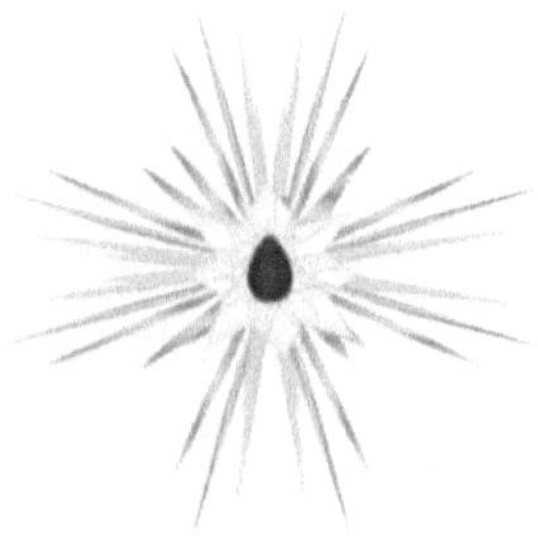

CHAPTER THIRTEEN: ENSHRINED IN TEARS

I

ALEX

Orison Crossing, Early Autumn 2021

Officer James looked up as the door chimes jingled. He nudged his chin in greeting. "Chief's in his office."

"Thanks, man." With a stiff wave, Alex headed down the horridly lit hall, passing officer portraits and awards, and knocked on Walter's door.

"Hey, it's me." The convincing smile he'd mustered for Officer James fell. No pretending here.

"Come on in," Walter called.

Alex whistled. He had to dodge collapsing paper stacks and maneuver around crates of files and scattered pages that drifted with the door's draft. The filing cabinets were empty, desk drawers were stacked against the wall, and boxes were piled on the floor and desk.

Hunkered over a pad of paper, Walter scribbled with an inkless pen. It landed into the metal garbage can with a sharp *twang*. By the looks of things, it hadn't been the first to go.

A genuine grin lifted Alex's cheeks. "Are you that desperate to delay the inevitable? You don't have to retire."

"Meh, you just don't want me to go." He grabbed another pen and popped the cap off.

Alex bundled a bunch of coats off a chair and glanced at the other, stacked with bulletproof vests and duty belts of increasing girth. He mentally shrugged and added the coats on top. Sitting back, he propped a booted foot on his knee. "Well, I do like working with you. You're the only normal pillar this community has left."

"I've done my time," Walter grumbled, his wrinkles drooping as he frowned and tossed the pen.

"Does it really save the bottom line to keep the one pen that works?" Alex asked.

"There are markers, too."

"Ah, yes. We must save the markers. There should be a campaign for that—especially the scented ones." Alex held out his hand. "Come on. Stop for a minute and talk to me."

Walter leaned back and ran his ink-stained hand over his balding head. "You know, when I first met you, I never imagined we'd be here, like this."

"I can't help it," Alex said, pretending to primp his hair. "You like me so much better than Raven."

"I thought you were going to kill us. I shielded Molly with my body praying that my vest would protect her more than me." He quieted. "And then a different monster killed her the next day."

Alex sobered. "Damn, you're in the *real* zone. Man, none of that should have happened. None of *this* should be happening. I wish Raven was here instead of me."

"Shoulda, coulda, woulda," Walter said with a heavy sigh. "None of that matters. It is what it is." He jabbed his computer monitor with yet another dead pen. "Say! You know how Heron and Cyp talk Greek to me?"

Alex smiled and flipped his eyes to the ceiling. "Like, they actually speak in Greek to you?"

The pen flew at him. "No dumbass, I'm an ancient history buff."

"Hey! Hey!" Alex laughed. "Yes, yes, I know. What about it?"

"They told me that Alexander the Great was Cleopatra's brother, and I couldn't believe I didn't know that!"

"Well—"

Walter held up a hand. "Now give me a minute, here, it's my story."

"Yes, but—"

Patting the air, Walter continued, "Now, she and Marc Antony had twins that they named Alexander Helios—after the Titan of the Sun, of course—"

"Of course." Alex nodded. "I had no idea...I mean Apollo's predecessor, whaaat? Who knew—"

"Smartass, dumbass—whatever, you're an ass. I'm the one retiring, so listen," Walter said, pointing a thick finger. "And the other was Cleopatra Selene—after the Titan of the Moon. So, that got me thinking…do you have a middle name?"

"Uh…are you trying to determine if *I'm* Alexander the Great?" Alex asked. Something about this sounded familiar. "You do realize there's a massive difference in age here? And besides—"

"Do you want another pen? I have plenty of ammo, buddy."

"Well, but they're also precious commodities, so yeah, sure. Like, duh!" Alex ducked another pen attack. That was it—when Lucifer attacked Eric. Paresh had distracted him with random facts behind the false sunflower's name.

Interesting that Helios and Selene are coming up again, now.

"Okay, so it's all B.C., yeah, but *that* Alexander and *that* Cleopatra were born hundreds of years apart," Alex said.

"But…" Walter leaned back and pulled out his keyboard tray. "It said she was his sister, I looked it up."

"He did have a sister named Cleopatra, but she was successful—history would rather remember the one with all the dramatic love affairs and romanticized suicide by *asp*."

He swept his hand toward Walter. "But! That Cleopatra *did* descend from one of Alexander's generals. So there's that."

Walter gawked at his monitor a moment before slamming his keyboard under the table. "Damn it. I thought I was onto something."

"Ohh!" Alex laughed. "You thought I was one of the twins? Walter, man, I wasn't born human. And I'm not *that* old! A.D., man. A.D."

Red splotches spread from Walter's neck to his scalp. "I know that. I just thought that maybe…I don't know—"

"That Cleopatra and Marc Antony had vampire babies?" Alex slapped his leg and laughed harder. "Oh, that's one I haven't heard!"

Walter crossed his arms. "It's just…*that* Alexander disappeared, like history erased him, and I know we live by an *altered* history, so…"

"Yeah, yeah. I think I get it. Sorry to laugh, man, but I needed that. Thanks." Alex wiped his eyes and pulled out his coin. The weight of it was comfortably familiar even after years of neglect. He flicked it to Walter. "You won't find *me* anywhere in history, either. I honestly don't know the actual origin of my name. Raven was the one who linked me to Alexander the Great. She gave me that coin."

Walter traced the outlines and turned it over in his hands. "Who are these guys? Which one is The Great?"

Alex smiled. "Neither. One is Zeus on his throne and the other is Hercules."

"Are you kidding me?"

"Cross my heart, man. I swear."

"Then why is it an Alexander the Great coin?"

"I don't know? Why isn't a five dollar bill called a Lincoln?"

The coin flew at him. "At least *his* picture is on it!"

Alex tucked the coin into his pocket. "They were minted when he was King. It's not about who's on them—it's about who made them."

Walter sat back. "Hmph. Guess that makes sense."

"You learned something new, right? And more importantly—"

"Now I know Cleopatra didn't have vampire babies."

Alex snorted and slapped his boot. "Not as far as I know!"

"Hm." Walter quieted. "So, uh, are you checking on him today?"

Alex's head bobbed slowly. He wouldn't say more. He didn't want to deliver false hope like he'd done so many times before. He wanted a sure thing this time.

"Expect any change?"

His eyes deliberately met Walter's and the lawman shook his head. He collected the remaining pens and markers and dropped them into the garbage. "I don't know what's going on in that head. He should've torn this world apart to find her."

"Yeah." Alex ruffled his spikes. "I'd ask if you want to go, but—"

"Yeah." Walter leaned back with a huff. "You never know what you're gonna get. Does he even know I'm retiring?"

"I told him months ago, but he doesn't open his mail, so he hasn't seen your invitation." Alex hung his hand off his neck. "But we got ours."

"Please, come! Have you ever been to a retirement party before?"

Alex shrugged. "We don't retire."

"Figured as much." Walter ripped the top two sheets off the notepad and crumpled them into a ball. "Well, it usually involves a bar and lots of drunk people telling stories."

"I'm your designated driver. Got it. I see how it is." Alex wiped away a fake tear.

Walter threw the paper at him. "I do wish Raven could be here, though. The town's nervous—changing of the old guard and all that. They'd gotten used to that blinding spot of neon pink on the street in the short time she was here."

"We all wish she was here," Alex said quietly, his gaze dropping into his lap.

They sat in a somber silence as the clock ticked. Raven would energize this moment, grinning and slapping Walter's back to irritate him or make him laugh. She'd make it a celebration. He wondered what Walter was thinking.

"Hey, man, at least the new chief, your old lieutenant—"

"Kyle Waggoner."

"Yeah." Alex nodded absently. "He didn't freak out *and* he caught up pretty quick—"

"He's having a hard time understanding Eric, though," Walter said. "He was always suspicious of him."

"He wants to know things," Alex agreed. "But he handled seeing Michael's avatar the first time better than you did. It didn't smell as bad."

"Hey now!" Walter leaned over his desk and stuck his finger in Alex's face. "You left me there with strangers. Farran? That one still does *not* know how to interact with humans! At least he had you and me there with him."

Alex chuckled. "That's on me, I suppose. But that should ease any concerns you have about the town. I'd still rather have you in that seat, but he's a decent guy. I'll probably be here for the next one, too."

Walter eyed him a moment, chewing over a thought. "He wants you to appoint a hunter to work here as a liaison. Said it makes sense to have a force that represents the population. But I didn't tip you off."

"I'll mess with him and claim I had a great idea," Alex said with a wink. "I'll give him Farran—for *pest* control."

The notepad flew at Alex. He ducked with a laugh.

"Don't you dare!" Walter said, smiling even as he tried his hardest not to. "You'd better offer someone from the Crimson Guard!"

Alex curled an arm around the neighboring chair and grinned. "Ah! Every true blood's dream: office work!"

"You said you wanted the lives of men, right?" Walter threw his hands out to the sides. "Welcome to the glory!"

☽ ✳ ☾

Tossing up Raven's two-fingered salute to the Officer James at the desk, Alex left the station with the heavy pit returning to his gut. Despite Eric's newfound hope, and remorse, the new chief's mind would churn over his previous behavior, a worrying aspect of the cop mind that might lead him to conclude that Eric is a threat—and rightly so. Eric wouldn't deliberately harm a human, but his blind rages—and his beast—didn't care who was in the way, and *he* hadn't yet thought of a way to help.

Alex waved at people on the street and smiled when they waved back. *This town...*

There was no other place like it on Earth. Vampires and humans knowingly coexisted with virtually no crime—maybe a petty theft or minor fight here or there. When people felt safe and stopped worrying, they poured that wasted energy into their lives and their families. Strangers made them nervous, though, and the town made sure they passed through—quickly.

Main Street faded as he entered the residential district bordering Sunset Grove's north end. Beyond it, the forest loomed tall, the rustling canopy stretching into the sun's embrace, with the quiet buzz of insects and faint emergence of recent animal chatter.

Butterflies fluttered in his chest as he hit the dappled driveway. He longed for the days when he raced to the flagstone, eager to see Paresh's smile. Hope had done his anxiety no favors. He couldn't help being angry at Eric's sudden change of heart, bitter about what could have been if he hadn't given up before they'd even started. He hated what Eric had become and what they'd done to him.

His dragged his feet and scuffed his boots. Eric wanted to talk. And that meant he expected forgiveness, or, at least, a gateway to it, and Alex didn't know if he was ready. It wasn't just about Eric, not when Alex had taken his anger out on him and tortured him countless times, thinking that Eric truly deserved whatever he got.

But he hadn't. And Alex had known it. Paresh's hug yesterday morning had lit his guilt on fire. Eric wasn't the only one who needed to atone.

He puffed his cheeks and stopped on the flagstone, staring at his boots. Where would they start? Did they need to acknowledge the wrongs, or could they simply start over?

The cottage door opened and Eric stepped out. He seemed just as nervous. Alex scratched the nonexistent itch.

"Hey," they said in unison. Eric ran a hand through his hair. Alex pulled a vial from his pocket.

"Look, before we get into...whatever, remember when Paresh told you about the false sunflowers? Why do you think she talked about Helios, Selene, and Eos?"

Eric shrugged. "I thought it was just something to keep me focused on her, but we were in a field of yellow flowers and the titans preceded the gods of Mount Olympus, right? Maybe it was a metaphor about Lucifer trying to be a false god—she made a specific point that killing Lucifer would be a choice that I needed to remember. I didn't think much of the rest. Why?"

"It's nothing, really. Here" Alex gave the vial to Eric. "Does this still take you to the Elysian Fields?"

"It didn't last time. And they won't let her visit again." Eric nodded his thanks and broke the seal.

"Yeah, I figured. Is it helping, though?"

"It's more calming, like it used to be, but it has no stopping power against the beast. At the slightest aggravation——" Eric tossed his hand up. "It takes over——or tries."

Alex kinked his neck to protect his ear from restless fingers. "So, uh, back on topic…did you…did you actually *want* to die? Or were you strictly starving the beast?"

Eric sighed. "At first, no, I was too lost to think about living or dying, but later…yes."

"Do you still want to die?"

Eric shook his head. "I'm so ashamed, Alex. I don't how to begin…" He shrugged helplessly. "I can only imagine that Jonathan felt something like this after his confessions——everything he'd done to Paresh's family——"

Alex shifted on his feet uncomfortably. "I can get that. Hey, uh…"

He went to scratch behind his ear, but grasped his nape instead. "Who knows what life will look like, right? But-but, Walter's retirement party is next weekend. Your invitation is in the stack of mail inside." He gestured at the open door.

Eric glanced over his shoulder. "Retirement?"

"It's been fifteen years——the dude's gotten old."

"I should go see——"

"No, you really shouldn't." Alex huffed at the sky. "I've got this handled, and if you go in…he hears that we *might* be close, *at last*——and he doesn't retire. In fact, he'll want to help, and he can't."

"But I——"

"Haven't been around!" Alex threw his hands up. "Don't mess this up! Look, Heron and Cyp have been with him, in some capacity, all this time. They've got the department covered and we've broken in the new chief——I…"

He shook his head and put his hands on his hips. "I can't have him seeing you as a threat. You can't go like this, you just can't. You can't wreck what we've set up in this town."

Darkness shaded Eric's visage. Alex tensed. "Come on, control it!"

"You have no idea what this is like," Eric growled. "None of you!"

Alex tapped a prong on his Vampiric Star to get Jonathan's attention. "Okay, fine. I don't understand it. I can't. I know your heart and the beast are like water and oil, and only Paresh can bring them together—so, let's go see *her* and see if that helps."

Fear lurked deep in Eric's simmering eyes. Alex's guilt chomped hard at his ribs. All that time angry and blaming Eric, but what had *they* done to him?

Alex closed the gap between them and grabbed Eric's hand. "Look, you apologized, but I didn't. I've been a cold-blooded asshole to you, but you're just as hurt as she is. Your soul died with her and we did horrible things to control you…to p-punish you. *I* did horrible things to you, and I'm sorry I didn't see it, that I didn't *help* you."

Eric jerked him forward and slammed their skulls together. Jonathan came running from the southern trail. Alex didn't let go. He pulled Eric closer.

"I'm sorry!" he cried, seeing stars as he clung to Eric's neck. "We need to wipe it clean and start over! It's the only thing we can possibly do!"

Jonathan stopped beyond Eric's reach and Alex quickly said, "He can't control the beast and you understand better than anyone else what that's like for him. Her blood isn't enough."

"I don't want to hurt you," Eric growled, visibly straining not to gnash at Alex's ear, "but *it* wants to kill you…*both*."

The color of blood draped the world as Alex matched Jonathan's transformation. Jonathan approached Eric from behind and locked himself into place by bracing arms with Alex.

"Brother," Jonathan said in a calm, raspy voice, "come back to us. She needs the man in you. We need you."

The warning rumble continued to build. Alex shot Jonathan a "try again" look.

"I've missed my brother," Jonathan confessed in earnest. "I've missed the honorable *man* you are, the *man* who never let me win. That *man* wouldn't lose now, not now, not this close."

Moisture surged into Eric's darkened eyes. His teeth chattered as he blinked and fought for control. His entire body was as hard as stone. A low grunt gradually grew into a throat shredding howl.

"We need you back, man," Alex said in a quiet voice. "We really do—forget our transgressions…we need to pull together—we all need to man up for Paresh."

Her name brought Eric's scream down to a whimpering cry. His grip on Alex's hand loosened. Alex embraced him and cupped the back of his head when Eric leaned forward on his shoulder. Jonathan's face signaled alarm, but Alex only nodded, acting in good faith that Eric wouldn't tear out his jugular.

"I trust you—maybe it's stupid, but I trust you, Eric," Alex whispered into his ear. "And I've got you now. Okay? We've all got each other. And we need to be together to be here for Paresh."

Eric's knees wobbled. He hugged onto Alex like a life raft. His whole body shuddered. Alex shook his head, so wracked with remorse that his voice was a hoarse whisper over the rock in his throat.

"I wish I'd understood sooner. I wasn't helping you; I was *breaking* you. Over and over, but you were already fragmented and I couldn't see it. I didn't want to see it. You were an easy target and I am such an ass for everything I did to you. I wish I could take it all back."

Eric released a choking sob and started to sink. Jonathan and Alex went down with him, not letting go. For the first time since Paresh's death, Alex saw Jonathan's eyes mist up, his jaw grinding, his expression hardening.

"I should have been my brother's keeper," Jonathan said sharply, turning his loathing inward. "Instead, I abandoned you to Alex and ran away...I hid at the mansion where I could pretend. Where what was out of sight was out of mind."

Jonathan huffed. "And when I did see you, I'd get so angry. I was angry with myself, but I couldn't let it out in front of the Elders, so instead you got it."

Jonathan's countenance crinkled with pained lines. "I couldn't handle it. I couldn't even accept what was really happening. I refused to see any of it...including your struggles—how hard you had to battle within yourself. I turned it all out on you and I am sorry, Brother."

Eric was crying so hard he couldn't catch his breath. Tears spilled from Alex's eyes as he patted Eric's shoulder, finally allowing himself to feel the grief he'd kept bottled up. "Everything became about you and Paresh, but I lost...Rav...Raven, too. We lost them both and ourselves. I miss the life we had. I want that life back. I want Raven back. I want it all back."

"Me, too," Jonathan whispered. "I don't think I ever said it, but I loved having a real brother. I loved our new relationship and I wish I hadn't thrown it away. I hope we can get it back."

"We've got you, now, okay?" Alex said, his voice whining softly over the catch in his throat.

Eric nodded his head against Alex's shoulder and reached back to grab Jonathan's hand. Jonathan clapped his other hand onto Eric's back.

"We'll do this together, from now on," Alex said. "We'll forge a better future through this. I know we will."

"She's coming back, Brother," Jonathan said. "She's a fighter, a survivor. She didn't let Death stop her before. It won't stop her now. Believe in her."

II

KESTREL

Orison Crossing, Early Autumn 2021

Something strange happened last night during their final grid search. Sarah must have seen it coming—she'd thrown herself over Kestrel to block it, but it'd sailed right through and rammed into them both, a wave of energy that penetrated through the silver and into the eternally raw skin underneath. It'd knocked them out, and when they awoke, her vines were different, like they'd learned a new language that she didn't speak. But their insistent urge to go to the cottage didn't need interpretation.

She'd tried calling Alex and Jonathan and hadn't gotten a response. When they got there, they saw smoke puffing from the chimney, and Kestrel detected three bodies inside, one of which Sarah's sight confirmed was Eric.

They jogged up the flagstone. Sarah moved to enter like she usually would, but Kestrel held her back. "Something's up. I think we should mind our posts—just this once."

Annoyance flickered over Sarah's façade as she stepped in place as First Officer. Kestrel knocked. The door opened a crack and Alex squeezed out with air heavily scented of blood, whispering, "Pleeeease tell me you have good news. We're barely keeping him stable."

At the look Sarah shot him, he said, "We didn't dose him. But he's calm and we need to keep it that way. No triggers."

Then, at the grim look Kestrel gave him, he pulled them halfway down the flagstone. "Damn it—okay, what's going on?"

"You tell us. I felt…*something*—" Kestrel started, protectively covering her belly.

"What happened to Eric?" Sarah interrupted, staring hard at the blinds covering the windows.

"The beast came completely untethered. We thought we'd calmed Eric down, but then he suddenly snapped to attack me and Jonathan intervened and got it instead. Paresh's blood barely takes the edge off.

We managed to get him inside where it's dark, and Jonathan's keeping him talking about mundane boring stuff—and I mean like the history of type setting type of boring."

He grabbed his neck with a lost look in his eyes. "I think this is it. Our last chance. So again, please tell me you have good news."

"I can't." Kestrel threw up a helpless hand and pointed toward Grandfather Wisdom. "We can see her there and watch her essence move through tree roots all across town—"

"But?" Alex motioned for her get to the point.

"We also see Lord Eric's light at the cemetery—it was brighter than ever last night—"

"But?" Alex crossed his arms, unease thrumming through his aura.

"We don't see her body," Kestrel said.

"Anywhere," Sarah added.

Alex slumped and grabbed his head. "No, no, no...*no!*"

"We looked for voids in the roots, high concentrations of energy—" Kestrel started.

Sarah continued, "She's even in the roots at the cemetery. Her light interacts with Eric's when he's there, but we don't see—"

Alex clutched Sarah's shoulders. "Wait—she interacts with him there?"

Sarah was still nodding when Alex zipped down the flagstone. He mumbled too fast to understand anything beyond, "Wait, wait, wait..."

They shared a bewildered look and chased after him to the carriage house. Metal and wood clattered until he emerged with a shovel.

"I think I have it!" He yelled as he ran down the lane.

"Where are you going?" Kestrel called, running after him.

"There! She's there!" Alex skidded off the lane as he hit the main road. He was so far ahead that he was almost out of sight.

"What the hell is he talking about?" Sarah asked. "We would have seen her! An extra light or a void—"

Understanding slowly awoke within Kestrel. She grabbed Sarah's hand and pulled her into the woods. "We assumed it was Eric's light because he's always there and he's never felt her there."

"Oh God." Sarah rushed ahead. "We should've looked closer."

When they arrived, Alex was already digging up Lucinda Ravenscroft's grave. "He lost control. You felt *something*," he said. "She's ready to come home. It's not a coincidence. It's not. *It's not.*"

"Alex, I sense something new from the one beside you." Kestrel pointed. "It feels...different. I don't understand this. It's like the Earth is talking to me. It feels...organic *and* celestial."

Sarah stared at the headstone. "But no one's buried there."

"He was drawn here *every* night." Alex pivoted and started a new hole, and his words jumbled together. "Not *there*, even tho'she would've felt'im. When he did man'ge t'sleep, he slept *here*. *She lured him here. That's why he never went to the tree!*"

"Donovan used his empty grave—" Kestrel stopped as a charge appeared in Sarah's aura and her claws dug into Kestrel's flesh.

"Tell me you feel what I see."

Pouring energy into her vines, Kestrel got stung by an unwelcome essence and flinched with a groan. "That's impossible!"

Alex froze. "What's impossible?"

"Salea," Sarah whispered, turning in a circle with her eyes closed. She pointed at Lucinda's grave. "Her blood is there."

"It's smeared into the grass," Kestrel said. "It's recent, too."

"What about the brighter light we saw the past few nights?" Sarah asked. "Did she deliberately interfere with our baseline for Eric's presence here?"

"No way!" Alex kicked the shovel into the earth. "Eric would've ripped her apart!"

"Eric's never seen her," Kestrel said. "He doesn't know anything about her—"

"If she was here, does that mean—"

"That Lucifer told her? If Paresh broke her rules, does that free him to break his?" Kestrel gaped in horror. "What if he told Salea? What if she led us here and it's a trap? We need back up!"

"No! Don't panic." Alex shoveled faster, throwing a near constant stream of dirt over his shoulder. "Just us until we know more. You'll see her if she's around—or smell sulfur if *someone else* shows up. If we need help that badly, I'll tell Jonathan to set Eric loose and put his beast to good use for once."

☽ ✳ ☾

ALEX

Of course, Paresh would lure Eric to sleep on her grave. *If* she was meant to spend all those years in the tree, then they were meant to find her *now*. Eric's essence would've kept her cells active enough to survive regardless of when Donovan stopped delivering his blood. Alex kicked the spade down and threw out another shovelful.

"Come on, come on," he muttered impatiently, wishing he could dig faster.

Sarah caught the shovel's handle. "I can see her light and it's faint, but you're close."

"He probably didn't put her in a box, so be careful." Kestrel squatted at the edge of the hole.

Alex tossed the shovel to Sarah and scrabbled along the bottom. He brushed something solid and shoved his hands into the dirt, pulling up what appeared to be the seam of a cloak—an Aegis Cloak. He found her arm and followed it up to where her head would be. Carving away at the soil, he cried out when he saw the outline of her face.

"P-Paresh! *Paresh!*" His vision swam as he scooped faster.

"Don't pull on her!" Kestrel slid down beside him. "She'll be fragile."

Sarah gasped behind them. "Oh, God," she whispered as she uncovered the bones of Paresh's toes.

"Oh no…" Alex held his breath and delicately uncovered her exposed nasal cavity. Rot had eroded the soft tissue around her forehead, cheekbones, and chin.

"Her left hand is bad, too," Kestrel said. "Bastard didn't tuck it under the cloak for protection like he did the other one. It's not entirely skeletal, but it's down to the bone."

Together they finished uncovering her in silence. Once they could see her whole body, Sarah winced.

"We can't move her like this," she whispered. "Eric needs to be here. And Jonathan, too."

"I don't think we should risk calling anyone," Kestrel said.

Alex snapped his fingers impatiently. "Call Walter. On his phone. Tell him to get Cyp and Heron, and book it to the cottage. They need to take vials—plural—of her blood to keep Eric calm and then they can bring them. And yeah, of course—without drawing attention."

As Kestrel made the call, Sarah said, "Despite the rot, she still smells like Paresh."

Alex stroked the dehydrated skin on her face. "Oh, Pare."

"They'll be here soon," Kestrel said. "We should set up a perimeter—"

"The Chthonic Knights have medical supplies at the mansion," Sarah said. "What if they brought a gurney and we take her there?"

Alex shook his head. "Just keep watch. I think you're right about Salea—a few nights ago, Eric encountered a cloaked hunter who was chasing a COMS signal. He thought it was Donovan, but it could've been her—and she must've known it because she was gone by the time

I got here."

"How would he not find a teenage vampire odd enough to mention to us?" Kestrel asked.

"Who says she's still a teenager?" Irrationally afraid that Paresh would crumble to dust or disappear, Alex couldn't look away. "She's one of the damned—she must be aging, too."

"As the only one here who lived through those awkward years—I bet she doesn't look anything like we remember." Sarah shook her head as though clearing a bad memory. "She's not getting another shot at my head, I promise that."

She and Kestrel climbed out to stand watch. "But think about it," Sarah said, "fourteen-year-old humans don't look the same at thirty."

Alex brushed at the dirt around Paresh's crown and freed a few brittle hair strands. The bounce and shine was gone. He wanted to hug her so badly that he instantly understood Eric's torture in the Elysian Fields—having her so close, yet not at all.

"We can ask him later." Tears dripped off Alex's cheeks as he kissed Paresh's skeletal forehead. "He's coming, Pare—they both are. Can you feel them?"

He wiped his nose on his filthy arm. "Hey, do you guys see any change in her light? Does her soul know we're here?"

Kestrel and Sarah both faced the direction of the forest and clasped hands. "There's no indication," Kestrel said, while Sarah simultaneously replied, "They're not letting her out."

They stared at each other a moment. Sarah closed her eyes and lifted her chin. "Michael is aware—he's keeping her there so we aren't discovered. He's watching."

"So she probably knows," Kestrel added, "but can't feel or hear you if they're blocking her signal. She's not in the roots."

In the distance, a car flew around a corner and skidded on the gravel. The tires caught and the engine roared, and Eric suddenly appeared, flying through the arborvitae, eyes darting wildly, hair an unruly mess and feet bloody. "Is she...is she...?"

As Alex felt his skin leap off his body, Eric slid into the pit, his scared countenance twisting in distress upon seeing her face. He sank slowly, reaching for her. "P-P-P...oh, God, what did I do?"

"She's too fragile to move," Alex said, delicately. "The, uh, damage is extensive."

Eric shredded his wrists and poured his blood into Paresh's wounds. Alex stepped aside to give him room to move along the rest of her body. Eric choked when he saw her bony hand and toes.

Alex dreaded seeing her abdomen. He tried to offer a steadying hand for support, but he was shaking too badly. "You didn't do this, Eric. If you hadn't come here every night, she'd be far worse—probably beyond saving."

Eric stared at him in alarm. "What? What if…we can't…"

Damn it. He hadn't considered that, you dolt. Alex brushed dirty fingers through his hair.

Eric gasped for breath. "Save her?"

"Look, look, look—" Alex got Eric to make eye contact. He grasped his shoulder as a reassurance. "Kestrel and Sarah said Michael's watching. We *did* get here in time, okay?"

Alex didn't let go until Eric nodded. "You're doing what you can right now. Keep going."

"Okay."

Alex cringed at how frightened Eric sounded. Jonathan appeared above them and jumped down beside Eric.

"Pare!" Jonathan rolled up the sleeves of his already bloodied shirt and clawed into his veins, following Eric's lead. "Alex, why didn't you tell us to begin with?"

"I didn't really know what I was doing." Alex scratched his ear. "I had a thought—"

"He took off like a madman, is what he did," Sarah said.

"We were reporting to him," Kestrel added. "And he picked up on something."

"How bad is the damage we can't see?" Jonathan asked. His throat had healed, but he hadn't yet cleaned off the dried blood from Eric's bite.

"I hadn't looked yet." Alex pulled apart the seams of Donovan's cloak. Dirt packed the sunken cavity of her belly. He threw the seams back into place and turned away cursing.

Eric moved in slow motion, jaw gaping, and lifted the hem. "Oh honey…"

As Eric's ragged breaths came quicker, Jonathan crouched beside him, covering his mouth. "Wh-who did this?"

Alex swung a deliberate gaze over Kestrel and Sarah to keep them quiet before answering, "Salea."

Paresh's scream ricocheted through his mind. "I shot her twice that day and haven't seen her since."

Sarah tossed Alex her cloak. He mouthed his gratitude and used it to cover Paresh's belly. "We'll cause more damage if we try to remove the soil here. Please—"

He gestured at Paresh's face, where bright red tissue was regenerating over the parts of exposed skull. She was still missing her nose, but her body was ravenously soaking up their blood. "Keep doing what you're doing. The more hydrated she is, the safer it'll be to move her."

The car finally screeched to a stop at the entrance and the doors popped open. Heron and Cyprian appeared first, followed by Walter.

"Holy Hell," Walter whispered, his knees shaking. Heron pulled him back from the hole.

"I don't want to take her through Animus Hollow." Alex visually queried the hunters.

"We can take her home in the back of Walter's squad," Cyprian said. "We brought coolers of blood, too."

"But she should go to Eido," Kestrel said.

"Like hell." Jonathan tossed up a glare. "She's going home."

"The blood bath—"

"Lucifer's still out there. We can't risk the Hollow. There's a tub at the cottage," Alex said softly. "That's where she belongs—once we're moving and you sense a shift in Michael, start pulling in heavy security. The entire forest, the town, the outskirts, neighboring areas—and tighten down all Hollow points anywhere near Orison Crossing. It'll draw attention, so—"

"I'll coordinate with the Commanders, don't worry," Kestrel said. "We'll lock it all down."

"If I may, when it's *safe*," Sarah said, "I'd like to go to The Greenery— she'll want soup." Her voice cracked. "I really want to make her soup."

Eric sniffled and bit down on his lip. Drops fell to his cheeks as he squeezed his eyes tight. Alex looked from him to Sarah in agreement. "But you and Kestrel need to be on watch. Don't let your guard down."

"Yes sir," they said in unison.

Eric gingerly cupped Paresh's face. "She can't stay here, discarded like this. We have to get her out."

"We need her tissue to regenerate or she'll break," Alex said gently. "But she would heal faster if we could get her home. Do you have any thoughts, Walter?"

"Um…" Walter pointed over his shoulder. "The farmer down the road is with the fire department's EMS unit. He'll have a spine board, straps, trauma bag—whatever you need—in his truck."

"Okay, good. Can you make it happen?" Alex asked. Walter nodded and pulled out his phone, so Alex gave Heron and Cyprian the go-signal. "Walter—tell him to stay put, though."

Minutes after Walter disconnected the call, Heron and Cyprian returned with a bright orange board and equally bright bag. Cyprian held up another piece. "He said to make sure we use the head immobilizer."

"Good start." Alex climbed out. The pit was about four feet deep and narrowly angled around her body. "We can't get to her like this. We need to dig it out more."

"That guy said he has a digger," Heron said. "He wanted to come with us to help."

Cyprian nudged Heron's elbow, prompting him to add, "He also asked if we needed blood." He shrugged. "I think he's *in the know*."

Alex looked to Walter, who also shrugged and said, "The way things have been—I mean, the Fire Chief knows what I know and they're best friends. Plus, he's used to situations like this—well, as much as one can be, anyway."

"Fine, call him, get the digger—and shovels." Alex grabbed his spade. He couldn't stand there doing nothing. "Cyp, head back and help with anything he asks. Bring whatever you think we'll need."

He felt Jonathan's eyes on him. Alex had never seen so much fear there before. Wiping his cheeks merely slicked them with mud as Alex tried to pull himself together. They needed the Crimson Commander—all of them.

To Jonathan, he said, "You and Eric keep at it—this is what you're supposed to do. Stay focused down there and leave everything up here to me. We'll expand the hole out this way to extract her safely. The plots are far enough apart that we won't...eh, hit Lucinda."

He winced at the expression on Eric's face, but straightened his spine and kept his momentum, mentally ticking off a list and planning. Kestrel was on security. Sarah was on...soup. "Heron—as soon as she's immobilized on that board and in the car, take Cyp to Eido and get the oxygenating machine, as much blood as you can, and hoof it back to the cottage. They're going to pour every ounce of their blood into that tub, so we need to replenish it faster than it's going out."

Heron nodded and said, "Walter?"

Walter dragged his gaze away from Paresh. "Wh-what can I do?"

Heron locked onto Alex's gaze and quietly suggested, "Fresh blood?"

Walter paled slightly, but he caught on quickly. "R-right...Juliet runs the blood bank and has supplied Eric for decades. She can mobilize a drive real quick without needing to explain a thing."

"Fresh blood would be better…and we could use it to supplement theirs in the tub, too. Yeah, do it." Alex clapped Walter on the back as he turned away to make the call.

"What about Lord Lucien?" Heron asked quietly.

Jonathan cut Alex off. "I'll tell him later."

"But his blood saved Eric that night," Alex said. "He could—"

"No," Jonathan said with finality. "We can't all be in the same location, and we need him at full health while we're weakened. He'll notice—Michael's not the only one watching. Lucien will come if he's *needed*."

Alex reluctantly nodded. The ants started crawling again, disorganized and wandering, jamming hundreds of spiked feet into his heart. He absently rubbed his sternum and noticed Eric watching him.

"You can do this," Eric said. "I owe you everything, Alex. You found her. *You* saved her…and me. You kept your promise."

III

LUCIEN

The Great Holy War, Continental Europe, 897 A.D.

Jonathan sluggishly paced the horizon, shoulders hunched, filthy, and exhausted. Dissent was growing in the ranks, but that wasn't the cause of his frustration.

Endymion sidled up to Lucien with a sly smile. "Something's wrong with your pet, First Born."

"Fear and instinct do not drive him." Lucien gestured at the bloody mist that obscured the front line. "Unlike your army there. Battle has always been his thrill."

"Ah, 'tis the moment when thrill becomes the everyday that it turns into monotony."

"He's bored, *again*," Lucien said. "And that threatens your vision."

"'Twould appear so," Endymion agreed, "but we can salvage your war machine and the future, yet."

"How so?"

"'Tis a unique moment—remember the girl vampire? Rescued like a damsel by the Deceiver wearing the guise of a chained angel?"

Lucien warily nodded. "What about her? We don't yet know his intentions."

"'Tis true, but I have learned her whereabouts. She's on an isle not too far to the North." He flicked his tongue over his lips. "She has befriended a human."

Endymion's gaze landed on Jonathan. "Which means a virgin village awaits *slaughter*. Perhaps that shall satiate his boredom?"

Lucien waved him off. "If he's bored with war, killing a village won't change anything."

"I agree, but, meeting *her* will shift his focus."

Doubtful, Lucien said nothing.

"Give him Rainne and Alexander and tell him to go. I shall follow. I desire to meet her and will ensure that your pet doesn't kill her."

Silhouetted against the mire of the War's never-ending battle, Jonathan stopped pacing. Lucien turned cold eyes on Endymion. "Call him Jonathan or Second Born. You promised reverence."

Endymion shrugged. "Someday. For now, I'm bestowing upon him a great gift that will serve you both well. She is the leader of the rebellion."

Lucien's jaw clamped shut.

"And she's immune to Rainne."

Lucien silently prodded Endymion to elaborate.

He drew in a contented breath. "See? That tantalizes even you. We can pique his interest——"

"We agreed to burn out his bloodlust. This won't *interest* him. He'll kill her," Lucien interrupted. "She is our only measure of success without knowing the Morning Star's end game. So yes, we are in agreement that he mustn't kill her, but you cannot use that as an excuse to kill *him*."

"'Tis why Alexander shall travel with him and know that I am there."

"I won't fall for your word play, Third Born. Jonathan must not die, regardless of the hand or means. He lost his mind in Japan——I cannot risk that happening again if your plan works."

Endymion covered his heart and swept into a partial bow. "I intended no such implication, I swear on my title. I only meant that Alexander is her ally and he's…eh, *good*…with Jonathan. *This* is the moment we need to get Jonathan into a place between control and boredom, so we can negotiate our withdrawal."

Lucien pulled his aura in close. "Target the human's village and lure this girl out. I expect to see renewed fire in Jonathan…and hear an in depth report about the girl, her immunity, and the rebellion."

"If I am correct, she will absorb his attention," Endymion said.

"Which is why we must keep her alive," Lucien replied coldly. "We know the risks, the possibilities, and many of the unknowns. We're both tired of playing this game. We need to end it."

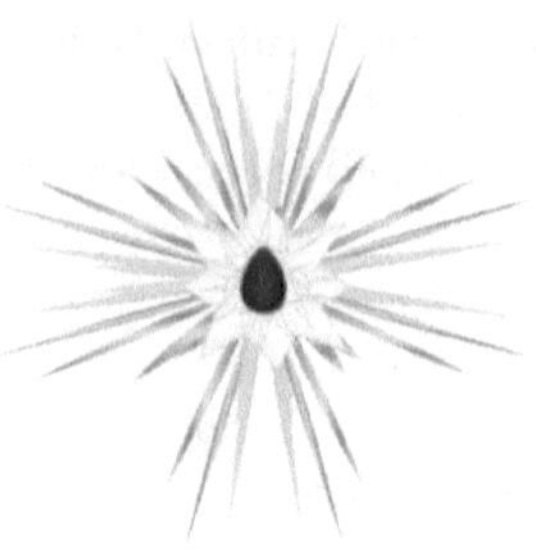

Chapter Fourteen: De Omnibus Dubitandum

I

ERIC

Orison Crossing, Early Autumn 2021

Cyclic whirring coaxed him in and out of consciousness. He'd expected a setup like the heart and lung machine that surgeons used in cardiac bypasses, but that was overkill for a "patient" that was already dead, so instead, a small pump suctioned and oxygenated blood from their veins and drained into Paresh's tub. She was regenerating faster than they could supply her—half of the fresh units from Juliet's impromptu blood drive went into the tub and the rest dripped into their IVs.

The folding chair's metal frame gnawed into his shoulders. He couldn't move without disturbing Jonathan—asleep on the toilet with his feet propped on Eric's lap and a sizeable bloodstain trailing down his collar. As though aware of Eric's guilty eyes on him, Jonathan groaned to life, his head lolling and eyelids fluttering.

"Stop it with that already," Jonathan grumbled.

"Do you feel any better?" Eric croaked. Fatigue ached in his joints and his head weighed so much he didn't know how it stayed upright.

"Blood loss is blood loss," Jonathan said. "Heartbeat?"

"Not yet."

Drifting back into a semi-conscious state, Eric dreamed that she was sleeping. To think otherwise was unbearable. She'd taken ten pints, but her nose was still an open cavity. Once submerged, her body had prioritized healing the damage to her belly and heart over everything else.

Alex slid into an open pocket by the vanity. The two silicon vials in his hand were remnants of a quickly dwindling supply. He hovered with anxious energy and dutifully came in every hour to deliver a nutrient and stamina boost via Paresh's blood. The infused blood didn't stay in them long enough to do *them* any good. It merely picked up enough of their essences to be useful to *her*.

Alex popped off the tops and poured the contents into their mouths. Deep lines etched his forehead as he studied Eric. "Do you need more?"

"Can you spare it?" Eric tried to stay alert, but gravity tugged at his lids as the machine whirred its lulling rhythm.

"…hey!" Alex sounded far away.

Air broke on his cheeks from fingers snapping in his face. Stars shot through the blackness as his head slammed into the wall. Hands landed on his shoulders, pulling him forward. Someone was talking.

Hazy vision drifted over Paresh. No heartbeat. No breathing. No giggles or smiles. No nose.

He hoped Saint Michael wouldn't release her soul while she was in this state. How painful would that be? When he did release her, would her soul come home? Or would they need to take her body to the tree?

"P…Pare…"

"Take it easy," Alex said softly. Another vial streamed into Eric's mouth. "Swallow."

"How much is left?" Jonathan yawned. "We only had three pints to start with—"

"Yeah, and it's been stretched as far as it can go while still being *her* blood." Alex gripped Eric's shoulder insistently. "Is that better?"

His head felt like an anvil on spaghetti. "One more."

Alex gave Eric a third vial and lowly said to Jonathan, "This is the last in silicon. We only have one unopened tube left."

Jonathan cursed under his breath. "It's more important that he gets it. Bring me a warm bag to drink."

Gravity crushed down. Eric grabbed his head and groaned.

"You guys should have your hearts level with your heads—like between your knees."

He removed Jonathan's legs from Eric's lap and helped him fold in half. Alex squeezed back into the vanity's pocket beside Jonathan. "You, too."

"I am not planting my face into the base of a toilet," Jonathan said dryly. "Bring a fresh bag and I'll be fine. I should feel better than he does."

"But you took a hit right before we found her and, as you said," Alex insisted, "blood loss is blood loss. You're her only hope right now. You need to do whatever you can to be strong for her."

Eric imagined the look Alex got for that, but Jonathan let him reposition him. Alex left for supplies and new bags for their IVs.

"How big is a tube?" Eric asked.

Porcelain muffled Jonathan's response. "A hundred milliliters."

"So there's only about six ounces left?"

"After fifteen years, we're lucky to have anything. Lucien extended part of the initial supply with his blood the night he drank from her and placed it in a separate reserve for emergencies—"

"This qualifies—"

"Except that we used most of it to finish delivering the Second New Age to the Nation. When it became obvious that this was going to be a long haul…and with Hawkiel's curse in motion—"

There was a finality to the unfinished statement that held Eric's tongue hostage. He was slowly catching up on the horrors he'd missed over the years.

"When did you last speak to Lucien?" Eric asked at last, pulling himself up to lean on his knees.

Straining under the weight of his body, Jonathan also propped up and mouthed, *yesterday*. He shook his head at Eric's querying brow. "I'm out of his loop. Something's going on, but I don't know what."

"I thought he told you everything."

A lock of hair loosened from Jonathan's ribbon and fell over his face. "Not always. And he's been *different* since Endymion died. He was like that with him sometimes during the War, too—there's a dynamic between them that I've never understood."

"Or questioned?" Eric got a look for that one. "I'm not being a jerk. I mean it. Did you ever ask about it?"

"I rarely challenged him on anything *ever*," Jonathan replied. "I didn't have a reason to, until—" He looked at Paresh.

"I suppose it's safe to assume, then," Eric said, following his gaze, "that this *emergency* hasn't moved him to give you access to the arc?"

Jonathan's tongue curled over the tip of a fang. He gestured, *no*. "I hate seeing her like this, but…I love *seeing* her again."

Eric rubbed his forehead. His consciousness was swimming into the darkness. "I think I'm going out again."

"Hold on for Alex." Jonathan weakly kicked his foot. "Hey! Do you think her Star is still unlocked?"

Eric slipped off his elbows and moaned for Alex. "Maybe. Probably. Who has it?"

"Me."

"Haven't tried?"

"I didn't think about it."

"You can't go now. She needs us here."

"I was thinking of *after*. No one else can go—I don't know Lucien's rationale. Salea's the only threat to Arc Cyber Security. She can manipulate the Hollow in ways not even Lucifer can, but Lucien can easily kill her."

"So, can't risk…sending someone—"

"He might kill. Exactly. We've dealt with too much death as it is."

That hit Eric hard. "I'm s—"

"I don't want your apologies. You don't owe me anything. I pushed you off on Alex instead of being here."

A gravelly chuckle rose from somewhere deep within Eric. "Some penitent heart you've got."

He got a lethargic slap across the cheek. "The rulebook didn't mention being my brother's keeper."

"That's…a default with brotherhood, you idiot." Eric half-laughed and half-sighed. He moistened his lips and managed to raise his head. Connective tissues were building over Paresh's nasal cavity. "Look!"

"Come on, Pare," Jonathan whispered. He gripped the edge of the tub. "You've got this, I know you do."

Hope sparked in Eric's chest and a feeling of peace settled over him. He smiled. Paresh's regeneration quickened. "Alex! *Get in here now!*"

"What is it, Brother?" Jonathan asked, leaning forward.

"The shift in our energy is affecting her." Eric yelled for Alex again.

Alex squeezed in holding three blood bags. "Sorry, sorry! They had another donor finishing up and asked if I could wait."

"Give it to me," Eric said, holding out his hand with newfound strength. He opened the valve and drank as fast as he could. Jonathan did the same, which left Alex with only one bag for the IV. At Jonathan's motion, he swapped it with Eric's depleted bag and ran out to grab one from the chilled supply.

Eric leaned back into the biting chair and wiped his face. He tentatively stroked Paresh's fragile hair. "Come on, honey. Come back to me."

Jonathan shifted uncomfortably on the toilet seat. "Why did I get stuck over here anyway?"

"If you want this chair to torture your back, I'll happily switch."

Jonathan watched Eric pet Paresh with soft eyes. "No…you belong over there, Brother."

II

RAVEN

———————————

Endymion's Compound, Early Autumn 2021

Machinery droned through the darkness alongside a voice that floated near and far without connecting. She reached for it, clutching only air, and the whirring stopped. Silence descended as the darkness lightened and her consciousness slowly awoke. She cracked open a gooey eye.

A shaft of light. A glass wall. A flash of neon pink. Blackness returned with something warm and moist over her eyes. The voice was there again, beyond reach. The damp heat scrubbed, blotted, and wiped with slight pressure and the texture of cotton. It was removed, replaced, and the movements repeated.

She couldn't swallow or choke even though she felt a desperate need to do both. The voice belonged to a girl. Sensation began to return. She groaned. Had her body always felt so heavy?

"Exhale to remove the intubation tubes," the girl said. "Keep it coming. Go. Go. Go."

Quick and steady, the tubing scratched its way out. She coughed uncontrollably and whined with tears dripping from the corners of her eyes. Another warm cloth, soaked in blood, was shoved into her mouth.

"It'll get better soon. Waking up sucks." Her voice sounded familiar.

Raven whimpered. Spasms rocked her lungs, expelling the cloth and spattering her face with hot droplets. She tried to sit up, but a firm hand held her down.

"Not yet. I've shut off the regulator, but it hasn't been flushed from your system quite yet."

The Sandman beckoned through the darkness. She stopped fighting him. The muscles in her esophagus relaxed and she stopped choking. The black was comforting as she sank further. This had to be a dream. Otherwise, Endymion would be——

Her consciousness blasted her eyes open. She saw a blur of rainbow and neon pink.

The girl put a cold finger to Raven's lips. "Sh, Mama Bird."

No! No! No! Raven's silent scream vanished into the void as she squeezed her eyes shut, wishing she'd escape this nightmare. It only got worse every time she woke up. Was Endymion so twisted he'd actually let *Salea* wake her up?

Cloths returned to her eyes and mouth—one to remove protective ointment and the other to leech moisture into her soft membranes. Bringing someone out of deep sleep was a deliberately slow process to avoid shocking the body. That much she understood after seeing it done at the Arc of Celestial Night.

Metal clanked above her head. "I'll open the drip all the way, but that means the sponge bath might hurt," Salea said.

Raven moaned but her heart was screaming.

"You'll need a touch up and a cut—even the tips are barely pink anymore." Salea's fingers swept over Raven's forehead and through a long length of hair. Dread sank into Raven's gut. Her hair had been measurable in inches and now it was in feet. How long had it been?

"I met Eric," Salea revealed dreamily. "He's so handsome. A gentleman. Caring and respectful. He barked at Alex, but was nice to me."

Water splashed in the sponge pan. Salea daubed her arms and torso. Raven silently shrieked at the sensation of millions of needles piercing her skin.

Salea was oblivious. "They look the same, but his attitude is *so* different from Lucifer's. He just radiates power, you know? Ironic, I guess, since they both do."

A splash. Dripping. Blotting. More needles. Raven groaned low in her throat and clamped down on the bloody cloth.

"I miss talking to you like this," Salea confessed. "Lucifer was as fascinated with me as I was with him. I was robbed of a decent male role model and look how important it's become for girls to have their fathers in their lives. They're so involved these days."

Salea moved down her legs where dulled sensation reduced the sponge to annoying scraping. Stuck between dread and nostalgia, Raven had to admit that she missed this version of Salea—brimming with the sweet innocence that she'd stolen.

"In those early days, I'd hoped we'd form a family. Maybe we would have if Hawkiel had been anything like Eric."

Her voice soured. "But he wasn't. And he needed me to go with you to the race that killed my real family."

A bitter laugh. Splashing. Dripping. No sensation below the knees.

"I searched for him almost every day," Salea said. "I went to war zones, to evil places. You never asked, but I know you looked for me. I'm sorry I disappeared on you, but when I found him—*baited* him in 1099—I wasn't about to let him go. I became the demon that haunted the Devil. I'm the only voice in his ear; he doesn't have a better angel."

Her laugh rode an undercurrent of pain. Raven moaned. Salea rushed up to refresh the bloody cloth.

"I was so angry. I wanted him to destroy the world—to kill me and everyone else, vampire, human, whatever." Her voice was down by Raven's feet. "I pushed and pushed and pushed. It took him ages, but he finally saw my vision. Mine! A once-human girl, part of the scourge that had divided his brothers into warring factions."

She quieted. Raven heard water dripping and cloth shuffling. Salea wiped her eyes again and removed the cloth from her mouth. Raven blinked, desperate to focus and too confused to think clearly. "Sahl—"

The swelling in her throat hit her gag reflex. She choked again. Salea stroked her hair and cooed soothing noises.

"I go by Seren, now, Mama Raven," she whispered sadly. "I've grown up, too. My heart was too vile for redemption. I look older than you. I don't take many chances, but nobody recognizes me."

She hovered out of Raven's sightline.

"I can't say I didn't earn this punishment. I thoroughly enjoyed pushing every boundary I ever found, but now—" She sighed. "Eric has confused me. Part of me wants redemption, but I know I'll never seek it genuinely enough to get it."

"Wha…Er…an…Luc…?" Raven's eyelids fluttered. The glass wall with Endymion's bush was on her right, so he hadn't moved her from his room, but she was up higher, in a medical bed—like those used at the Arc of Celestial Night.

"Ooh, right!" Salea cried. "I suppose we've never seen Hawkiel the same way. I've always seen his true face. I hated that he gave it to that bastard Second Born."

"Luc…fer?" Raven croaked. Understanding finally dawned. She remembered—

"But *Eric* is his real twin because they have the same father!" Salea laughed. "If only he was more like Eric. Things would've been so different."

Raven felt sick. Salea was ripping open Lucifer's betrayal all over again.

"I'm honestly torn," Salea said, "it must be a sign from God, right? Maybe I'm meant to be with Eric instead of Lucifer?"

"Wha…what?"

"I know, I know." Salea patted her shoulder. "He's so much younger, but he thinks quite highly of you. I could get a do over—we could be the family we should have been!"

She leaned on her elbow in thought. "But I can't see him as a father figure now. He's moved something in me. He's like…the perfect man."

Salea fingered her hair. "You've missed so much, Mama Bird. He's magnificent—his beast is strong and brutal. He shredded the Crimson Guard to bits over Donovan!"

Icy shock raced down Raven's body and stabbed the tips of her toes. "The Crim—Don…? *What?*"

"Poor thing. You don't have a clue. That dumbass arrogant son of a bitch Corben killed Paresh and Donovan took off with her body. It was hidden for fifteen years! Can you believe that? And—get this—the Crimson Guard had to protect that traitor from Eric's wrath!"

Goose bumps lifted Raven's flesh at Salea's disquieting laugh. "They sooo got what they deserved, like he was delivering retribution for Papa Alexander shooting me in the head."

"Sahl…" Raven tried to swallow again. Her throat was too raw.

"Sh, sh. Don't rush it," Salea whispered. "Your lover is quite daft, isn't he, though? Shooting me with silver bullets? *You* had to know that it wouldn't work, right? And then he did it again! With a crap aim, I might add."

She kissed Raven's forehead. "I tried to give myself wings like yours, but Lucifer only intended those for you. Papa Alex's bullets didn't give me much to work with this time. But then I couldn't have gotten to know Eric. He thought I was you at first."

"What…did you…do?" Raven asked, finally able to meet Salea's hazel gaze. The girl she'd once known had grown into a woman, the soft curves of her youthful face replaced by refined angles, with subtle crinkles creasing her forehead, eyes, and mouth. There was a well of insanity swirling within her pupils.

"I talked to him," she said as though it was obvious. "He didn't want to visit with Paresh's soul and slept with his wife instead. I thought he'd reject me when I wasn't you—"

A genuine smile lit her face. She gnawed her lip. "But he welcomed me. He invited me to come back and protected me from the VaSH."

"No…" Raven tried to shake her head. Railroad spikes slammed into her skull.

"Be patient!" Salea insisted. "Endymion's at the Arc of True Blood sucking up to Lucien. It's just us."

Salea rolled her eyes. "I wish I knew his game. He's pretending and I don't know for whom. But!"

Her grin widened and her fang pierced her delicate skin. "They found Paresh! I thought it was odd, the whole time, that Eric always ran to his wife and never to his soul mate. But I figured it out on my own! Appearances are deceiving—but, well, you know that, don't you?"

The girl excitedly kissed Raven's crown. "You and Rainne are going to bring it all down!"

"No," Raven whimpered. "No."

"I wish I'd met Eric sooner. I really do. But I can't stop it now, even if I take you away. Lucifer promised to make this world burn and he cares enough about me to make it happen."

"He can't. It's not…too late," Raven struggled to get out, pleading silently with her eyes. "He lies."

"Not to me. Not once." Salea shook her head. "And it is too late. I can't be saved now and Darkesiel is almost here."

She tapped Raven's nose. "You and Rainne are supposed to be there to greet him so he forces Hawkiel to choose to leave his cell. But I don't want you to go. You're so lucky that you got such beautiful wings."

Blood dribbled down her chin. "He apologized to me, Mama Raven. When I asked for wings. To be reunited with you. You think he doesn't care? Who else would the Devil apologize to?"

Salea's aura shifted angrily. "Everyone thinks they know him—what drives him, what he wants. But I!" She smacked her chest, still as flat as when she was fourteen years old. "Listened. I saw his vision. I nurtured his desires. He was made of love incarnate—he's not incapable of care. He was abandoned. Worse, even! He was denied, cast out. Who cared about him? What do you think happens to love when it's rejected like that?"

"Salea," Raven begged, desperate to reach her.

"Seren!" she yelled, shoving back from Raven's bed. "Salea is dead. She's lost and can't be found. I'm here to protect her."

"But you are her."

"No, I'm different! You all destroyed her—that innocent girl. You turned her into a monster. She only wanted love, the same as him. We found it in each other. You can't understand."

"But…you couldn't love," Raven croaked.

Salea scoffed. "Because of you, you mean?"

Her smirk shot daggers into Raven's heart. "Lucifer kept my heart unlocked. Salea never lost the ability to love. That's why she spiraled into madness—why I had to pick up her shattered pieces after Alex finally killed the final piece of her shredded soul. She wanted your love, but you were utterly incapable of giving it to her. But not Lucifer. He cared—not at first, I'll give you that—but he did. Didn't you think his grand plan was to take over Heaven? He told you that's not it now. Lucifer wants this world, and he wants it for Salea—I need to see it through. She's the voice in his head thanks to you and the world is going to pay for it."

III

LUCIEN

Lady Rainne's Dwelling, Arc of True Blood, Summer 2006

Enrobed in white silk, the body at his feet was still, and yet, despite the bloodstain over the heart, there were faint tells of life—a pulse and shallow breathing no one else would hear but him. "Raven is off to avenge you. Are you aiding our enemies now?"

Sucking in a rush of air, Endymion sat up. He pulled his robe open and examined his healed chest wound. "'Tis apparent Salea can override Arc Cyber Security."

"Stating the obvious, as well."

"If you hadn't given Raven permission to put Salea in the Arc of Celestial Night, I wouldn't have been forced into this position. She was sent by Lucifer."

"Playing the victim is beneath you." Lucien sneered coldly, his brow dipping between his eyes as a roiling simmer sparked in his gut. "Did you help her kill the Crimson Guard, as well?"

"'Tis nothing beneath me," Endymion retorted, rising. "And I shall do whatever is necessary, though I greatly dislike this manipulation."

"As do I."

"That girl should not be alive, but she is, and she has Lucifer's ear— 'tis not a simple matter to resolve."

An ancient, unwelcome sensation prickled Lucien's skin. Dark lines patterned his hands. "I am not prepared to lose you."

"'Tis no longer our choice." Endymion adjusted his robe and retied his sash. "I must meet with *him*, and I don't have a body double for you to give to Raven."

"I'll deal with it." Lucien's internal chill was icier than it had ever been. "You must destroy Rainne."

Endymion shook his head. "You removed your mark and restored me to the third seat, so *I* shall decide how to proceed. Neither of us ever learned how Rainne plays into Lucifer's final plan, but while we're deducing things, just how do you intend to 'deal' with my body now that you've promised it to Raven? I can disappear much easier with incineration."

"I may have removed my mark, but she has not." Lucien's gaze hardened as his scales returned for the first time in more than two thousand years. "I intend to honor her claim."

"I don't intend to die." With a scoff, Endymion pondered the horizon. "I've lost count of how many times I've marked and unmarked myself as hers. It's possible I no longer belong to her."

"That's irrelevant. She believes you are hers and you claimed her as your queen. Does she even know that marking is removed the same way it's given?" Lucien waved a dismissive hand—a hand darkening in color. "I should kill you myself and be done with it. Let her bury you."

"No, you *should* have killed Salea and given us the ability to do this on our time after gaining more information—time to secure our future. I must tread carefully with Lucifer—his goal has become unclear."

"The prophecy's timing was never ours to control," Lucien retorted. "Salea's actions are a byproduct of the dark spot moving—that must play into the Morning Star's planning."

"Raven's going to seek out the one she thinks is Hawkiel," Endymion said. He shared a look of mutual uncertainty with Lucien. "I must get to him first so he doesn't kill her as a threat to Rainne."

"Will—"

The air pressure changed. Animus Hollow was opening. Lucien held his hand out. "It's Alex, with Raven. You must be dead. *Now.*"

"Hello?" Alex called. "What the hell—"

"Alexander." The timbre of Lucien's voice had deepened alongside his regression in appearance.

"Okay, that's scary as hell," Alex muttered. "My lord, I apologize for breaching protocol. Raven's out cold and I don't know what's happened. She said Lucifer has Lady Rainne?"

"Come to Rainne's." Lucien glared at Endymion and pointed at his feet. "Play dead."

Endymion's eyes narrowed. "Don't enjoy treating me like a dog or I shall enjoy returning the favor in the aftermath."

The scales on Lucien's neck bristled. "Do you wish to battle to the death? Here? With no army?"

Endymion lay at his feet. "'Tis irrelevant who would win—we'd both enjoy it."

He smirked at Lucien's glare.

"Worry not," Endymion whispered, his body going lax. "I am an ally."

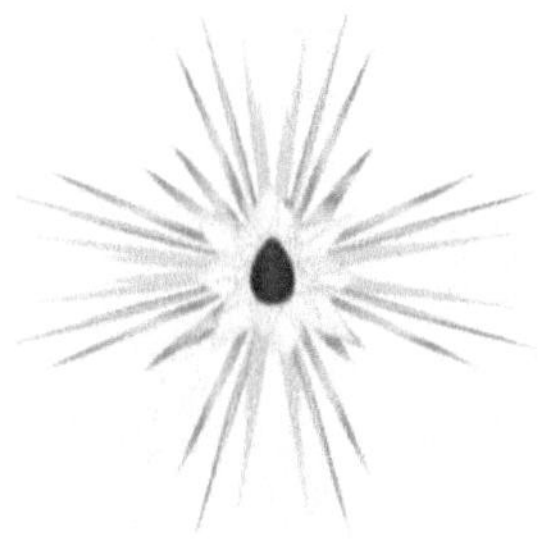

CHAPTER FIFTEEN: CUSP OF INNOCENCE

I

ERIC

Orison Crossing, Early Autumn 2021

Slimy mud and gelatinous blood filtered down the drain as the gentle spray of the handheld showerhead slowly revealed Paresh's restored body. Eric added shampoo to her hair, which had thickened, yet lacked a healthy luster, and worked her soap into a gentle lather to cleanse her face, working delicately over the curves of her new nose.

As the level lowered, he rinsed her shoulders, her décolleté, her breasts, her upper back. When it sank below her ribs, he caught his breath. The showerhead clanked against the tub.

"Oh honey," he whispered, his voice catching. He reached for her blood-slicked belly and curled his hand over the bump——their daughter, *Celeste*, was there——not yet alive, but *there*.

He hoped. What if Paresh's womb had only regenerated to its previous size? What if it was empty?

Afraid to breathe, he imagined their fetus adrift in the river, flung out like the innards of a gutted fish. His strangled cry brought Alex in running. Wiping tears on his t-shirt, Eric sniffled and whimpered, "Wh-what if sh-she's not in *there*?"

Alex looked in the tub and collapsed beside him, scrabbling to confirm the bulge. His fingers dusted over Eric's hand and curved around the bottom side. "The baby——"

"Please!" Eric's tears were too thick to see through. "Tell me she's not in a river. That she regenerated, too!"

Shocked as though slapped, Alex looked at Eric and then at Paresh, his jaw slowly dropping open. "She had to! There's no way she's not in here!"

"B-but—"

"No!" Alex grabbed his shoulder. "Look, there's lots of stuff in there, right? There—there's the placenta, th-the…amniotic sack, the…fetus, the blood—right? *Right?* Some part of her remained or this wouldn't exist—and her soul wouldn't be waiting for her."

Eric reluctantly nodded. The tremor in his jaw chattered his teeth.

Jonathan slipped in behind them. "Is she…?"

"Not yet," Alex whispered. "But, look."

"The baby?" Jonathan asked, dropping his hand to Alex's shoulder.

Alex fixed a firm, but teary, gaze on Eric.

Sarah rapped on the doorjamb and poked her head in. "Sorry to interrupt, but the clearing is totally lit up. I think they're ready."

Eric swallowed over a lump. "Sh-she can't go out like this."

The showerhead slipped out of his grip again and crashed against tub's side. Water sprayed the three of them. He was shaking so hard he couldn't regain control of the damn wand.

"Easy, easy," Alex said. He nudged Eric to switch places. Alex retrieved the sprayer and Eric nervously lathered the soap. Under Jonathan's watch, they cleansed her until the only dirt or blood that remained was caked under Paresh's nails.

"She deserves dignity," Alex said, looking up at Jonathan.

"Her maternity clothes are at the mansion." Jonathan faced Eric.

"The heralds took my clothes back to my house and she won't fit into anything of hers here." Eric sighed and nodded for them to hold her up. "Let's towel her off. I'll wrap her in her mother's quilt and carry her."

He wiped away his tears and stroked her cheek. "I won't let anyone take you from me again, my love."

☽ ✳ ☾

Swaddled in the king-sized quilt, with her hair curling as it dried, Paresh looked like a fragile doll. Shadows of night danced ribbons under the canopy, practically skipping with excitement the farther down the path they walked. Ahead, gilded light beckoned like a beacon in a dark tunnel or the spark of hope on flint. Anticipation built from all around: Jonathan and Alex trailed him closely, followed by Kestrel, Sarah, and Walter.

The woods were alive with noises of the old forest: scurrying and pattering of feet on dusty leaves, sharp cries and excited whimpers, and the humming of frogs and crickets, while melodious songbirds mixed unnaturally with whooping calls from owls and crows. Time had kept them all distant, but not forgotten. This symphonic orchestra had gathered for a cherished and exalted guest.

The entirety of Grandfather Wisdom blazed with golden light. The darts supporting the casements sizzled in the same azure color of the avatar that pressed its attention upon them the instant they stepped off the path. The instruction was clear. Only Eric may approach.

Time slowed to an ethereal crawl as though he no longer walked in the Realm of Man. Harvest dust and decaying spores hung suspended, illuminated like fairy dust that twirled lazily in his wake. He dragged his feet the closer he got, hesitant and curious, and more than a bit anxious. Paresh's arrival had triggered the Second New Age. This resurrection would likely spark the beginning of the end. She was the catalyst to bring an angel's curse to life.

Saint Michael's pulsing avatar exuded a cool wariness of what this moment truly meant for the world. A blanket of stars should dazzle the heavens, but beyond the casements the sky was black. The dark spot was going to land, a muted star that had journeyed to Earth for a decade and a half, a star that carried Paresh's vision of Hell.

The tree's radiance reflected off hundreds of eyes in the shadows. Expectant energy thrummed the air like a guitar string vibrating against his skin. He wanted to hold her there in that moment and prevent the world's continued rotation, entangled in time and spirit, spellbound by a magic only Mother Nature could weave.

But he walked.

Gabriel's voice boomed beneath the concealing casements. "This is her path, child."

Eric dipped his chin in understanding even as the pit in his stomach deepened and his heart entered free fall. He squeezed her closer and kissed her crown. "My love," he whispered.

Gone were the scents of honey and green clover, of summer sun and warmth, of feminine pheromones and innocence. She smelled only of soap and the light floral perfume of her shampoo. He stopped at the base of the grand tree and closed his eyes, his lips lingering atop her head.

He placed her between the glowing roots, watched closely by the eagle-eyed avatar. Eric withdrew her hand from within the quilt's folds and kissed her newborn fingertips.

"Our baby?" he whispered.

"Their souls are linked. Where one goes, the other shall follow."

Tears burned his eyes. *Please wake up, my love.* It was a bare wisp of desire too fragile to utter aloud.

He pressed her palm to the trunk.

Orbs jumped to life, giddy with energy, and the tree pulsed, like a blinking lighthouse on a foggy night. Darkness cascaded in thick ribbons as the light returned to where it belonged.

"Please, please, please," Eric begged. "Wake up. Come back to me."

Her heart thumped faintly.

Air shallowly touched her lungs.

His tears splashed her face as he kissed her hair, her cheeks, her eyes, her nose. He couldn't hold her close enough.

Hands on his shoulders leant him strength. The others gathered around and waited in silence. Eric looked up for reassurance from someone—he didn't care who—and gasped. He gathered Paresh to his chest and stood, turning to present her to the horde of animals emerging from the forest.

Led by a doe and buck, raccoons and foxes, rabbits and coyotes, and skunks and opossums closed in. Birds in every color and shape flew out in oddly structured formations, singing and calling, and swooping down to feed her spirit—he could feel it growing, her essence radiating out to them, her kind heart calming their frayed nerves.

"She's home," he whispered, kneeling and bowing his head. He held onto her hand, desperate not to lose the frail pulse in her wrist.

The others knelt behind him like statues. Walter had little to worry about, but the others contained their auras to avoid spooking Paresh's truest friends.

The doe approached first, nudging the quilt near Paresh's head before turning away. Rabbits hopped over, standing on their hind legs to see her face. He peeled back layers of the quilt and their little noses wiggled. They hopped back behind the doe and the others all came forward, blessing her, nuzzling her, bestowing her with much needed energy from the Earth itself.

Walter gasped when the coyotes licked her cheek like domesticated pets. They sat with Eric the longest, impossibly comfortable with a predator they should instinctively fear. The alpha eventually whimpered and the pack departed.

The doe flashed her tail and the animals retreated, no longer quiet in fear. The forest was alive again, breathing and thumping with the unstoppable force of the natural world's spirit.

Eric couldn't bring himself to move. The mystical motes of light and the golden stream were gone. Time had resumed. Only Saint Michael remained—a visible sentinel for Paresh's soul.

And Celeste's, Eric thought with a surge of emotion.

He hugged Paresh close, warm with love and relieved of grief's pain. Scents of summer wafted up and he imagined her giggling in the Elysian Fields. He smiled.

Alex knelt at his side. "Let's get her home, yeah?" his voice was gentle as he nudged a lock of hair behind her ear.

As Eric stood, Alex slapped a staying hand on his arm. Pressing his ear into the quilt, his face lit up with joy. "It's there! The echo!"

Leaping up, he threw his fist high into the air with a *whoop!* before bending over her once more. "Oh, sweet music, little bean," he whispered.

Alex's smile thinned. He squinted, pressing closer. "There are two echoes. It's not the same as it was before."

"Arrhythmia?" Jonathan asked, leaning in for a listen.

Eric bumped them back with his elbow. "Let's get her home and let her rest. Her heart's working harder than ever right now. She's alive. We'll figure out the rest when she wakes up."

II

RAVEN

Endymion's Compound, Early Autumn 2021

Salea froze when a thundering force rammed the door. The breath that broke over her lips shook with fear.

"No," she whispered, "he's back too soon."

Gaze darting wildly, Salea bounded over the bed and threw her weight into the glass. She bounced off. "Can you move? Walk? Or rather…*fly?*"

The door thundered again, painfully loud in Raven's ears. She couldn't think, let alone process her disbelief or the situation.

The girl gritted her teeth and kicked, and kicked again, each failed attempt darkening her expression with frantic desperation. "Come on, come on," she whined. "They found her! The world's time is up, Mama Bird."

A cold sweat broke down Raven's back. "Salea! What were you trying to do here?"

"Come on!" she shrieked, throwing the dream regulator at the glass.

She hunkered down at Raven's side, grabbing hold of her hand. "He's going to kill me! I didn't know what I wanted until now because I thought I should live for Salea, realize her dreams, but then I met Eric—"

She broke down sobbing. "*I* don't want to die!"

Raven squeezed her hand. "Sal…Seren, I'm sorry."

The door cracked. The latch rattled loose.

Salea shuddered. "Tell Alex, *if you can*, that he did kill her—she died in Animus Hollow fifteen years ago. That's when I woke up and saw a new world, but it's not enough, is it?"

Raven paused a moment before whispering, "No, it's not."

She tightened her hold on Salea's hand as Endymion finally broke the latch. He raced inside, first casting a worrying glance over Raven and then monstrously charging Salea. Raven didn't let go of the girl until he had her.

Raven expected to feel something at the betrayal and fear in Salea's wide eyes. But even as Endymion slammed her against the glass and the girl screamed, Raven felt very little. No guilt, no responsibility, no respite—just a sense of completion. Whether or not Seren was a true personality, Salea was finally going to die. If Raven had done her job, none of this would be happening.

Pinned in place by Endymion's throat crushing arm, Salea kicked and fought, but his patience was gone. He pulled a dagger from his robe and drove it into her heart so hard the tip struck through her back and fractured the glass into a giant web. He yanked the dagger out as he spun on his heel and hurried to Raven's side. Salea's corpse collapsed on the floor.

"My dear!" Concern etched lines throughout his porcelain face. He took in every bit of her all at once, searching her bare skin for injuries with his eyes and hands. "Did she harm you?"

"N-no," Raven said, shocked by the emotional intensity within his aura. Her heart recognized this care, this version of Endymion that was so different from the one she'd last seen. As that memory returned, she flinched at his touch. "Cruel torture…love…loyalty. You asked if I'd claim you as you are…but that I didn't know you."

He lowered his hands.

Raven rubbed her forehead and whispered, "I *don't* know you, do I? I never did."

He drew her hand up to his chest and held it over his heart. "'Tis true you don't know my secrets, my dear. But you do know the core of my being. I have never hidden that from you."

She hated the haze that blurred her vision. "B-but...you *commanded* me, like *Rainne*. Like some *thing* that you could just put to sleep and hide away to forget about." She tried to pull her hand away but couldn't. And not because of him. She could feel the truth of his words and it didn't make sense.

"I did not wish to forget you, my dear Raven, *ever*," he whispered, solemnly. "'Twas too painful to make you suffer unnecessarily so. My commands do not work on you as they do the others—"

His fingers curled around her hand as though it pained him to continue, "'Twas never my intent to ever *try*...I did not want to know if I could do that to you. I never *wanted* to do that to you. Circumstance forced my hand."

He eyed her tears and opened his aura.

His raw regret and fear stole her breath. "But you always enjoy the path you walk—"

"Not of late," he said sadly. He kicked Salea's body. "Seeing *her*...I thought I was losing you forever."

Raven feebly reached for his face. He pressed her palm against his cheek and exhaled relief. Her heart screamed that she knew him even if she didn't. That his cruelty had somehow been a necessary evil that tormented him more than her. That his commands and the sleep regulator had been a mercy for them both. She didn't understand it, but she knew her heart. She blinked slowly and released hot tears.

"I think—" Raven choked. Endymion pulled her up and braced her back as her wings hung limp and heavy. "I think she was rescuing me? She didn't make much sense."

Alarm briefly flared from Endymion's aura. "She wasn't here on Lucifer's order?"

Raven shook her head. "She was infatuated with Eric—she insisted...I don't—"

Endymion's enveloping lavender scent and his rattled gaze made her heart erupt. "You were really afraid she was going to take me to him, weren't you? This is...it's *you*? The you I've always known. I...don't understand what's happening. Why would you work with him in the first place?" Her voice broke. "Let me believe that you were a traitor if you weren't?"

"Oh!" he breathed, dropping a Wraith Reaper dagger on the bed to embrace her. "I'm sorry, my dear. I thought I could follow through to the end, but I love you too much, and everything is happening too fast now."

"Please tell me what's going on!" she begged.

"Had that girl died in 1888, we'd have more time." He kissed Raven's forehead. "But, 'twould still be happening—it began with Eric, the dawn for the Second New Age, and now Lucifer will expect you, but he can't know yet."

Raven went rigid in his arms. "Know what?"

"That I killed Salea—his driving force. He'll know I'm not—" He hugged her tighter and kissed her again. "I've missed you, my dear, but I cannot stop this before it's begun. I can only hope for a chance to save your life. 'Tis been my sole goal."

"There's no time for sentiment, Third Born," Lord Lucien coldly said from the splintered doorway. "If Raven and Rainne Blood Pathos don't go to the village, he won't appear and Darkesiel may not land."

Fear locked Raven's arms around Endymion's torso. He murmured assurances in her ear. "'Twill be alright, my dear. We've found Paresh at long last—"

"And that set everything into motion at once! You need to mobilize your army!" Lord Lucien yelled, marching over to break them apart. "*She* needs to go save the world."

Lord Lucien's cold hand on her skin gave Raven access to his heart. This was the same leader she'd always known. "But I can't! Lucifer told me that I f-failed when I took Salea's innocence. I didn't give her a choice. I broke my heart," she said numbly. "There is no justice there. There never was. I can't trust what I feel—"

Endymion shoved Lord Lucien aside and tucked her to his chest. "Lucifer is mistaken, my dear. I killed you after you bit her. I reset your heart. I couldn't break your bond to *him*, but I could save your mission. I vow it on my life."

"Mobilize your army or people will die," Lord Lucien warned. "Your Knights are here with Rainne's casket."

Endymion snarled, "Raven can't move yet! The instant she enters his range, she'll fall under his control, and I can't prevent that. Paresh needs to be in place first or he *will* use Raven to activate Rainne."

"Please!" Raven cried. "Tell me *what the hell is going on!*"

"The *King* here didn't explain it to you?" Lord Lucien asked on a current of sarcasm as Endymion withdrew into himself and gathered his aura into swirling layers. A jagged seam appeared in the fabric of reality and his aura shot inside.

"Lord Lucien—"

"High Commander, the Apocalypse is here," he interrupted. "Endymion was searching for a way to save you, but I fear that's not possible, and he refuses to acknowledge that. But you know the truth of the matter."

She exhaled a shaky breath. "I s-see. Is it Darkesiel or Hawkiel?"

"Perhaps both. We don't know, but we think Kestrel found the real Hawkiel."

"You know there's an imposter? How?"

Lord Lucien shot cold daggers at Endymion. "He's known from the moment of your birth."

All the air disappeared from her lungs. Sucked out like a vacuum. Angry tears needled her eyes.

"And so have I." Withdrawing into his usual apathetic self, Lord Lucien tucked his hands into his sleeves. His skin was patterned with dark lines. "Because he told me, immediately afterward."

"Then why keep it a secret *from me?*" she cried.

"Would you take back all the good you've done in the world for that knowledge? You would've imploded, hunted Lucifer, doubted yourself—failed to lead as you did so honorably, for so long. You would've doubted your heart, but it never led you wrong."

The emotion he tried to hide was painful to witness. "D-did you know this was going to happen to me?" Raven swallowed hard and pointed at her wings. *"He ripped me open like a coveted hatchling."*

"No," Lord Lucien admitted quietly. "Everything that we didn't know forced us to keep secrets. He and I know more, still."

"What about Master Jonathan?"

"He knows nothing of this."

Her heart was the only thing holding her up against uncertainty's circling sharks. "What's the plan, then?"

"I can't tell you—"

"Because if I know, I may counterattack unwillingly."

"Or tip off Lucifer."

"I'm not going to make it am I?"

Lord Lucien didn't answer.

"I expected I wouldn't. But it's scary to face when it's here. It's been an honor to serve you, my lord. You've always treated me differently, with kindness and consideration—thank you."

"Regardless of your role, you've earned everything you've received, High Commander." He dipped his chin.

Endymion's aura returned and the seam closed. "I've mobilized the Chthonic Knights and distributed orders to Kestrel and Sarah—Lior's soul responded and shall proceed accordingly."

"*That's* your army?" Raven asked.

He stared at her blankly. "No, my dear, they're *all* my army. You're the only one I can't control."

Shock almost rendered her speechless. "All of the VaSH?"

"Think bigger, my dear." He leaned in for a kiss and whispered against her lips, "I am the Vampire King, and you, my dear, are my Queen— you have been from the moment we met. Lucien and his ilk are cousins, not true vampires. I am linked to anyone of my bloodline—true blood and altered alike—and they cannot defy me. Only you can."

She breathed shallowly and pushed him back.

"'Tis much to take in, I know." He combed through her hair and gripped the back of her head. "But your spirit broke my will and I fear my future without you. I enjoyed every moment we had, my dear."

"But…but, the High Council, Lord Lucien." She gestured helplessly at her eternal lord.

Lord Lucien's face of stone gave nothing away. "It is as he says. We formed a pact millennia ago."

"And we shall return to that once we avert catastrophe," Endymion added. "Kestrel and Sarah, and a select few know of this arrangement."

"What about Alex?" she asked softly, afraid of the answer. "If I'm your…your—"

"Queen, my dear," Endymion said. "It's not such a hard word. Alexander shall also go on as before, if he survives."

"Survival is a guarantee none of us have," Lord Lucien reminded coldly. "But one obstacle is down, so let's take care of the rest before the world goes to Hell, shall we? We've already told her too much."

III

LUCIEN

Endymion's Compound, Summer 2006

Lucien exited Animus Hollow into a room that would appear blacker than tar to most. To him, it was a cube of hollowed gray stone. A fitting tomb for the fair Elder there to greet him.

He didn't think his skin could get any tighter. But it had. "They killed Paresh—"

Endymion paled. "I can—"

"—and Donovan hid her body, so, no, you *can't*." Lucien glared with icy eyes. "No one else *on Earth* knows where she is."

"I will—"

"Do nothing," Lucien interrupted. "We have a security detail on him to protect him from Eric and Salea alike. Apparently, she and Corben deviated from Lucifer's plan. What do you have to report?"

"He placed Rainne and Raven into my care."

"Raven is here?" Lucien's body felt infinitely heavier. "So he did reveal himself to her?"

"And carved into her flesh—she has wings."

The floor seemed to give way. Lucien had never felt such confounding rage. It flared into his aura.

Endymion approached a wall and a black portal appeared. He beckoned Lucien. They stepped into a dimly lit hall of carved stone and medieval sconces lit by modern energy. He followed Endymion to a wooden door studded with iron. The Elder pressed his thumb to the electronic scanner and stepped back as the door cracked open. "She hasn't yet awoken."

Inside was a sparse room with one wall of glass. His pink-haired High Commander lay unconscious on a down futon. Wings of iridescent blue sprouted from her shoulder blades. Crimson began to drape the room. His control fled faster than it had in millennia.

"That explains the blood Alex found." Lucien pulled the door shut. "You can't hold them together."

"Agreed. Take Rainne to the Arc of True Blood. It's safest to hold her in her chambers."

"The ventilation system was damaged by the fire," Lucien reminded stonily. "It is not secure."

"Another gift from Salea," Endymion said with disdain. "Put the arc on full lock down. That'll offer enough protection. Lucifer believes I am his ally—Salea shouldn't show up unannounced."

"It will be her end if she does—which puts you in danger."

"No matter. 'Tis as it should be—she's survived on borrowed time for too long."

Lucien's eyes shifted sideways as hunters bearing the crest of the Chthonic Knights approached with Rainne's casket. Before they could bow, he impatiently waved them into the portal.

Once they were safely inside, Endymion lowered his voice and said, "Lucifer believes that Paresh can unlock Rainne. He wants her found. Eric may not be Donovan's largest threat."

"Unlock? As in deprogram?"

"As in, restore her free will. He believes he'll retain his control, but I think he's wrong. When he releases her—"

"I'm not letting her out of that arc. You're lucky I agreed to keep her alive."

"Find Paresh and keep Rainne alive," Endymion demanded. "I must fulfill my role in preparing them both, and that includes delivering them when the time comes."

"Our future will hinge on your ability to shield Rainne from his command," Lucien snapped. "If she kills a single innocent—"

"'Tis not her will!" he seethed through tight lips. "She's never wanted *any* of the control we've exerted over her! Thousands of years and she could *never* say no. Those twin angels hold in their hands the lives of every single planetary soul—"

Lucien's hand shot up. "Your guest has awakened," he said lowly. He gave another disapproving look and followed the hunters into Animus Hollow.

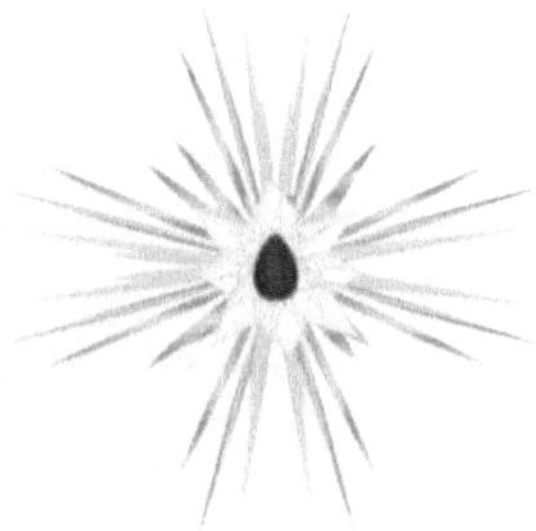

Chapter Sixteen: Dost Thou So Fall

I

PARESH

Orison Crossing, Early Autumn 2021

Like a breath exhaled, a fiery, sable cloud rushed past, burning her eyes and throat. As before, flames ravaged a broken city torn asunder by devilish growls. The very air seemed to melt under intense pressure. Buildings crumbled into screams of the tormented.

Unlike before, she didn't scrape at her throat or gasp for air when thick black smoke snaked down her esophagus. This time, she knew it wasn't real.

Yet.

The male figure stood unnaturally tall at the epicenter, tugging at chains that crossed his chest. He possessed the same spiritual imprint as Gabriel—Hawkiel, his brother, screaming as his skin burned like a candlewick.

The moment he saw her, everything went quiet. Flames continued to devour everything in a downpour of brick and glass. His eyes burned with the holy blue flame she'd come to know so well. She was too far away, but reached out to him anyway. The heat evaporated the tears in her eyes before they could spill over.

Instead of breaking his restraints to unleash his wings of light, he sucked in the largest of breaths, and the whole of the scene disappeared into his mouth, leaving behind only velvety blackness. It struck her odd: it was the sky, but there were no stars and the moon was gone.

Darkesiel, a voice whispered.

A speeding fireball illuminated the atmosphere and sucked the darkness into it. Prisms of light sparkled beyond the silver crescent, but as the last of the black was absorbed, time itself split in twain.

She stood on the borderline, not understanding. She hadn't seen this before. On one side of the line, she reached out as though to catch the fireball. It looked so small, that high up, like a baseball. The ground rushed away and blended into the ruddy hue of every color mixed together. The source within the fireball became clearer. Humanoid. Giant. Flaming blue.

She whispered his name and he accepted her hand.

Suddenly, she was back on the line. One the other side, she merely watched. The fireball streaked through the sky, the force of its speed discharging kinetic layers that broke the laws of physics. He crashed into Orison Crossing, cratering downtown and obliterating homes and businesses with waves of superheated energy.

She braced against hot wind that threatened to erase her, as well, but refused to look away from the man in the crater. He, too, wore chains, connecting wrist cuffs to ankle shackles. They didn't restrict his wings—beautiful, inky, and reflecting the cosmos. Like Hawkiel's, they flexed with greatness and stretched so high they knocked satellites from orbit.

Fire encircled the crater and hungrily demolished the land, buildings, and trees. People and animals alike didn't have time to scream. They were vaporized.

Painlessly, she hoped.

As with Hawkiel, time seemed to stop. She noticed that it corresponded to her shift in emotion. The flames continued, but the wave of death stalled. Darkesiel cocked his head. He stretched out his arm and turned his palm up. She mimicked him and was pulled to the crater, where she stood palm to palm with him.

His restraints turned to ash and hovered in a thick cloud. She could barely see the flame in his eyes, flickering at intervals as he blinked, but she felt them in her soul. Darkesiel recognized Gabriel in her, but that wasn't enough.

When she tried to speak, a cold gust swept her off her feet and deposited her into a creepy dungeon with walls of flesh and throbbing webbed veins. She covered her belly instinctively as she turned in a circle.

Demonic growls came from grotesque shadows that crawled over the outside. An open door led to a tunnel with faintly quivering blue light at the end. She completed the turn and a cot appeared. A chained man—Hawkiel—sat on the edge, elbows on his knees and head hanging between his shoulders.

"I can't leave." His voice was melodic but coarse, his hair and skin coated with thick layers of dust—it covered the bed and floor, too. She stepped back and left deep footprints that caved in at the edges.

She tried to speak, but, as before, her voice was gone. She ran to Hawkiel, stirring up a cloud scented of sulfur, and crouched with her hands on his knees, squeezing in urgency.

He looked up and let his eyes drift into hers. His flame was muted, a husk of what it had been, of what it could be again.

"Hope is a pitfall, Child," he said. "If I leave—"

He spared a passing glance at the door and then gazed over the crawling silhouettes. "They will follow and unleash Hell on Earth."

Moisture surged into her eyes. His cell alone seemed like Hell.

"You must tell my brother that I've made my choice." He locked eyes with her and briefly released his true fire. "I can only leave if he chooses me."

She tried to talk again, to tell him about her dual vision, that his brother had already made a choice. But nothing came out. She couldn't tell them what they couldn't tell each other.

"Do not mourn for me, Child," Hawkiel said. "I chose this torture by not choosing long ago."

He covered her hands and gripped them tightly, but not painfully so. "Only you can pass him my message. He will recognize Gabriel in you, and once you see me—"

He squeezed tighter and poured energy into her hands. "He will recognize me, as well."

Intertwined crescent moons against a twelve-pointed star appeared on her hands. A sucking wind developed in the tunnel. She wanted to scream for him to wait, to tell her why he'd made his choice, but he let go and returned to his original position, the dust of his tomb flowing out with her. She saw the shine of his golden hair and skin and realized for the first time that Darkesiel was his opposite—his other half—which meant his hair and skin likely gleamed like polished obsidian.

She remembered Gabriel's tale of the siblings Helios, Selene, and Eos, and thought of Hawkiel as representative of the Sun, which would make Darkesiel the Moon. Without each other, the balance would tip, and without Eos, they couldn't function. They had to maintain an equivalent state or a false god would rise. So who represented Eos, the Dawn Bringer?

As the vortex sucked her into the tunnel, she realized this went beyond the twins and their curse. Gabriel had sent her back without the vital third piece of the equation and nothing in her vision had offered a clue about finding it on her own.

II

SARAH

Endymion's Compound, Early Autumn 2021

Sarah got lucky and ducked in with the troop of Chthonic Knights carrying Lady Rainne's casket. She paused behind them to use her sight on the compound and found multiple familiar lights in Endymion's room.

So, he does have Raven here, she thought indignantly. *The whole time, I bet, too. So why is he bringing Lady Rainne here?*

She charged ahead of the Knights and turned them back to the entry cube using hand signals. Until she knew more, she wasn't letting him continue this charade. She crept down the hall. Endymion's door was in fragments.

She thought she was out of sight, but she felt Lord Lucien's undeniably cold gaze hit her like a slab of frozen marble. A creeping sensation wound within her gut as she stepped through the broken door and saw the special bed and connected tubing, blue feathers, bloody webbed glass, and a body on the floor. She looked again with her eyes closed and confirmed Raven's presence in the bed and a faint, unwelcome essence that ignited her into altering.

As crimson took over her vision and her fangs descended, she heard Endymion ask, "Why are you here?" while Raven whispered, "Sarah?"

"I came to double check the security protocols on Rainne's casket." Sarah sidestepped Endymion and unsheathed the gold dagger at her back. "Now you answer—why didn't you tell us Raven was here? No— why did you *hide* her from us? Deliberately. You wouldn't let me in because you knew I would've seen her."

"You need to return to your post," Endymion growled. "All is as it should be here."

"I disagree." Sarah gestured in the direction of the cube's entrance. "Nothing is right about this. We have blindly and loyally followed you our whole lives." Sarah licked her lips as she inched closer to Salea. Her light was growing brighter. "So you tell me where your head was when you let that girl live *after she cut mine off?*"

"*Your* head?" Raven gasped. "Lior? How is this—"

"I always respected you, Raven. And Alex. I still do," Sarah said, briefly lifting her gaze. "But you have always been *his* weakness, an obsession that outweighed all else. Seeing you here? Now?"

Sarah pointed the dagger at the door and glared at Endymion. "Makes me wonder why Rainne Blood Pathos is here. You told us she was leverage to get Raven from Lucifer! But here's Raven! *So why is any of this happening?* Putting them out there is an unnecessary risk! Paresh needs to touch Rainne, first!"

"Lucifer is making his move and Paresh is not yet awake," Endymion said thinly, his eyes flashing with warning. "If we don't deliver, Darkesiel may not land."

"Yeah, I recognize that 'no one talks back to me' look, but I'm a Black lesbian who grew up in a small white town. None of that shit matters in our world, but *ohh boy* does it change things in theirs! Welcome to my *human* mechanism for survival—perhaps if I'd had it back then, I might've saved *my head*!" Sarah was yelling. She could calm down, but what was the point? "I am not disposable, and I refuse to blindly follow you when the whole reason we retreated from the War was to get away from a creator that didn't care about our lives!"

"I value your life greatly," Endymion said through his teeth.

Sarah rolled her eyes and pointed at Salea. "Right."

"Would you have said no to Raven's request?" Lord Lucien asked emptily. "After she confessed that Salea was damaged because of her actions? That you were dead because of her mistakes?"

Sarah faltered a step, but only because Lord Lucien was the one asking. "Perhaps not. But that still doesn't excuse Rainne's presence here."

She unclasped her cloak and let it slip down her left arm, keeping Salea in her sightline as she glared at Endymion. "Haven't you seen the sky? Nothing we do is going to stop Darkesiel—he's already coming down. Lucifer holds *nothing* over you, now—well, actually, he never held anything over you, did he?"

"He holds Raven's will," Endymion protectively embraced Raven, who was staring at Sarah in slack-jawed disbelief.

"How are you connected to Lior?" Raven whispered in the same moment Lord Lucien said, "She is right—with Salea dead, I can return Rainne to the Arc of True Blood and safely lock her beyond Lucifer's reach."

"Oh, that little bitch isn't dead. Yet." Sarah pointed the dagger at the blade on the bed. "No weapon with silver in it can kill her. I forged this in iron and gold—"

Behind her eyelids, the girl's light was nearing the level of consciousness. "In case I got a happy little moment alone with her."

"No!" Endymion's voice festered with quiet rage. "Lucifer maintains his control over Raven and I can't break it yet!"

Sarah's spine stiffened. She whirled around yelling, "*With that again? The world has gone to shit the last decade and a half, and now that Hawkiel's Apocalypse is upon us, you're hinging the entire world's fate on your obsession? How does Raven feel about that?*"

Raven's eyes widened and she made a squeaking noise just as Salea's bladed claws pierced through Sarah's abdomen from behind. Sarah swore under her breath and threw her cloak up into the air.

"So. Fucking. Annoying!" Sarah lurched forward and ducked low, pivoting on her heel to slam a fist into Salea's knee and stab the dagger into her opposite thigh.

As the cloak fluttered down, Sarah popped up and shattered Salea's hip with another punch while angling the dagger to rip through her spleen. She wrapped the fabric around Salea's face and whipped around to her backside, jabbing the dagger into both of Salea's lungs repeatedly.

She yanked Salea onto her heel as she rolled onto her back and kicked the girl into the manzanita's atrium. Glass shattered and sliced into Salea's thin frame as she flew through and landed on her back. Sarah wound the cloak around her arm and jumped on top of her, pressing it into Salea's snapping mouth. The girl tried to strike with her silver monstrosities, but her movements were sluggish and easy to dodge as she choked up blood and labored to breathe.

Sarah grinned. "I'd hoped to watch you scream, but you're breathing far too easily—"

She shoved down on Salea's breastbone and crushed her chest cavity before stabbing straight through her neck, carotid to carotid. She smirked at the girl's gurgled attempts to gasp.

"See, *this* is how it should have gone the first time," Sarah cooed quietly. "But back then, I preferred the challenge of fighting without weapons."

She leaned in close. "Lesson learned since it cost me my head."

Salea's eyes suddenly widened in recognition.

Sarah grinned. "Ahh. There…you've got it now, yeah."

She withdrew the dagger slowly and put the tip to the girl's forehead. Raking her tongue along her teeth, Sarah sneered. "I wish I shared your affinity for decapitation, but I kind of enjoy good old fashioned vampire hunting."

She rammed the blade down, getting slight pushback against Salea's skull before it sank into her brain. The girl's body went limp. Sarah closed her eyes. The light was fading.

"You're not too comatose not to hear me in there, yet, right?" she whispered into Salea's ear. "Because I wanted to tell you…that baby you enjoyed tearing from Paresh's womb? She regenerated, too. You and your filthy comrades were nothing but an irritating glitch that history will forget. Our lady has blossomed at last, and our peace will reign despite your chaos."

She yanked the dagger free and staked Salea's heart. The light finally went dark.

She threw her head back with a satisfied howl and flinched at a bright light far above her. She opened her eyes. A winged shadow loomed over the shaft's skylight. The frosted glass dome shattered.

"It's the Deceiver!" she yelled, diving back into the room as glass rained down.

An angel with six wings descended and hovered over Salea. Sarah gawked at his appearance. Hadn't she known what he looked like? How could she possibly forget *that* face?

"*Lucifer!*" Raven screamed, leaping from the bed and landing on his back, fully demonic, viciously ripping out tufts of skin and feathers.

He threw her off. Her wings slapped the air. She flew at him again, jerky and awkwardly. Endymion charged behind her. Lucifer kicked him away and again threw Raven off. When she came at him again, he turned to catch her, and held her tightly to his chest, his flaming eyes sorrowfully landing on Salea's body.

"Where is Rainne Blood Pathos?" His gaze pierced through Sarah to Lord Lucien, who said nothing.

He pointed a perfectly sculpted finger at Endymion. "I underestimated you, Third Born. Do not make that mistake with me."

Raven's ribs cracked in his arms. "Deliver the weapon or I'll snuff out your queen."

His eyes flared when they hit Sarah. Searing pain dropped her to the floor clutching her chest.

Endymion lunged again, but the seraph flapped all six wings and shot up the shaft. The gust blasted Endymion into the room.

"What," Sarah panted, "just happened?"

"Endymion bet Raven's life against the world's fate and gave Lucifer his leverage." Scales gleamed on Lord Lucien's face.

"B-but, we have Paresh!" Sarah cried.

"As much as I agree," Lord Lucien spat, "I cannot give up on Raven. She was charged with protecting this world by Gabriel. Endymion— you will deliver and recover Rainne. Do not fail me."

☽ ✳ ☾

RAVEN

She thrashed and slapped in vain. Thrusting with powerful wings, Lucifer held her in locked arms. As they flew farther from Endymion's range, she felt herself slipping away, like her mind was tethered to that bed and hadn't stayed with her body.

But it was still her body. She sank her fangs into his arm and clamped her jaw shut to force his muscles to spasm. Her wings ballooned open and caught the current. She sailed away from him, but the winds shifted and carried her right back to him. She flexed her shoulders on instinct and flew over him as he dipped to catch her.

He yanked on the brown hair that dangled below her feet and laughed bitterly. "Enjoy the uncertainty while you can, Little Bird. Your will won't hold out much longer."

She frantically kicked at him, but couldn't connect. Her mind felt fuzzy. She tucked her wings to her back and let herself fall. More of her awareness returned as the Earth rushed up at her.

She didn't have time to be scared or to question what had happened. If she couldn't escape Lucifer, she had to remove herself from his equation. She twisted into a dive and sped up.

She could make out shapes on the ground. It was all red and wavy and rocky. It was a desert. A red desert. But she'd sworn she saw trees and even the ocean after Lucifer shot up the shaft. She'd briefly thought it looked like South Africa, but this…this looked like the Middle East.

What does it matter? That red sand is about to get a bit redder.

She felt Lucifer gaining on her. His fingers tangled in her hair and swept the bottom of her feet. His hand started to close around her ankle. She kicked with everything she had and got free. She didn't look back. It wouldn't do her any good. She only had one way out.

She could never look back. Ever.

I love you, Alex.

She hooked the air to veer toward a limestone plateau. Surely a vampire would go *splat* from that height regardless, but blasting into rock seemed more absolute than into grains of sand easily blown and arranged by the wind.

So many moments of her life wanted to scroll through her mind. She steeled her focus. She'd had no control over her life. It couldn't even be called hers. From the moment of birth, she'd been Lucifer's pawn, and later, Endymion's plaything. She soured at the thought but knew in her heart that she was wrong about him. That Endymion had loved her. That the Hand of Divinity had touched him and granted his psychopathic mind the ability to care about her. He hadn't enjoyed hurting her—and he enjoyed everything.

The ground was rushing up faster. She knew it wasn't—not really. She'd hit terminal velocity. It only looked faster because she was closer. The end was coming. She closed her eyes, frightened to watch her own death even though she knew she wouldn't feel a thing.

III

JONATHAN

Arc of True Blood, Early Autumn 2021

Undisturbed layers of dust and pollen did not give Lucien's dwelling a *dwelled in* look. Neither did the open courtyard wall with damp rotting frames or a view overrun with decaying petals from the eternally blooming cherry tree. Nor the unfixed China cabinet damaged from their last fight or the fifteen-year-old hole in the entrance's shoji screen. The bamboo fountain was dry and motionless on the deck. Planting his hands on his hips, Jonathan glanced down the slope at his abode and shook his head at its equally appalling landscape.

"Lucien, where are you?" he asked.

Paresh's unlocked Vampiric Star let him Hollow-hop to check Snowblood Square, the bathhouse, and Lucien's favorite gardens—all wild with neglect. He searched the rarely used equipment rooms for Arc Cyber Security and the structural access ducts. Everything was working, a surprise since nothing had been maintained. Lucien hadn't merely locked down the Arc of True Blood; he'd put it on a path to ruin.

Where the hell is he? His frustration mounting, he marched from building to building, stopping only when he noticed the refurbished doors on Rainne's residence. Curiously, the pathway was clean and manicured, and the shady trees seemed to breathe with the only enviable life in the whole arc.

Unease shifted in his gut.

The familiar *clunk* of Rainne's bamboo fountain echoed down the hall. Not a trace of damage from Salea's invasion remained, and fresh clove oil and wax saturated the air over the ripe scent of Rainne's metallic blood. Rather than going past her chamber door, he took the shorter path to her sitting room—a space that definitely looked kempt *and* lived in. There was a tea tray and cushion on the deck and the courtyard had been tended.

Why would Lucien stay with Endymion's body instead of repairing his own—

"Why are you here?" Lucien rounded the corner from Rainne's chamber, moving with the fluid grace that belonged only to him. Dark lines and scales patterned his teal skin and his hair gleamed like polished hematite. His black eyes landed on Jonathan with crushing intensity, but his aura walled him off.

Shocked into silence, Jonathan tried to understand, but there was no understanding. Not this. Not now.

Warning rumbled deeply in Lucien's throat. "You should not have left Orison Crossing. Lucifer is making his move—he's forced our hand. *You should be there!*"

Jonathan staggered back a step. "How do you know what he's done? She's not even awake yet!"

"You are supposed to protect her," Lucien growled, his scales darkening. "Why. Are. You. Here?"

Jonathan's internal fire flared and he let it blast Lucien. "Why are *you* here? If Lucifer's moving, we need you! And, why are you *here*? Do you want solitude so badly that you'd damn the world?"

The scales on Lucien's throat bristled. His aura emanated dangerously quiet fury. "I do not enjoy being alone and I never asked to shoulder the Nation's burdens, but I've been stuck with both time and again. *Everything* I do is a furtherance toward our future, my own desires *be damned!*"

The friction between them crackled.

"Then why are you *here*?" Jonathan demanded, pointing at Lucien's ritualized set up outside. "Why did you lock yourself up instead of helping us? *Me?* You left me there to deal with Eric and forced me to lead the Elders while you sat up here *playing house with a corpse!*"

"*I was guarding Rainne to keep her out of Lucifer's hands!*" Lucien roared. "And that sacrifice? Withdrawing and putting all of that responsibility on you for a few measly years? *It was for nothing! Endymion's taking Rainne to him as we speak!*"

Jonathan's ears rang too loudly to hear his own response, if he had one. Lucien had blown all thought from his mind. He just stood there, struck dumb, but somehow standing even though he'd swear his legs were gone.

Lucien's chest heaved under his wrath and his aura was completely open, blazing with emotions far beyond anger. Loneliness, loathing, regret, doubt. His skin hardened into armored scales as he regressed more than Jonathan had ever seen.

"Endymion's alive?" Jonathan whispered, his eyes wide and mouth moving silently in between words. "And...R-Rainne—"

Lucien clenched and unclenched his fists, a terrifying exercise that Jonathan recognized from the only time Lucien had ever lost his temper with him. He took a step back.

"Just...tell me what's going on," he said, forcing his voice to level out as his mind whirled out of control. "We're not seeing the same picture."

"We never have, and as much as I hate to admit it, that predates Endymion's arrival in our lives."

"Things changed when he showed up." Jonathan held his hands up. "But we don't need to go back that far. I don't understand the *whys*, but here's what I see, all right? He was dead, but now he's not. Lucifer had Rainne, but she was here. And now she's with Endymion who's taking her to Lucifer. What do you see?"

"Handling the Elders has changed you." Lucien's fists clenched and unclenched. "Even more than *she* did."

"We don't need to fight, Lucien." Jonathan sighed. "I'm sick of fighting with everyone. I want to understand for once."

Lucien fumed awhile. Finally, he said, "It goes back to an evolving strategy Endymion formed during the War after Kestrel and Lior acquired their sights. He saw the Deceiver take Raven off the battlefield the day she was born. Endymion has known since then—and so have I—that Lucifer was planning something bigger than the War. We never definitively figured it out, but we got most of it. That left us to determine how his plans affected the Treaty and Hawkiel's curse."

"Okay, okay," Jonathan whispered. "That's a lot. The Deceiver—"

He gasped. "*Hawkiel?*"

"Was Lucifer all along. Kestrel and Sarah believe they've found the real one."

"H-how do you—"

"They report to Endymion. He reports to me."

The knot in his gut became a heavy stone swiftly gaining weight. "Circle back to Endymion being alive, please."

Lucien's fists tightened. Jonathan subtly added to the distance between them.

"Neither of us foresaw Salea's attack. Endymion chose the path of sympathizer knowing that Lucifer wouldn't question it."

"But he's on our side, right?"

Jonathan patted the air at Lucien's piercing gaze. "It's a fair question. I want to understand."

"He wants the same thing I want."

Questions collided and twisted together in Jonathan's head. He needed to pluck the right one or Lucien was going to attack. A few strings suddenly connected. "Salea took Rainne…who was under Endymion's care. So…he 'died' and went to Lucifer to maintain his guardianship?"

"He's fond of not failing, as you know." Lucien's jaw bulged. "And he inadvertently gained guardianship of *Raven* under Lucifer's order, as well."

Jonathan stumbled over his feet. "Ra-Raven's alive?"

"I've clearly stated that Lucifer has Raven many times. Why would you assume she was dead?"

"Wh…why *wouldn't I think she was dead?*" Jonathan sputtered. "You…you shut down every attempt to search for her! We should have…I can't believe you abandoned her like that!"

"She was with Endymion," Lucien growled, fisting and unfisting.

"Was?"

"Lucifer is moving. He took her."

"We should have rescued her!" Jonathan insisted. "If Rainne was here and Raven was with Endymion, why did Endymion need to keep up the ruse? We could have regained control of both of them!"

"*They murdered Paresh!*" Lucien screamed. He whipped around and threw Rainne's loveseat through the wall. "*And Lucifer disappeared after he attacked Eric!*"

Jonathan froze as his thoughts rapid fired over his fear. He stared at a spot on the floor as the threads connected. "You didn't have a choice," Jonathan whispered. "Endymion had to stay on the inside to know what Lucifer was going to do. You couldn't blow his cover."

Jonathan looked up. "Pare was the lynchpin; she stopped everything. That's why they kept her in stasis for so long. Lucifer could've started his assault years ago—wiping out humans and wreaking destruction before Darkesiel ever landed—he would've won."

Lucien's monstrous fingers slowly flexed at his sides.

"Finding her put everything into motion at once, didn't it?" Jonathan asked quietly.

Lucien nodded. "Lucifer discovered Endymion's betrayal and kidnapped Raven."

The stone dropped *hard*. "The demand is Rainne—"

"If we don't deliver her, he'll go after Paresh," Lucien said. "He still might—and *you left her!* If you loved her, you wouldn't have left her side. *You're supposed to be there to protect her because you love her the most!*"

Tendrils of jealousy wove through the rage in Lucien's aura. They coiled in tightening layers around Jonathan.

"The most? What are you talking about? That's not how love works!" Jonathan yelled, sliding off the edge of diplomacy into panicked confusion. "I can love her and prioritize! I can *trust* the others who love her to protect her, too, and still love you! Why do I need to love anyone *more?*"

"Love is an ugly emotion. A lie. You never lived under the nameless god," Lucien said, rough and simmering. "You were born with the privilege of knowledge. I had to learn. I had to question, to think, to wander, to overcome. *Survive.* I saw what false gods did to humans and what humans did to them. Excuses. All of them! And Lucifer is *exactly* like them! Blamed for everything bad thing that happens even though they do it to themselves!"

"What...?" Internal alarms blared under a suffocating blanket of fear. Jonathan was missing a crucial piece of Lucien's picture.

"Everything I've done to this point has been an effort of holding our nation together while trying to determine Lucifer's end goal." Lucien took a step toward him.

He took a step back.

"Before you were born, I already knew that the nameless god had created this planet for the Children of Earth—this is their playground to love, consume, replenish, or destroy at their will. That's the point of this realm. Lucifer's battle has never been about them, or he would've given me the knowledge he bestowed upon you and Endymion."

They each took another step. "Because when you *think* and *survive* like I did you realize blatant truths about your existence. I was a prototype for *function*, a half-hearted test without real purpose, because humans are Lucifer's excuse as much as he is theirs. He uses them to lash out at the one who created him like the spoiled child of a loving parent. But us? We've never known love or entitlement. All we wanted was peaceful coexistence and the ability to enjoy the Earth as humans do— and I had intended to deliver that."

Another step. Jonathan backed into the wall. Lucien kept coming.

"I *know* change is never easy. I have adapted time and again to achieve my goals and the life I want, and I will never stop. I put in the effort, the work, even if it means sacrifice. But all I've ever wanted is a companion and a place to call home—"

Sorrow bounded to the front of his aura as he closed in. Jonathan reached for him but was too scared to touch him.

"I saw his face, Jonathan. Lucifer saw Salea dead, and I saw the emotion there, the anger, the *love*—I recognized it, and now I'm left questioning everything I've done. Everything Endymion's done. Change, by nature, doesn't give you what you want, but I thought that as long as I had you, even if you weren't *here*, I'd never be alone—"

"You said you'd rust for me," Jonathan whispered. "I love you in a way I will never love Pare or anyone else—we were made for each other—"

"By a being of love incarnate. A being who desired this planet's demise *before* we killed the object of his affection."

"*Salea?*"

Lucien closed the gap between them and pressed Jonathan's hand against his chest painfully hard. Beneath the silk kimono, his heart thundered through his armor. "I'm sure he denies his grief to himself, but love is a limitless and powerful force acknowledged or not. So tell me, how can we ever trust such an unstable, fickle emotion? *Love is going to destroy this world.* How can I rust for you? How can we say that our love possibly matters in a world like this?"

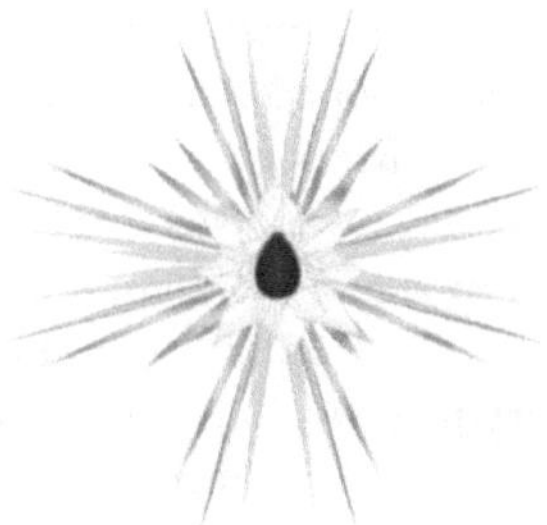

CHAPTER SEVENTEEN: STARS DON'T FALL
LIKE FIGS

I

PARESH

Orison Crossing, Early Autumn 2021

Something sharp tugged on her arm. For a second, she allowed herself to revel in the ability to *feel* anything, regardless of pain. She'd experienced every emotion imaginable while in stasis and, through Gabriel's vision, had seen the various fibers of the world's path, but she missed physical touch.

The blinds were drawn, so the room was dim—but not dark enough yet to be night. She hadn't known if she'd awaken in her bed at the cottage or in Eric's bed. Either would've made her happy. She was finally awake, after all, but seeing the furniture from her childhood home came as an unexpected relief. She smiled at the animal chatter outside.

Lightly fingering the catheter in her arm, she followed the line to Eric, asleep at her side, and carefully rolled over to kiss his cheek. An IV blood bag dripped into his other arm.

He seemed stuck in a dream as he caressed her cheek with his thumb. "Im…ist…you."

She kissed him again, sighing at the feel of his lips so cushioning and perfect against hers. "I 'mist' you more."

The door burst open and Alex blew in in wide-eyed amazement, looking both elated and determined to fight off a horde of demons. If he only knew what she knew.

Now who's keeping secrets? she thought as she stretched her free arm out to him. He melted into her embrace, weeping quietly. "Oh, Alex, I know it's been hard. You've done so much and grieved for Raven all alone—I am sorry. You'll see her soon, I promise. But..."

She glanced sideways at Eric, who oozed exhaustion in his struggle to wake up. "Thank you for taking care of him."

At the guilt in his averted gaze, she gave him a gentle squeeze. "I know, Alex. I know everything. It's okay. Really. It is."

As Alex choked on a sob he'd held in for the last fifteen years, she nudged his head to her shoulder and stroked his hair. Eric leaned up on his elbow and cupped her cheek.

"You...you're—"

"Alive? Yes, my love. I'm home now." She nuzzled his palm and held Alex in place, trying to absorb as much of their pain as she could. "I love you both and you've done nothing wrong, so please don't waste another second on regret or what might have been. Outside influences necessitated the current path. I knew it was going to take a long time, and I promise you both that I am thinking clearly, feel greater than great, and am well aware of the situation. You don't need to protect me anymore. But...where's Jonathan?"

"Checking on Lucien," Eric murmured, as Alex made a dreamy sound of agreement.

"That's not going to go well," Paresh whispered. She patted Alex's shoulder. "Can you see the moon?"

He looked up, puzzled. "It's three o'clock in the afternoon."

"Can you check anyway?"

Understanding slowly crested. "Oh shit...Darkesiel?"

She blinked deliberately and let her eyes direct him to the window. He pulled up the blinds, but the room's lighting didn't change.

He slowly backed away. "He hasn't blocked the sun, *yet*. Lucifer will—"

"Endymion's on that, don't worry." Paresh took in the inky veil beyond the glass and whispered for Gabriel. He'd gained permission to enter the Realm of Man after she awakened.

Confused, Alex said, "Endymion's dead...don't you remember?"

"He's not." Paresh kissed Eric again and swung her legs over the side of the bed. She was dressed in a lightweight nightgown with cap sleeves. *How fittingly Dracula-esque to save the world in,* she thought with an internal giggle. She touched her belly and grinned. "Good, they're safe."

"Th-they?" Eric asked, inching closer. "Paresh, where are—"

"I can't explain. Gabriel will be here soon and I need to go with him." She held the catheterized arm out to Alex. "Remove this, please."

"What do you mean, 'he's not?' I saw his body!" Alex pulled out the catheter with a deft touch.

"You saw what they wanted you to see." Paresh held onto Eric's hand as she stood and adjusted to the weight of a physical body. The world teetered for a moment under gravity's pull. She'd missed so many things about the corporeal world, but she'd missed things like this— like the heat of Eric's hand in hers—the most.

"Th-they?" Eric sputtered again as Alex asked, "They?"

She smiled over her shoulder at Eric. "I haven't met the other one yet. I only met Celeste." She arched a mischievous brow. "She's going to be a fifteen-year-old infant. Prepare yourself."

To Alex, she said, "Lucien and Endymion. After I leave with Gabriel, you need to trust them. This is much bigg—"

She couldn't say that. Instead, she clasped Alex's hand and squeezed Eric's. "I'm alive! It was an ordeal and a feat—a miracle, really. Yes, Lucifer is coming, and Endymion is on it—so work with him, and Lucien while I'm gone with Gabriel—and hope I get back in time."

Eric gasped as though she'd knocked the wind from him. "In time for what? I can't lose you, again!"

Smiling for them, she glanced from one to the other. "I love you both, so much. I can't say more, but it's a safe assumption that if I fail, we're all going to die together. Eric, you are integral to what's coming. Don't fight with Lucien. Jonathan must be angry with him, but, like you, he only did what he had to. It was the only way. I know things got ugly between all of you, but we need to have faith in the balance and not fight amongst ourselves."

A bolt of blue lightning struck the clearing, blowing out the windows and violently shaking the entire cottage. Alex and Eric folded protectively over her.

Old habits, she thought as she peeled them off. "I love you." Her lips dotted Alex's crown before sharing a lingering kiss with Eric. She fought the urge to prick her tongue—if he'd sought her blood on his own, he'd have an advantage, but if she gave it to him, she'd break the rules. "I will return to you, my love, I promise."

She was only vaguely aware of glass cutting into her feet and of Eric crying out to her as she approached the window. Through a dusty cloud, Gabriel's form materialized, magnificent in a rippling pale robe with two pairs of wings splayed open. In stasis, she had seen his four faces often, but now he wore only one under a crown of light.

He approached the cottage and offered his hand through the window. As she accepted, he phased her through the wall. A seam in reality ripped open and a wheel-like structure rolled out. It ballooned around them and lifted into the blackening sky.

☽ ✳ ☾

The transparent globe sped above a crosshatched earth, the monochromatic coloring growing darker as they traveled east. They entered clouds, which didn't move like the Hollow's haze and beaded water on the exterior. A rainbow of ripples exploded beneath her fingers when she touched the orb. It was viscous like the casement material at the Arc of True Blood.

They cleared the clouds. The fireball was visible high above them. At that distance, it looked smaller, like a marble. Gabriel's hands twitched at his sides and their transport responded. They rushed away from the fireball, farther into its wake of absolute black until no sunlight broke through.

The globe lowered over a vast city. People were gazing up in wonder as Paresh gazed down in amazement. "Is that St. Peter's Basilica over there?"

Gabriel nodded.

"Then that's…St. Peter's Square? But it's not a sq—"

The limestone paving and people rushed up too fast, but Gabriel didn't twitch and the globe didn't shudder as it phased into the ground. Soil and stone replaced the black sky. They dropped into a large cavity lit by a solitary flame. She recognized its flicker from her vision, and watched it grow smaller and more distant—a wish, a hope, an impossible promise—as they moved through the tunnel.

"We do not have bodies like yours, Little One," Gabriel said. "Our hearts must supply our bodies, our wings, and our spirit. I cannot fathom my brother wearing flesh for millennia. Behind the Celestial Curtain, we are energy. We do not have hearts; we cannot bleed. But we do *feel*."

Hawkiel, in his dust-free prison, on the same cot she'd seen, looked up. Shadows slithered over his cell's fleshy walls. Paresh shuddered.

"We *feel* too much, I'm afraid." A note of sadness hid within Gabriel's whisper. "I know what you've chosen, Brother."

"Can he see us? He's not moving."

"He can see *you*. The casement will allow you to pass through, if you so choose."

She pushed through the gelatinous layer until her palm hit the solid exterior. Gabriel's hand flattened against her back and the orb's texture changed, allowing her to exit.

Paresh stared into Hawkiel's muted flames. The air was stifling and drenched with sulfur. Her throat seized and moisture surged into her eyes. Fire roared to life in her lungs as she knelt before him. She put her palms up as she had done with Darkesiel in her vision. He contemplated her a moment before pressing his hands against hers.

She drew in his spiritual energy. Heat gathered and a bright light pulsed. A twelve-pointed star beneath two intertwined crescent moons, and a twelve-armed sunburst beneath an offset four-pointed star, marked her hands. They alternated in color between maroon and navy. A pattern leaped at her——numbers easily divisible by three to form the only perfect number that could break any God-fearing man.

"Transformation, creation, imperfection. Six means many things, Vessel. For us, it is the *balance* of three," Hawkiel said softly, his voice a resonant, musical hum.

Explosive pressure shoved down on her lungs. Blackness glimmered at the edges of her vision. She grabbed his hand and willed him to see her vision of Darkesiel. He nodded and shoved her into the orb.

She collapsed at Gabriel's feet gasping for air. She locked onto Hawkiel's brightly burning gaze. Relief bloomed in her heart. "You'll…see each other…soon."

She gulped for more air, but there wasn't enough. The flickering blackness blurred as they reentered the tunnel and passed by the lonely blue flame. Gabriel lifted her into his arms as the Earth itself raced around them. Her eyelids drooped heavier. She glimpsed the black sky. Gabriel's robe.

"That was quite brave, Little One," he said, using the same hushed tone as Hawkiel.

"I'm…miss…ing…"

"Sh," Gabriel whispered, "everything in time, Little One. Let's go meet Darkesiel."

II

RAVEN

Saudi Arabia, Early Autumn 2021

Lucifer's hand clamped onto her ankle. She hurtled sideways. Instead of *splatting* into the limestone, she crashed into red sand, her wings instinctively protecting her as she tumbled over hot grains and finally rolled to a stop.

The heat distorted Lucifer like a mirage as he charged toward her, fuming mad. He looked so much like Jonathan then, from the old days when he'd beaten her, and beaten her some more, while Endymion watched. Had he enjoyed *that*?

She felt her mind slipping with every step Lucifer took. The air was sweltering and the sand burned into her skin. She tried to crawl away. Her wings had prevented major injury, but her body had taken that fall. It screamed from bruising pain. Snapped and popped as everything squeezed back into place.

She yelped when Lucifer jerked her up by the arm. His flaming eyes drilled into her. "Did you have fun, Little Bird? *I should have clipped your wings.*"

He kicked off the sand, dragging her with him, her mind growing fuzzier. "Then why carve them out of me at all?" she snapped. "I don't want the damn things!"

The subtle timbre of a growl vibrated his throat. "None of this has gone as it was supposed to!"

He let go and punched her down, landing a fraction of a second before she careened into a dune. She forced herself to get to her feet. She imagined Jonathan there, shirtless and barefoot, ready for the kill. She clung to that imagery. To that fear. That hate. How had their relationship evolved into mutual respect after that?

You fought back. It was fun for him. You made yourself worthy of his attention. Then it wasn't about him, but you. What he could teach you. How you could reach your peak. How you became the best of them all.

Lucifer scoffed. "Are you trying to convince yourself? Or trying to delay the inevitable?"

Because I'm already in your head, Little Bird. Lucifer's voice felt like a worm burrowing through her brain. She grabbed her head and staggered backward.

"With Rainne delivering destruction on the ground, you would have been my angel of death from above, swinging that scythe you love so much." He grabbed her arm again. "If I hadn't miscalculated with Endymion, I'd have a mindless, unstoppable army—most of them highly trained and skilled hunters thanks to you—unlike the tepid creatures I churned out before."

He tugged her to his chest and took off again. Clouds began to populate within her mind. Her thoughts had difficulty connecting, like they were there, but beyond reach. The white mist closed in and she lost sight of them altogether—forgot they were ever there.

"I was in control for so long, but you managed to get in there—somehow, you did," he said, "and mucked up everything."

Raven laughed. For a moment, she wasn't sure why. But then she visualized an urn filled with blood. "Psh! You wanted so badly to kill the Servator before she arrived that you saw to her death personally. And *you* failed. That wasn't me. Not any of it. In fact…you wanted me to broker the peace that led to that prophecy! You set up the dominoes wrong so stop lying to yourself."

"Then permit me to illuminate to you a brutal honesty that pains even me." He squeezed her tighter. "*You* brought Salea into my life. That girl twisted my wants into her wants—and they were so similar, it began not to matter. Instead of storming the gates of Heaven, she wanted me to seal them shut, forever closed to an Earth under my dominion where she could have all the fun she wanted without you hunting her down. Now that she's dead and Endymion has revealed his farce, I see my folly, the tiny mistakes, and asinine choices that added up over time."

He flipped her around so that his eyes plunged into hers with scorching fingers in search of her soul. The heat of a sun erupted in her chest. He secured a vice on his target and grinned when she howled its first death rattle.

"There, Little Bird," he murmured. "I put cruelty in Endymion's heart, but misjudged the weight of Father's counterbalance. I overestimated Salea's sanity and underestimated her abilities. I fell for a betrayal and a disappointing failure who proved to be too fatally human to be of any real worth. She loved me and thought I loved her back, but then she met *him* and discovered that the heart truly makes the man—"

"Somethin's…al…ways…fall…in'…with you, huh?" Raven panted as he hollowed out her soul and began prying out the final embers of rage. But as long as she had even one, she could fight. She latched onto his back and sank her fangs into his jugular. She clawed into the central wings' muscles required for flight.

A ghastly screech raced off Lucifer's lips. He struggled to peel her off and his fiery probes released her soul. She sucked his blood as hard and fast as she could, her fingers clawing deeper to paralyze his wings. The top and bottom pairs weren't strong enough to hold them both. The air whistled past with a chill as they fell back toward the desert.

What goes up, must come down, asshole. If you're always falling, then how hard do you land? she screamed in her head. *I refuse to be your angel of death. I will never ride your pale horse!*

He scruffed her neck and ruthlessly ripped her off, flinging her clear with a violent heel to her gut. As his wings blew open, his eyes burned into her with fierce intensity. "Those impulses of yours—always rushing in and not thinking, right Little Bird? Who do you think that stunt actually hurt?"

No! No! No! Dread seized her in a merciless grip as the vile blood in her veins crawled into her heart.

Lucifer's fiery tendrils latched onto her soul and trapped it into a constricting, writhing knot. Her muscles spasmed and wound tight like steel cables. He tossed her screams into a box in her head where only he could hear them, and scorched her thoughts and free will, reducing her to a fleshy sack filled only with base fear—but even that was fading. His gaze swung up at the sky. A black sheet was about to cover the sun.

Smirking victorious, he said, "Alongside my brothers, you and Rainne Blood Pathos will usher in destruction and death, and I shall slip between the veils to burn the gates to Heaven and Hell. I *will* bring the celestial dawn of dominion to this world."

III

KESTREL

Orison Crossing, Early Autumn 2021

The bolt of lightning radiated power that blasted her vines and blew her past the tree line. Another bright light pulsed behind the cottage and then an orb rose into the sky. The spiritual presence went with it. She raced past Cyprian and Heron—doubled over with bleeding ears—and flashed a hand signal to *stay*. She burst into the cottage and jogged down the hall. It was wrong. It felt *all* wrong.

Her vines drew her attention from the shell-shocked expressions on Alex and Lord Eric's faces to the shards of glass that glittered with blood. "*Where's Paresh?*"

Like a lost child, Eric pointed at the window. The IV that had connected him to Paresh dripped a bloody trail on the floor. "Gabriel."

She pulled his arm straight to remove the dangling line. "Please say that's a good thing, because it does not feel particularly *good* out there."

Alex dazedly asked, "Where's Sarah?"

"She's on a special assignment." Kestrel blew a burst of air over her lip. "Where did Gabriel take Paresh? Why didn't they go that way—"

278

She pointed in the direction of the business district. "That's where I feel him going."

"Darkesiel will land *here?*" Eric asked. "We need to get the people—"

The Hollow's hazy mouth opened in the bedroom and Lord Lucien's voice preceded his exit, "You may speak honestly, Commander."

She and the others took a collective step away from the portal when an *armored creature* came out. Alex swore under his breath. Energy ripe with fury and dejection battered Kestrel's vines.

Jonathan appeared behind the *creature,* saying, "Yes, do *please* tell us all about Sarah, *Endymion,* and the Chthonic Knights who are in possession of Rainne Blood Pathos, *for now.*"

Jonathan held up a hand before she could speak. "No, let me, since they're preparing her *for Lucifer* since he stole *Raven* from Endymion's custody after he killed Salca."

"*R-Raven?*" Alex whispered, paling.

The chilled shock in his aura brushed the vines on Kestrel's back as her own cold fear draped her body like a wet cloak. "Why would Lucifer *steal* her?"

"So you do know Endymion's alive! Do you know about *all* of his treachery?" Lord Jonathan's façade befitted an enraged demon.

Dropping to bended knee, she glanced at Lord Lucien before saying, "I-I have orders, yes, but I didn't know he had Raven! Why was Salea there?"

"It was a misguided rescue attempt. Endymion and Sarah killed her." Lord Lucien's eyes drifted over Alex. "Lucifer took Raven as retribution."

"B-but…you said Lucifer already had her!" Alex's shock quickly heated into anger. "Y-you *refused* my requests! I could have found her! *Where was she?*"

"She was never lost to find," Kestrel said quietly. "He knew she was with Endymion, but I swear I didn't. I thought he was looking for her."

Alex snarled in her direction, but his eyes blazed with murderous intent at Lord Lucien. "*Why didn't you tell us Endymion's alive? Holding Raven captive?*"

"I owe you no explanation, High Commander," Lord Lucien said coldly.

"I think you do—you owe all of us, because the way I see it, *you and Endymion were working with Lucifer!*" Alex's eyes darkened. "And now you say she's gone for *retribution?* For what? It's not like he cares about anyone beyond himself!"

"Apparently, he did," Lord Lucien said tightly. "We might have learned that sooner had *that girl* died as ordered, *when ordered,* or perhaps that *care* would've died and not brought us to this day."

Master Jonathan jabbed Lord Lucien in the back. "*You* let her live. Don't you dare go after Alex. He took the shot."

"He also suggested putting her to sleep," Kestrel added, feeling like a true traitor.

"Don't you think I've beaten myself up for that every single day?" Alex yelled. "*I heard them murder Paresh! That never would've happened if I'd killed Salea! And now Raven's…she's…*"

Alex screamed and lunged at Lord Lucien like a savage beast. "*Start talking! I should have rescued her! Why in Tartarus would you work with Lucifer?*"

"Stop!" Eric blocked Alex's attack. "Think about Paresh—she told us not to fight! Can't we do the one thing she's asked? I'm tired of failing her. Aren't you? Because we *all* failed her. It doesn't matter how, why, or when."

Alex eased off as Eric whispered to him, "She said you'd see Raven again. Focus on that."

Eric wearily sat on the bed with his head in his hands. His sorrow manifested as condensation on Kestrel's vines. She stood and hesitantly touched one. She shivered from cold. "What is this?"

Alex gulped down air as he put more distance between him and Lord Lucien. "She told us to trust *them*, and that Jonathan was angry with Lord Lucien. That seems true enough."

Kestrel scoffed. "Are you actually questioning what she said?"

"No!" Alex threw his thumb at Master Jonathan. "It was an observation! Clearly, she's got it all right and we're intent on killing each other while she and Gabriel are…doing whatever they're doing right now!"

A daggered claw on her vines jolted Kestrel stiff with electric pain. Lord Lucien scraped damp beads off a silver loop and let them pool into his palm.

"Silver tears…cleansing waters…a mirror to the soul. May we all seek purification from a hard look within." He gave a respectful nod to Eric. "Anointed Strength."

Lord Lucien cupped his hand over his mouth and swallowed. Kestrel held her breath as his energy rapidly fluctuated and an emotional vortex formed within his aura. His skin gradually reverted to its normal pale blue and his hair lightened. His eyes returned to quartz crystal and focused on her.

"Breathe, Commander." To the group, Lord Lucien said, "I now understand how you all perceive me. Nothing I say will regain your trust, but know that I do not wish harm upon this world and am not in league with Lucifer. So…I turn to Eric for the words spoken to us from the Sacred Vessel on *that night*."

Sighing heavily, Eric scrubbed his face. "Gabriel told her that you are an honorable leader. And she also asked us to trust you—and Endymion—so…that's what we should do."

Lord Lucien's energy quieted. His aura draped him loosely. He gestured at Kestrel's belly and sought permission with his eyes.

She nodded.

"View yourself as others see you," he directed. "Gain clarity and understanding so that we may unify for this final battle."

Master Jonathan and Alex gathered Eric's silver tears onto their fingertips and licked them off. She looked to Eric, who was watching her.

"It's your turn," he said. "I should be last."

She didn't understand what was happening, or the change in her vines, but she copied the others. Emotions assailed her from every direction, none perceivable by her vines. They came from within—fear, suspicion, blame, respect, trust, anger, sadness—and plunged her into the undulating darkness of deep thought.

She'd arrogantly assumed that her vines gave her more awareness of the self than the others could ever reach. But that wasn't true or enough. The secrets she guarded altered the way others saw her and their ability to believe in her, which, in turn, affected their thoughts and actions, and how others saw them—it created an unending cycle of choice made by perception based on perception and choice.

She'd never cared what the others thought. She'd been happy with herself and with Lior, and that shortsighted view had a ripple effect that she'd never noticed. There were real world consequences surrounding the secrets that weren't hers to divulge.

Kestrel returned to the room, dazed and looking at the others as though seeing them for the first time. She recognized Alex's anger and grief over Raven, his guilt over Salea and Lior, and his reluctant trust for *her* based solely on the fact that Raven had chosen *her*. She felt Master Jonathan's distrust toward her, Endymion, and the situation with Lady Rainne, and his hope for Raven's return. She cringed at Eric's pain and the realization that despite everything said and done, he trusted her only because of Sarah. Lord Lucien left himself deliberately open, allowing her to see his unquestioning trust because of her true self—but he also knew the same secrets.

Everyone but Lord Lucien tried to speak at once and shut down into an awkward silence. She swept a silver tear onto her fingertip and studied its distorted reflections.

"I carry confidences that aren't mine to disclose," she started softly. "I am true to myself and loyal to the Vampiric Nation, always. None of us know everything—not even Lord Lucien or Lord Endymion—but that shouldn't change our ability to trust each other here and now for the greater good. We all want the same things. We must understand that and come together to mitigate the damage until Paresh returns if we want this world to survive."

☽ ✳ ☾

The Hollow delivered them downtown. The streetlights had come on. People spilled from the shops and restaurants, leaned out of their cars or turned them off and got out. All were looking up with gaping mouths.

They pointed. Asked where the sun was. Gasped about a "cool" solar eclipse. Some tugged at each other to get off the street, whispering about portents of doom—as if brick and mortar from the Romanesque Revival could possibly save them.

Walter appeared at the door to the police station, gaze skyward, rubbing his balding scalp. Outside, a father tried to use sheets of paper to show his kids the eclipse's shadow, but all they got was darkness.

Fitting, Kestrel thought as she tapped her communicator. She'd forgotten Cyprian and Heron. She advised them to hold position in case Gabriel took Paresh home or they were wrong about Darkesiel's landing.

"Did you know this was happening, today?" Walter asked the father. "They made such a hoopla the last time—sold special glasses and everyth—"

He saw Kestrel's group down the street. He surveyed the people. It was busier than usual, or so it seemed—she didn't know what a normal day in Orison Crossing looked like. His eyes asked a question. She shook her head. He paled.

How do you protect anyone at the end of the world? she wondered as Eric patted her shoulder and followed Alex over to Walter.

The others were studying the sky. Energy began to gather densely beside them.

"Lord Endymion is about to open Animus Hollow here," Kestrel said. She took next the half second to belly breathe and scout with her aura. Pinging and chirping phones echoed off the buildings, and the organic essences of the villagers and the chemicals from the cars struck her vines. Each sensory input tied into the next and developed a mental blueprint.

As Lord Endymion's portal opened, she reported, "Lucifer's not here yet. There are approximately fifty people in the immediate area, maybe more. If Darkesiel lands—"

"He'll kill all of them," Sarah said, emerging from the Hollow's giant mouth, followed by Lord Endymion and a squad of Chthonic Knights with Lady Rainne's casket. She locked eyes with Kestrel and held a bloody hand up.

Kestrel flinched, stung by Salea's toxicity even in death. An impish grin split Sarah's lips.

Shoulders squared and chin up, Sarah sauntered over and slid that hand over Kestrel's naval and around to the small of her back. A satisfied laugh softly dropped between them as Kestrel shivered and Sarah tugged her in for a kiss. "She's *dead* dead, with the Knights at Eido, awaiting your order to incinerate."

Sarah's lips dusted hers again. "The honor to destroy her is yours, m'lady."

Kestrel bunched Sarah's hair into her fists and kissed her deeply. She didn't care about the Elders or the hunters or protocol. In minutes, everything she knew might disappear. She wanted this moment, this kiss, and she was taking it.

☽ ✳ ☾

ERIC

He saw the virginal wings of a seraph coming down before Alex or Walter did. Eric quickly pulled the station door open and urged Walter to get in, beckoning the father and kids, too. "Get inside, away from the windows!"

The teaching papers tumbled to the sidewalk. Alex shot a bewildered glance at Eric and then looked over at Kestrel and Sarah, who were kissing while Lord Endymion told Lord Lucien about the enhanced locks on Rainne's casket. Eric crouched before the kids and forced a grin as he tousled their hair. "Hide under Walter's desk like it's a fort, okay?"

Entrusting them to Walter, Eric didn't wait for confirmation before grabbing Alex and dashing into the street. The angel was descending faster and no one else had seen him yet. His glowing bronzed skin and golden curls were deceptively peaceful—but those eyes, flickering blue around the edges of a hellish orange flame—Eric knew those eyes.

He yelled a warning, but it was too late. Lucifer blasted sulfuric fumes at Kestrel that dropped her to her knees. She grimaced and instinctively covered her vines as a thick, ashy cloud bloomed around her and the others.

Slamming his heels against the pavement, Eric took a running leap, his view stained crimson and animalistic growls rattling his throat. He landed on Lucifer's back, tearing at the feathers on any wing within reach.

"Ah! My imposter has rejoined the game! Little Bird?" Lucifer snapped his fingers.

An attacker from above kicked Eric into a parked car across the street. An angel with blue wings and brown hair began to dive after him. Alex whipped out his revolver and aimed at the back of the angel's head, but Sarah rammed him before he could take the shot. Lucifer whistled. The blue angel stopped.

"Reacquaint yourself with your friends." Lucifer turned his blazing stare onto Endymion. "Release Rainne Blood Pathos."

Through the ash, Eric saw Endymion drop a hand signal. The Knights shimmered out of the visible spectrum and the casket hit the ground with a solid *thunk!* The electrical odor of their cloaking mechanisms fled up the street and dispersed into the crowd. More confusion ensued as they moved people—to their shock and surprise—into the buildings.

Kestrel blocked the blue angel's access to the casket. A shock of familiarity registered in her eyes and an expression of anguish scraped Endymion's face as the angel lunged again. He glared pure hatred at Lucifer before rushing over to where Alex was trying to escape Sarah's restraint.

Endymion scooped Alex into his arms and ran for an ally up the street. As Alex sputtered in protest, Lord Lucien quietly said, "Crimson Commander, you and Endymion must protect Paresh when she returns. Kestrel and Sarah will handle this. The Knights will evacuate humans."

Eric jumped off the car as Lucien and Jonathan dove for Lucifer. A wing clap blew them back. He slapped his wings against the street and shot up into the black sky. "Let the blood rain, Little Bird!"

The blue angel robotically echoed Lucifer and the casket began to hop on its own. Sarah yelled at Eric to go after him and joined Kestrel's fight.

Jonathan and Lucien tailed Eric as he led the chase. Eric jumped onto Lucifer's back in mid-air a few blocks over and speared the central wings' muscles. The horrid sound that came from Lucifer's mouth drew attention from people on the ground. They screamed and scrambled to get out of the way. He and Lucifer crashed out of control into a storefront window.

"Get away from here!" Eric yelled to anyone who could hear him as Lucifer kicked him off. Eric hit the shop across the street and sprang up. "Go! *Go! Clear downtown!*"

Lucifer climbed out and stepped to the center of the street. He slammed his wings down. The blast threw Jonathan into a store display with Eric and knocked down fleeing people. He slammed his wings again and generated a visible shockwave that shattered windows, exploded bricks, and crushed mortar into powder. Eric threw himself over Jonathan as a tower of debris collapsed on them. He snarled in pain as rebar and glass gouged the muscles of his back.

"Why did you do that?" Jonathan asked, partly angry, partly stunned.

"I single-handedly set your healing back by decades. *He* doesn't get to make it worse."

Hidden within a rising debris plume, Lucifer laughed hollowly. "The Imposter rescues the damaged Second Born as the First Born pushes humans out backdoors? *Pathetic!*"

"We're pathetic?" Jonathan yelled.

"You created an army to fight your war and then fell in love with an altered vampire who twisted your grandiose ambitions into her own." Lucien's voice came from up the street. "Do you even know what you're fighting for?"

Eric shook off debris and scoffed. "Why are you wearing that false face? All golden and cherubic—so you don't look like *me?*"

The Hellfire orange flared to life as Lucifer puffed out his chest. "Why would I want to look like a lowly cherub? I'm not just a seraph! I am the most beautiful and treasured—"

"Were," Eric corrected as Jonathan said, "Egotistical bastard."

Kicking a mannequin out from under his legs, Jonathan added, "All we have to do is insult you to death. Such a fragile mind you have."

"I'm sick of seeing my face on the two of you," Lucifer snapped. His golden curls straightened and darkened to black, his bronzed skin paled to ghostly white, and his flame fizzled into irises of electric blue.

Lucien dashed down the street, and Eric and Jonathan charged, all pouncing at once, kicking and pummeling, and circling as Lucifer ducked and dodged. He hurled them off, but they attacked again and again, and beat him down until a wing clap lobbed Lucien and Jonathan into a sandwich shop up the street and threw Eric into the wall directly at his back, ramming the glass and rebar into his lungs. Eric dropped to his hands and knees wheezing and spattering the sidewalk with blood.

He heard whimpering inside some of the buildings, but the street was clear, at least. He tried to yell another warning, but only choked instead.

Lucien charged with an infuriated, inhuman shriek, but Lucifer pivoted and kicked him into Jonathan. They crumpled limply into a pile of debris and their eyes went vacant.

"Cheating coward! Get out of their heads!" Eric roared, leaping up and crushing the central vertebrae in Lucifer's back under his fist. "Jonathan found his penitent heart and Lucien has Gabriel's respect! You can't break them to avoid a real fight!"

"My fight isn't with *them*, Imposter. I created them. I can kill them." Lucifer whipped around smiling cruelly and caught Eric's next punch. "Easily."

The bones in his hand crunched and snapped. Eric folded down to his knees, refusing to give Lucifer the satisfaction of his pain even as the ulna and radius cracked and shattered as Lucifer twisted his arm.

"*You* are the problem," Lucifer sneered. "*She* saw you and unraveled! Because of you *I* was beholden to ridiculous rules—"

Jonathan raced past Eric and planted his shoulder into Lucifer's solar plexus. He flew backward, straining to spread his wings to freeze his momentum. With a quick sidestep, he deflected Jonathan into the brick facing and demolished the corner block.

Eric tucked his arm to his side as it healed. Lucifer approached, pointing at him. "She thought you could *kill* me. Perhaps Michael does, too, and that's why he intervened when he did. What do you think?"

Reserve strength and fury surged into Eric's core. He butted heads with Lucifer. "That you need to shut up!"

He charged again, head-butting harder and shoving Lucifer back despite his bracing wings. The flame of Hellfire returned and consumed every bit of blue. He grabbed Eric by the throat and hurled him through back-to-back buildings. Eric landed on the next street over, winded and choking up bloody globs, and Lucifer was there in an instant, kicking him into another wall.

As Eric thudded onto the sidewalk, people screamed and ran, and Lucifer scoffed, gesturing at his face. "Since we already share so much, and because *you* ruined it, I can't let it go. My *pride* won't let me."

An image appeared in Eric's mind—the girl with the bouncing red fruit, with Raven at a riverside. Lucifer, wearing his false face, walked along the bank and the girl beamed a joyous smile at him.

"Meet Salea," he said to Eric sourly. "I still question it, though I cannot deny that I cared for her in some capacity. Now that she's dead…I'm lost…"

His voice trailed as Jonathan and Lucien emerged from the wreckage. He clapped all six wings to thrust them back. "And that's somehow fitting since once she saw you, she was lost to me. She saw *you* as the *perfection* she needed and *you* changed her goal."

Lucifer's lips curled in disgust. "And to think…she only approached you to *confirm the location of the Sacred Vessel's body*."

A chill raced down Eric's spine. He choked. "You…told—"

He laughed again, resentful and bitter. "And break my brother's rules? She found it on her own. Intended to deliver it as a *gift*."

He yanked Eric up nose to nose. The flame sparked and went out, returning his eyes to hardened electric blue. "She found it first. Before you. But Alexander's last bullet lodged in her brain and changed her personality. And this is really the best part, *for you*, what I really want *you* to hear, because *that shot*? In retaliation for the Sacred Vessel's *womb*? Gave birth to *Seren*."

Stones dropped into Eric's stomach. They grew heavier as he felt a guilty shift in Lucien's aura. Lucifer loosened his grip so that Lucien was visible over his shoulder. Eric shook his head in denial at the grim line splitting Lucien's face.

Crinkles etched Jonathan's forehead. "Why does that matter?"

When Lucien and Eric both remained quiet and Lucifer didn't move, Jonathan hesitantly asked, "Eric? Who is Seren to you?"

Eric clenched his jaw. "I met a girl at the cemetery. After Kestrel and Sarah's new plan. She…helped me process what I'd been through. It was only a few days—"

"But she *really* helped you, didn't she?" Lucifer jeered.

"And betrayed *you*," Lucien jabbed coldly.

Lucifer shot upward like a bullet. Lucien and Jonathan raced to grab Eric and kicked through a store's door to tug him inside. An instant later, Lucifer cratered the street. Windows and walls exploded and mammoth dust clouds rose as whole buildings collapsed.

Lucien and Jonathan charged the Morning Star before his shielding wings could unfurl. Lucien restrained him, rendering him powerless to fend off Jonathan's clawed fists.

Eric tried to shake his head clear, but his mind was reeling—as intended—and that pissed him off more than anything. The revelation about Salea and Seren changed nothing.

But it shows how fallible Lucifer's grown during his life on Earth—and if he's fallible, he's killable.

The hairs on Eric's arms stood on end. A bolt of blue lightning struck the street and another six colossal wings stretched high into the sky. Enrobed in white, the seraph held a sword of light and bore the face of the avatar that watched over Grandfather Wisdom. He said nothing as he manifested a charged gust that blew Lucien and Jonathan away from Lucifer. Saint Michael lifted weightlessly and took up a guarding stance between them and his brother—who looked less than grateful.

Saint Michael raised his sword when Jonathan stepped forward, but did nothing as Eric lunged for Lucifer with a beastly growl. Under the power of Eric's fist, Lucifer crashed into the remains of a brick column. Eric attacked again, talons extended, thrashing the face that had cursed his life. He heard Jonathan yelling at Saint Michael to let them pass.

The memory of Nicole's evil smile broke over his mind and Eric felt the dagger plunge into his heart all over again. He pulled a length of rebar from his chest and rammed it into Lucifer's gut. Pouncing onto Lucifer's back, he hammered on the broken vertebrae and tore at the bloodied muscles of his middle wings.

Lucifer screeched unnaturally and bucked Eric off, struggling to stay on his feet. The wings protecting his face and legs unfurled to propel him away. His middle wings hung limp as he clutched at the steel bar. Eric kicked Lucifer into a crumbling building and launched into the air. He brought his elbow down onto Lucifer's back and they collapsed into the rubble, rattling the planks of the floor above.

The beast's roar built pressure within Eric's chest. It rattled its cage and screamed for the kill. But then, an expanse of glowing Heliopsis and the warmth of the Elysian Fields ran over him like a train, leaving the scents of honey and green clover in its wake, and Seren's angry voice echoed in his head. *Life will throw obstacles at you, but you need to determine how they affect you.*

Paresh's voice trailed faintly. *That makes it a choice...*

"You cheat with psychic attacks!" Eric growled, huffing for air and control. "You messed with Salea to manipulate her like you would anyone else, but it backfired, didn't it? She got access to *your* head and was in there as a constant voice, wasn't she? Always there. Even as she slept at the Arc of Celestial Night. And now she's gone. Silent. You feel empty and don't understand it. You lived eons without her, so why is this different? *That's* what you don't understand. *That's* what you interpret as care—as love, *but it's not!*"

The beast cowered in its cage as Lucifer groaned in pain.

Eric dragged himself to his feet. "I don't care that Salea was Seren!

The girl I met wanted to do good in the world and she did!"

Eric glanced at Saint Michael before looking back at Lucifer in his pitiful state. "You brought your fight to humans to strike at your father, so *he's* here to prevent *your* children from interfering because they were never human. *This isn't their fight.* But I was human once—"

Eric pointed at the sunless sky beyond the smashed windows. "So *that* is."

Dust trickled into his eyes, and he heard a loud *crack!* The floors above buckled. Then everything came crashing down.

IV

PARESH

Orison Crossing, Early Autumn 2021

The globe descended on downtown. Below, Sarah and Kestrel were blindfolded and fighting a blue-winged angel and a blur of a woman in motion. Kestrel was fending off the angel with her broadsword and Sarah tried to keep the woman contained within a cluster of cars that limited her reach.

The woman stopped and looked up. The scarlet glow of her eyes sharply contrasted skin that was whiter than snow. Gorgon-like hair reflected the inky black of the sky and rusty hue of the buildings. Paresh felt her soul dive into that mesmerizing pop of color, transfixed by the weapon that was Rainne Blood Pathos.

Gabriel covered her eyes. "Leave them be, for now, Little One. You and I cannot yet intervene."

The globe came down in an alley. Gabriel pulled her forward and kissed her forehead. "I may remind you once to wait for him."

"But I'm missing a huge chunk of the puzzle!" Paresh cried, bunching his robe in her fists. "What's the final piece? What do I do after I meet Darkesiel?"

Gently loosening her fingers, Gabriel smiled sadly. "Trust that you will find the answer, for only you can."

The floor gave way and deposited her onto the alley's asphalt. Gabriel and his globe lifted out of sight.

Paresh's heart sank as she contemplated the superheated glow above the clouds. The clash of metal on metal and exhausted battle cries boomed against a background of rumbling engines, radios, and dinging phones. She approached the alley's mouth, curious for another look at Lady Rainne, but sharp pressure built within her head and the world tilted askance.

The scent of lavender wafted over her. She weakly fell into arms bound with corded muscle that lifted her easily. A gentle voice whispered, "Ah, my dear Sacred Vessel, leave this to the warriors."

"H-ow can they…see?"

"They have special sights to guide them," Endymion said.

Alex pressed a cool hand to her forehead. "You're burning up—"

She struggled to swallow. Sweat dripped from her brow. "It's…Darkesiel. He's—"

A blinding flash sparked an energy wave that demolished masonry and glass as it rippled down the street. Endymion yanked her and Alex into the safety of Animus Hollow to shield them from explosive debris, but urgency flared in her belly.

"I can't run away!" She escaped before the Hollow closed. "I have to stay here!"

Gabriel's globe returned. He slipped through the bottom and floated down to Paresh. The globe stayed above him and moved in harmony with his movements. The barest trace of worry lined his face. He reached for Paresh's belly but stopped shy of touching her. "Little Ones!"

"I'm okay—we're okay." She gasped in horror at the shattered business district engulfed in flames, black smoke, and thick dust.

Endymion's fingers encircled her arm. "I must keep you safe."

She pulled free of his grip, looking from him to Alex and back. "You can't! This is why I'm here!"

Gabriel threw out a blocking arm before Endymion could grab her again. "Third Born, while in stasis, she watched the fibers of light and dark bend and twist and saw how the gray fibers of probability work. She has seen what's to come and played it through countless times— now, she must navigate reality to achieve a desirable end. Would you deny her destiny?"

Gabriel nodded at her, not permissively, but in understanding. "Only she can choose the path now."

She shared a final look with them as Endymion's arm lowered, and took off, running hard into the heart of her nightmares. She had lived this moment so many times within Grandfather Wisdom that the pain and heat registered more like memory than experience.

Stepping into the cloud of choking air was like entering another world. Under crackling and roaring flames, the silence of what should have been heightened the noises of what was—bricks crumbling, walls creaking and collapsing, engines hissing, radios blaring, survivors crying under layers of destruction. But above all was the agonized screaming of one man.

"Darkesiel," she whispered.

He quieted. Through growing flames, searing heat, and thickening smoke, she soldiered on, one foot in front of the other, even as black lights flickered in her peripheral and oxygen grew scarce. Glass and debris shredded her feet. She reached the edge of his crater.

Steaming smoke rolled off his skin, dark as obsidian and muted as ash. Two pairs of wings blew out from his back, reflecting the darkness of isolation and the expanse of the cosmos. An orb, like Gabriel's, floated above him, centered with his wings.

She offered her hand. He mirrored her. Taking the first step, she slid down the crater's face, scraping her legs and arms on exposed concrete and pipes, and scalding her skin on water steaming under the fire's heat. She grimaced and bore it all with nary a sound, keeping at least one palm out in offering.

He, too, moved closer, flames popping to life within his footprints. Soon, they were face to face and lifting their palms in unison. They connected and the world spun away like a top. Darkesiel absorbed the ache in her heart as his energy cycled through her body. She felt the depth of his loneliness, the toll of his seclusion, the grief of forgetting his brother's face—a face he shared. He'd nearly forgotten himself, unsure if he even existed at all. Only the vision of a distant blue marble kept him sane, for the memory of his brother, faint though it was, walked there, and he knew, someday, they would reunite.

In touching her, the spirit of Gaea, the mother of nature, and planetary nostalgia returned to him—the scents of the Earth, the organic green, the musk and pheromones of animals, and the pollen of flowers and trees. The simple molecules of water and the complexity of the sensations they delivered. The crisp edge of a fall breeze. The charred ribbons of fire's smoke. His love for these things reawakened in his heart, which for so long had been cold with hate.

She willed him to see her visit with his brother in the fleshy prison of Hell, to hear the message only she could deliver. Hawkiel's marks came to life, and she knew Darkesiel recognized not only Gabriel's presence in her, but also his twin's. The chains linked to the shackles around his wrists and ankles rattled and dissolved into embers. The restraints dropped and burned up before touching the ground.

The air shifted and circled like a sucking breath, and relief tingled within her burning lungs. But then a thundering crash shook the ground and a new heated wave blasted her into Darkesiel. Another orb—crudely formed and damaged—emerged from the wreckage behind her.

No! she screamed internally. *You can't be here yet!*

She'd known that Hawkiel's freedom came with a cost, but she'd misunderstood the meaning of his message.

She turned to face the angel who burned like a candlewick. He screamed and grabbed the chains crossing his chest. They smoldered orange from the heat of his hands and melted into pools of iron at his feet. Fire flew all around him, flaring and consuming everything, an angry beast ravaged with a hunger that fueled the shadowy creatures crawling through the rubble at his back.

Devilish growls tore through the broken town. Whimpering cries from the injured became tormented howls. Tears scorched Paresh's eyes. She'd never seen this. The twins had never united this way in the fibers of probability.

She pushed herself away from Darkesiel as Hawkiel's four wings flourished from his back and caught the air like sails. He floated over to his brother. They stared at each other in disbelief, each reaching for the other's face. Hawkiel's flames sparked brighter and Darkesiel shone faintly with dark light. They embraced and sank into a fire that burned black, blue, and red. The tips of Hawkiel's light wings began to emerge.

Paresh screamed at last, but they continued to rise, spreading far beyond his back, annihilating anything they touched. They stretched high into the atmosphere where electric blue cracks formed in the fabric of reality. The Hollow's wispy fog spilled through ripping seams.

"Please, no!" she screamed. Flames scorched her skin and black smoke snaked into her lungs. Her sweat and tears evaporated from cauterized blisters, and her vision swam with ash. Gabriel's voice whispered within her head and she echoed it aloud, "Enlighten the eyes of your heart to hope!"

She sprinted into the fire and threw her arms around the burning twins, urging Darkesiel to acknowledge the love that had awakened in him—willing them both to see that they weren't alone anymore and never would be again. As they locked gazes with her, she saw a reflection of the holy blue flame that burned in her eyes.

The cracks stopped growing. The flames froze. All of time seemed to stop except for the three of them. She repeated Gabriel's words and added a plea of her own, "Even when it seems there is too much to bear, true love can endure. It deserves that chance—that hope—to endure."

Michael and Gabriel touched down lightly at her sides, their wings dusting the flames from her skin and puffing air as a balm. Michael extended his hand to the twins and Gabriel said, "Your hate for Lucifer counters your love for this world. That is the choice presented to you now, my brothers."

His globe morphed into a Wheel of glowing bluish-white. The twins nodded to each other and pressed their foreheads together in unity. Darkesiel's globe became a Wheel that absorbed the veiling darkness and returned the sky to the sun's rule. The returning solar light energized and repaired Hawkiel's globe until it, too, became a Wheel that glowed golden-red.

Darkesiel accepted Michael's hand and Hawkiel followed. The three brothers embraced with Paresh at their center. The energy they emitted blew out the fires and joined with the sun's rays to eradicate the demons that had followed Hawkiel from his cell. The trio, one Seraph and two Cherubim with their Wheels, flew high into a blind spot where the sun's light shielded them from view.

Gabriel remained at her side, his attention focused on a fallen brick column and a cone of debris. He pressed his hand to her womb and whispered, "Be reborn and live the life that was stolen from you by the hand of deception." Confused, Paresh followed his gaze to the limp body of the blue-winged angel.

Something flew out from under a collapsed building on the next street and slammed into Gabriel. Her breath stuck like spider silk in her throat.

"Eric?" she whispered, turning in slow motion as they crashed through the remains of a two-story brick wall.

She scrambled after them, frantically trying to climb the crater, slick and muddy in the absence of the flames' drying heat. She managed to get one hand onto the street before she lost her footing. Protectively shielding her belly, she slid onto a sewer pipe, and ducked as a six-winged body zoomed overhead and slammed into the crater. Gabriel followed and pinned it under his foot.

"Eric!" she screamed, slipping off the pipe. She slid and stumbled in her rush to reach them. "Gabriel? *What are you doing?*"

"He only looks like Eric, Little One," Gabriel said. "I promise your love is protected above—inadvertently shielded by the wings of this one—"

He ground his heel into the angel's chest. "Who sought to kill him, *again*. Lucifer, you know Brother Michael will deal with you when the time comes. Now, will you make your body whole and free the twins of your despicable influence?"

"What...?" Paresh asked breathlessly with disbelief. She felt the world slide out from beneath her feet. She dropped into the mud, mesmerized by the hellish flames in the angel's eyes. "Lucifer?"

He was injured and appeared drained and weakened. His hardened stare drilled into her, and she swore she could feel him rooting around within her, searching for something, anything, but not finding what he wanted.

"How is that possible?" he demanded. "How can you have no trace of useable sin? That's an impossibility in this world!"

He glared at Gabriel, huffing in frustration. "She's not supposed to exist!" he yelled. "It's against the rules!"

Gabriel grinned smugly. "*Brother*, those are our rules. She was born of *His* will and imbued with the power of Gaea, herself. Who are we— nay, *you*—to question a greater existence?"

He gestured at the hidden trio. "Since the *dawn* of time, humans have seen us, you, *them*, tying us into their mythologies and bestowing names upon us. They saw us watching from the constellations in the heavens and called us down, designating some of us as sacred watchers of the sun and the moon and every earthly wonder, until *your war* came to this world and we fled, only to return to fight. Your war trapped the stars of Orion in your orbit."

Gabriel's expectant gaze buzzed Paresh's nerves. Her lips moved to form words, but none spilled forth. She knelt and reached for Lucifer's face, no longer seeing his emotion, instead focusing on his black hair and the blue of his irises behind the flame. She expected to feel love's warmth, as she did with Gabriel, but Lucifer was cold and distant—there but not there. Energy zapped her fingertips as she neared a connection.

"You look like him," she whispered. "But you don't."

The flames flourished. "We're identical—"

"You're not." She shook her head gently. "You're completely different on the inside and that's what makes the person. That's what makes the man I love. And that shines through his appearance."

The blue-winged angel tumbled down the wall of broken earth, rolling and bouncing with alternating views of deathly pale skin and azure feathers. She splashed into a large puddle and blew bubbles of labored breath to lift her face.

Icy barbs in her aura needled Paresh's gut, and when the angel's dull eyes snapped up, the flames of Hell re-erupted to sear Paresh's soul. In those eyes, the sapphire color had once burned so fiercely, full of a life that was no longer there, and the brown hair, crudely cut, was missing more than its formerly vibrant color—it lacked the radiance that reflected Raven's personality.

That wasn't Raven. Not anymore. Bloodied and beaten, she moved on autopilot with drool dripping from a sagging mouth. Her wings drooped as she staggered to her feet and swayed off balance, one straightening to hook the breeze and hold her crookedly on her feet. The right arm hung broken and useless, and the other feebly pointed a scythe at Paresh.

Atop the crater, Rainne, too, rose from beneath the crumbled column, aglow with that horrific scarlet, but the effect dulled by the dirt and dust coating her skin. Lucifer scurried away from Paresh's touch and growled, *Let the blood rain*, except it didn't come from *his* mouth—it came from the empty shell that had been Raven.

Gabriel's gaze flew up to the blind spot. "Brother, I need Time!"

As though unaware that her mask was already off, Rainne went through the motions before lifting onto her toes and throwing her arms out parallel to the ground. She swung into a wide arc and began to spin through the wreckage as dings, chimes, and cries returned with Time.

Paresh screamed Rainne's name and jolted with surprise when she leaped into the crater. Raven's husk charged Paresh with the scythe raised high, but a crimson blur rammed into her. The weapon dropped into the mud as Raven's body impacted the crater's far wall. Alex had his hand over his eyes as he ran in Paresh's direction.

Paresh quickly tossed a look at Gabriel. "He doesn't know?"

He didn't need to answer. The sharp pang in her heart was enough. "Oh Alex..." she whispered.

Paresh caught her breath as she returned her gaze to Alex. Rainne was behind him. He wasn't going to make it in time—Rainne was moving too fast. Her bladed toes nipped his heels and he tripped, pumping his arms and legs hard to stay afoot. Paresh could hear Eric and the others groaning under the debris. No one was coming to save Alex.

Paresh caught Gabriel's eye and he nodded. She saw Raven charging across the crater in her peripheral vision, but she was already running and leaping as high as she could. Gabriel clapped his wings and propelled her over Alex. She slapped the hand on his eyes to get his attention and blindly threw her hands out to catch hold of Rainne. Alex cursed and swiveled on the ball of his foot, and Rainne snapped backward with Paresh's momentum. Paresh looped an arm around Rainne's waist and narrowly evaded a deadly swipe. As the Elder's muscles tensed to strike, Paresh took her chance and slapped her palm against Rainne's neck, skin to skin.

Time seemed to stop again. But it hadn't. Rainne froze under her touch, Lucifer and Gabriel were motionless observers, and even Alex had stopped. Disbelief cracked throughout his aura—his horrified stare locked on—

"Raven?" he whispered. His mouth kept moving but he had no voice. Paresh could feel the paralyzing power of his emotions as he warred within himself, likely replaying the happiest moments of his life with Raven and trying to reconcile them with the threadbare version he saw before him.

He ran and collided into her, clasping his arms around her and falling with her into the mud, his eyes wide and searching. "Are you in there? No! It's not true! Raven! R-Raven! You're in there…I know it! Raven!"

He pulled in a soul-heaving breath as he struggled to hold onto her. "Raven! Please be in there. Come back to me! Come back! I love you. It's me…it's Alex. Please—"

He evaded her gnashing mouth and cried into her ear, "Come back…please come back. Please…this can't be you. It can't be. Without you, I'm always on the outside. You got me…I got you. *How can I live this life without you? I need you. You have to come back! I need you! I need you—*"

She lashed at him with her claws and roared like a feral creature. The mud weakened his grip and she slipped free, popping the good wing open to lift her to her feet. He folded in on himself, sobbing into muddy hands as she dashed for her weapon.

"*Alex!*" Paresh screamed.

Raven's husk kicked up the scythe and swung it at Paresh and Rainne, who was still immobilized by Paresh's touch. The blade tangled in Rainne's exposed weaponry. The husk wrenched it free and swung again. A shot boomed and rebounded off the crater walls.

Raven's body collapsed. Blood oozed and smoke coiled from the hole in the side of her head. Alex sat back on his heels staring at his hands like they weren't his own. Paresh let go of Rainne and ran to him, diving into the mud to sling her arms around his neck.

"*Alex!* I'm so sorry, Alex. I'm so sorry! *Oh Alex!*"

The revolver slipped off his fingers. He dragged his arms up Paresh's back. Unsteady breaths hit her shoulder. She choked out a whimpering cry and held him close as he finally hugged her to him.

"I loved you so much, Raven," Alex whispered as he looked across the crater. "I loved you more than I thought was possible. I loved you so much…it hurts. Oh, it hurts, Raven. It hurts *so much*. I wish…you could come back to me. To be well. To never have had that damn curse. To live your life…a life you actually *wanted*—"

He choked and sucked in a jagged breath through clenched teeth. His whole body heaved as he cried devastating tears…world-shattering tears, and clung to Paresh in desperation.

"I n-need you h-here! *H-here!*" he sputtered, his voice cracking, broken. "I know it's selfish, but I n-need y-you. Don't leave me…you can't leave me…you can't—"

He covered his face with one hand. "I was closer to you than anyone. I loved you…and it wasn't enough. *Come back to me! I can't. I just…can't…*"

Paresh's heart was ripping in two. She cupped his head and kissed his cheek. "It was enough, Alex," she said sadly. "You have to know that."

Snot trailed from her shoulder to his nose as he sat up. "How can I?" he squeaked, his red face streaked with tears and mud.

"Because you *did* get each other better than anyone and when you have that with someone, how can you not have love? How can that not be enough?"

She hugged him tighter as tears dripped from her eyes. "I love you, Alex. I always will. And I will selfishly never let you go, so thank you for saving my life. I know what it cost you, but that wasn't her. You did her memory justice with your mercy and your heart. You had love—it was enough. That was her nightmare—and you gave her peace."

Alex clung to her and hoarsely whispered, "I love you, too, Pare."

Endymion appeared beside them, patting Alex on the back before pulling Paresh up to his chest and kicking off with a spray of mud. He glared at the archangel as he returned Paresh to Gabriel's side and then trekked back over to Alex. He gave him a hand up and together they went to Raven's body, where Rainne was on her knees, cradling Raven's head in her lap. Her misty eyes were a glittering shade of gold and her hair was a radiant copper-brown. She was finally free of control, a real true blood with a virgin will that was all her own.

Gabriel called to Alex, "May it bring you solace to know that Raven's soul was predestined to return upon the contractual fulfillment of a life that was never truly hers."

Alex stared emptily at Gabriel a moment. Anger seeped into the heartache on his face as his eyes focused. "I'm sick of your riddles and wordplay! *I don't understand what that means!*"

Gabriel solemnly looked down at Paresh and doled a kiss upon her crown. "She does."

He swept her up and half-hopped, half-flew to Lucifer, who was dragging himself through the mud. "It's been hard, but you've done well so far, Little One. It's almost over."

Gabriel kicked Lucifer onto his back and pinned him beneath his heel again. "Your fight is with the Almighty and only He may settle it at this juncture."

Gabriel directed Lucifer to acknowledge Michael. "That is why he is here. Eric had the choice—and the power—to kill you, but his choice here was designed to affect this realm, *not you*. Had things gone differently with the twins, Michael would have struck you down, as he is destined to do in the Apocalypse, but the Sacred Vessel found the correct path. In the future, her Anointed Strength may do whatever is necessary to protect her and this world, even if it means striking you down. Right now, I require an answer."

He set Paresh onto her feet without looking away from Lucifer. This was it; she knew it, felt it, despite not knowing what *it* was.

"He was tempted," Paresh whispered. "And didn't kill you."

She sank into thought, seeking a thread to tie it all together. "Since the dawn of time...your fight started long before any of us existed. It's not our fight to win, which means...this isn't about you or us."

She crouched at Lucifer's side. "The sun, the moon, the stars...the dawn...the Dawn Bringer was Eos."

Shielding her eyes, she glimpsed the silhouettes of the twins above. "And Helios and Selene...Eos lifted the veil so they could function. But what do the stars of Orion have to do with that?"

"Lucifer, as *Hawkiel*, told Raven that he once watched Earth from that constellation," Endymion said quietly as he combed his fingers through Raven's hair.

Paresh took that in and bit down on her lip, feeling *it* slip away any time she got close. What else was she missing? Gabriel was forbidden from helping her, but she could ask specific questions. "What is the choice again?"

To Lucifer, Gabriel asked, "Will you make your body whole and free the twins of your despicable influence?"

Lucifer snarled and tried to scoot beyond Paresh's reach. "How is this *my* choice?"

"Oh, Brother," Gabriel cooed, "you made *that* choice long ago. I never said this one was yours."

Paresh studied her hands and the fear in Lucifer's eyes. "I touched

Rainne and gave her freewill. What happens if I touch you?"

Lucifer seethed at Gabriel. "How is this *her* choice when she doesn't even understand what she's doing?"

"She'll get there," Gabriel replied with a small smile. "Have *faith*."

The metaphorical light bulb popped on in Paresh's head. She snapped her fingers. "It's not about Eos. It's about the veil she lifted. Before I died, Raven said that Lucifer couldn't control Rainne Blood Pathos if he's not in his body. Is this not your body? Is it another illusion? A trick to mess with our heads? A veil to be lifted? Do you really not look like Eric?"

Her fingers zapped with energy the closer they got to Lucifer's skin. He squirmed under Gabriel's foot.

"It's my body!" he spat. "I wouldn't voluntarily take on a used face!"

"No, you merely chose to recycle it yourself because of your pride and then threw a tantrum when Father bested you at your own game. Again," Gabriel said.

"But he's not whole…" Paresh said to herself. "And he holds the twins under his influence—the stars of Orion, where he once watched…so, if I touch him—" She moved to cup his face, a face that fit so perfectly into her hands, but didn't belong there. "Then they will be free, his influence returns to him, and he is whole. The veil is lifted. Yes. The choice is yes."

She flattened her palms against Lucifer's face. The marks on her hands flourished to life, the red of Hawkiel's starburst and blue of Darkesiel's sunburst illuminating through the blue crescent moons and the red intersecting star. White fire erupted along the edges, embossing the outlines with gold light.

A visible energy cloud lifted from Lucifer's body and floated like an ethereal specter up to Hawkiel, and another came down to him. The wheel hovering over Hawkiel's wings burst into golden-red flames. Darkesiel's erupted with bluish-black sparks.

"Very good, Little One," Gabriel said, lifting his foot from Lucifer's chest. "Brother, the twins have chosen, and you no longer exert any control over them or your children—they are all free at last—so a new choice comes to *you*. Will you face Brother Michael today? Or return to the background of humanity's world as you were and face him later?"

Lucifer stood with a huff and spat on Gabriel's foot. "What do you think?" He threw his hobbled wings open and fled into a Hollow portal that opened in the sky.

Pulling Paresh into an embrace, Gabriel whispered, "Know that I shall watch over you and your wee ones always. Hawkiel and Darkesiel will remain as guardians of the Earth to maintain the balance until it tips beyond sustainable measure. Live and love well, Little Ones."

He kissed the top of her head and flew up to his brothers. A bolt of blue zapped the heavens and they were gone.

☽ ✳ ☾

"Paresh!" Eric yelled, leaping into the crater with Jonathan and Lucien practically on top of him. She ran into his arms and clung tightly as he asked, "Are you hurt anywhere? Is the bab—"

"I'm good," she said. "We're *all* good."

Eric diverted a somber gaze to Raven's body. "Did you know—?"

A pang of sorrow struck Paresh's heart as she nodded. "Raven's fate was written the day she was born. Like mine."

She reached out to Jonathan and threaded their fingers. The twins' marks were tattooed onto her hands. The golden line resembled her stream in Grandfather Wisdom. She studied it a second before grabbing hold of Lucien's silk kimono and pulling both him and Jonathan into an Eric-smashing hug. "Thank you all for enduring. I know it wasn't easy and that only time will heal the wounds, but I will take away the pain that I can. It's energy, you know, for the *wee ones*, as Gabriel called them."

She released them to rub her belly. "We're having twins."

Eric palmed her bump. "Do you know who the other one is now?"

Biting her lip, Paresh nodded and jogged over to Alex, followed closely by Eric, Jonathan, and Lucien. She held up a finger to them and squatted beside Alex, pulling his hand from Raven's body to her belly.

"She's alive in me," she whispered. "You heard two heartbeats, but only one had a soul at the time. She'll get to live a new life of her own choosing this time."

Alex stared at her like he couldn't believe what he was hearing. But then he threw his arms around her and sobbed so hard he choked. She turned a teary smile up to Eric who knelt to embrace them both. Eventually, Alex sniffled and wiped his face, and pressed his ear against Paresh's womb, closing his eyes to listen to their beating hearts. Endymion and Rainne turned their attention to her, and Sarah and Kestrel emerged from the wreckage above, jumping down to join them.

"What shall you name her?" Endymion asked softly.

Paresh glanced uncertainly at Eric and the others. "Raven, right? That's her name?"

Alex shook his head, unable to speak yet. Sarah ruffled his hair and said, "You should give her a new name. One to call her own. She was never free in this life—"

"—and she knew it," Kestrel finished. "She knew she wasn't making it out alive."

"Well, then, I don't know yet," Paresh said. Eric clasped his hands under her bulging belly without disturbing Alex.

Jonathan and Lucien suddenly tensed in alarm. Hunters materialized around the crater's rim and stretched back in rows as far as Paresh could see. She recognized insignias from every squad. Heron and Cyprian broke through holding Walter—with a splinted leg—between them. Every hunter but them dropped to bended knee in a gesture of respect and mourning.

Paresh tapped Alex's shoulder. He glanced up and slowly stood, his mouth falling open. The ranks circled the entirety of the crater. In unison, they covered their hearts and tucked their chins, and Walter gave Raven's two-fingered salute. Heron and Cyprian did the same. Alex saluted them and circled in place, covering his heart and nodding acknowledgment at each turn.

"Raven deserves a proper funeral," Eric said to Lucien. "I know that's not tradition—"

"We will honor her sacrifice with a tangible memorial, and we will never forget," Lucien said. He, too, and Jonathan, covered their hearts. Endymion and Rainne, and Kestrel and Sarah got down on their knees.

"Here," Alex said, softly, his tears flowing freely. "We'll bury her here, in the first vampire-human haven in the history of the world. This is where she'd want to be."

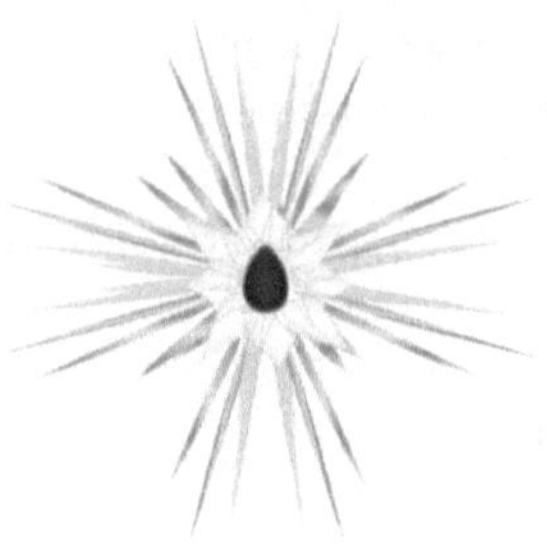

CHAPTER EIGHTEEN: BY THE WINDS OF AURORA

PARESH

Winter Solitude, Arc of True Blood, 2029

To the outside world, a miracle happened that early autumn day eight years ago. A freak asteroid demolished nearly every business and half the homes in Orison Crossing, but no one died—no humans, anyway.

The citizens who remained remembered. They'd chosen to retain what they'd experienced as hundreds of military clad vampire hunters shuttled them to safety in the aftermath. And they, along with every member of the VaSH and High Council, attended the first ever funeral for a vampire, to celebrate her sacrifice at the end of the world. Paresh couldn't help but smile as she'd nursed the very soul they were mourning during the ceremony, but few had known about that then.

In addition to a marker in the cemetery, Eric erected a beautiful mausoleum and garden on the mansion grounds as a place where hunters could imbibe and pay their respects beyond human eyes. As the Elders' permanent home under Lucien's restructuring, the mansion was a busy hub and embassy for the Vampiric Nation, especially in the years of rebuilding.

Jonathan delivered a surprise to Eric when the village's library excavations were underway. Someone found an old trunk filled with journals written by James Adam Ravenscroft. Paresh knew Jonathan had planted them there, but never let on to either that she knew the truth. His gesture restored a tarnished reputation, reset the town's history, and led Eric to discover the broken headstone of his sister's plot on their old family land. In turn, that prompted him to work with the Fausts to find his mother's unmarked grave on their farm. He had both interred with his family. Unfortunately, all records of his father's body were lost, and while Eric sometimes wondered how his father's life had gone so wrong—and eyed Jonathan suspiciously—he never asked. It was easier, and less painful, to remember the mood and changing attitudes of the era. Given the Ravenscroft's work with the Underground Railroad, pro-slavery secessionists could've easily targeted them to smear their name.

Walter pushed his retirement back a few years, but he got there eventually. He borrowed the Ravenscroft and Faust journals and frequently read them to Molly—and Raven, even though he was *in-the-know*—at the cemetery. He also helped Heron and Cyprian set up an outreach and assistance foundation that they operated out of Molly's house, in her name. They loved playing with the kids in cul-de-sac basketball games. The kids nicknamed them *Moon Rabbit One* and *Two* because of their crescent crests and their "unfair" jumping skills. They always fought over which team got which hunter even though it didn't really matter. Every now and then, the matches got heated and ended in a tie that they let the kids break, because if they didn't, Sarah entered the picture, and no one could beat her.

Kestrel petitioned the High Council for Sarah to be her Co-Commander. She didn't like the hierarchal dynamic that restricted their official dealings, and, as she put it bluntly, they were a whole that should operate as a whole. Lucien agreed. He'd been more agreeable since that day—strangely, a day no one wanted to name. The outside world called it "A-Day." To locals, it was a day of remembrance—they'd never forget the name *Raven Hawkings*.

Of course, to the humans who'd learned firsthand that God and the Devil did, in fact, exist—alongside old spirits like Mother Nature—the itch to carry on with life came with renewed purpose or newfound repentance. Paresh had never gotten time to ponder how she'd change her decisions with absolute proof like that, but the villagers had the time, and they took it. They still see mysterious golden-red and bluish-black lights in the forest at night—Hawkiel and Darkesiel running through the woods playing tag with Gaea's woodland nymphs.

Living in Orison Crossing came with strict rules to protect its secrets, but also steep rewards. No one worked because they needed money; they did it to maintain the structure of small-town life and because they wanted to. Whether volunteering, running a shop or coffeehouse, policing or firefighting, or working at The Greenery, most saw it as a token of gratitude to the one who had always been there for them—and many of their ancestors. All money earned went back into the community. With the backing of the Vampiric Nation, no one was left wanting.

Alex retained his hybrid post, and he and Jonathan split their residential time between Eric's house—they refused to let him give it to them—and their dwellings at the Arc of True Blood. Lucien programmed additional Animus Hollow exits to ease the minor annoyance of traveling between points in the village. Living in both places was as easy as walking from one room to another.

With Paresh's essence and the spiritual nexus restored, Sunset Grove thrived with life. It didn't hurt that the Earth's guardian angels called it home, either, but Paresh was relieved. That had been her one worry with the vampiric influx. The forest had been so desolate in the years of her absence. She never wanted to see it suffer again.

She and Eric decided to tear down the cottage. They could hold onto their happy memories and let the bad ones go with it. Her parents had built it knowing they'd never have another child. She and Eric didn't know how many they'd have. They built another cottage in its place, with bedrooms to spare and room to grow. Like Jonathan and Alex, they split their time between Sunset Grove and the Arc of True Blood, wanting their girls to grow up as forest sprites with privacy. The unfortunate side effect of that day was the spotlight it put on them and their family—vampires were as insatiably curious as humans when it came to royalty, and that's what they were, whether they wanted to be or not.

Safety wasn't a concern for anyone in Orison Crossing. All known COMS, save one, were eradicated. Many aging rogues who knew they'd never repent grew weary of simply waiting to die and took control of their deaths, and others formed support groups to seek meaningful change or to help others *want* meaningful change. Regardless, the aging factor made it nearly impossible for them to hide. Most of the non-repentant were held for their crimes at Eido.

After the happenings of that day, Paresh pulled Endymion and Lucien aside, urging them to come clean about their secret alliance. They declined and Endymion offered to relinquish his title, pointing out that with Paresh as the most powerful and influential of them all, his real identity was inconsequential. He'd offered to use his connection to seek out all rogues and make them self-terminate, but Lucien had been surprisingly adamant that choice and atonement were part of human life, and that those within the Vampiric Nation deserved the same right to choose their own fates. The Second New Age had finally delivered the lives they'd wanted: the lives of men and the judgment that came with them.

Endymion had asked for a private moment with Paresh to address the one surviving COMS rogue, and, with one question, exposed her inner darkness. What did she want to do about Donovan? She'd had ideas, that's for certain, but none that she'd say out loud. Endymion presented the easy option—killing him—and another option that more or less forced Donovan into the life he'd bargained for. Endymion hadn't needed to go into the details, but he had, including ways to prolong Donovan's life despite the years that he'd aged, and he'd watched Paresh's reactions closely.

She'd smiled and bluntly asked what he was looking for, because if he wanted to know how powerful she really was, she'd show him the same courtesy he'd shown Lucien.

"The path you choose is up to you," she said, "but I'd really like to remain allies and friends. I can't return to being that bright-eyed girl in awe of a new world, but I can continue to respect your guidance and enjoy your company. I know where your heart is."

She'd looked down at her hands, folded atop her bulging belly, and thought of the second fetus growing there. She'd locked eyes with him and thought, *You protected her and gave her the best shot at having her own life. I can never repay that, and I will forever be grateful. How she interacts with you when she grows up is up to her, because I believe she'll regain her memories. But you must recognize, now, that I am no longer on the same level as any of you. And you no longer hold the leverage you once did over anyone.*

The surprise in his eyes was enough of an acknowledgment. She'd smiled wider. *Give Donovan the life he wanted and enjoy every moment of it for me, Endy.*

"As you wish, m'lady," he'd purred, grinning as he swept down into a bow. "Oh, the secrets we keep, indeed."

Eric and Jonathan, and Alex and a host of others, had decried "Endymion's" decision, but they grew to see its worth. Donovan became a vampiric version of the Ancient Roman's Accursed Man. Yet, instead of becoming killable to everyone, he was killable to none, banned from his nation, and implanted and tracked every moment of every day to be hunted for sport—his only protection being that one taboo. And if he let himself be killed…well, he landed in the hands of Endymion and the Chthonic Knights. Death never lasted and it tasted increasingly bitter each time. Now he put up "good" fights worthy of sport—

"…absolutely adores him." Eric draped his arm over her shoulders. "Are you still with me?"

"Of course." Paresh looked away from Endymion and Lucien, and snuggled closer to him. "The peace here makes it easy to drift off sometimes."

The arc was dark. The casements clear. The majesty of the snowcapped Treuter Mountains on full display under the dazzling stars.

Their sector of the arc was reserved, and its fortified sound grid gave them quiet privacy, even from Lucien and Endymion. The "public" side was abuzz with energy and activity as members of the Vampiric Nation and the Elders enjoyed their annual festival and visitation. The only Elders who lived there fulltime were Lucien, Endymion, and Rainne, making Winter Solitude a refreshing indulgence for the remaining High Council, more than it had been in the past.

"But it's happening more lately," Eric insisted. "Are you sure everything's okay?"

She breathed in the crisp bergamot of his cologne and shyly grinned at the fluttery tickle it gave her. A flash of crystalline gray caught her eye. She motioned for their daughter to join them. "Everything's perfect, I promise."

Looking very much like her father from her glossy black hair to her equally dark clothes, Celeste shoved an untamable lock behind her ear and plopped melodramatically next to Paresh, huddling close to get under Eric's arm. He gave them both a squeeze.

"The forecasts say they should start any time. I know it's weird, but the wait is my favorite part of Polar Midnight." Celeste's gentle cadence matched her tranquil nature. She was eight years old, but appeared sixteen and had a mid-twenties mentality. She sighed and peered up at the casements, awaiting the show.

They'd expected fraternal twins, but their daughters were identical, except for their birthmarks—crescent moons on Selene's shoulder blades and a star in the center of Celeste's back. They'd aged at twice the rate of humans until their last birthday, when their cellular growth showed signs of slowing and transitioning to regeneration. Endymion believed they'd stop aging in another four to six years. The twins thought it was funny that they'd eventually look older than their mother.

He saw you watching them. And he's right, you are spacing out more, Mom. In her head, Celeste's voice was a melodic hum—a feminine version of Gabriel's that came from the bond they'd shared in death and stasis. For better or worse, Celeste had seen and heard the same things as Paresh in those years, and could visualize the patterns in the fibers of light and dark to project them into the future. Although Gabriel tried to limit her access, she was connected to his sight and could watch the fibers of probability, too.

You're having a boy this time. Celeste hummed. *You should tell Dad.*

Paresh gasped aloud and faced Celeste in shock, which drew a suspicious eye from Eric that shifted to their daughter. "Use your voice, please."

"Sorry, Dad, but Mom's got something to tell you." She hopped up and ran over to Alex and her sister.

"That little snot." Paresh laughed.

Eric pulled her in for a kiss. "What's the big secret?" he murmured, resting his forehead on hers and tracing her lips with his thumb.

"I'll tell you soon, don't worry." She shot a sideways glance at Lucien and Endymion.

"What's going on with them?" Eric asked, his brow dipping slightly as he followed their gazes to where Alex sat with his arm around their other daughter. "Endymion's not going to…?"

Endymion's peridot orbs locked onto Paresh. *I know you meant what you said,* she thought to him and got a slight chin dip in return.

"He watches her all the time," Eric added, unaware of Paresh's abilities outside of her connection to Celeste.

"If you think about it, he's never known loss—she's his nostalgia. He'll always love *his* Raven, but our daughter's heart clearly belongs to Alex. Endy is content enough to see her smile—he only wants for her to be happy," Paresh said, deliberately not mentioning the question that had sparked the conversation in the first place.

Lucien had asked Endymion what he intended to do about his *queen.*

"Raven was always doomed to die by that pact," Paresh said, echoing Endymion's answer as he and Lucien headed toward them, "so he did what he could to give her a life she could call her own. This version of her no longer needs him."

"Should we be concerned as parents about Alex?" Eric asked. "They've gotten a lot closer recently and old soul or not, she's got the hormones of a teenager."

"It's not like he's going to get her pregnant, right?" Paresh laughed, but Eric's expression went from humored to puzzled. She wrapped her arms around him. "I think she's fine and they're cute, and not that it matters, but Endy's given them his blessing. Alex's affections face no challenge from him. It's up to her, honestly; she's not a normal child, after all. She loves them both, but with Alex——"

"They're soul mates." Eric mused to himself. "I guess only Sarah knows what it's like to remember a previous life like that. I can't imagine cramming over fifteen hundred years of memories into an eight-year-old brain."

"I'm just happy that she likes her name and loves her sister. I worried they wouldn't bond like twins usually do." Paresh tilted her head in thought and softly confessed, "When Alex suggested 'Selene,' I also worried about the implications given all we'd just gone through, but he was right—it connects her to both Endymion and him."

"He's rarely wrong." Eric grinned. "The *daft idiot* is surprisingly insightful."

Paresh snorted and covered her mouth as she bent over laughing. Eric playfully smacked her on the back. "I won't ever let him live that down—stealing Selene's first words like that."

"Well…at least we got the confirmation we wanted!" Paresh wiped her eyes. "If I wasn't so connected to Celeste, we might've mixed them up and swapped their names!"

Eric chuckled and offered a stiff wave when Selene and Alex peered suspiciously back at them. Celeste merely shook her head, not lowering her focus from the sky for a moment. She wanted to see that first sliver of color. She'd guessed it'd be green tonight.

Paresh had never seen Alex this happy. She blew him a kiss and winked at her daughter. Selene gave her a toothy grin and wrestled Alex into a headlock to run her knuckles through his hair.

"Ow, ow, ow, Goody!" Alex yelped, his squeak coming out extra high-pitched thanks to his adorable nervousness under *parental scrutiny*.

Selene's knuckles dug deeper and rougher. "Stop calling me that!"

Strolling leisurely into their privacy grid, Jonathan asked, "May I join you?"

"Tired of mingling with the masses?" Eric asked, patting the spot beside Paresh.

"Being responsible is tiring." Jonathan sat and kissed Paresh on the cheek. "I suppose I'll be homeless soon," he said, dramatically gesturing at Alex.

"What do you mean?" Paresh asked.

"She'll want to live with him, and a *real* Ravenscroft should live in the Ravenscroft house." He shrugged. "Maybe I'll stay here fulltime or take over the mansion's basement."

"Oh…" Paresh flattened her palm to her chest. "I hadn't thought that far ahead. I'm not ready to be an empty nester."

"Huh," Eric said, his unreadable expression proof that he hadn't thought about it either.

Sarah and Kestrel waved from the edge of the grid. Eric sighed and waved them in. "Sometimes I wish more of the Sarah I knew was still in there. She would've just run over here before."

Jonathan made a thoughtful noise. "Lior was too respectful for that. She's still got that human spunk you loved—don't read too much into it."

As if to prove the point, as Kestrel stood back in a respectful stance, Sarah rushed Eric and wrapped him into a firm hug. She embraced Paresh more gently and then dropped down beside Eric. "Granddad would've loved to see this," she said. "I wish I could've brought him up, just once."

"He's probably got a better view now," Eric said, nudging his chin at Kestrel to join them.

"Yeah, maybe." Sarah yanked Kestrel down to lie on her back. She tenderly stroked Kestrel's gold and black locks as she nestled her head in Sarah's lap. "Maybe someday I can bring my nieces?"

She sounded hopeful. If not for the fact that Celeste and Selene had befriended her older nieces, it would never happen, but now…well, things were different now.

Paresh threaded her fingers with Jonathan's and laughed as Alex broke free and pounced on Selene, mercilessly tickling her ribs. She kicked him square in the gut, knocking him on his rear, and took full advantage to return the favor, the pink tips of her black hair swinging past his cheeks as he threw his head back laughing. Their immature squealing chased Celeste back to her parents. She wedged herself between Paresh and Jonathan.

"Hey, Uncle Jon," she said, dusting his cheek with a kiss. "Are you staying up here awhile?"

As he nodded, Paresh tugged on Celeste's sleeve and pointed.

"Look! You were right!"

The aurora started with a green spark and blew into ghostly curtains that cast vibrant reflections of green, red, and blue onto the surrounding snowy canvas. The overhead effect was like a psychedelic trance of weaving plasma and a kaleidoscope of shimmering color that dropped like the sky was falling, yet snaked away before gravity could grasp it.

"I'll never tire of this view," Celeste whispered. She leaned her head back against Paresh's shoulder.

Paresh kissed the top of her head, and spied Alex and Selene settled on their backs, hands clasped, shoulder to shoulder. Alex's love radiated in tangibly warm waves. She wasn't surprised when he propped up on his side and hesitantly kissed Selene on the lips, but Paresh did make an appropriately stunned noise as her hand flew to her belly.

She thought she'd had more time.

It is in line with when Dad felt me for the first time, though. Celeste hummed. *And ignore them. She kissed him first in private—it's just the first time he's done it in front of you.*

"Ah!" Paresh gasped again, drawing the others' attention. *That explains his extra cute nerves tonight, then.*

Come on! Come on! Are you going to tell them or what?

Paresh smiled up at Eric. "Um…y-you're going to be a dad again."

"Another b-baby?" Eric's mouth dropped open. He cupped the new bulge in Paresh's belly that she'd been concealing with her clothing for the past day.

"A son." She gnawed her lower lip. "His name is Sora and he said it means *sky*. That's why I've been spacey lately—the coincidence with that day…Gabriel and Hawkiel put such an emphasis on the sun, moon, and dawn, and the balance of three. And now we have a star, a moon, and a sky."

She gestured at Celeste, Selene, and her belly before covering Eric's hand. Sora kicked and got a half-laugh and half-gasp from his dad, which made him kick harder.

"Congratulations, Pare." Jonathan gave her shoulders a reassuring squeeze.

"Yeah, you're a great mom." Celeste cooed at her belly, "I can't wait to meet you little bro!"

Eric pulled Paresh against him, breathlessly whispering, "God, I love you," before kissing her deeply. Their auras interlocked swirling with joy and love.

She couldn't help wondering what her children meant for the next generation of the world. Too much had happened to discount Fate and Destiny having a plan. But, as Lucien pulled Jonathan into his embrace, and Endymion and the others closed in around Eric and her, Selene and Celeste touched her womb and connected with their brother, and in that moment, she knew her kids would grow up in an ocean of love and close friendships.

She melted into Eric's kiss, into his passion and his unyielding care. Under ethereal dancing ribbons and prismatic stars at the top of the world, she it felt in her very soul that as long as they had each other, they would conquer any obstacle thrown in their path. They would always work it out because they had each other and the support of their extended family. And that meant she didn't need to worry anymore about what was going to happen in...

THE END.

NOTATIONS

<u>Author Note</u>

Thank *you* for sticking with Paresh and Eric through the end! Maybe we'll see more of them in the future? Anything's possible. Thank you to Megan. I cannot overstate how much you helped me. You kept me sane, among *everything else*. No easy feat! To authors M.K. Deppner, Serene Conneeley, Ruth Miranda, Andrew Franks, & Julie Embleton for support, friendship, & guidance. To my friends and family, especially Mom & Brenna. To my husband, who supported me through every grueling minute of the entire series. I should thank my cats one last time. And anyone I may have overlooked. I am so grateful to everyone who's been on this journey with me. Thank you.

Reviews are lifeblood to authors! Please let other readers know what you think of this book by reviewing on Amazon and/or GoodReads! It's as easy as telling a friend! Thank you for your support!
www.kastiepavlik.wixsite.com/author

<u>Timeline (Continues Next Page)</u>

2000 B.C. Lucien created 1901 Lucien hunts human prey 1849 Lucien's first major injury 1799 Lucien discovers pleasure, alters self 1713 Lucien named "Waira" by humans; discovers meditation & his aura; maintains humanoid appearance	2100-1200 B.C. tales of the Epic of Gilgamesh are told/written (end c.200B.C.) Neolithic & (end c.300B.C.), Jōmon cultures, Japan; Jōmon culture produces some of the world's oldest pottery
1446 Lucien kills tribal leader; is hunted; forest home is burned	c.1600 change in Earth's orbit/axis leads to desertification of Sahara & population movement toward Central & South Africa
1194 Lucien ponders the Watchers & false gods; witnesses the Siege of Troy off the Northwest Coast of Asia Minor	1194 Legendary Trojan War begins (end c.1184)
1000 Jonathan created, given to Lucien; first tactile sensation-rain in South Africa	1010-970 reign of David, King of Israel 970-931 reign of King Solomon
c.950 In Egypt, Jonathan introduces Lucien to strategy & utilizes regional conflict to increase comfort; Jonathan set free on his own for first time	c.950 Egyptian Pharaoh Psusennes II dies; his Libyan general, Shoshenq I ascends; regional history & Biblical history blur—possible uprisings, possible region stabilization, possible attack on Jerusalem
	700 Homer writes *The Iliad*
c.4th Century B.C. Lucien & Jonathan travel early routes of the Silk Road	c.476-221 China's Warring States period; (Qin Dynasty unifies China 221)
370 Jonathan thrills in killing warring combatants; Lucien gifts Jonathan ribbon	300 B.C. Yayoi Culture, Japan (end c.300 A.D.); early practices of Shintoism appear
	b.356-d.323B.C. Alexander the Great
	250 construction begins on the Great Wall of China
200 Lucien returns to the foothills of Mt. Fuji, Japan; hopes to calm Jonathan with meditation & "tea" ceremonies; Resides in a village of peaceful monks	b.70/69-d.30 Cleopatra VII Queen of Egypt; births twins Alexander Helios & Cleopatra Selene with Marc Antony (40 B.C.)
	c.2nd Century B.C. Silk Road begins
	c.27 B.C. Roman Empire Rises
	Heron of Alexandria, 10 A.D.-70 A.D.
c.36 A.D. Jonathan slaughters village of monks in blind rage; the Great Holy War begins on Earth; Lucifer creates Vampire King Endymion; Lucien meets Endymion & accepts his proposal; Lucien & Jonathan leave Japan for Africa	c.36 A.D. Lucifer expelled from Heaven Altered History Begin Date Unknown
c.40 A.D. Donovan, Alex, others created	
150 A.D. Kestrel & Lior experiment with purified silver on the European Continent; Lior invents liquid silver	306-337 reign of Constantine the Great, Roman Emperor; Christian convert c.312
5th Century Raven created; witnessed by Kestrel & Endymion; attempts suicide; rescued by Not-Hawkiel (Lucifer); begins rebellion; c.455 Kestrel & Lior camp on Swiss Plateau, final carving; save Alex wounded on frontline	c.300-500 A.D. Altered History reflects Roman Empire Collapse c.5th/6th Century Buddhism enters Japan 536 volcanic eruptions, famine, starvation, war, no sunlight 18 months, extreme weather; period of suffering lasts into 7th century; Bubonic Plague 541 & more volcanic eruptions

Timeline markers (center): 2000 B.C., 1500 B.C., 1000 B.C., 500 B.C., 1 A.D., 300 A.D., 400 A.D.

Vampiric History | Human History

Vampiric History		Human History
897 Lucien & Endymion conspire, send Jonathan to eradicate Salea's village using Rainne Blood Pathos; Raven reveals her immunity to Jonathan; Endymion meets Raven, forms alliance	700 A.D.	8th Century tea arrives in Japan 793-1066 A.D. Vikings invade England
c.920 Kestrel & Lior deliver scroll to Raven in Norway, discover the Aurora		
c.998 Lucien signs Treaty of the Lasting Peace; builds arcs; creates Vampiric High Council of Elders	1000 A.D.	c.1000 A.D. Leif Eriksson settles L'Anse aux Meadows
1099 Lord Connall's execution; Salea influences the Crusaders		1099 First Holy Crusade 1346 Black Death
1692 Wraith Reapers execute rogue inciting Puritans to kill each other; Donovan's first innocent kill	1690s A.D.	1692 Salem Witch Trials
	1840s A.D.	1841 Eric is born 1842 Eric's sister dies
1847 Jonathan meets Eric; destroys his life		1851 Eric's mother dies c.1854/55 Eric's father dies; Eric meets Thaddeus Hawthorne
	1860s A.D.	1860 Eric marries Lucinda 1861 U.S. Civil War begins; Eric enlists Feb.1864 Lucinda becomes pregnant
Apr.1864 Jonathan alters Eric Oct.1864 Eric awakens as a vampire		Apr.1864 Eric "dies" in battle Oct.1864 Eric awakens, altered Nov.1864 Lucinda & infant Darien die
Nov.1864 Eric slaughters Confederate Camp; Rescues Willy (Weaverly) 1866 Eric becomes Hawthorne guardian		Nov.1864 Eric returns to Civil War May 1865 Civil War ends 1866 Hawthorne Legacy—Lucas is born
	1880s A.D.	1887 Nathaniel is born
1888 Salea, in London with Lucifer, copycats Jack the Ripper; beheads Lior; shot in head by Alex		1888 Jack the Ripper stalks London
	1900 A.D.	1905 Joshua is born
1908 The games begin: Jonathan corrupts Hawthornes; Eric fractures Joshua's mind		1908 Elizabeth Hawthorne's suicide; Nathaniel's paranoia;
	1930s A.D.	1914-1918 World War I 1935 Daniel is born; later becomes Senator Hawthorne
Jan.1936 Eric kills Joshua Hawthorne; Jonathan kills Nathaniel & Lily; burns the mansion; attempts to rape Eric		Jan.1936 Eric rescues Clarence Weaverly & infant Daniel; seeks redemption
1936-1960 World wars & global political climate restrict Jonathan	1950s A.D.	1936-1956 Eric raises Daniel Hawthorne 1939-1945 World War II 1956 Andrew is born 1957 David is born
1960 Jonathan begins molding David	1970s A.D.	1960 David begins fighting with Andrew 1975 David murders Daniel & Sandy, & Felicia's parents; Molly meets Eric 1976 Andrew & Felicia marry
Jun.1988 Eric resurrects infant Paresh 1988 Jonathan sets & frames David for Sunset Grove Parish Arson		Jun.1988 Paresh stillborn Summer 1988 Sunset Grove Parish Arson
Aug.1996 High Council orders Paresh's abduction; Jonathan uses David	1990s A.D.	Aug.1996 David murders Andrew & Felicia, & kidnaps Paresh

Summer 2006: The events of *The Arrival* end in the pre-dawn hours of Paresh's 5th morning home following her death & resurrection. The events of *Confessions of the Second Born* begin on Paresh's 8th day home & end on the 13th day after Molly's funeral, which is where the events of *Last Born Daughter* begin. They end on the 15th day, where the events of *Eternal Light Descendant* begin. The finale jumps to 2007, 2010, 2021, and ends in 2029.

The Elysian Fields

In Greek mythology, it was generally part of the Greek Underworld alongside Hades and Tartarus. It was a place of happiness for gods and the righteous to enjoy after death.

Waira - Lucien

The Waira is a yokai from Japanese supernatural folklore described as a green forest dweller with a taste for humans and a single claw for a hand.

Alex's Sayings

Alex makes many references to Greek and Roman mythology that tie into the series thematically. Here is a *brief* guide:

✳ Apollo's Laurels (on the laurels of Apollo, etc.)—Apollo, Greek God of the Sun (and poetry and music and much more), was cursed by Cupid (Roman—Eros in Greek) to love Daphne, a water nymph, who turned into a laurel tree to escape his advances. In her honor, he wore a crown of laurels upon his head.

✳ Deimos (dreaded…with a capital "Deimos" in Ch10)—Ares, Greek God of War, and Aphrodite, Greek Goddess of Love, birthed Deimos (terror/dread) and Phobos (panic/flight), the gods of fear. Deimos and Phobos are the moons of Mars, named after Ares' Roman counterpart (Venus is Aphrodite's Roman counterpart and is considered the astronomical Morning Star).

✳ Daughter of Night (I swear on the Daughter of Night in Ch11)—Nyx, the Greek personification of night from the dawn of creation, was sister to Gaea and Tartarus, and daughter of Chaos. She produced many offspring, to include the Fates and Charon, but the daughter referenced here is Lyssa (Rabies in Roman), the embodiment of mad rage and frenzy.

✳ Prometheus (Curse you like Prometheus to suffer eternally… in Ch11)—Viewed as the Thinker Titan who championed for humanity, Prometheus was punished by Zeus for giving fire to humans. He was chained to a rock and doomed to have his liver eaten for eternity by an eagle. He was eventually freed.

✳ Charon/River Styx (Fate was like Charon…the dead…couldn't afford…trapped like a wraith on the banks of the River Styx in Ch10 and referenced again in Ch11)—The dead wishing to cross the River Styx into Hades needed a token to pay Charon, the ferryman. Those who couldn't pay wandered the banks of the river as wraiths.

✳ Tartarus (Why in Tartarus… Ch17)—As referenced above, Tartarus was among the primordial divinities who preceded the Titans and Olympians. He was the embodiment of the Underworld, a place of torment, a dungeon, a prison of punishment. Tartarus is a place lower and worse than Hades.

Gaea/Helios/Selene/Eos

Continuing the Greco-Roman theme, Lucien provides references for Gaea and the Titan trio Helios/Selene/Eos, among others. Here is a *brief* guide:

❋ Gaea, the representation of Earth and Mother of the Natural World, was among the primordial divinities who preceded and birthed the Titans and Olympians. Zeus was her grandson.

❋ Helios/Selene/Eos, were the sibling Titan representatives of the Sun, Moon, and Dawn, respectively.

☽ Eos, or Aurora in Roman, the Dawn Bringer, lifted the veils of twilight for the Sun and the Moon, and mothered many offspring after being cursed by Aphrodite, Greek Goddess of Love, to fall in love eternally. She mothered the planet Venus (not the goddess, however), also known as Lucifer, the Light Bringer. Eos/Aurora is sometimes referred to as Light Bringer as representative of bringing the early light of dawn with the sunrise.

☽ Helios, or Sol in Roman, the Sun, is often depicted as driving a four-horse chariot across the sky. His name forms the basis of Heliopsis, the false sunflower. He was replaced in Greek mythology by the popular Apollo.

☽ Selene, or Luna in Roman, the Moon, fell in love with the mortal Endymion and was associated with Artemis, Greek Goddess of the Moon.

The Watchers

Watchers are angels in the Book of Enoch sent to Earth to watch over humans. They began to lust after human women and became fallen angels. Watchers/Nephilim are also mentioned in the Bible's Book of Daniel and Genesis. In the Book of Enoch, Satan leads the Watchers astray in revolt, and later condemns and tortures them.

The Trojan Horse, Troy, & Helen

The debate continues as to the Trojan War's place in history or mythology. The story is most notably known from Homer's *Illiad* and *Odyssey*, and for the tale of the Trojan Horse sent by the Greek army to Troy to retrieve Helen, who had been taken by Paris of Troy from her husband, the King of Sparta. Helen was said to be the most beautiful woman in the world, possibly birthed from Zeus and Leda, and used as a lure by Aphrodite to win the Judgment of Paris as the fairest goddess. Archaeological finds strongly suggest that the city of Troy did exist in the modern-day city of Hisarlik, Turkey, off the coast of the Aegean Sea.

Geminid Meteor Shower

The Geminids usually peak in early-mid December. They get their name because they appear to come from the constellation Gemini. In Greek mythology, the Gemini twins, Castor and Pollux, are brothers to Helen of Troy (Sparta). In Homer's *Iliad,* they are not at the siege of Troy because they are dead, even though in Homer's *Odyssey,* which takes place after the siege, they are alive. In most stories, Castor is mortal and Pollux is immortal. Castor and Pollux are the brightest stars in the constellation and are representatives of immortality and death. The symbolic meaning, if any, of this backdrop to Lucifer's attack on Eric is up to the reader.

The Silk Road

The Silk Road was a series of trade routes across East Asia into Europe. Origin dates vary within the 2nd Century B.C., although some routes were already in use in previous centuries.

The Warring States Period, China

Some historians believe this centuries-long period of war began in 475 B.C., although it could be much earlier, and ended in 221 B.C. when the Qin (Chin) conquered and unified the remaining states as China under the First Sovereign Emperor, Qin Shi Huang.

Celeste/Selene/Sora Names

The meanings of the names: Celeste (Star), Selene (Moon), and Sora (Sky) and are meant to be interpreted by the reader within the context of the story. However, "Selene" also connects Raven's soul to Endymion and Alex.

✳ Selene and Endymion—One version of this myth says that Selene, Titan of the Moon, fell in love with the mortal shepherd/prince Endymion. As she rode her moon chariot across the sky at night, she visited Earth to be with him. She wished to enjoy his beauty forever and asked Zeus to make him immortal and put him into an eternal sleep. She birthed fifty daughters by him.

✳ Selene and Alexander—Alexander the Great (356B.C.–323B.C.) had a successful sister, Cleopatra of Macedon, who is sometimes confused with Cleopatra VII, Queen of Egypt (70/69 B.C.—30B.C.). She descended from Ptolemy I Soter, a general to Alexander the Great and the successor king to his empire who founded the Ptolemaic Dynasty— under which Cleopatra VII ruled. She and Marc Antony spawned the twins Alexander Helios and Cleopatra Selene in 40 B.C. Cleopatra VII lived and died in city of Alexandria, founded by Alexander the Great.

Gabriel/Hawkiel/Darkesiel & their Globes

The notations in *Last Born Daughter* for Seraphim and Cherubim excluded the Wheels that accompany the Cherubim. Wheels are mentioned in the Bible's Book of Ezekiel and Daniel, and are referenced in the Book of Enoch. The author once read that after the Holy Rebellion, God created the Wheels—and *only* the Wheels—without freewill so they could never disobey Him; however, the source material has been lost and is unconfirmed.

Enlighten the eyes of your heart to hope

Reference to Ephesians 1:18.

Orion—the Stars of Orion

In *Confessions of the Second Born*, Jonathan enjoys stargazing upon the Orion constellation. In *Last Born Daughter*, "Hawkiel" (Lucifer) tells Raven that he once watched the Earth from that constellation, "The Hunter of Night," and that his mark is blue and red because those are the colors of blood. They are also the colors of Orion's brightest and most famed stars: the red supergiant, Betelgeuse, and the blue supergiant, Rigel. The constellation is listed in the Bible as "Kesil" and was called Osiris (God of the Dead, Resurrection, and Life) in Egyptian mythology. In Greek Mythology, one version tells of Artemis, Goddess of the Moon, falling in love with Orion and killing him—unknowingly set up by Apollo due to jealousy—and then sending him to the stars as a constellation. The Orion Nebula is astronomically important as a stellar nursery and in the *Epic of Gilgamesh*, Orion is known as the Light of Heaven.

Homo Sacer — The Sacred or Accursed Man

This Ancient Roman law is a complicated subject beyond the scope of this narrative. Within the context of this story, this may be viewed as someone who may legally be killed without punishment, but not sacrificed, and who is under no protections by the government, but possibly by the gods—extrapolated to mean that this person may survive only by divine will because humankind will not intervene. Endymion uses this concept to disavow Donovan, only placing him under the Vampiric Nation's protection *if* he is killed. Endymion then intervenes to save or resurrect him, and ensures that he remains immortal, thus preventing a natural death due to Donovan's Initial Judgment. In a reversal of the human law, Donovan may legally be hunted, injured, or maimed by anyone without retribution, as long as he is not killed.

KASTIE PAVLIK is a gamer, artist, techie, and hopeless bibliophile who grew up loving all things macabre and creepy crawly, with an affinity for mythology, vampires, the paranormal, and psychology. Diagnosed with Multiple Sclerosis in 2008, she has subsequently beaten breast cancer, and manages a rare genetic disorder, Ehlers-Danlos Syndrome. She spends her days entertaining (annoying?) her feline overlords while adapting to her endlessly changing needs. Surrounded by the starry cornfields of Illinois, she enjoys a quiet life with her husband and their cats. She is the author of the *Children of the Morning Star* vampire series and the horror novelette *How to Make Lemonade*. Her writing influences include *Edgar Allan Poe, Anne Rice, James Herbert, Alfred Hitchcock,* and *Hideyuki Kikuchi*. She is a member of The Alliance of Independent Authors.

www.ingramcontent.com/pod-product-compliance
Lightning Source LLC
Chambersburg PA
CBHW051215190726
48288CB00006B/1973